To: Verna

Beyond This Mountain

Exie Wilde Henson

Warmest Regards ~
Exie Wilde Henson

PublishAmerica
Baltimore

First printing

ISBN: 1-4137-2125-7

PUBLISHED BY PUBLISHAMERICA, LLLP

www.publishamerica.com

Baltimore

Printed in the United States of America

Dedication

With profound gratitude
and in
loving memory
of
my parents,

Joseph Stokely Wilde, Sr. and Ethel Phillips Wilde

This is their story in fictional form.

Acknowledgments

My deepest gratitude and love to my husband, Gene, for helping me realize my dream of writing this book and its sequel, *Mountain Song*. His support has covered all facets, including an adjustment of our lifestyle to provide time for me to write. His greatest gift is his unwavering, expressed belief in me.

Much love and thanks to our children—Melody and Steve Fifer, Rebecca Dobson, and Scott and Kristy Henson for their encouragement and helpful suggestions through the writing process. Thank you, Scott, for help in designing the book cover and in navigating the technicalities of a computer.

I am grateful to our grandchildren – Amy, John, Kelly, Matthew, Carrie, Anna, Ben, Ashley and Aaron – for the joy and promise they bring to our lives. My thanks to our first grandson-in-law, Kevin, for helping keep me and my computer on speaking terms.

As the youngest of nine children in the Wilde family, I am indebted to my brothers and sisters – Dorothy, Nell, Oneda, J.A., Marie, Stokely, Festus, and Kadez – for affording me opportunities they did not have, and for a lifetime of love and shared memories.

My gratitude and love to Jerry Dempsey for her gift of true and abiding friendship, and for praying with me and for me across the years.

My grateful acknowledgement to Dr. Dennis Hensley, my editor *par excellence,* consultant and friend, who took the journey with me, word by word, through this book and its sequel.

My appreciation to the late Reverend Thea Rose for sharing his knowledge about the logging industry in the 1920s and 1930s, and for the inspiration of his life.

My thanks to Doug and Sally Boenau for the beautiful photograph of our North Carolina mountains which is used for the cover of this book.

My thanks to James and Judy Poe, the professional and personable photography team, who took my photograph for the back cover.

Chapter One

Justin stood when the doctor walked toward him. It was late afternoon, and he had been waiting since one o'clock when they had wheeled his wife, Laurel, into surgery. Fear clutched at his throat and choked his voice. "How is she, Doctor?"

"I'm sorry, Justin," Dr. Leighton said. "We've done everything we know to do. I'm afraid she lost too much blood before coming in. Then she hemorrhaged in surgery."

His weary voice paused. "She's slipping away from us. I really don't expect her to last through the night."

The color drained from Justin's face. When he reached for support, Dr. Leighton grabbed his arm. "Here! Sit down!" The doctor pushed Justin's head forward. "Take deep breaths!"

He watched Justin carefully. "Are you alone?"

When Justin was finally able to speak, he said, "No. Some friends are in the lobby. I sent the older children home so they could help care for the young ones."

Dr. Leighton sat down facing Justin. His eyes communicated his own pain and helplessness. "She should have had this done just after your last child was born two years ago, you know." There was no reproach in his tone. Both men knew that the Depression that had been gripping the country for three years had presented crises which had overshadowed Laurel's need for surgery.

"You need your older children here with you. I'll send for them." Dr. Leighton stood to go. "You can go in to see her now. The nurse will be here if you need her. I'll be back in a little while."

He impulsively embraced Justin. "I'm so sorry, my friend." He rubbed his hand over his eyes, trying to brush away the fatigue and defeat, then walked away. He could not allow Justin to see his personal dismay over losing this capable, courageous woman. In the ten years he had known them, Laurel had delivered babies, battled diphtheria and typhoid, and had nursed loggers through snake bites and accidents in the rugged North Carolina mountains where Justin ran a logging camp. Leighton had delivered four of their children. He considered Justin and Laurel special friends.

Justin sat where the doctor left him, unable to move or think clearly. Laurel was dying. His Laurel…who had given his life meaning for the past eighteen years. Laurel…his emotional and mental companion, his comforter and friend. The only woman he had ever loved.

She knew him better than he knew himself. She had accepted his dark side and had loved him anyway…had shared his life more completely than he thought anyone ever could…had borne him three daughters and two sons …

As the realization of the children's loss swept over him, he shook his head. "No! No! No!" he protested, hanging his head in his hands.

Someone touched his arm. The nurse stood there, a sympathetic look on her face. "You can see her now. She's not conscious, but you'll want to be with her in case she wakes up."

Justin walked numbly into the room. Laurel's auburn hair tumbled over the pillow, making her fair skin look waxy and lifeless. Justin gently pushed back the one curl which always fell over her forehead and caressed her face with a touch as light as a feather. His grief was etched so clearly on his face that the nurse slipped from the room, not wanting to see it.

"Laurel," he whispered. "Laurel…don't leave me…and the children. Come back to us. Please…come back!"

He took her small hand in his calloused one and stroked it as he talked. "You haven't had your big house, and I owe you that flower garden. I never meant for us to live so long in logging camps. You've worked too hard. There's still so much I want to do for you."

He sat down suddenly, no longer able to stand. An overwhelming desire to gather her in his arms consumed him. He wanted to breathe his breath into her, allow his blood to flow through her, to give his own life to her!

He couldn't see her breathing, and suddenly he couldn't breathe. He stood quickly, leaning over her. "Breathe, Laurel! Breathe!" Then, almost angrily, "Don't you know that your breath is my breath? Your life is my life?" He turned away, desperately running his fingers through his black curly hair while he looked out the window at the sun, now slipping toward the horizon. Darkness was on its way.

"God," he questioned angrily, "don't you understand? If she dies, my life…my reason for living…is gone! And the children…they must have their mother!" He paused, closing his eyes for a moment and then he looked out again. "If you hate me so much, God, why don't you take my life instead of hers?"

He turned again to her. He rubbed her arms. He stood and retrieved a washcloth from the bathroom. He washed her face gently, talking to her all the while, willing her to live. He turned the lights on and pulled the drapes early, not wanting to see the darkness come.

After awhile, Justin, realizing he must get himself in hand before the children came, washed his own face and combed his hair. The stubble on his chin and cheeks would have to stay. He didn't have his razor.

When the three older children came through the door, he looked at their concerned, solemn faces and gathered them close. The four of them went into a group hug without a word. He could not bring himself to tell them their mother was dying, but he knew they knew. Sarah, at sixteen, was like a mother hen to the others. Adam, fourteen, and Caroline, ten, followed. David, six, and Alexis, two, were at home.

The nurse entered and came over to the children. "Why don't you talk to your mother? She might hear you even if she's not awake enough to talk back. I'm sure you can think of something she would like to hear."

Sarah walked to the bed and took her mother's hand. "Mama, I've been watching after David and Alexis. This morning David came in, holding Alexis by the hand." She swallowed hard, then went on. "He said they had been out by the wood pile praying for you to get well. He said that God told him that you…that you would be well soon. Oh, Mama!" She suddenly broke into sobs and ran to Justin, who held her close and stroked her head.

Adam, his chin quivering, was next. Shoulders straight, he took Laurel's hand. "Mama, uh…you know that hen that was setting but we couldn't find her nest? Well, I found it this morning." He looked around at the others as if to gain their support and then went on.

"When…when you get home, there'll be some yellow baby chickens like you love so much walking around the yard." Bending over, he kissed her lightly on the forehead and whispered in a husky voice, "I love you, Mama." Then he straightened and walked over to stand beside Justin. He wiped his eyes with his fists. He looked at his father and Justin read Adam's plea not to baby him, but just to let him stand by his side.

Caroline, already crying, slipped over to Laurel's bed. Her voice rose. "Mama, you can't die! I want you to come home!" Justin put his arm around her and guided her out into the hallway. Sarah and Adam followed him, trying to help comfort their sister.

The hall was busy with people, so Justin took the three children to an empty room nearby. He cleared his throat and summoned his courage. "Your mother is very sick," he said, "but she is still alive and, as long as she's alive, we have hope." He put his hand under their chins, one by one and raised their faces to look into his solemn blue eyes. "I love you…and you…and you!" He hugged each child as he spoke. "And I'm proud that you're so brave. I'm going to stay with her tonight and I want the three of you to go back with Aunt Hannah and take care of each other…and especially David and Alexis. Your mother is a fighter. I believe she's fighting now. I promise to send somebody to tell you how she is early in the morning."

He asked Hannah Owen, whose husband Jed had been Justin's foreman in the logging camps, to take the children back home and to stay with them. Her sister, Nora, was already there keeping David and Alexis. Hannah and Nora had helped raise them, and all the children dearly loved both women. He looked Hannah straight in the eye, daring her or anyone else to think differently, and said, "I'll send word when she wakes up and is better."

He felt grateful in a detached sort of way for all the friends gathered to be with him. He was gratified by their kind words and wishes, but relieved when Dr. Leighton told them it would be better if they waited in the lobby. The doctor and nurse would be checking in with Justin and Laurel through the night.

After their friends left, Dr. Leighton sat down with Justin.

"We've done all we can to save her life, Justin. Now it's up to her and a higher power."

"What do you mean, 'it's up to her'?"

"It's hard to explain because we don't understand it, but sometimes people live despite awful odds…when it doesn't seem physically possible. It seems they choose subconsciously to live. They won't let go. So, their body responds and fights for life."

"Are you saying she could…live?" Justin whispered.

"Well, I didn't think she'd live this long, Justin, but she has!" There was a spark of hope in Dr. Leighton's eye. His voice even sounded different.

Justin's solemn blue eyes did not waver from the doctor's as he went on. "First, I want you to eat something and drink some coffee. I know you haven't eaten all day. Then, I want you to sit beside her, hold her hand or rub her forehead, and talk to her. Go over some of your memories. Talk about the children. Tell her things you always wanted to say about loving her, but could never voice. In other words…call her back to you and the children."

"Do you think it might work?"

"I can't say, but at least you'll know you've tried your best."

He was quiet a moment, then continued. "After you say everything you want to say to her, I want you to leave her for awhile." He waved his hand toward the door. "The lobby is full of your friends and they say they'll be here as long as you're here. So, go talk to them, or if you can't do that, slip into the room across the hall and rest a while. I've asked them to keep that room for you."

Tears pooled in Justin's eyes. He hadn't cried since he was a child, and was alarmed to think he might start now.

Dr. Leighton stood. "They have some food and coffee for you in the kitchen. Shall we go?"

Justin grasped his hand. "Sure…Okay. Thank you, Doc."

Justin made his way to the kitchen and, indeed, the food and coffee did make him feel better. He decided to walk around the hospital grounds and get his thoughts together before going in to talk to Laurel. The street lights held at bay the darkness he had dreaded as he walked slowly, his head bowed, trying to formulate a plan for talking to Laurel.

11

They were so close words weren't usually necessary for them to know each other's thoughts. He could anticipate her stance or reaction on most issues, as she could anticipate his. In the beginning, this had irritated him or made him feel restricted because he tended to live by his moods. But, as the years had come and gone, he had begun to feel comforted by her…her steadfastness. He stopped in his tracks as the truth of what Laurel meant to him crystallized. "Laurel," he whispered, "you are the only constant in my life. You are my stability…my anchor."

Fear of losing her struck him again like a physical blow. He felt sick at his stomach. *This is no way for a man to act*, he thought. *She's always there for me. I must be there for her.* Straightening, he took several deep breaths and started walking again. This time there was a purpose to his stride. He was not aware of anything else but the smell of honeysuckle…and after a little while he was ready.

In the years to come, he could never remember how long he talked that night. Only that he started at the beginning…the night they met.

"Laurel, I fell in love with you the first time I saw you. It jolted me like a thunderclap. I've never gotten over it and I never want to. People say that's the best kind of falling in love." He held her hand in one of his, caressing it softly as he leafed back through the pages of his memories…

He had been visiting friends in Knoxville who had invited him to a charity benefit at the school. The proceeds were to go to the orphanage, and it seemed that the whole community was there. After some singing, the master of ceremonies announced, "Before we have our box supper and cake walk, Laurel Kingsley has agreed to do some poetry recitations for us. This is by popular request." Laurel walked to the platform in the midst of applause.

As Justin looked at her now, she seemed his same young love.

"I carry a detailed picture in my mind of the first time I saw you, Laurel. You had put up your hair…I couldn't decide if it was bronze or copper. Anyway, you had put it up in a kind of puff that was in style then. You had a big dark green bow at the back." He smoothed her hair and leaned down to kiss her forehead. "You had the fair skin of a redhead, so I was surprised when I saw your eyes were brown instead of blue. Those unusual brown eyes make you even more of a striking beauty, Laurel. Did you know that?

"You had a fancy high-necked white blouse with sleeves that puffed out at the top but clung to your arms below the elbows. And there was a row of little buttons that ran from your wrists to the bend in your arm." He rubbed her arms as he talked. "You wore a dark green velvet skirt that matched the bow in you hair. The only jewelry was a wide, gold bracelet on your right arm. I bet you didn't think I'd remember all that."

Unable to stand her stillness any longer, he got up and went over to the sink where he washed his face and got a drink of water, but his memory carried on.

With a mixture of poise and liveliness, Laurel had recited some poetry, then some rhymes for the children, asking them to join her.

When she finished, Justin whispered to his friend, "Who is she?"

"Professor Kingsley's daughter. She teaches with him now."

"Who is Professor Kingsley?"

"The dressed-up gentleman on the front row on the right. He's taught school here for about forty years and is considered the most educated man in these parts."

"Sh-h-h," hushed someone behind them who wanted to hear the instructions about bidding on the supper boxes.

But Justin had to know. "Is she married?" he whispered again.

"No," his friend answered, "but it's rumored that she's about to get engaged to that fellow in uniform sitting beside her."

Justin was quiet. *We'll see about that,* he thought.

Chapter Two

Suddenly realizing he was supposed to be talking, Justin said. "Laurel, did you know your papa and I liked each other from the minute we met? I was immediately jealous of that fellow you were going around with. Do you remember the professor inviting me to your house the day after we met? He and I sat on the porch and talked politics. He warmed up even more when he found out I was a Republican.

"But it was you I was aware of as you came and went, serving cake and coffee. I was surprised…and pleased…when you gave your honest opinion of President Wilson's policies and made some comments on the war in Europe.

"I remember the magic and excitement I felt just to be near you, and when you looked at me or talked to me. There I was…almost thirty years old…acting like a lovesick schoolboy."

He outlined her face gently with the tips of his fingers.

"And our wedding on that ferry boat on the Pigeon River! Laurel, I couldn't believe you agreed to that. I figured someone like you, one of the belles of Knoxville, would want a big church wedding. I was only teasing when I told you I wanted to get married on a boat so you couldn't change your mind at the last minute. You amazed me when you agreed. Most of our friends had to watch from the bank. I saw then that I was marrying a strong-minded woman."

His voice dropped. "Strong-minded…and so beautiful."

He brushed her hair back and touched his lips against her forehead.

"You still are."

He remained silent for a few minutes, unable to find the words. Then he whispered, "I love you so much!"

He went to stand by the door a moment as someone rolled a cart down the corridor. The nurse, seeing him, slipped in, checked Laurel's vital signs and smiled. "She's still holding steady. I'll go tell the doctor."

Encouraged, Justin returned to the bed and continued.

"Laurel, I'm really proud of our children. You have been a great mother. I guess it's partly from being a teacher. You seem to know how to handle them. You bring out their best.

"I remember our move to the first logging camp as if it was yesterday. You really didn't want to live like that, and you let me know. But you made the best of it. Your touch made a cozy little house out of that rough old shack. Do you remember putting up curtains, not only in our shack, but also in the mess hall?

"You somehow turned that unlikely group of people into a family. Most of them…maybe all of them…are here, Laurel, in the lobby. They're waiting to hear…hear that you're going to be all right."

She lay so lifeless he couldn't bear it. He turned his back and paced around the room until he knew he could talk again.

"There are so many things about you I admire. The way you care about people. The way you have of turning an ordinary situation into something special. I admire the way you fight for what's important. When we have arguments, even when I'm disagreeing with you, I like the way you hold your ground and won't give in." He laughed a little. "I don't think I could stand a woman who agreed with me on everything.

"You sure are one stubborn woman! But I've learned that when your temper flares and your eyes flash, that means you're fighting for something that's important to all of us.

"Like that argument we had about me taking Sarah to school on Tattoo and going back and getting her in the afternoons. When the time came for me to start taking her, it looked like it would be impossible for me to cut into my work schedule that way. But when I told you so, I've never seen you so angry! That was the biggest fight we've ever had. You never knew I got drunk over that one, and Jed had to rescue me.

"The problem with the job worked out fine. The crew carried right on without me. They would do anything for you anyway. Besides, they thought your request sounded normal, as long as it was you asking."

He smiled. "And, you know, those are some of my favorite memories, Laurel. Holding Sarah, and later Adam, in the saddle in front of me, wrapped up in a blanket. We enjoyed the snowy days best. Sarah and Adam and I still have a special bond because of those days together."

He knew he needed to keep talking, but he didn't want to say what he had to say next. It was the only important thing in his life that he had never talked to her about. He moved around the room again until he was ready. He took her hand as he spoke.

"I know I've hurt you many times over your belief in God. You've looked at me often, pleading silently for some kind of explanation that would help you understand that side of me. After awhile, when you realized I wasn't going to explain, you just accepted it and lived with it the best you could. You've kept your faith and taught the children well by yourself. A lesser person would have given up a long time ago."

As he talked, he allowed himself to open the door on some memories that still hurt so much he had kept them locked away…

Younger than his brothers and sisters by about five years, he had adored and been adored by his mother. She knew he was her last, so she had enjoyed him fully. He was six when she died of pneumonia. He tried for a long time to retain a picture in his mind of her laughter and love of life, but it had faded until sometimes he wondered if he had imagined her. In less than a year, his father had married again, an old maid, very religious, who didn't like little boys. His stepmother catered to him when the family was around, but when he was alone with her, she was different.

She would beat him severely for a childish accident. Then, she would set him in a dark corner, or lock him up in a dark closet, and pray over him in a loud whining voice, asking God to keep him from being such a bad, bad boy. Since God never helped him avoid regular beatings, he figured his stepmother and God were in cahoots. His childish mind had somehow figured that he was responsible for it all…his mother dying, his stepmother, and his beatings…so he never told anybody. He left home as soon as possible and had kept a respectable distance from his stepmother—and God—ever since.

"Laurel," he heard himself say, "I still can't put words to the hurt I received. My mother dying, my stepmother beating me and locking me up in the dark. I know I blame God. It's a confusing and dark place within me where

I try to keep the door closed. All I can do is ask you to forgive me for the hurt I've caused you over it."

Drained, he knew he couldn't go on yet he had to say one more thing.

"I want to repeat to you a promise I made when we moved to that first logging camp. I promise you a big house and a place for a flower garden. No more moving around. I promise you some roots."

He didn't know how, but he knew if she lived, he would do it.

"Come back to us, Laurel. The children and I need you!" He stooped and kissed her forehead. "I love you, my darling."

No further words would come but as the night lengthened, he sat still beside her, holding her hand, and occasionally rubbing her face or touching her hair.

Dr. Leighton came in an hour or so later. "She's holding her own. That's a good sign. Let's leave her awhile and, if there's any change, I'll call you."

Justin knew he could not lie down and just wait. "I'll be in the lobby with the others if you need me."

As he entered the lobby, the conversation stopped. Everybody looked at him. He could sense their fear and concern. *They all love her*, he thought. Their solemn faces helped him find his voice. "She's holding her own. Dr. Leighton says it's a good sign."

Jed Owen, his foreman for the logging crew for almost ten years, put his arm around Justin's shoulders. "Come sit down awhile, Justin," he urged. "We believe Laurel's going to be all right. People like her need to live a long, long time."

Ethan Stewart, a young man who had lived with them seven years working in the camp, even moving with them when the Depression had struck, gave Justin an embrace. Neither could speak and didn't need to. Justin clung for a moment to this young man he considered a son. He knew how much Ethan loved and admired Laurel.

Bulldog Aiken, one of his best loggers, walked over and put his hand on Justin's shoulder. "I'll never forget the way she fought to save our Joanie from diphtheria. I don't know how she kept from getting it herself."

Her eyes swollen, his wife Bess said, "We were just talkin' about the day she jumped into that flooded river above the falls to save Adam's life," she said. "She's had plenty of chances to die if she was goin' to, but she's a fighter, and I know she's fightin' right now."

Alice and Tom Raines were there. Tom was one of the youngest loggers Justin had ever hired and he had turned out to be a good one. Laurel and Hannah had delivered both of their children. "We come as soon as we heard, Mr. Worth," Alice said. "We've been praying for her and you and the children."

Tom grinned like an overgrown kid as he said, "I keep remembering her gettin' us to build them outhouses. She had us all workin' like a bunch of school boys."

"How could any of us forget?" Abe Johnson, another logger, said with a laugh.

Justin's eyes swept over the group. The whole crew had respected and liked her from the beginning. They had accepted her being different and, instead of rebelling as he thought they might, had even become proud of her expectations. Besides, they had never eaten so well in their lives.

These same weather beaten men in their work clothes stood around the room now. He couldn't understand how they had all gotten here so fast. Some of them lived a long distance away. But each one had a handshake or a touch and an encouraging word for him.

As Justin looked at their faces and listened to them, he felt the knot in his stomach loosen. He had left the logging business three years ago when the Depression had hit. These people no longer worked for him. They were here because they cared. They all had shared life and death, happiness and hardship, for almost ten years. They were friends for life. Their concern for him, and their absolute faith that Laurel would beat the odds again, somehow reduced his fear to manageable proportions.

He knew he needed to rest a little while he could. As he stood to go, Jed said, "We'll be right here, Justin."

Justin gripped his shoulder briefly and looked around the room again. "Thank you…all of you…for coming. I…told Laurel a little while ago that you were here, waiting to hear she's all right."

He walked down the hall to Laurel's room. The nurse spoke quietly. "There's no change for the worse, and that's encouraging. Go rest a little while. I'll be here with her."

He went across the hall, lay down and closed his eyes, finally allowing the guilt he had been avoiding to wash over him. If Laurel died, he would be to blame. The cruelly hard life and work in the logging camps, while bearing and caring for the children, had taken its toll. Then the Depression had exacted its price. Their life's savings had been wiped out when the bank folded, taking their dream of a home and farm of their own. The logging business had closed down quickly, forcing him to find another place to live and some way to make a living for his family.

The past three years had been the most difficult of their lives. Moving, renting, share cropping. Money was hard to come by. They missed the closeness and support they had come to depend on from the people in the logging camp. They had been like a family and they'd been abruptly ripped apart. Laurel's life with him had been hard. She deserved better. If he could just have a chance to make it up to her…

The crisis that had happened three days ago and caused her collapse kept running through his mind. He had not remotely considered the consequences when he ran Toby Rapp off the place where they were living. He had rented the farm from Mrs. Rapp, Toby's mother, an elderly widow. Fearing her two drunken sons, Toby and Bud, both in their thirties, would burn the house down on her and themselves, she had gone to live with a married daughter. Mrs. Rapp had put her sons out, hoping to make them responsible. She desperately needed the income from the rent and part of the crop Justin would grow.

Toby and Bud had gone to the timber fields in Oregon for awhile, but had lost their jobs because of drink. When they returned home, they asked to live in the canning shed behind the kitchen that had a stove and two cots. Justin agreed until they could find a place. Laurel had even given him some quilts for them. He soon realized, however, that they were mean, sneaky, worthless bums. He couldn't tolerate that kind of men around his family. After he asked them to move on, they harassed him at night, causing disturbances among the animals and stealing food. He brought home a large shepherd dog that took the responsibility of keeping them away. Then they changed their tactics again.

On Wednesday afternoon, Toby, drunker than usual, had shown up with his bottle of moonshine asking to spend the night. Only this time, he had a woman with him. When Justin saw them coming, walking unsteadily, passing a quart jar back and forth, he asked Laurel to keep the children in the house.

Justin spoke as if to a child. "Toby, what are you doing here?"

"Me and her is goin' to spend the night in that shed where me and Bud's been sleepin'," Toby said. He gave a man-to-man grin of conspiracy. The woman stood behind him, saying nothing.

"I can't let you do that, Toby," Justin reasoned. "I told you and Bud that you can't stay here anymore."

The whiskey and the woman's presence fueled Toby's belligerence.

"What'cha mean, I can't stay? This here's my mama's house. You can't keep me from stayin'!" He took a step toward Justin.

Justin took him by the arm. "Toby, listen to me. I'm renting this house from your mama. I pay her rent every month and she gets part of the crop in the fall. You know that. You're not supposed to be coming here at all."

Toby's voice rose as he started toward the shed. "Don't you tell me what I'm supposed to do! Get out of my way!" He turned to the woman and said, "Come on."

Justin stepped in front of him again. "Toby, I said go on home. You can't stay here tonight."

Toby swung hard at Justin with his whiskey jar, but Justin caught the jar and wrenched it out of Toby's hand. "I'll keep this. You've had enough for tonight. Now get out!" His voice was hard.

As Toby turned unsteadily and walked away, he yelled, "I'll get Bud and we'll be back. We'll put you out of here!"

Toby lurched down the road with the woman clutching at his sleeve.

Justin stepped to the corner of the porch and poured out the rest of the whiskey. Laurel came outside.

"Justin, I heard what he said. Is there going to be trouble?"

Justin slipped his arm around her as they went back into the house. "No, Honey. That's just drunk talk. He'll sleep it off and be all right tomorrow."

But this time Justin was wrong.

The next morning, Justin had just started plowing the lower field when he saw Toby and Bud coming. He felt a pang of pity as he watched them shuffle along in their dirty clothes. He stifled his impatience at having to deal with them when he had so much work to do. As they came closer, he saw their uncombed hair and stubble of beard stained with tobacco juice. He moved upwind to try to get away from their smell. Their eyes were bloodshot but they were not drunk.

"Good morning, gentlemen," he said. "What can I do for you this fine day?"

His irony was totally lost on the two men as Toby said without ceremony, "We come to tell you to get off this place. We want you gone by the end of the week."

Justin looked at Bud who was considered somewhat more responsible than Toby. "You lettin' Toby do your talkin' for you these days, Bud?"

Bud shifted from one foot to the other as he looked at Toby, then Justin. "Toby says you run him and his woman off yesterday."

"I did. He was drunk and wanted to spend the night with her in the shed. You know I can't have that in front of my family." Justin spoke slowly, but firmly.

Toby spit a stream of tobacco juice to the side and jabbed his finger at Justin. "You ain't got no right to run me off. This here's my mama's place!"

"Your mama rented this place to me, Toby. She doesn't want you here. She needs the rent and part of the crop I'm planting." He was getting tired of repeating himself. "You boys have a place to live. You don't need to keep coming hack here."

Bud looked belligerent. "Toby says you took his whiskey away from him, and his woman made fun of him."

"I did," Justin said again. "They both had had enough. Toby tried to hit me over the head with his jar of whiskey." Suddenly, he decided he was through explaining. "You boys get on your way now. I've got work to do."

As he turned to go, Toby blustered. "If you ain't gone by the end of the week, we'll be back with the sheriff."

Justin whirled around. The look on his face made both men take a step backward. "Don't threaten me, you good-for-nothing bums! Your mama had to move out of her home because you're not men enough to take your drinking somewhere else. She's afraid of you, but I'm not!" He took one more step toward them, his blue eyes cold with anger. "Now, get out! And don't come back as long as I live here!"

They both turned without another word and left faster than they had

21

come. But their anger showed clearly on their faces.

As Justin plowed, he thought about Toby's threat to bring the sheriff. Big Jim Potts was everything that Justin thought a sheriff shouldn't be. He was ignorant and cocky, and ran his job on bluff and bluster. At election time, Justin had voiced his opinion clearly. He was sure that Big Jim knew of his opposition. After awhile, Justin dismissed the whole thing from his mind. He had more important things to think about.

Laurel was still getting over her papa's death just two months earlier. But it was more than that. Something had been wrong with her for some time. She was unusually pale and that vital energy that characterized her was gone. He had mentioned taking her to the doctor several times but she always insisted she would soon be all right. He knew she was concerned about the money and he resolved he would take her within the next day or two and work something out with the doctor about paying. He felt better after making that decision.

Friday afternoon brought events that he had never believed would happen. After finishing supper, he sat down to rest a few minutes and read *The Grit* before he and Adam went to feed the animals. He was happy because Laurel had agreed to go to the doctor on Monday. She and the children were back in the kitchen when he heard a car coming.

He went out on the porch with the paper still in his hand and saw the sheriff's car approaching. He stood quite still and waited until the car was as close as he wanted it, about forty or fifty feet from the porch. Then he stepped to the edge of the porch and held up his right hand, signaling the sheriff to stop. The car stopped and Big Jim Potts, Toby, and Bud got out. Toby and Bud looked triumphant.

Justin's voice rang out across the yard like ice. "Stay where you are, Jim, and keep them with you. You can say what you have to say from there."

Toby was fairly prancing with excitement. "I told you we would bring the sheriff," he babbled.

Jim Potts spoke. "Be quiet, Toby, and let me handle this."

Justin was suddenly aware that Laurel and the children were standing behind him. Without turning or taking his eyes off Jim Potts, he said, "Laurel, take the children into the kitchen and keep them there."

22

"Justin…." Laurel began.

"Go right now, please," he interrupted. "You stay with the children. You're hardly able to stand up."

He knew her normal behavior would be to send the children to the kitchen and stand by his side, no matter what he said. When she did as he asked, he felt relieved, but curiously alone and alarmed. She must be weaker than he realized.

"Now, what are you going to handle, Sheriff?" The sarcasm was evident.

"Toby and Bud here say they are renting this house to you and they asked you to leave by the end of the week. Is this right?"

"Part right and part wrong. They asked me to leave, but I'm not renting from them. I'm renting from their mother."

"Same thing. They say they're speaking for the mother."

"They're lying. Did you happen to go talk to their mother before you came out here?"

"No. I didn't think it was necessary."

"It is necessary. You need to check out facts before you blunder into something that's none of your business."

The sheriff straightened and angrily hooked his thumbs in his belt. "I still say they have the right to ask you to move. This is their home place."

"Look at them!" Justin shot back. "They ran their mother off from her home with their drinking and carousing and womanizing. She didn't have a minute of peace because she was afraid they would burn the house down on her. She put them out, I didn't. The only income she has is the rent I pay plus part of the crop. They're not men enough to take care of their own mother, so don't talk to me about their rights."

Bud looked sideways at the sheriff to see how he was taking this information, but Toby could stay quiet no longer. "If I burn the house down, I'll make sure you and your family're in it." He grinned and added. "Yeah, I'd like that!"

Justin, looking at Toby's leering face, knew he meant it. White hot anger coursed through him. Without being consciously aware of his decision, Justin whirled, went inside the house and came back through the door with his shotgun leveled on the three men. Toby and Bud crouched and darted behind the car. The sheriff, as if in slow motion, unhooked his thumbs from his belt, ran his tongue over his lips and edged sideways toward the car.

"Stay where you are, Jim, and listen! You get those rats in your car and get them away from here! Don't come back without legal documents!"

Laurel was suddenly beside him, her face very pale. She took a long look at the sheriff and back to Justin. Her eyes rested on the gun barrel for a moment before she sank to the floor in a heap.

Justin forgot the men. He was through with them. He laid the gun down and dropped to his knees beside Laurel. He straightened her carefully and cradled her head in one hand as he called, "Sarah, Adam, bring some water and a cloth! Hurry!"

He rubbed her hair back and held his head down to listen to her breathing, whispering, "Laurel, Honey, it's all right!"

Sarah brought some water and a washcloth. All the children gathered around with scared faces. No one made a sound. Adam brought a pillow and Justin slipped it under her head. He washed her face gently, still calling her name.

He had so totally forgotten the sheriff that he looked up, surprised, when he heard a step on the porch behind him. With an anxious, abashed look on his face, Big Jim asked, "Can I help?"

"No," Justin said, without lifting his eyes from Laurel's face. "You've done enough damage. You're supposed to be protecting law-abiding citizens, not threatening them."

"I thought…" the sheriff began, but then stopped and stood silently looking on as Justin tried to bring Laurel around.

When she didn't respond, Justin said to the sheriff, "She's worse than I thought. We'll need to use your car to get her to a hospital right now." He stood and faced Big Jim. "But, before we go, I want you to order Toby and Bud off this place and tell them not to come anywhere near here while we're gone."

Big Jim did as he was told. Toby and Bud, still remembering that shotgun leveled on them, went without protest.

Justin quickly gave instructions to the children and tried to comfort them. He, then, carried Laurel to the sheriff's car and they drove away in a hurry.

Laurel only partially regained consciousness on the way to the hospital, with a murmured, "No…no…"

After examining her, Dr. Leighton told Justin that Laurel needed a hysterectomy immediately. She was in shock. He would wait only until she was stabilized before he operated.

Justin shook himself, trying to get rid of the fear that threatened to consume him. He sat up quickly, in a panic, and went to Laurel's room. He couldn't stay away. He had to be with her.

The nurse understood. "There's no change. We're taking that as good news."

When she left, Justin sat down by Laurel again. A very faint pulse beat in the hollow of her throat. After a few minutes, he said, "Laurel, you won't believe who all is in the lobby waiting for you to get better. I think all the families and the crew from the logging camp are there except Nora and Hannah, and they're taking care of our children. There're so many people out there, there aren't enough places to sit. They're telling tales on you…especially about that first logging camp."

The talk today…and the way his former crew had closed ranks around him and Laurel, with love, had brought it all back as clearly as if it had been yesterday…

Chapter Three

Justin was surprised and elated when he was picked as supervisor of the new logging job for Beck Lumber Company. They had purchased a large boundary of timber in Pisgah Forest that should take a few years to log, and Justin knew that several men, including some of his friends, had applied.

He also knew that logging in Pisgah Forest was a challenge that any serious timber man would love to tackle. This section was remote, about four hours south of Asheville, by horse and wagon. Since the depletion of timber reserves in the northeast, large timber companies were moving into western North Carolina where some of the most extensive virgin hardwood forests in the eastern region of the United States grew. The mountains, besides their incredible beauty, offered a climate that encouraged the growth of the biggest variety of hardwoods to be found in the entire country; a climate that offered four distinct seasons, without any season being overly harsh on its flora, fauna, or people.

The job offer had happened so fast there had been no time to contact Laurel, who had taken the children to visit her folks in Knoxville. He knew that his photography alone was not going to support them without Laurel teaching, but she needed to stay home with the children.

Hiram Beck of Beck Lumber Company hadn't wasted time or words. He was a man in a hurry. Justin walked in, held out his hand, and said, "Justin Worth, Mr. Beck. I'm interested in the logging job." He and Justin talked about fifteen minutes with Justin answering his rapid-fire questions as quickly as they were asked. Mr. Beck suddenly pushed his large body back into his chair which rolled slightly under the impact. He hooked his thumbs in his suspenders, stuck out his chin, clamped down on his cigar, and glared at Justin, his steel-framed glasses outlining steel blue eyes. Justin lifted his chin a little higher and faced him steadily. They both were silent for a few minutes.

Finally, Hiram Beck took his well-chewed cigar out of his mouth and placed it in a large ash tray. "Can you go to work for me on Monday?"

Justin sat forward. "Just like that?"

"Yes. I've interviewed twelve men and some of them have more logging experience than you, but I believe you're the man for this job." He paused, then hurried on. "You're an educated man, Worth. You don't have to do this kind of work. Why you are doing it is your business. How well you do it is my business. You're your own man. That means you're likely to be a leader of men." His eyes glinted briefly, and his mouth turned up into a half smile, "And, you haven't said 'sir' to me once!"

Justin laughed and relaxed. They understood each other for starters, anyway. Now they could get down to business. When Justin left the office on Main Street about an hour later, he knew he needed to get home and think. The word that he had the job would travel fast, and he didn't want to talk to anyone until he had made his plans. He quickly unhitched Tattoo, his chestnut bay, from the shady side of the street, mounted and rode out of town.

He wished Laurel was home. She had a way of helping him simplify things. On his way, he stopped and sent her a telegram: *Have new job supervising logging crew Stop I'll meet your train Sunday at 5 pm Stop Love Justin Stop*

It was now Wednesday and there was much to do. He had to develop and deliver some pictures, and he was scheduled to photograph a wedding on Saturday and a homecoming after church on Sunday. He'd have to find directions to the churches. Only then could he turn his mind to hiring a logging crew and supervising the building of a logging camp.

As he and Tattoo approached their white bungalow set back from the road, his glance swung over the picket fence, the two oak trees, Sarah's swing, and the ruffled curtains at the windows. He had his first qualm about how Laurel might react to this move. She was happy here in Deerbrook. As he rode by the house toward the barn, her jonquils caught his eye – the courageous heralds of spring, she called them – and he saw green shoots that would soon grow into red tulips. Stopping, he leaned over and rubbed

Tattoo's neck. "I hope I've done the right thing for all of us, Tattoo."

Laurel, meanwhile, was enjoying her visit. The past Sunday afternoon, Papa and Laurel's stepmother, Madeleine, had given a reception for her, inviting her three older sisters and their families and her old friends, who came with their children, to meet her children. The women sat on the wrap-around porch drinking lemonade and eating pound cake while the children romped on the shady lawn and the men played horseshoes and baseball. The conversation soon moved from "Do you remember?" to questions and answers about the present. Laurel was glad to catch up with their lives.

Isabel, her best friend growing up, said, "Laurel, of all people to move to a little backwoods mountain town! Is it awful? Are you happy? Do you have friends? What do you do?"

Laurel laughed. "You're still the same, Isabel! If you'll stop for breath, I'll try to start answering.

"The people of Deerbrook would be amused that you call them backwoods. It's a small mountain town, but we like it. I've taught school there two years, so I know a lot of people. And it seems like everybody knows Justin. He travels and takes pictures of family groups, weddings, homecomings, reunions, baptisms. When anything is happening, people want Justin there.

"I have several friends from church where I teach the children's Sunday school. We get together and quilt and trade recipes and canning secrets. And, you know how most of my life is spent because you have a husband and children, too!"

As if to prove it, Madeleine placed Adam in her lap saying, "A little boy just woke up and he's hungry."

When Laurel left to nurse Adam, Isabel turned to the others. "During those years Laurel taught with the professor, she was always doing something that women don't usually do. Remember how she'd speak out on issues like Prohibition. She saw a lot of misery in her students' lives because of their fathers' drinking. She would have faced a snarling tiger for those children." She was quiet a moment, then added softly, "I wonder if she's really become as tame as she sounds."

As twilight came that evening, after everyone had left, Laurel sat alone on the porch swing allowing the atmosphere of home to enfold her. She had been gone five years. Long enough to realize how privileged she had been growing up in this family. The spacious two-story white farmhouse and grounds stood in understated elegance that only comes with age and loving care. The first floor held the living room, dining room, Papa's study, Papa's and Mama's bedroom, and the large comfortable kitchen with a fireplace, chairs, and reading lamps well out of the busy work area around the stove. A round oak table stood in the center, dividing the two areas. During the four years she had taught with Papa before she married, they had done their school work together at night at the kitchen table, while Mama sat in her rocker mending or knitting, or breaking beans.

A curved staircase led from the foyer to four bedrooms on the second floor. Laurel's bedroom was much as she had left it with the wild rose wallpaper, lace curtains, rose and green bedspread, and that wonderful feather bed.

Laurel smiled as she looked at the two luxurious magnolia trees that dominated the front lawn where the croquet wickets were still in place. Then she allowed her thoughts to encompass the grounds. There was the shed out back with the table and benches where the family ate in summer, the horseshoe stakes, the ball field in the back corner, the arbor with benches, the bank house for canned goods, potatoes, and apples. *This place, inside and out, shows a lot of living,* she thought.

The next afternoon, Laurel peeked into her father's study. He was busy at his desk. She watched him quietly for a moment. Hunter Kingsley was well named. The strong bone structure of his face suggested strength of character and revealed his Cherokee heritage. His lighter skin and hair coloring were gifts from his mother.

His father, full Cherokee, was eight years old in 1838 when the Congress and President Andrew Jackson forced the Cherokee from their ancestral land. About one-fourth of the seventeen thousand perished on the "Trail of Tears" before reaching the land allotted them in Oklahoma. Hunter's grandparents were among the nearly one thousand Cherokee who escaped and hid in the mountains. Four years later, after lengthy negotiations with the government, this nucleus was allowed to remain in North Carolina and land was purchased for the Qualla Reservation.

Hunter's grandfather, a wise chief named Strong Hunter, knew he must integrate his family into the white society around them. His children were educated, and Hunter's father, Forest, married a strong-minded redhead from an old established Knoxville family, who were proud to have him for a son-in-law.

He established quite a reputation for himself. Forest Kingsley's name was brought to the attention of the public as the first man successfully to ride the remote and dangerous mail routes between North Carolina, Tennessee, and Virginia. His exploits equaled those of the Pony Express in the West. When the Civil War came, he joined and served with the Union. He was an American before he was a Southerner. He owned considerable land and, after the war, became a successful planter. It was no surprise when he was elected a state senator where he served the State of Tennessee with distinction for several years. He and Hunter's mother died before Laurel was born, but she wished she could have known them.

She spoke softly, "Could I come in and visit for a few minutes?"

Her father stood and motioned her to come in. "Yes, please! I was wondering when we could have our talk."

After a few minutes of catching up on some details of each other's lives, Laurel smiled at him and the words she had been thinking about since the previous night tumbled out. "Papa, do you have any idea how important you – and this house – are to this community? I was watching and listening Sunday when everyone was here. You have taught most of the people in this area under forty. They all feel welcome here and cared for. They also know you will tell them, without being asked – but kindly – if they are wrong or about to be wrong. You expect certain behaviors at forty because you knew their abilities at twelve." She paused, raised her chin, then asked, "Am I right, Professor?"

He sat looking at her, amused. "So you still have the gift of impassioned speech. Good!"

"You didn't answer me, but that's all right. I'm not through yet." She had to finish; she had been thinking about this all day.

He leaned back in his chair and listened to her solemnly.

"You are a constant, Papa. People depend on you. You are authority and knowledge and wisdom and kindness and love to these people. This house serves as a haven, a church, a courthouse, a school, a hospital, and, above all, a home." She moved around as she spoke, touching his schoolbooks, his Justice of the Peace license, his Bible – the tools of his trade. Then she stopped and stared at him, too full to continue.

He stood, held out his arms and she went into them. "Papa, I love you," she said, her eyes brimming.

"And I love you, Sweetheart." He held her close for a moment and rubbed his hand over her hair, then he fished for his handkerchief and handed it to her. He took off his glasses and rubbed his eyes. After a moment, they both sat down.

"Laurel, you've paid me the highest tribute I will ever know in this life. If I'm only a fraction of all those things you said, I will have fulfilled my purpose." He smiled. "Most people don't get to hear their eulogy. I'll take your words as mine, and I will treasure them more because they have come from you."

"Papa, I want to thank you, officially, for raising me the way you did, for my education and values, and the encouragement to stand for what I believe, and for your love." She swallowed hard. "I will not waste what you've poured into me. Someday, maybe I can mean as much to the people around me as you do."

"Laurel, all that you are didn't come from me. You are your mother's daughter. You never knew her because you were only three when she died, but you are much more like her than your sisters in temperament and appearance." He stood. "Let's walk around the yard and maybe sit under the arbor a little while."

As they went out, he called to Madeleine, who came to the door of the kitchen with flour on her hands. "Laurel and I are going outside to visit a little while."

"Good," Madeleine said. "Laurel, I'll listen for the children while I make you some of your beloved fried apple pies."

Laurel said, "Thank you, Mama," and went to hug her. Madeleine, always flustered by open expressions of affection, held her hands aside to keep the flour off Laurel, but her smile was like a hug as she said, "Go on, now, before the children wake up or somebody comes."

The grape arbor was cool and the smell of fresh-mown grass surrounded them. Papa continued his previous comments. "Your mother had the most profound love of life I've ever known in anyone. She had a great capacity not only to live, but to love, to feel, to enjoy."

He spoke hesitantly as if searching for the words. "She had your color of rich auburn hair that shone like polished copper. Her eyes were brown with hazel flecks, and her skin just as fair as yours. I couldn't believe that she loved me – a dry, bookish young school teacher. But she did and I adored her. She created magic out of ordinary, even dull, circumstances. She was the one who started calling me 'Professor.' When you tilted your chin a few minutes ago and said, 'Professor,' I saw her so clearly in you."

Laurel's eyes filled. She laid her hand on his. "Papa, don't…if this makes you sad."

"No, you need to know so you can understand yourself. I called her my 'redbird' because she brought a sense of freedom and color to my life. To this day, a redbird – more than anything else, except you – brings her back to me. She had studied to be, and probably should have been, a teacher. She felt deeply about injustice and human misery, and she was always pulling me along to get involved."

They sat a while with their thoughts and emotions.

"We had twelve years together. When she died suddenly of a ruptured appendix, leaving me with four little girls to raise, I only wanted to die, too. I couldn't even think of you girls and your loss; my own was too great. Your Aunt Sarah helped take care of you girls until I could function again normally. I continued with my teaching. I had to. But my grief almost consumed me.

"Then, one day several months later, my mind took over again. I could not change her death or my loss, but with God's help, I could change my attitude. The day I accepted her death, I went into the woods and stayed a long while. I made a private little ceremony out of it. I asked God for His guidance and strength. I knew that my life and the lives of my four little girls depended on it.

"After a while I knew what I had to do. I promised her I would not retreat to my introverted academic world, but would live in the larger place – the marketplace – with people. She had led me there. I would try to look at life through her eyes as well as mine. And I promised her I would attempt to raise our daughters in that larger, people-filled, happy place. You have described that place today." He paused and put his hand over his eyes.

Laurel sat without moving.

He continued almost in a whisper. "Then, I deliberately let her go, Laurel, and I sensed that she let me go. I let her…go!" He was quiet. Tears flowed down Laurel's cheeks. She pressed his folded handkerchief to her face over and over again as he continued.

"After awhile, I stood up and walked away into my life – our life – without her. I made a choice that day to live my life as fully as possible for myself, for you girls, and for her. All you say I have done is mostly because of her gift of opening up a richer life to me. Your mother must have some of the credit."

"But, Papa, you, yourself, chose…"

"Yes, I chose, but it was because my back was to the wall, Laurel. I don't think I would have been able to do it without the memory of her."

She put her hand over his and they sat together, each with private thoughts, before they willed themselves back to the present.

"And Mama – Madeleine… You've been happy together." It was a statement.

"Yes, we have been. We are. We married when you were six. Madeleine's a good woman. She took us all in hand and raised you girls as her own. We're a good match. She keeps my feet planted on solid earth; and we wouldn't have this home you love without her. She has made the life you described possible, Laurel."

"And you love her." Another statement.

"Yes, I love her. There are different kinds of love. We have a good life. I've been blessed."

Madeleine hurried toward them with Adam in her arms and Sarah in tow. "I'm sorry to disturb you, Hunter, but a young couple is waiting to talk to you about getting married. They said they need you to help them make some decisions."

Laurel took the children. She gave Papa her "I told you so" look and a smile as he turned to go inside.

The rest of the week went by quickly. As she watched her children enjoy her family, play with their cousins, she wished she and Justin lived closer. She realized she also enjoyed the status she still had here, as her father's daughter and as a successful and well-loved teacher in her own right.

This made her feel slightly disloyal to Justin, turning her thoughts in that direction. In Deerbrook, she and Justin were beginning to be known and respected. Many parents as well as students were disappointed when she decided not to teach this year, but she had needed the time with her children and had enjoyed fixing up their little home. She felt like she had turned their house into a home that reflected who she and Justin were. She had finally bought the furniture she had wanted for a long time – a Victorian sofa and two wingback reading chairs, along with Chippendale tables. Then Justin came in one day with a beautiful old oak desk. It was small, but full of cubbyholes, similar to Papa's big desk. Her last purchase was a brass oil lamp with a translucent china shade, with a mantle which gave off a bright light.

She had been so busy with babies and Justin, house and church, she had not missed teaching. But several times lately, she had felt restless, as if something important was missing from her life – as if she should be doing more – was supposed to be doing more.

Justin's telegram, which arrived just as they were sitting down to supper, caused a flurry of discussion between Laurel's brother-in-law and Papa until Papa realized Laurel was very quiet and turned the conversation into other channels. Laurel was subdued, wondering what this would mean, what was involved.

For the remaining days of her visit, her mind was divided. She enjoyed being with her family, but she felt a growing apprehension, tinged with resentment toward Justin for making this decision while she was away.

Papa seemed to know instinctively what she was feeling. He held her close and said, "Let us know as soon as possible about this logging job and your plans."

When Sunday morning arrived, she said her goodbyes and boarded the train with a mixture of anticipation and dread. The rhythm of the train lulled the children to sleep after the bountiful lunch Madeleine had packed. Laurel leaned back and watched the varying landscapes glide past her window. A mountain range, a valley, a farm, occasional tunnels. After relaxing a few minutes and absorbing the beauty, her thoughts turned to the speech she was scheduled to make in Deerbrook on Women's Suffrage, as soon as the nineteenth amendment was ratified by Congress.

Last night she had asked Papa how he felt about women getting the right to vote in Tennessee the previous year. His answer pleased her, showing his usual common sense and fairness. She took a small notebook and pen out of her bag and jotted down some of his comments.

The invitation to be the principal speaker for the Women's Suffrage Rally came from Mrs. Henry Sargent, president of the Women's Temperance Union. Laurel grimaced slightly, then smiled as she thought of Mrs. Sargent with her tall, ramrod straight posture which pushed her ample bosom forward to an intimidating degree. She was vocal and opinionated, with the conviction that everyone was waiting to hear her views on everything. She had made Laurel uncomfortable when they first started working together. After awhile, however, Laurel recognized that hiding beneath the formidable public manner was a warm hearted civic-minded crusader with common sense and courage. They became an unlikely team, balancing each other as they led the fight for Prohibition in Wildwood County.

Last October Laurel had given her first serious public speech since she had moved to Deerbrook. About one hundred and twenty-five women, brought together by the Women's Christian Temperance Union, heard the reasons for Prohibition and how they could help Wildwood County "go dry."

Her facts were documented. Her arguments answered the opposition. At her request, Justin had argued at home with her against Prohibition – some valid reasons he really believed – and helped her to think through and strengthen her arguments for. She used as emotional fuel her own stoked anger from seeing her students in want and abused by drunken fathers. In conclusion, she quoted a poem entitled, "The Drinking House Over the Way," which described in stark detail the effects of drink on a family. Because of Laurel's speaking skill, the audience could imagine the woman who lay dying of want, of hunger, and cold in a bare room with snow drifting through a broken window pane. Nearby stood an empty cradle where the baby had died a few weeks before. The husband and father was, of course, where he was likely to stay – in the drinking house over the way.

When Justin read the poem before her speech, he said, "Not your usual literary level, my dear. Are you sure you want to use this tear-jerker?"

Her answer gave a clue as to why she was a good speaker. "Yes, I plan to use it. I can give them the facts and they will leave there well-informed but unmoved. I must get their emotions involved. This poem is grim but true to life. They can live it in their imagination. I hope to inspire and possibly arouse some anger which will result in action."

It did. More than one hundred women went out to crusade. Wildwood County went dry. It was a great day for them when the Eighteenth Amendment passed in January and Prohibition was in force for the entire country. Their next battle was voting rights for women.

When the train pulled into Deerbrook on schedule, Justin was the first person she saw. His joy at seeing her and the children was transparent and contagious. As he held her close, she realized how happy she was to have his arms around her again. She thought, *I love this man and I know he loves me. We'll work out the differences about this job.*

She could sense the pent-up excitement that always gripped him when faced with a new challenge. However, it was Sunday night after the children were fed and in bed before they had a chance to talk seriously. Laurel felt refreshed after supper and a bath. She and Justin finally sat down in their reading chairs with their cups of coffee to discuss this change in their lives.

Justin sat forward as he told her about Hiram Beck's remarks and sudden decision to hire him. He would never brag, but she heard the pride in his voice and saw it in his eyes.

He put his cup down and walked around the room with his hands in his pockets as he continued. "Laurel, I know this will be hard and very different for you, but I need a job that will bring in a steadier income than my photography. I'll continue that on weekends.

"The money you saved from teaching that we have been using all along is almost gone. I believe I can make a good living at this job and have enough left over to buy us a place – maybe a farm – near Deerbrook, if that's what you want."

"Justin, if you're worried about money, I know I could get another teaching job this coming year, and you could set up a photography studio here in Deerbrook like we've talked about several times."

"But this logging job is an opportunity to make some good money fast. We could do it for maybe three or four years and get out."

"You've mentioned twice about it being hard. What do you mean? I don't know one thing about logging camps. What would this mean for our family?" She sat on the edge of her chair and looked at him solemnly.

He stopped pacing and stood in front of her, equally serious. "It means we'll move into a lumber shack in Pisgah National Forest. The shacks are crudely built because they are temporary. They are torn down once we finish cutting one tract of timber and they are built again at the next tract."

"How many shacks will there be in our camp?"

"We're planning to have four shacks, a kitchen and mess hall, a bunkhouse, and a barn. There's a crew already at work building them."

Laurel was reluctantly intrigued. "That's almost a community in the woods. How do you know about all this?"

"Mr. Beck and I rode through the tract of timber we'll be cutting first and I estimated about how many board feet of lumber we can cut, about how many men we'll need, and about how long it will take."

"I didn't know you could do that. Did you learn it in that logging camp where you lived when you were young?"

"Most of it there. But, you know how far back in the mountains my family lived. I grew up logging. Cut my teeth on it. Our only choices seemed to be logging or making moonshine. My family logged, but our neighbors made moonshine. I learned how to do that, too! Hey! Now that's an idea! How'd you like to be a moonshiner's wife?"

She laughed. "Well, maybe we could do both. I'll hide the moonshine under my petticoats and peddle it around town."

He reached for her hand, pulled her up and looked into her eyes. "You'd make us rich."

They stood a moment, holding each other close, but still aware that there were currents pulling them apart. After a satisfying kiss, Laurel said softly, "Justin, we're off the subject. Tell me the rest."

So he did. There would be three other families in the shacks and about sixteen men in the bunkhouse, making a crew of twenty men to begin the job.

"You'll need to be in charge of the cooking, Laurel."

"I'll what?"

But he didn't even hear her as he continued. "We'll be feeding twenty men, four or five women, and several children three meals a day from Monday through Friday. The other women will help you. We could hire somebody, but I told Mr. Beck I wanted you to do it."

Laurel was dumbfounded. She let it sink in for a minute and faltered, "What about our children? Who will watch them while I'm in the kitchen all day?"

"Oh, all you women will work that out together," he said airily, dismissing the subject with his hand.

"Why would you rather I be in charge?" she persisted.

"It's the reasonable answer. You would have to help any way, so why not be in charge? You're capable and educated and nobody's going to want to be telling you what to do. You'll have plenty of help. I know you'll do a good job. We'll eat well and save money!"

Anger coursed through Laurel. She stood and looked at him for a long time. "You've totally disrupted our lives. You've signed me up for a job I don't want! And I don't even have any say in it?"

"You do have a say, Laurel. That's what we're talking about."

"Not really – not in the turn our life has taken. I only get to choose one of two bad choices that you have imposed on me. Do you know how that makes me feel, Justin? Like I've been kidnapped and held against my will!"

His anger sparked against hers. "Laurel, I have the responsibility to support this family. I'm doing it the best way I know how. I thought you would be willing to help us get ahead. But I sure don't need a kidnap victim to deal with!" He swung out of the room and she heard the kitchen door slam as he left the house.

She didn't know where he was going and didn't care. She looked around the room. The Aladdin lamp cast a glow over the room, showing her furnishings and decorating efforts. The deep wine fabric of the sofa matched the floral print of the wing back chairs which was a soft green with varying shades of rose, deepening into wine. Two dainty Chippendale tables sat at the ends of the sofa and one between their reading chairs. She was particularly pleased with the oak desk, where she had arranged and rearranged books, papers, and figurines until it had just the look she wanted. She had just finished putting up her wild rose pictures on the wall above the sofa before she had gone to Knoxville. She had thoroughly enjoyed turning this house into a home. It mirrored who she was, and she didn't want to give it up!

She looked slowly around the room. Saying goodbye to it would be like leaving a part of herself behind. When she realized she was crying, she deliberately quieted her thoughts and suddenly felt very tired. It seemed a long time ago that she had left Papa waving at the train station. What would he think of her cooking in a logging camp? She would have to be careful how much she told him. He still liked to treat her as a fragile southern belle. She smiled, then her mouth tightened. It seemed Justin's expectations of her were quite different.

She turned off the lamp, undressed, and went to bed, lying as far on her side as she could. She was asleep in a few minutes.

Chapter Four

When Justin's anger propelled him out of the house, he had no idea where he was going. He was getting away from Laurel before either could say any more things they would regret. Her words bit deep. Kidnapped! Against her will!

He headed, without thought, for Tattoo's stall. He felt for the lantern that always hung on a nail just inside the door. When he lit it, Tattoo snorted and jerked his head up and down in greeting. Justin picked up the currycomb without a word and started brushing Tattoo's coat.

The horse had been an important part of Justin's life for two years. He had a reddish brown coat with a white mark the shape of a small map on his forehead. White markings called stockings on each leg reached halfway to his knees. Justin had named him Traveler Too, after General Robert E. Lee's famous horse, Traveler. Sarah, with her baby talk, had changed that to Tattoo. The name had stuck.

Justin had wanted – had expected – Laurel to be proud of him for getting this job. Couldn't she realize how many men and their wives would jump at this chance? He knew she was used to more than he had been able to provide for her so far, but if they would work hard at this together for a while, maybe they could get ahead and buy a home.

Then, because he could be totally honest with Tattoo, he started talking. "Tattoo, I do want to provide and get ahead. But I also want the challenge this job offers. I want to be my own boss on the job. I want to work outside with other men. I like to work hard and see what I've accomplished with my own two hands."

He brushed awhile then continued. "Tattoo, I'm not a studio man. For all that talk about a photography studio, I know I can't do it. I need to be out where the action is. I know Laurel would like to tame me, but in some ways I can't be tamed and still be who I am."

He gave a few long strokes. "Yeah, yeah, I know I'm asking a lot from her, too."

As he carefully worked some knots and snarls out of Tattoo's mane, his emotions and thoughts smoothed out, but his resolve strengthened. He patted Tattoo, hung up the currycomb and turned out the lantern. He walked slowly back to the house, got in bed quietly without waking Laurel and went to sleep actually looking forward to the next day.

Because they both made an effort, breakfast was outwardly normal. Justin said steadily as he fed Adam his oatmeal, "We have two weeks to get ready. I want to be in the woods with the crew cutting trees two weeks from this morning. I've already hired about half the crew. I'm hoping to have the rest in a couple of days. Lots of people need work, so I can pick and choose."

After looking at her expectantly for a moment, he went on. "I'll also ride up and check on the camp today. I've asked the crew to have it ready by Friday."

Laurel stayed busy with the children. She said nothing.

His voice rose and sharpened. "Laurel, please stop busying around and look at me!"

She stopped in her tracks on the way to the stove, turned and looked at him impassively.

"We need to move on Saturday or Monday at the latest," he said. "We have to get settled, buy what we need for the camp kitchen, and buy groceries to feed the crew the first week."

Laurel spoke for the first time. "I'm not ready to talk about moving. I need a day to think about all this and figure out what to do. The children are tired and I need to wash clothes." She turned and went to the bedroom.

Justin stood. He talked to Sarah and Adam a moment, tousled their hair and kissed them. Then, he took his jacket off a hook by the door and headed out. As he left, he called, "I'll see you tonight."

Laurel was actually relieved when she heard him leave. She dressed herself and the children, and made up the bed quickly, her frustration driving her. She felt betrayed by Justin; her desires and opinions were of no value.

She was a pawn to be moved as he wished. She went through her routine of housework automatically. *But I'm not helpless,* she thought suddenly as she scrubbed his work shirt on the scrub board. *I can make a living for myself and the children. I do have a choice.*

This thought comforted her until she thought of Sarah and Adam without their daddy. He was so good with them and they adored him. What's more, in her heart, she knew she did not want to live apart. Even so, she still held the thought and turned it over several times during the day to examine the possibilities.

When Justin came home, tired and hungry but mostly excited about his progress, she heard him out, then said in a rush, "Justin, I've been thinking today about staying here with the children. I can get a teaching job in August. You could come home on weekends like most of the men in camp will do."

He looked at her, bewildered. "You want us to live apart except for weekends?"

"That's what most of the men do, isn't it? And we would sure have a more normal life here than in a logging camp."

"You call living apart more normal? The children will forget they have a daddy."

"How much will they see you at the camp? And how much will they see me, for that matter, if I'm the chief cook? What kind of day will it be cooking three meals? Tell me the schedule."

"I told you it will be hard work, Laurel, but it won't be forever."

"Tell me."

"Breakfast at six, lunch at twelve-fifteen, and supper at six-fifteen. The crew will work from seven to twelve, then from one to six. A ten-hour day. They can walk to the job in ten minutes."

"So that means being in the kitchen by four-thirty in the morning and finishing about eight-thirty at night. A sixteen-hour day for the cooks."

"There will be four other women living in camp. I expect all of them to be willing to work. You could work shifts." His tone became impatient. "You know I don't expect you to work sixteen hours a day with two children, a husband, and a home to take care of."

"Maybe you can hire one of the other women for your chief cook. I'm going to check tomorrow about a teaching job. I'll pay the rent on this place and you can still save money to buy a house."

He held his voice steady. "Why are you fighting me on this?"

"Because I don't choose to raise my children in a lumber camp away from civilization. Some people can't do any better. We can!"

He stood. "Laurel, my dear, you do whatever makes you happy. I'm planning to start this job on time, whether you're there or not." He picked up his coat and went to the door. "I'm going to ride Tattoo into town to deliver some pictures. Good night!"

She sat for a few minutes staring at the door. She heard him leave, riding hard, then she walked through the house slowly, looking and touching some of her favorite things. It had taken five years to get her house as she wanted it.

After awhile, she tiptoed in, checked on the children and then went to bed. She found herself listening for Justin's return. Finally, she slept.

Justin's anger was evident. Usually gentle with Tattoo, he now threw the saddle across Tattoo's back, jerked the girth tight, and pounded out of the yard.

Laurel had never stood so fiercely against him in anything. He admired her strong-mindedness, but didn't enjoy having it pitted against him. He had actually expected her to be caught up in the adventure of this job, just as he was.

The spring night was clear and the brightness of a full moon lit his way. After a mile or two of hard riding, Justin gradually slowed Tattoo to a walk and allowed the quietness around him to seep in and help him relax. He thought again of the job.

The lumber industry was expanding in the area. It was said that Pisgah Forest had the greatest variety and number of hardwood trees per square mile to be found on the continent. Southern Railway was constructing a logging railroad to bring out the logs. He had watched a crew of Italians laying rails last week. Their rhythmic action reminded him of Walt Whitman's poem, "I Hear America Singing". The railroad already went past their logging camp and would continue to the end of the Beck Lumber Company boundary.

Last week, when he had walked alone over the first tract of timber he would be cutting, he had felt a sense of belonging and a peace that surprised him. The woods – the smell, the sounds, the sights – met a hunger he had not realized he had. It was a homecoming. He knew this job was a part of his destiny. He would find a way to win Laurel over. He finished his business dealings in town and rode home quickly. Tomorrow he would spend some unhurried time with her and the children.

True to his word, the next morning he was up and had the coffee perking when Laurel awakened. The children were awake and ready to be fed. Justin went to feed the animals and milk the cow while Laurel fixed breakfast.

Laurel was still on guard, wary of any overtures. After the children were fed and dressed, and the table cleared, Justin said, "Let's have another cup of coffee and you tell me about your visit to Knoxville. I've been so wrapped up in this job we haven't even talked about it. What's the Professor up to?"

She was hesitant at first, but with a few sips of coffee she loosened a bit. She told him about the family, the reception, and news of people he knew. Then she said musingly, "I fully realized for the first time how important Papa is to the people in that community and I told him so. He was touched and told me some things about my mother, Alexis, that I never knew."

Justin leaned forward and put his elbows on the table. "Was she like you?"

"Papa says I'm more like her than any of us girls. He says I look like her, act like her and, well, that I have her same capacity to enjoy life."

"So that's where you get that special quality! You are different from your sisters."

"Papa made me cry when he talked about my mother." She spoke softly and slowly. "He said he adored her, that she brought him out of his introverted, pedantic world into the world of people and their needs. After she died, he made a promise to her that he would try to look at the world through her eyes and raise us – and I'm quoting him here – 'in the larger, people-filled, happy place' she had led him to enjoy."

Laurel's eyes filled. "Justin, I wish I could have known my mother."

He reached across and put his hand over hers. "But I think you do know her, Laurel. It sounds like you are very much like her."

"Papa called me my mother's daughter."

"I'm sure you are, but you know something? You're also your father's daughter. You have a big dose of your papa in you."

"Do I really?" she asked, giving him her first real smile in two days. "I'd like someday to be like Papa."

He came around the table, pulled her to her feet, and held her close. "Laurel, I just want you to be you – the woman I love."

"I love you too, Justin." She looked at him with pain in her eyes. "You know I do…but, right now, I'm so confused."

"I realized last night I hadn't told you all I need to about the logging job. You need to know as much as you can about what we're getting into and why. Then you can make a decision based on facts rather than pressure from me."

As Sarah and Adam played around their feet, he told her about the expanding lumber industry in western North Carolina, the logging railroad being built, the opportunity of good jobs for men who badly needed them. She found herself becoming interested in spite of herself.

He was honest with her about his loss of interest in the photography studio and he shared his feelings about being in the woods again. "You married an adventurer, Laurel. I need to be outside and on the move."

He picked up Adam, who had pulled up on his daddy's legs, and finished by saying again, "I haven't been able to provide you and children with a home and living like you grew up with. You deserve more than I've given you so far. I think this is my best chance to make enough money to buy us a home."

He paused. "The professor is right, as usual. You do have a love for life, and I know you like a challenge just as much as I do. Could you look on this as a challenge? I thought this might appeal to your adventurous spirit and, hey, you don't get a job offer like this every day!" He laughed at his own bad joke.

She almost smiled. "You're a charming rogue, Justin! But I still have some hard thinking to do."

He pulled her to him and looked into her eyes. "Laurel, you choose. You and children could stay here and I'll see you on weekends. I want you with me but I won't try to force you. We could save more money for a house if we're together. You think about it today." He handed Adam to her, put on his jacket, hugged and kissed them all and said, "I hope to finish hiring my men today."

He paused at the door. "I need to know your decision by tonight."

As Laurel washed the dishes and made the beds, she allowed herself time to consider moving and living in the logging camp. Since she had never seen a logging camp or shacks like Justin was talking about, it was hard to imagine. Justin's offer to leave the decision up to her dispelled most of her resentment and her common sense took over. She usually made her decision on facts rather than emotion. Justin was the impulsive one.

So, when the children went down for the naps, she sat at her oak table with a notebook and pencil to write out her mental dispute: the pros and cons. Things inevitably became clearer to her if she wrote them down. She had once joked that her brain was really in her elbow.

On the first sheet of paper she wrote *Con – Against*. On the next, she wrote *Pro –For*. Her hand flew across the paper with her reasons for not wanting to live in the logging camp:

Complete change of lifestyle...Changing from teacher to cook...Long hours of hard labor...Isolation from civilization, friends, church...Primitive living conditions...Type of people we'll work with...Effect on children... She got up and paced the room, worried, not knowing what all this would do to their family.

Finally, she sat back down. On the "Pro" sheet she wrote:

First, financial gain – owning a home. She had weighed one financial choice against the other as she worked that morning. If she taught school she would have to hire someone to come to the house and keep the children, besides paying rent and expenses for a separate household. It would take almost everything she made. On the other hand, if they lived in the logging camp together, they could save what they would have to pay another person to be in charge of the cooking. That would get them out of the camp sooner.

Secondly, Justin would be doing the work he enjoyed.

Third, they would be living together as a family. She did not want to live without him and the children needed to be with their daddy.

The "Pro" page was not as full but the reasons weighed heavier. They tipped the scales. She decided. She would keep those heavy reasons in her mind and look on this as a temporary adventure. She would write exciting letters to Papa about their new life.

Once she had made up her mind, she was ready to get on with it. She made a list of things to do about moving and a tentative schedule. When Justin got home that night, she was well under way with her plans.

When they were able to talk, she said, "Justin, hear me out on this. I have reasons for and against." She knew he was anxious to know her decision but he needed to know her deep concerns, too. In fact, he should be concerned about the same things. She took her time and shared her questions on the negative sheet.

He listened without emotion, then said, "We've covered this ground before, Laurel."

"I know. But I want us both to go into this with the understanding that this is a major change that may have lasting consequences, especially on our children."

"If we can't make it as a family, we'll get out as soon as we can," he said.

"Then, here are my reasons for…." She shared her financial reasoning, mentioned his love for this kind of work, and told him it was important to her that their family stay together. She finished by saying, "I guess the essence of it is this: You're moving to the logging camp because you love the forest and the work. I'm moving to the logging camp because I love you."

He stood and pulled her into his arms. "And I love you. I didn't want us to live apart. We'll face the problems together as they come. And, you, m'lady, will be the best logging camp cook in history!"

"I've got a bunch of questions about moving. Can you answer them now?"

"Sure." He was so relieved over her decision, he would have answered questions patiently all night.

"You'll need to store some of your nice things and all of your living room furniture." He spoke gently because he knew how much pleasure she had received from having her house the way she wanted it. "There won't be room for it in our shack and it's way too nice for a lumber camp, anyway."

"But we have to have some place to sit and something to sit on," she objected.

"We'll maybe have room for two comfortable chairs plus the kitchen table and chairs. We'll be living in a two-room shack. One bedroom for all of us and one room that will serve as a kitchen and living area. Of course, we'll eat our meals in the mess hall during the week, but I'm sure we'll want our own kitchen."

Laurel tried to digest all this. She asked, "Are you going to the camp tomorrow?"

"Yes. Why?"

"I want you to measure the rooms in the shack and draw me a sketch showing where the doors and windows are. Then we can figure what will fit."

"Okay. Good idea."

"And, Justin, where will we store the things we can't take?"

"Let me think about it. I'll try to figure out something tomorrow."

They were working together again. That night as he held her close, just before they went to sleep, he thought, *I should take her with me to see the camp but then she may back out entirely. It's better if she doesn't see it until we move in.*

With just a trace of guilt, he went to sleep.

Chapter Five

The next few days were a flurry of activity. Laurel packed on Wednesday and Thursday. On Friday, Justin moved their things to store them. He had bartered with an elderly couple who lived in a two-story farm house just out of town. They would allow Justin the use of one small bedroom upstairs which they no longer used in exchange for his taking pictures of them, their children, and grandchildren.

Laurel lovingly wrapped her sofa in an old sheet, then a quilt and tied it down around the legs. The Chippendale tables were wrapped in old blankets. She packed her best dishes, bric-a-brac, and pictures in boxes. With a goodbye rub on her sofa just before Justin pulled the wagon out of the yard, Laurel determined to look forward, not backward.

A couple of men from the logging camp crew helped Justin move two wagon loads on Saturday. Justin introduced them as Zeke and Odell. They were helping to build the camp.

On Sunday, Laurel and the children went to church and said their goodbyes. She kept her emotions under tight rein as she talked to her friends cheerfully about the move, but she could tell they were concerned and she would miss them!

As she taught her last Sunday school lesson with the children gathered around her feet, she felt close to tears, which spilled over when one of the little girls hugged her and aid, "Miss Laurel, you've been our best teacher ever. Who's going to teach us now?"

As she drove away in the wagon, she felt all alone and vulnerable. This church and these friends had become a significant part of her life, a part Justin chose not to share. She could not just sever it without pain.

Monday was a good moving day weather-wise. Zeke and Odell were back to help Justin load the rest of their furniture and belongings on two wagons. They had brought one wagon from camp for the remaining furniture. Laurel's and Justin's wagon was filled with things they would need when they arrived: clothes, pots, pans, and dishes. She had also packed a lunch and had food accessible for cooking supper once they arrived.

When they were almost ready, she and Justin placed the children in their traveling boxes. As Justin hitched Tattoo to the wagon, Laurel walked unemotionally through the empty house one last time. She had put it behind her. She walked out the front door to survey the house once more for memory's sake. Her jonquils and tulips were a bright stretch of yellow and red on each side of the walk. Her hyacinths were sprouting and the long blue blossoms would soon join the red and yellow ones. *The primary colors,* the teacher in her thought irrelevantly, *which, when mixed, make other colors such as green, orange, and purple. Primary – the beginning – the most important.* She would look on this move as primal, essential; it would be a move that would enhance their future moves.

Reality claimed her for a moment. This was the third time she had planted bulbs in the fall and had moved before she could enjoy the flowers. She quickly broke off some jonquils and tulips for a bouquet for their new home and headed around the house without looking back.

When Justin saw her coming with the bouquet, he felt a pang of regret. He said quickly, "Here, let me fix them so they'll stay fresh." He retrieved a piece of folded newspaper from a box, went over to the pump and wet the paper thoroughly. Then he wrapped the flowers carefully and laid them in the back of the wagon.

"Thank you," she said, as she settled Sarah and Adam. When Sarah was little, Laurel had asked Justin to make a large, sturdy wooden box about three feet long, two and one-half feet wide and about eighteen inches high. She had lined it with an old quilt. It was good to move from room to room when Sarah was little, serving as a bassinet at home and as a traveling box for the wagon. They, of course, had fixed another one for Adam. The boxes fitted behind them in the wagon bed. With the boxes, she could take the children places by herself, without bothering Justin. It gave her some independence.

Today, however, they were all together, heading toward an adventure –

from Justin's point of view anyway. As they drove through Deerbrook, Laurel was impressed by the number of men calling out, "Mornin', Justin," or "Mornin', Mr. Worth," as they tipped their hats in her direction. Everybody seemed to know him and like him.

The day was bright and warm with spring sunshine working its miracles. Delicate green buds adorned the limbs that had still looked naked and lifeless just a week earlier. Birds celebrated with singing as they built their homes. As a robin flew by with some building materials hanging from its beak, Laurel laughed and said, "If the birds can do it, so can we."

"Do what?" Justin asked.

"Build a new nest. They do it every spring, so that means we've picked a good time to move. We'll have spring and summer to adjust."

We'll need it, Justin thought, remembering how bleak winter can be in a logging camp. He said briefly, "Yes, we've picked a good time."

They stopped to eat their picnic lunch near the river just after entering the forest. She nursed Adam and put him down for his nap on a pillow in his box while Justin set out their food and helped Sarah eat. As they ate, Laurel realized there was a drop in temperature. She shivered and put a sweater on Sarah and shrugged into hers as well. "Am I imagining it, or is it getting colder?"

"It's always cooler in the forest with all the trees and undergrowth," Justin explained.

Laurel felt as if she was seeing life through a green haze. The huge evergreen trees, the rhododendrons, the buds of new green on the oaks and maples, and the undergrowth all shimmered in the afternoon sun. The river rushed around the bends and over the rocks, babbling and splashing, yet with a deep soothing sound as though moving relentlessly toward a destination. She took a deep breath of the pine-scented air. "I can see how the forest works its magic on you, Justin. It is quite beautiful to see, to hear, and to smell."

Justin had been amused watching her trying to take in all the gifts of the forest in one gulp. "There's no place on earth – that I've been yet – where I feel so alive as in this forest, Laurel. I…I hope you'll enjoy it with me."

"Well, I am so far."

A sharp clap of thunder suddenly reverberated in the distance, waking

Adam and sending Sarah scurrying into her daddy's arms. Justin looked around puzzled. "I didn't see any lightning, did you?"

"No," Laurel said, quieting Adam. "It's not even cloudy."

Justin stood up. "It's further in the forest, in the direction we're headed. See? It's come up all of a sudden."

Laurel looked in the direction he pointed and saw dark thunderclouds in the distance. "What do we do now?" She glanced at the children.

"Wait and see where it's going. Maybe it won't come this way. If it does, I have a tarp to put over the wagon to keep us dry."

"I hope they made it with the furniture before the storm hit." Laurel looked worriedly toward the direction of the storm.

Justin took out his pocket watch. "They should be there by now."

The thunder made Tattoo skittish. Justin, still holding Sarah in one arm, went to the river and dipped a pail of water. As Tattoo drank, Justin rubbed his head and talked to him gently while Sarah traced the tattoo on his forehead with one finger. Justin spoke quietly, "Tattoo, there's a bad storm coming. We have to get Laurel and the children through it as fast as we can. I'll be right with you all the way." The thunder was moving closer and the wind was up, swaying the trees.

"Laurel, let's get the things back in the wagon. I'll put the tarp over the poles on the wagon and tie it down while you get the children settled in their boxes. Put their pillows around them so they can sit up."

There was an urgency in his voice, and Laurel hurried to follow his instructions. Then she was beside him, holding the flapping tarp so he could get it tied. It covered the top, sides, and back of the wagon. *Like a covered wagon going west*, she thought.

The first fat drops of rain plopped around them as they secured the tarp to the last pole. They scrambled inside just before the curtain of rain fell. Justin pulled the reins to turn Tattoo and the wagon toward the road, facing the storm. Lightning played around them and the thunder was right above their heads. Adam and Sarah began crying. Laurel started to get them on her lap, but Justin said, "No, leave them in their boxes. You may have to help me."

Laurel knew they were in serious danger. She turned and said sternly, "Sarah, hush crying. Get over into Adam's box and play peek-a-boo with him. I need to help daddy."

Sarah's crying dried to a hiccup and she soon had Adam quiet. Playing peek-a-boo was his favorite game.

Tattoo pulled them out to face the storm. Justin called, "Giddy-up, Tattoo, Giddy-up!" He slapped the reins up and down.

"Laurel, we're going to meet the storm head on and go through it as fast as we can. It's moving this way and we're going the other way so we should be out of it before long. It's just as safe moving as it is sitting it out, maybe more so." He looked at her. "You okay?"

"Yes. I'd rather be moving, too."

The tarp could not protect Justin and Laurel totally from the driving rain but Adam and Sarah and their household belongings were dry. Tattoo pulled the wagon at a fast trot at Justin's urging, shying sideways when the lightning struck close. The wagon bounced over the rough road. Laurel held on and the children were wide-eyed. Sarah held Adam in her lap as they bumped along with the pillows around them. An explosive crack of thunder stopped Tattoo in his tracks. He snorted and jerked his head in fear. "Take the reins, Laurel. I'm going to help Tattoo. He needs me."

Before she could protest, he was over the tongue of the wagon and had swung himself onto Tattoo's rump, scooting up toward his neck, rubbing him as he talked.

"Come on, boy. Keep going. We've ridden through a lot of storms together." He lay down, almost on the horse's neck. "Giddy-up, Tattoo! I'm here with you! Move out!"

Tattoo shuddered and snorted. With seeming great effort, he put one foot before the other and started pulling again.

Laurel's breath came in a rush. She held the reins loosely, waiting for instructions as she watched Justin transmitting courage and determination to Tattoo. And Tattoo's response was touching. He trusted Justin enough to move out against his own will and with obvious fear. When Tattoo was in a full trot again, Justin sat up and took the reins. He kept up a running monologue for Tattoo as he rubbed and patted him. Occasionally, he raised his face to the storm almost as if he welcomed it.

She watched him. He was in charge, riding bareback through the storm, one with his horse, facing danger to get his family to safety. Suddenly the kaleidoscope in her mind that defined Justin shifted and she saw the real man. A moment of truth assailed her. She knew, that even while fighting him, she didn't want him to change. She wanted him to be who he was – different from any man she had ever known. He had talked about her capacity to enjoy life, but he, too, had a voracious hunger for life. He gobbled it up.

She had been trying to cage an eagle!

It was as he said. One moment, they were totally immersed in the storm; the next moment they were in startling bright sunlight. It was if they had driven through a waterfall into the land beyond.

"Whoa, boy!" Justin called. He was off Tattoo in a moment, hugging him and rubbing his head. "Good job, Tattoo! I knew you would bring us through!"

Soaked, with water still running down his face and from his clothes, he looked at Laurel and grinned. "That was quite a storm!"

Her love and pride glowed warm. "And you're quite a man with quite a horse, Mr. Worth. A match for any storm!"

"Tattoo and I have ridden out of a lot of storms but this time we were afraid for you and the children. Are all of you okay?"

"We're fine", she said, looking back at the two children who were playing again. Then she looked him over. "You're the one who's not okay. You need to change clothes."

His clothes clung to him and he could still feel water running down his back. He shivered in spite of the sunshine. She climbed down quickly and went to the back of the wagon. "If you'll help me untie the tarp back here, I'll find you some dry clothes."

She rummaged through two boxes and found a complete change of clothes and a towel. While he dressed at the back of the wagon, Laurel went to Tattoo. She rubbed his forehead and said, "You're the bravest and best horse in the whole wide world, Tattoo."

When Justin came around with his dry clothes on, she was feeding Tattoo an apple left over from lunch. She pulled the horse's head down, gave him a hug, and laid her face on his.

"Do I get one of those hugs?" Justin asked, holding his soggy clothes well away from him.

"You do, after you lay those clothes down."

He put the dripping pile on the wagon tongue and she went into his arms the way he loved, signaling she was his. "Thank you for taking care of us and getting us out of danger so fast." She pulled his face down and kissed him.

He tightened his arms around her. "I was scared for awhile with all that lightning playing around. I was afraid the metal on the wagon might attract it or it might strike a tree and knock it down on us."

"You didn't act scared. You acted like a part of you was enjoying it."

"You know me too well, woman!" He looked at her, pleased. "It was a challenge."

A little voice from the wagon spoke, "Daddy, hug!"

Laurel laughed, "Somebody's jealous."

Justin climbed up, handed Adam to Laurel and climbed down with Sarah. He hugged her tight. "You were a big girl and helped mommy and daddy with Adam."

"I know," she said and nestled her head on his shoulder.

Laurel changed Adam's diaper while Justin wrung out his clothes. He laid them out on top of the tarp to dry. Steam started rising immediately. Soon the wagon was rolling again.

Nothing could have prepared Laurel for her first sight of the logging camp and the shack they would live in. Justin brought Tattoo to a stop at the edge of the camp. Her eyes traveled across the clearing. Raw muddy earth, trampled undergrowth, stumps of various sizes and heights, and piles of scrap lumber and sawdust comprised the center of the clearing which was about the size of a ball field. Rays of sunshine, made visible by moisture from the storm, streamed down around the camp. It was as if she had gone back in time.

Justin was pointing out buildings to her, so she made an effort to listen. Their shack was the first one on the right. Her eyes grew wider. They were going to live in *that*?

Justin's information kept coming. The longer building closest to their shack was the mess hall. Another shack that looked identical to theirs stood next. The bunkhouse, the longest building in camp, had been built a sensible distance from the other buildings and finished the circle except for the barn and shed, which stood in isolation to the left of the camp. She could hear some hammering coming from that direction. All the buildings backed up to the forest and faced the mutilated clearing. *We're lined up in a circle like a wagon train,* she thought.

She had never seen such crude buildings. They looked like they had been thrown together with rough scrap lumber by a bunch of boys playing at building.

A wall of tall trees which looked impenetrable surrounded the camp. Glancing at her, Justin said, "The trees aren't as thick as they look when you get closer. There's a path between the mess hall and the next shack that leads to two more shacks hidden by the trees. And that makes up our logging camp! What do you think?"

He was so proud and she was speechless with dismay. She forced herself to look at him squarely. "It'll take some getting used to." Her eyes rested on the shack again and she swallowed hard. "Let's go see our new...uh...place"

When the wagon stopped in front of the shack, Justin carried Sarah and Laurel carried Adam. He lifted the wooden latch and the door swung open to darkness inside. He felt his way in and opened two wooden shutters, one on each side of the room. Light spilled in, showing a haphazard pile of furniture and boxes.

Laurel's gaze traveled the walls of rough splintery boards, full of knot holes. Green studs, still oozing sap, supported the walls. The shutters hung open, showing windows without glass. The same rough lumber rose above their heads to make a roof line through exposed rafters.

"It's dry, even after that storm," she said, glad to find something positive to say. "What kept it from leaking?"

"Tar paper is nailed on top of the roof."

He went into the bedroom and opened the shutter. The one window in the room was in the middle of the end wall. It was straight across from the door into the room. She could see the forest and a corner of the mess hall. From where she was standing, she could see out on three sides. She knew she would never be able to keep those shutters closed. "Justin, why aren't the windows in yet?"

"These are standard logging camp windows. If we want glass windows, we pay for them ourselves. We won't have the money until I get paid."

"Could we use a little of my teaching money or do we need it for something else?"

"You check how much we have left and we'll see. I did have the men to cut the window openings to the size of a small six-pane window. I knew we would be having this conversation."

She smiled. She had never considered glass windows a luxury. "I can see my education about logging camp life is just beginning."

Justin went in search of someone to help them move the furniture. And Laurel was in a quandary. She couldn't put Adam down. The floor was too rough and full of splinters for a crawling baby.

When Justin returned with Zeke and Odell, they brought in the children's boxes first. After she settled Adam in to play again, she could turn her attention to the furniture.

"Let's do the bedroom first," Justin said. "We've already started it."

The two double beds with iron bedsteads were already set side by side facing the door, with about two feet of space between them for getting into bed. She had Justin place a small table between the heads of the beds under the window. She was greatly relieved when the wardrobe fit at the foot of their bed on the right and the chest of drawers at the foot of the children's bed on the left.

"Oh," Laurel said, "I believe there's room for my trunk in the corner beside the chest of drawers." She was relieved when Zeke and Odell lifted it high over the rail at the foot of the bed and wedged it in. There was barely enough room to open the wardrobe and chest of drawers but she could do it if she stood to one side.

The kitchen and living area presented a bigger challenge. She stood at their only outside door, which faced the clearing, and surveyed the room. Her handsome cook stove with its warmer cupboard on top and hot water reservoir on the right side, was standing in the center of the wall at the right end of the room, opposite the bedroom. Someone had already fixed the stove pipe so it looked ready for a fire to be built. There was also a small pile of dry stove wood.

"Let's put the cabinet in the corner to the right of the stove," she said. She was proud of her Hoosier cabinet with its flour bin, roll down front, and white enamel counter top trimmed in red. The enamel matched the doors on her stove. "Let's put it diagonally, out from the corner a little," she directed. "That way I can store things behind it." The men looked puzzled.

"She means catty-cornered, right here," Justin said. They understood then and hefted it into place.

Justin stood back and looked at the cabinet. "That leaves enough room to build a shelf beside the door to hold the water buckets and wash pans."

Laurel had chosen to bring their round oak table with claw feet and four matching chairs, their oak desk, and their two wing back reading chairs. She knew now she had made the right decision. She needed these familiar pieces around her.

"The table needs to go on the other side of the door under the window," she said.

The washstand with their only mirror stood in the corner near the table. "This needs to stay here. The light hits the mirror right for shaving," Justin said.

Laurel looked at the opposite wall and corner next to the bedroom. "Look, we have enough room for our reading corner after all! I'm so glad we brought the chairs." And they did fit with a small table between for their reading lamp. They both loved to read and looked forward to their reading time together at night after the children had gone to bed.

"I'll build a couple of shelves in that corner for our books," Justin said.

The last piece of furniture to put in place was the small oak desk. It fitted under the window straight across the room from the door into the shack. *The first thing I'll see when I come through the door,* Laurel thought.

The men waited patiently while she looked over everything and stopped in front of the stove. "I'll need some shelves here in the left corner by the stove, and a wood box to set beside the stove on this side."

Justin turned to the men and said, "We'll figure out what we need and I'll get you to finish this for us tomorrow."

Laurel said, "Thank you for helping us. Are you the ones hammering at the barn?"

When they nodded, she said, "We'll get a fire going and make some coffee. I have some gingerbread somewhere. Justin will call you when it's ready."

They nodded again. They seemed shy and ill at ease with her, and Justin blessed her in his mind for this kindness to them. He quickly built a fire and brought in two peck buckets of water.

When Zeke and Odell came for their coffee and gingerbread, they both stood as if struck speechless until Justin asked them to have a seat at the table. Laurel knew she had to try to cut through their shyness and embarrassment and help them feel at ease.

"Thank you for all your help in moving us. Justin says you will be part of the logging crew."

"Yes, ma'am," Zeke said. "We're mighty glad to get the work."

"Tell me about your families," Laurel asked.

"Yes, ma'am," Zeke said. He seemed to be the talkative one of the pair. "They's my wife and three boys and two girls."

"That's a big family. How will they get along with you gone all week?"

"My boys is big enough to help my wife a right smart. They're twelve and ten and eight, I think. The girls are younger. We're all glad I've got this job."

Justin said, "Zeke and Odell are cousins and live close together. Their families will look out for each other. I've been by their houses on my picture taking trips."

"Yeah," Zeke said. "The young'uns is always glad to see Mr. Worth comin'. He always brings 'em candy."

Laurel smiled at Justin. She could see it in her mind. "Odell," she continued, "tell me about your family."

"Ain't much to tell, ma'am." He clearly thought so much talk was unnecessary and required a lot of effort. "I got my wife, three girls and two boys." He looked at Adam in Laurel's lap. "Ain't none of them babies no more."

Hearing something in his voice, Laurel got up and set Adam in his lap. "Well, here's a baby. You hold him awhile. We can't let you get out of practice."

Adam turned around and felt the stubble on Odell's chin, then examined the buckle on his overall strap. Odell was so surprised and pleased, he forgot his shyness as he talked and played with Adam.

The rest of the day moved fast. Justin left to check on the progress around camp. He had to keep things moving in order to be ready to start in a week. As he walked across the clearing to check on the barn and shed, he started whistling. Everything would be okay now that Laurel was here.

Laurel, meanwhile, was having her struggles. She didn't dare stop and face up to her surroundings. *Not yet! Keep busy!* her mind told her. For one thing, she had no place to keep a crawling baby. She had carried him around so long, her arms and shoulders ached. While Sarah played with him on one bed, she quickly made up the other, then switched and did the same. She then put two quilts on the floor between the beds. She tied a long belt made of scraps around Adam with the other end around the bedpost, like a leash. She gave him only enough length to crawl on the quilts. He would get splinters and scrapes in his hands and knees if he got on the floor.

She unpacked the box of food they would need for supper and breakfast, putting it on the work area of the Hoosier cabinet. Her pots and pans were stacked on the cool side of the stove, over the water reservoir, until she had her shelves. She took out just enough dishes for supper and breakfast.

They were all tired at supper and the children were cranky. They had not unpacked their lamps and the shack looked harsh and cold and forbidding by lantern light.

At dusk, a din suddenly erupted, startling Laurel by its pitch and intensity. "Justin? What is that?"

He laughed. "They're serenading you. Cicadas and tree frogs and millions of other insects from the way it sounds. It happens every night. You'll get used to it."

"They're so loud."

"We're the intruders," he said gently. "This is their territory."

When she looked out the door, the dark was a dark she had never before experienced. She could feel it and the forest pressing in on them, swallowing them. She shivered and closed the door. She was glad Zeke and Odell were in the bunkhouse.

Later that night, snuggled in Justin's arms, Laurel still refused to think beyond the end of her nose. She was at the edge of sleep when she heard a scream. It sounded like a woman. She bolted upright, her heart hammering. "J-Justin, a woman screamed!"

He sat up and put his arm around her. "No, no. It was just a mountain lion. They sound like a woman screaming."

"A mountain lion? But it sounded so close."

"It probably is," he said placidly, lying back down. "Checking us out…after all…."

"I know," Laurel interrupted sharply. "We're invading his territory."

She lay back down. After lying wide-eyed in the total darkness a long time, still afraid to face her emotions, she finally slept.

Tuesday gave Laurel time to unpack and get her house in order. Justin got up early and built a fire, cramming as much wood as he could into the cook stove. The April air was cold and damp. Laurel woke with a sense of dread which she squelched. Justin was bursting with energy and purpose and she would do her part.

He left as daylight was trying to find its way over the mountains and through the trees into their little clearing. As soon as she had the children fed, dressed, and settled to play on the quilts in the bedroom, she sat down to finish her coffee while she assessed what she needed to do. Her jonquils and tulips in a quart jar in the middle of the table seemed as out of place as she felt. The absolute crudeness of the shack with the shutters closed and the lantern barely dispelling the darkness made her despair for a few minutes. She put her head on her arms and closed her eyes for a minute to shut it all out.

She refused, however, to give into the down pull and soon was on her feet. She hurried to her trunk, unpacked the Aladdin lamp and filled it with kerosene from the can behind the stove. In a few minutes, its bright glow bathed the shack in light. Sarah said, "Pretty, Mommy." Adam even gurgled his pleasure.

She enjoyed keeping house and got pleasure out of having everything in its place. As she unpacked her dishes and put them in the top of her Hoosier cabinet, the wild rose pattern on her plates somehow comforted her and she began to feel more like herself. The foodstuffs went into the bottom of the cabinet and she emptied a ten-pound bag of flour into the flour bin. That was all she could do in the kitchen until the shelves were built.

It was mid-morning when she opened the shutters and turned off the lamp. The air was still cold. In spite of the fire she kept going in the cook stove, she put sweaters on the children. Next, she unpacked their clothes and put them in the wardrobe and chest of drawers, the children playing around her feet. As she put his clothes up, the picture of Justin riding Tattoo through the storm yesterday kept coming to her mind. Her thoughts turned back to when she had first met him....

She was going through her poetry routine at the charity benefit when she first saw him. She noticed him immediately because he was sitting slightly forward, looking at her with total concentration. One expression after another crossed his face, catching her meaning and emotion. His intensity was such that she felt as if she were performing for him alone.

She found herself looking for him and wondering who he was after the benefit was over. Evan, her steady beau and escort that night, had gone to get her box which he had just bought for a high price. The custom of young men bidding on the privilege of eating a box of good food with the girls of their choice was the most popular way to raise funds. Laurel had been pleased and flattered, as any girl would, by the flurry and heavy bidding on her box.

The stranger she had been wondering about was suddenly at her side. "I enjoyed your performance, Miss Kingsley."

"Thank you, Mr...?"

"Worth. Justin Worth. I'm from Hartford, just here visiting a friend."

"We hope you like Knoxville and will come again," she said politely.

"Oh, I will come again," he said, looking at her. "I'm a photographer and I'm looking over the prospects of some work here."

"Oh, Papa may be able to help you with that."

She turned around and went to speak to her father who came over immediately. "Papa, this is Mr. Worth. Mr. Worth, meet Professor Kingsley. Mr. Worth is a photographer and is looking over this area for work."

The two men shook hands as Professor Kingsley asked, "Where did you learn photography?"

"In the army. I was in for two years."

There was something about Justin that Professor Kingsley liked immediately. On impulse he said, "Will you be in town tomorrow?"

"Yes, sir."

"If you could come to our house around three o'clock, we could talk awhile. That would give us time to get back from church and finish lunch. Is that time all right with you, Laurel?"

"Yes," she had answered.

"Thank you. I'll be there," Justin said, and walked away just as Evan returned with her box for their supper together.

As Laurel continued unpacking, past images and impressions of Justin flitted through her mind. Papa and Justin on the front porch that first Sunday afternoon, talking about the war in Europe, President Wilson's policies, and politics in general. They had included her in the conversation as she came and went, serving lemonade and Madeleine's famous Angel Food Cake.

She found out soon that he was a Republican – even more than Papa – and that he had graduated from college, planning to go on to law school. But he had joined the army for two years instead, where he had learned his photography. She remembered her strange excitement when he looked at her or talked to her.

Then Evan had arrived. He was in full uniform as he had been every time she had seen him during this furlough. He was on the porch, greeting Papa before he noticed Justin in the wicker chair. He barely acknowledged Papa's introduction before he turned to her, put his hand on her shoulder, and asked, "Do you have anywhere special you would like to go?"

His proprietary air and suggestion of intimacy between them irritated and embarrassed Laurel. She felt the color rise in her cheeks as she moved away. "I'd like to go over to Aunt Sarah's later. Why don't you sit down and have some cake and lemonade with us?"

The talk turned back to politics briefly, then Papa started asking Evan questions about army life. Justin, after a little while, got up and said he must go. Laurel thought, *He's going to leave here and I won't ever see him again!*

She said suddenly, "Papa, did you have any suggestions for Mr. Worth about his photography?"

"We talked about it while you were in the kitchen, I guess."

"He's sending me to see the editor of the *Knoxville Sentinel*. It seems they need a photographer," Justin said, smiling. "Thank you for your hospitality, Miss Kingsley. I enjoyed our talk, Professor."

"Yes, yes," Papa replied, standing and shaking Justin's hand vigorously. "So did I! It's good to talk with somebody who has some sense about politics. Please come back and let me know your plans when you have time."

"Thank you. I'll be back," he said to the professor. But his eyes were on Laurel.

A knock at the door brought Laurel back to the present. Zeke and Odell, definitely more at ease, were ready to build her shelves. Odell's poker face creased with a smile when Adam reached for him. He took him and went out the door, saying, "I'll show him around a little before we get to work."

Sarah, not be outdone, reached up for Zeke and said, "Me, too."

"Well, I'll be," said Zeke with a laugh as he swung her up and headed out after Odell. Laurel, watching them, thought, *Children are marvels.*

After a little while, they returned. Laurel showed them where to put the water shelf by the door and the shelves on each side of the stove. They went to work with their usual taciturn manner, and she decided this would be a good time to look around the camp herself. She carried Adam and held Sarah by the hand as they walked all the way around the clearing, circling the buildings to see the edge of the forest. She wondered fleetingly where the mountain lion that had stalked the camp last night stayed during the day. She did not go into any of the buildings because she knew Justin wanted to show them to her. Besides, she was looking for an inviting place where she could spend some time outside with the children.

Just behind their shack, a sparse stand of pine trees had covered the ground with a thick carpet of pine needles, discouraging the undergrowth. It was so soft and spongy, Sarah started jumping and falling, laughing with delight. Laurel found a comfortable seat on a log softened by age. There was even a tree to lean back on. However, after she sat a moment, she realized dampness was seeping through. Sarah held Adam long enough for her to run after an old quilt for her log seat and Adam's box to give her arms a rest.

She settled down to think as the children played at her feet. She needed to come to terms with herself and Justin over living here. Romantic notions of adventure fled before the stark reality facing her. She allowed herself to face it fully, knowing it was going to get worse before it got better. Her

64

agitation drove her to her feet. She paced back and forth as she sought to voice her fears. "I—I feel out of control. I'm afraid of living like this—of what it will do to me and my children."

Sarah tugged at her skirt. "Mama talking?"

Laurel stooped and hugged her. "Yes, I'm talking to myself, not you. Go play with Adam. I'm trying to figure something out."

Every time she looked over the clearing, she recoiled inside, as if the outer desolation might creep inside her very being. She continued talking in a low tone. "Can I stand against this—this overwhelming, invasive feeling of helplessness? Can I change this place enough to—to somehow be an acceptable place to live?"

She stared unseeing into the forest as she continued to struggle. "I can't let it conquer me for the children's sake as well as my own, but am I strong enough to fight it?"

A gentle breeze swayed the tops of the trees, a soothing sound. She looked up and her eyes were drawn to the mountains beyond. She thought of the verses from the Psalms she had known from childhood. "I will lift mine eyes unto the hills from whence cometh my help. My help cometh from the Lord." Was this her calm reminder that she had help beyond herself? For the first time, the mountains which surrounded her seemed comforting instead of threatening.

Adam was beginning to fret, so Laurel picked him up and sat down on the log with him on her lap. A redbird settled on a limb close to her and cocked his head so precociously she laughed and cocked her head in return. And that brought Papa to mind. What had he said about her mother dying? He could not change his circumstances but he could change his attitude. If he had not had the courage and character to go on in spite of grievous circumstances, what would her life have been like? He had said that life – or God—had handed him a challenge when he lost her mother. She remembered his serious expression as he had said, "Would I let my circumstances destroy me or would I face them like a man and learn and grow from them?"

If he had chosen the high road in far worse circumstances, could she do less? As she struggled with her emotions, the forest intruded on her thoughts with the smell of pine, sunlight etching the tops of the regal trees against the bright blue sky, a clump of lacy ferns to her left, squirrels scampering and birds singing. She absently ran her fingers over a patch of moss on the side of her log. It was like green velvet. And the hammering in her shack continued, preparations for a life she had not chosen.

That was it! She would deliberately choose it! She would not give into the downward pull of resentment, self-pity, and hurt pride over her circumstances. She would pick up the challenge Justin had placed before her, and she would give it her best efforts. Papa had given her a copy of a prayer that had given him comfort and courage after her mother had died. It was in her Bible. She would look it up.

Sarah had gathered a pile of pine cones near Adam's box. She handed one to Laurel. It was sticky with resin. "We'll take these in, Sarah. They'll be good to start fires instead of having to cut so much kindling. That will help your daddy."

Sarah smiled, leaned over, and told Adam, "I help Daddy." Then she added, "Mama, I'm hungry." Laurel realized it must be lunchtime. She lingered long enough to nurse Adam then took Sarah's hand and they went inside. The men had finished and gone. The shelves gave Laurel pleasure. She would cover them with oilcloth. *I can't control some things in our lives,* she thought, *but I can control my house. I'll make a decent place to live out of this shack.*

That night after the children were in bed, she and Justin sat down to talk over their day and to make plans for tomorrow. She wanted to tell him of her struggle and her resolve to give this job and life her best efforts. But she was not quite ready. She realized it was a very private battle and she needed to get it all in order in her own mind before she tried to tell Justin. They sat in companionable silence while Justin made some entries in his account book for the job. Laurel wrote some in her diary and looked through her Bible until she found a piece of paper. She sat looking at it in deep thought. When Adam cried out, she left her books and papers on the table and went to the bedroom.

Justin finished his paperwork and stood up. Her open diary caught his attention and involuntarily he read her struggle to accept this life, including the Professor's words about changing his attitude and being handed a challenge. Then he recognized the Professor's fancy script on the slip of paper on her open Bible. He picked it up and read. "God, grant me the serenity to accept what I cannot change, the courage to change the things I can, and the wisdom to know the difference. Amen." *Trust Laurel to have a poem or prayer for every occasion*, he thought.

As he read it the second time, it hit him. So, Laurel was still so unhappy about life – and him – that she was asking God to help her change things or accept them! Just go along with him because she was helpless to change things? Well, he wanted his wife to embrace life fully and enjoy it with him. He didn't see why an intelligent, educated woman like Laurel thought she needed God anyway. His stepmother – and her God – had turned their once happy home into a miserable abode. Under her strict religious pronouncements, Justin had seen his father change from a strong, happy, confident man into a sad, uncertain shadow of his former self. Justin would never allow a woman – or her God – to do that to him. He suddenly realized his hands were clenched and he felt a knot in his stomach. It had been a long while since that old, old fear and anger had gripped him.

Laurel was lying on the bed waiting for Adam to go back to sleep. She was thinking about the prayer she had just read. It condensed and clarified her struggle with an economy of words. She couldn't change the circumstance of living here but she would change her attitude. She would not, however, accept this, with serenity, as a permanent way of life. She would continue to fight for a decent place to live and normal circumstances for her children in the future. She and Justin had more education than most people. They didn't have to live like this. They had choices. This comforted her for the future. For now, they had a logging camp to run.

When she went back into the kitchen, Justin was sitting on the edge of his chair with his head in his hands. She rarely saw him show any weariness. In a rush of tenderness, she sat down and laid her hand on his arm. "Justin, I know you're feeling a lot of pressure right now. I'll help you all I can."

When he looked at her, his eyes were hard. "So, you've decided to accept what can't be changed!" he said. "I read that prayer. Your husband has made life so miserable for you that you have to have God's help to stand it!"

She flinched as if he had slapped her. "Justin," she said slowly. "That's the first time you've ever openly mocked my...my belief in God. Don't you think that is my business?"

"I just don't want you to go whining to Him about how bad I...how bad everything is!"

"Have you ever heard me whine?" Laurel asked. "I plan to help you because I'm your wife."

"I don't want a martyr for a wife!"

She had been mostly puzzled up to this point but now, stung into anger, she stood and looked at him. "You act like my life is yours to do with as you please without considering what I want! Well, I don't belong to you like – like Tattoo does!" She paused for breath. "And while I'm adjusting to this move, you talk about me being a martyr!"

He stood to face her. "What do you want, Laurel?"

"I want a say in making the decisions."

"And what if we can't agree?"

"We'll talk until we decide what's best for the whole family. You're not a bachelor any more. You can't just jump up and run to a new job every time you get the urge."

"Our life hasn't been that bad."

"Justin, I want what's best for all of us. I want you to do the kind of work you choose, but I have needs and wants, too. And I know what I want for the children."

"And what if I can't give you what you think you and the children need and want?"

"I'll let you know when that time comes," she answered. She paused a moment, then said more softly, "Right now we had better get some rest so we can get ready to run a logging camp."

He went to the door without a word, lit the lantern, and went out. She knew he was going to spend some time with Tattoo.

Laurel turned the Aladdin lamp low and sat quietly for a few minutes. Her anger had left as quickly as it had come, but she was still puzzled and hurt over Justin's remarks. She had enough to deal with right now without his anger. She was suddenly aware of how tired she was. She stifled the impulse to open the door to try to see if she could see Justin's lantern in the shed across the clearing. Instead, she tucked the covers around Sarah and Adam and went to bed. It took awhile, but eventually she dozed off.

Chapter Six

Meeting Nora was the best thing that happened to Laurel the next day. At breakfast, Laurel suggested that she and Justin should work on the grocery list for her first week of cooking for the crew. Since he had lived in a logging camp before, he should have an idea about how much food it would take and the kind of food the men would like.

He was keeping his distance this morning. His attitude toward her was courteous but brusque. The consideration and understanding she had felt from him yesterday was now gone. Well, she could carry on; she had before. She was still resentful and perplexed over Justin's behavior last night.

Just as they were finishing their list, someone knocked at the door. When Justin opened it, a cheerful voice said, "Mr. Worth. I come on over here to help this mornin'. I know Miz Worth has the children and a lot to do."

"Good morning, Nora." Justin said, "Come in and meet Laurel."

Justin introduced them and Nora launched into speech again. "Pleased to meet you, Miz Worth. You just show me what to do and I'll get right to it."

Laurel said, "I'm happy to meet you, Nora. Will you have a cup of coffee with us?"

"Why, yes, ma'am, I will. Then you can tell me what to do."

"Are Jed and Hannah settled in?" Justin asked.

"Yes. We got things put in their place yesterday. Jed says the other families should be gettin' here soon." Laurel could sense her excitement. This was probably Nora's first job.

"Everybody should be in today or tomorrow. We have a lot of work to do before the job starts on Monday," Justin said.

Nora was such a big woman it was hard for Laurel to keep from staring at her. She was not fat, but big, at least a head taller than Justin. Her face was wide and her features were somewhat uneven, as if a sculptor had left them unfinished. Her eyes were a light brown, almost tawny, color. She had short straight brown hair pulled over to one side and fastened with a child's red hair barrette. Her hand dwarfed the coffee cup. She was dressed in a faded, but clean, red and blue plaid dress that buttoned down the front. Her shoes were brown oxfords that tied and she had on white socks like a schoolgirl.

· Laurel recognized her problem immediately and her heart went out to Nora. She had probably been laughed at all her life. Laurel was very familiar with the way school children teased and taunted anyone who was different.

"I'm glad you've come to help, Nora. We'll get the children dressed and fed in a few minutes. Then I'll leave them with you while Justin and I go see what needs to be done with the camp kitchen."

"Miz Worth, I was thinkin' on the way over here. I'll help you a few days and you can see if you like my work. If you don't, you can tell me and I'll try to change, or you can tell me if you want to get someone else. That way you won't feel like you're stuck with me, good or bad, just because I'm right here in camp."

"That will be fine, Nora. I will be just as frank with you as you have been with me. I'll tell you in a few days how I like your work."

Justin was shaving with his straight razor at the washstand. He had lather all over his face. Laurel looked at him in the mirror and saw a smile touch his eyes. He had known she would like Nora with her cheerful and forthright way.

A call from the bedroom let them know the children were awake. While Laurel went to dress them, Nora got to work washing the dishes and straightening the kitchen. When Laurel brought the children out they looked at Nora shyly, but she soon had Sarah talking to her as she helped Laurel feed them breakfast.

After a little while, Laurel left them with Nora and went with Justin to the mess hall. It was a longer building than their shack and there was just one big room with a cook stove already in the corner just across from the door.

"Why didn't you tell me about Nora?" Laurel asked.

"How could I tell you without making her sound like a freak?"

"She has gigantism. It's caused by a malfunction of the pituitary gland. I'm sure she's been made fun of all her life, yet she's so remarkably likeable."

"I knew you would like her."

Laurel could sense some of the pressure Justin was under, and he was taking a lot of his limited time to help her get settled and provide the things she wanted.

"I've asked Zeke and Odell to build two long eating tables and benches for the men," Justin said. "What else do you think you'll need?"

"Let's see…I'll need shelves by the stove for the pots and pans and some big nails in this two-by-four to hang up my iron skillets right by the stove. And could they build a corner cabinet for the dishes here just opposite the stove?"

"Why don't we build a cabinet for the foodstuff in this corner and build some shelves over near the table for the dishes?" Justin suggested.

"That will probably be better," she agreed.

"You'll need to buy some dishes and flatware and pots and pans. I saw some heavy white plates at the company store. The company will pay a certain amount for supplies."

"That's good. You can show me the dishes and other things you think we'll need when we go get groceries. Oh, and I'll also need a table near the stove to work on. It will need to be almost as long as the eating tables but a little higher."

"I'll get the men to work on the kitchen today. The others will help when they get here. Now, before I go see them, let me show you the spring," Justin said.

About halfway between the camp kitchen and their shack, he led her onto a small path through the trees. Just at the base of a steep hill covered with laurel and rhododendron, the spring sparkled in the morning sun. It had created its own little cave. Justin had cleaned out the fallen leaves and the clear water showed a sandy bottom. It spilled over its sides and a small stream made its way through the undergrowth and fallen leaves. Laurel could hardly see it but she could hear an occasional ripple.

"Oh, this is a beautiful, quiet spot! You picked this place to build the camp because of the spring, didn't you?"

He nodded. "Because of two springs. There's another one on the other side of camp. The streams run together in the woods just past Jed Owen's shack."

She stooped, cupped her hands, and got a drink. "It's good water and as cold as ice."

"It's right out of that mountain," he said, lifting his eyes. "I believe it's the best water I ever tasted."

"Could we clear out some undergrowth from that stream and fix a place to set our milk?"

"Yes, we'll fix a place and, as soon as possible, we'll build a spring box to put the food in." He didn't add that some wild animals might get the food otherwise. He would wait to tell her that.

They both hesitated about leaving this quiet place. They knew they should make up their differences of last night, but neither one knew exactly how to make the first move.

"I had better go see how Nora is doing with the children," Laurel said.

"And I'll get the men started on the kitchen."

Laurel turned and walked quickly toward the house. Justin watched her for a moment with a sudden desire to hold her close. He was sorry for his outburst last night. He would find some way to make it up to her. She always surprised him with how much she knew. Her simple remark about Nora, as if anyone would know. He reminded himself that, besides being a teacher, she had almost earned a degree in nursing – and he was asking her to be a cook in a logging camp.

The next morning Laurel and Nora were unpacking and putting away clothes when they heard a wagon pull into the yard.

"Hullo! Anybody home?"

Nora went to the door. "It's Bulldog and Bess," she said.

"Who?" Laurel asked as she looked out.

"Bulldog is what everybody calls him. He's worked with Jed before."

Nora carried Adam while Laurel led Sarah out to meet their new neighbors. Nora took charge. "Mr. Worth ain't here right now but this here's Miz Worth and her children. Miz Worth, this here's Bulldog Aiken and his family."

Bulldog swung down easily from the wagon. He was short and stocky with brown hair combed straight back off his forehead. His pug nose had earned him his name early in childhood, Laurel was sure. His brown eyes were bright with humor.

"Pleased to meet you, ma'am. This here's my missus, Bess, and our little 'un, Jonah."

"Hello. It's nice to meet all of you. This is Sarah and Adam."

Bess Aiken stared at Laurel and smacked her gum for a minute. After looking Laurel up and down, she glanced down briefly at her own clothes before she drawled, "Pleased to meet you, Miz Worth."

Her dirty, blonde hair was pinned up loosely and her cheeks were bright with rouge. She had on a tight-fitting, low-necked blouse. Her green eyes were hard as she dismissed Laurel and turned to Nora.

"Well, Nora, I guess we're gonna be neighbors again."

"Looks like it. That's our shack right over there. Stop by and see Hannah. She'll show you your shack. It's back in the trees across the branch from ours."

Laurel's welcoming smile was gone. She stood a little straighter as she said, "I hope you get settled in all right, Mrs. Aiken. Maybe our girls can play together some."

"You'd like that wouldn't you, Jonah? Answer me, girl!"

"Yeah." Jonah looked to be about seven or eight. She peeked out from under brown bangs that needed cutting.

"Well, let's get goin', Bull," Bess urged.

"Mr. Aiken, I know Justin will be glad to know you're here. I'll tell him as soon as he gets in."

As the wagon pulled off, Laurel heard Bess say, "Mr. Aiken…Mrs. Aiken…Good Lord, where does she think she is?"

"Bess, be quiet! She's just bein' polite. You can tell she's a lady."

"Yeah. Wonder how long she'll stay one, living here."

Laurel was thankful Nora had gone back into the shack. As she turned to go in, Bess's laughter rang out across the clearing. It was not a pleasant sound.

After working with Nora all day and liking her more and more, Laurel suddenly asked, "Nora, would it be all right if we visit Hannah for a few minutes this afternoon?" She knew Hannah must be largely responsible for Nora's normal outlook on life in spite of her growth problem. Laurel was dismayed over meeting Bess and had wondered all day about the other women in camp.

"Sure. She's anxious to meet you. She would have been over here by now but she knew you would like to get unpacked first."

As soon as Sarah and Adam woke up from their naps, Laurel and Nora picked their way across the cluttered clearing to the Owens' shack. Laurel liked Hannah immediately. Her brown hair, drawn back into a bun, was softened by natural waves around her face. She was of average size, slightly shorter than Laurel. She wore a faded but clean blue gingham dress made like Nora's. After proudly introducing Laurel to Hannah, Nora took the children to look for Hannah's boys, Jesse and Thad.

"The boys are probably over at the stream looking for crawdads," Hannah called after Nora.

"Could I get you a cup of coffee?" Hannah asked. She had a quiet dignity and serenity that communicated itself to Laurel and put her at ease.

"Yes, thank you."

As Hannah got the coffee, Laurel looked around the shack. Everything showed its age but there was a sense of cleanliness and pride about the room.

They sat at the crude wooden table with four straight chairs. A bouquet of wildflowers in a pint fruit jar sat in the center of the table. Laurel turned the jar carefully to see all of them.

"I enjoy wildflowers," said Hannah, setting down the coffee. "This here's a Wake-Robin," she said pointing to a bright red, three-petaled flower with big leaves. "And these are Bluets," she continued, showing delicate light blue flowers with tiny leaves.

"Oh, I think I know the other one," Laurel said. "Is it Dutchman's Breeches?"

"Yes," Hannah said, smiling.

Laurel continued. "I've seen a picture of them somewhere." Then she added wistfully, "I had planted some of my favorite flowers where we lived in Deerbrook but we moved just as they started to bloom."

"I know how that is," Hannah said. "I used to try to plant flowers everywhere we lived but we move a lot, so now I just enjoy my wildflowers. They're like old friends."

"Would you teach me about the ones you know?"

"I sure will, and we'll try to find the names of the ones we don't know."

Laurel's eyes were drawn to a quilt that covered a metal cot opposite the table. The afternoon sun shone through the open window, lighting its dark, rich colors. The quilt pieces were all different shapes and each piece was framed with a heavy, black briar stitch.

Hannah's glance followed Laurel's. "That's Nora's bed. That quilt is the last one Mama finished before she died. Nora sure is proud of it. I wish she would put it up where the boys won't waller on it but she wants it right where she can see it."

Laurel went over to see it better. "It's beautiful!" She fingered the material.

"It's called a Crazy Quilt because it don't have a pattern. She just used different shaped scraps she'd saved."

"It reminds me of a stained glass window in a church in Knoxville," Laurel said softly. "Lots of rich colors and shapes. If it were mine, I would call it my Stained Glass Window Quilt."

Hannah studied her for a moment before a warm smile lit up her face. Laurel noticed the green flecks in her hazel eyes.

"Tell Nora that when she comes back. She'll be mighty pleased you like it. She's told me about your pretty things."

"Nora has already been a great help to me, and the children act like they've always known her," Laurel said as she sat down to finish her coffee. "Justin told me you've lived in logging camps before."

"Oh, yeah. Jed don't like workin' inside. It took me a while to git used to it. The hardest part is movin' around so much."

Laurel wanted to ask her how her family fared in a two-room shack during the hard, cold winter months, but she didn't want to sound snobbish.

"I'm worried if I can handle it all. I mean, cooking for the crew and taking care of my children, too." Laurel surprised herself by admitting this so freely to Hannah.

"I'm sure it's a big change for you. Jed said that you used to teach school."

"Yes, I taught four years with Papa in Knoxville before Justin and I were married. Then I taught two years in Deerbrook. I chose to stay home the past year to take care of the children."

"What grades did you teach?"

"The last year I taught first through seventh grades. I had twenty-five students, with a few in each grade."

"Lord 'a mercy! Anybody who can do all that don't need to worry none about cookin' for a logging crew. With you and me and Nora, we'll get it all done."

"It cheers me up just being around Nora. She's so happy and frank and likeable."

"She's tickled to get to work for you, and I can see why since I met you. She's plumb taken with you and the children and she's always liked Mr. Worth. Everybody likes Mr. Worth."

They heard Nora and the children coming and went outside to meet them. Hannah's boys and Jonah were with them. Hannah said, "Jesse and Thad, this here's Miz Worth."

Jesse inclined his head and said solemnly, "Howdy, ma'am."

Thad looked at her bashfully. "Are you Sarah's and Adam's mama?"

"Yes, I am," Laurel answered as she took Adam from Nora.

Hannah continued, "Jesse's my oldest. He turned ten last month, and Thad will soon be eight." They were both towheads.

Thad was excited. "Mama, we found the biggest crawdad I ever saw, didn't we, Jesse?"

"Sure did," Jesse replied. "He caught hold of a stick with his claws."

"He was all red, Mama," Sarah said, "and scary."

Jonah stood timidly in the background, still peeking out from under those long straggly bangs. Laurel's fingers itched for some scissors.

"Thank you, all of you, for showing Sarah the crawfish," Laurel said. "She's never seen one before. And now I think I have some sugar cookies and lemonade. Let's go get some."

It felt natural to have children romping and chattering around her as they crossed the clearing to her shack. She felt more comforted than she had since she had arrived. She believed she had found a friend in Hannah.

Chapter Seven

It was Thursday before Justin had time to take Laurel into town for groceries and supplies. They left the children with Nora. They had not spoken again of their dispute on Monday and the tension from it still hung between them. Justin had spent most of the previous two days in the woods with Jed and Bulldog, figuring out where and how to start the job on Monday. They had still been at odds, and so tired for the past two nights, they had gone to sleep without talking.

Justin, however, was rarely at a loss for words. As they drove out of camp under the canopy of spring green, he said, "There used to be a Forestry School near here. Jed Owen went to it for awhile."

"What's a Forestry School?"

"The men learn how to cut down trees without breaking or damaging younger timber; how to replant, when trees have been cut. You know, to continue the growth of the forest. That kind of thing."

"Did they teach safety too?"

"They must have."

"Who started this school?"

"George Vanderbilt, a very wealthy man from New York. He built a home, a castle really, in Asheville. He hired a fellow from Pennsylvania, Gifford Pinchot, who had studied forestry in Europe to look after his grounds. Pinchot talked him into buying 150,000 more acres, which is now part of the Pisgah Forest."

"Where did you learn all of this?"

"I read it in *The Wildwood Journal* last week. There's been some publicity about this logging job and the railroad. I kept a copy. After you read it, you may want to send it to the Professor. He'll be wanting to know what I've gotten you into."

"Who did they get to teach this forestry school?"

"Some German fellow named Schenck. The article said Pinchot was asked to work with the United States Government Forest Service, so Dr. Schenck took his place here. He operated the school for about sixteen years. It closed about fifteen years ago, but 350 or 400 men went through the school. The paper said it was the only one of its kind in the country."

"Then you're fortunate to have Jed working with you, aren't you?"

"Yeah, Jed's a good man. I believe the crew will respect him, so I can leave them with him sometimes."

"I like Hannah a lot, too."

"Everybody speaks well of Hannah. She's a good woman and a good worker, from what I hear."

They rode along in silence for a while. Then Laurel spoke. "Justin, what do you know about Bess?"

Justin threw back his head and laughed. "I knew I'd get that question sooner or later!"

"Well, tell me about her."

"Tell me what you thought of her first, "Justin said.

"She looks like a loose woman, a floozy. She didn't look real clean but she had tried to fix herself up so men would notice her. She stared at me like an insolent child and smacked her gum. I don't know any streetwalkers, but that's the way I would expect one to look."

Justin spoke quietly. "That's what she used to be, Laurel."

"What?" Laurel wasn't sure she'd understood correctly.

"Bess used to be a prostitute. Bulldog met her that way and ended up marrying her."

"How do you know all this?"

"Jed told me. Jed and Bulldog have worked together before. One night, Bulldog got drunk and told Jed the whole story. Jed said he and Hannah are the only ones who know, but he told me because he recommended Bulldog for this job."

"Aren't you taking a chance with a woman like that in camp with a crew of men?"

"Jed said she didn't cause any trouble at the last camp. She and Bulldog seem to be pretty well suited to each other and seem happy together. Jed says Bulldog is the best logger he's ever worked with."

Laurel rode along quietly for so long Justin said, "I wanted you to know, Laurel, because you women will be together a lot. I know you've never known anybody like Bess. I also know you'll treat her right in spite of the way she acts."

"I wasn't thinking about Bess particularly. I was remembering her little girl, Jonah. She was dirty and peeked out from under her hair like a little woods animal. She's old enough for school and Hannah's boys ought to be in school, too. I wish I could teach them a little so they wouldn't be so far behind."

Justin was quiet for a moment, thinking, *She'll always be a teacher at heart and she just doesn't understand yet how hard this life is going to be.*

He laid his hand on hers. "I wish you could, too, but you'll be too busy for awhile. Maybe you women can work out an exchange later. If you can teach the children, they would have to do some of your work. Don't take on too much until you get used to life in a logging camp."

"I won't. We'll work it out if I feel I can do it. And don't worry about Bess and me. We'll get along. I'm glad you told me about her."

They had arrived in town and Justin spoke softly to Tattoo, who turned into the office of the county newspaper, *The Wildwood Journal*. Justin jumped down lightly and hitched Tattoo to a post, then held out his hand to Laurel. "Come in with me a minute. I need to get my camera and to talk with Sam Parker about some pictures."

Laurel had put on one of her fancy white blouses with a cameo brooch at the neck. Her brown skirt matched her soft side-buttoned shoes. She wore a green belt and green bow in the back of her hair. As she stepped down beside him, Justin felt the pangs of pride and protectiveness she always aroused in him.

Sam Parker, the editor, a likeable man in his sixties, came to meet them as they entered. "I see you've brought the better half today, Justin. At the least the prettier half. How are you, Mrs. Worth?"

"I'm fine, thank you."

Barely pausing for breath, Mr. Parker continued, "Justin, those pictures of the locomotive and the railroad crew have brought a lot of attention to the article on logging."

"What pictures?" Laurel asked.

"Hasn't this man shown you the paper? There's an article about his logging job and two pictures he took."

"He told me about it but we've been very busy since I got back. Do you have an extra copy of the paper?"

"I sure do. Just a minute." He chattered as he scurried to the back of the office. "Here's one. Come sit at my desk and read it." He quickly made space on his desk for her to lay the paper.

Justin was amused at the treatment Sam was giving Laurel. He was usually a brusque, curt man, but here he was, actually hovering.

Laurel looked at the picture of the railroad crew. She could see every face clearly. They were grouped behind the section of railroad they were working on, with their shovels and picks in their hands. The picture of the locomotive was just as clear, as was the forest in the background.

"These are very good, Justin," she said as she started to read the article Mr. Parker had written about the logging job starting in Pisgah Forest. One paragraph was almost completely about Justin. She read, "The Supervisor of the logging crew is Justin Worth. Many people in the county already know Mr. Worth for his photography. He will also be the official photographer for *The Wildwood Journal* and will be taking on-the-job pictures of the work being done in Pisgah Forest. Two of his pictures are shown here."

Laurel sat quietly for a few minutes after she finished reading. She could see Justin and Mr. Parker outside talking. Justin was loading his camera and tripods on the wagon. He had evidently left them here during the move. She had conflicting emotions. She was proud of Justin and her love for him had become part of the fabric of her being. However, she was still troubled over their unresolved dispute. But she would cope, and it was time to get the supplies bought and get back to the children. She stood, straightened her skirt, and went outside.

"This article gives a lot of information, Mr. Parker. Justin had told me about the Forestry School. It seems this area is rich in history and you've made it sound very interesting."

Sam Parker looked at her and smiled. "That's my job, Mrs. Worth. You just keep that copy of the paper, and take care of this man. We're happy to have folks like you in Deerbrook."

Justin helped Laurel up on the wagon and unhitched Tattoo. "It may be a couple of weeks but I'll bring in some pictures of the logging crew on the job, Sam."

"I'll be looking for you. Good luck in beginning your new job."

As they drove to the company store, Laurel said, "This logging job is big news for Wildwood County, isn't it?"

"Yes, it means work for a lot of men, especially if you count both the railroad crew and the logging crew."

"Mr. Parker seems to think you can do anything, Justin. That was a good article he wrote about the job…and you."

"Well, Sam likes my pictures. He gave me some free advertising for my picture business."

"I guess a lot of men would like to have this job that you have."

"Yes, there were several who applied. That was one reason I decided on the spot when they offered it to me."

Laurel recognized this explanation as a plea for understanding. Justin was not one to defend his actions and seldom to apologize.

There was a crowd around the Beck Company Store. Justin pulled in between two wagons and hitched Tattoo. As he and Laurel walked toward the door, several men spoke to him. He kept his hand on Laurel's arm and kept moving, even as he greeted the men. Suddenly, a man, dirty and unshaven, lurched right in front of them.

"I hear you're goin' to be the boss of that new loggin' job in the forest, Justin. How about givin' me a job?" He asked this as he swayed on his feet. The smell of liquor enveloped them.

Justin put his hand on the man's shoulder and said kindly, "Curt, I've already hired my crew."

Curt's bloodshot eyes looked at Justin pleadingly. "You know I need a job."

Justin patted his shoulder. "I know you do, Curt, but I can't take on any more men right now."

He moved forward, leading Laurel around Curt to enter the store. Curt turned and called angrily after them. "If I was a Republican I bet you'd hire me. I bet all your crew is Republicans, Justin."

Justin's hand tightened briefly on Laurel's arm and he said something under his breath as he turned around.

Laurel said, "Everybody knows he's drunk, Justin. Let's go buy our supplies."

A young man walked over to Curt and took him by the arm. "You're drunk, Curt, and talking a bunch of bull. Come over here and set down and be quiet."

Justin nodded. "Thank you, Roy."

As they entered the store, Justin explained, "The problem is that some of those men out there will believe what he says and repeat it for the truth."

For the next hour, they were busy buying bags of flour, meal, sugar, grits, coffee, buckets of lard, dried beans, fat back, large cans of pork 'n beans, canned peaches, and on and on until Laurel felt they had enough. She was not sure how much it would take to feed the men for a week and she didn't want to run out of food in the middle of the week.

When they went over to look at the dishes, Justin showed her the plain off-white thick plates and cups he had told her about.

"They're so plain and ugly," she whispered. "Do they have any other kind of dishes?"

Justin looked at her to see if she was serious and saw she was. "Laurel, I ate out of tin plates when I worked in a logging camp. Would you rather have tin plates?" He grinned at her.

"No! I will not serve anybody food on tin plates. And stop laughing at me!"

Justin wiped his grin off and said patiently. "These men are used to roughing it. They're a logging crew. They're not apt to notice anything about their plates but the food on them."

"I will notice. I have to do this part in my way, Justin." She continued to look around.

In a moment, she called to him. "Look at these. They have some color, and they're almost as thick as the plain ugly ones. Aren't they pretty?"

Justin looked at the plate he held out to him. It was a good sturdy plate with a garland of autumn leaves with rust, yellow, green, and gold colors around the outer edge. On each side of the leaves was a small dark green border.

"Could we see how much more these cost than the plain ones?" Laurel asked.

"Let me have one of each," Justin said, "and I'll go find a clerk. We need to go as soon as possible."

He took a plate in each hand and went off while Laurel looked around for the last two items on her list. She hadn't asked Justin but she wanted to buy enough oil cloth for the tables and her shelves and some material to make a small ruffled strip of curtains above each window in the camp mess hall. It would bring some color inside.

She found the colors she wanted immediately. The oil cloth was rust-colored and the material, on the next counter, was a bright check with the same autumn colors that were on the dishes. She was figuring how much she would need with her pencil and paper when Justin returned with the plates.

"Mr. Jones says I can work out the difference in the price by taking some pictures for him. He'll put down the price for the plain plates on my bill for the company. So, m'lady, you can have your pretty plates."

She smiled briefly at him. "Thank you." She was aware that the dishes had taken on a significance out of proportion to their importance. The important thing was that she would feel she was in control of some portion of her life. "I also need some of this rust-colored oil cloth and some of this material and then I'll be finished."

This time Justin didn't ask any questions. He simply said, "I'll get someone to start figuring up this bill. Bring what else you need to the counter."

It took a while to get everything figured, then carried to the wagon. Laurel watched the packing and carrying of the dishes carefully. She felt ridiculously pleased over her purchases.

Just as they finished loading their wagon, Justin said, "I would like for us to send Curt Redmond's family a few groceries. Could you help me choose a few things?"

"He's the man who asked you for a job?"

"Yes, I've been by his house on my picture-taking trips. His wife's name is Cora and they have three small children. They live pretty hard, I think."

"He's drunk. How will he get the groceries home?"

"That was Cora's brother, Roy, who quieted Curt down. He'll see that she gets the food."

Together, they quickly gathered flour, meal, lard, coffee, sugar, fatback, potatoes, pork 'n beans, and canned peaches. Justin added some stick candy for the children. He paid for it all with cash from his pocket.

Justin called Roy as he carried the groceries out and they walked together to Roy's wagon. Laurel could see the pleasure on Roy's face as he and Justin talked for a moment. Then he held out his hand and said in a voice that carried clearly to Laurel and the men around the stores, "Mr. Worth, I'm sorry about what Curt said to you, but that was drunk talk. He knows you're a fair man and Cora and the children will be thankin' you for – for this food."

In the silence after Roy spoke, Laurel heard Justin's reply. "Well, maybe you can get Curt home and let him sleep it off. And tell the children the candy's from the picture-taking man."

On the way home, Justin talked about the logging job. He bragged on Jed's and Bulldog's knowledge of how to get the different parts of the job going. He talked about the swampers, knot-bumpers, teamsters, and cutting crew as if Laurel knew what it all meant. She didn't interrupt him to ask questions. She knew she would learn as she went along.

They rode in silence a few minutes. "Justin," Laurel said suddenly, before her courage failed, "I think we need to talk over our argument and clear the air."

"Okay, Laurel," he said warily. "Tell me what's on your mind."

"I'm a person, Justin, apart from being a wife and mother. I'm *me* first. Do you understand what I'm trying to say?"

"I think so. Go on." His tone was matter of fact.

"I'm struggling to adjust to this move and this way of life, and I'm making some progress. But while I'm reaching for help and strength from a source I have always found reliable, you come along and, in anger, try to take that away from me. I don't respect that very much."

"You should have been a lawyer," he said in a teasing tone. But when he looked at her, he knew she was not going to be teased out of this one. He sobered and said, "You're right. I'm sorry for my outburst the other night. You have a right to your beliefs." He put his hand over hers in a placating gesture.

Encouraged, she said, "But your protest was so spontaneous and forceful. I need to ask you a personal question."

"Go ahead."

"Why are you so afraid of God?" Her voice was softened by concern.

He removed his hand and sat up straighter. He scratched his head, a gesture she had learned was characteristic when he was puzzling over something.

"That *is* personal. And I'll give your own words back to you. I'm a person, too. I guess by our age we're products of what we've been taught and what we've come to believe through experiences, good and bad."

"So, you've had some bad experiences that you believe came from God?"

"He may not have engineered them but He didn't prevent them. And He didn't help when I…I couldn't help myself. He seemed to always be on the side of the opposition."

"You must have been hurt very bad. Can you tell me about it?"

"No, I can't, Laurel." His voice was sad. "As I said, you have a right to your beliefs and I have a right to mine. You trust Him, so you receive comfort and strength. I don't trust Him, so I only feel threatened. Like He's out to punish me. That's why I don't want Him interfering in our lives."

"I think that's a sad way to live," she said.

"I don't find it sad. It feels natural. I've been making it on my own for a long time."

"Justin, for the record, I want you to know I will continue to ask for God's help in our lives. And I plan to continue to go to church. I felt like I'd been given a gift when I saw that little church just inside the forest. It's close enough for us—the children and me—to go. And …I plan to continue to teach them about God."

"I promise I won't interfere with your efforts. I would rather Sarah and Adam grow up to know your God instead of mine. By the same token, I'll ask you to respect my beliefs."

Laurel recognized the sinking feeling in her stomach that she usually had when they discussed this subject. Their differences ran deeper than she realized. But this was the most he had ever talked about it.

She reached for his hand. "This is the only important part of our life that we don't share."

"And one isn't bad, m'dear. I know couples who have exact beliefs and don't have what we have." He reached for her. "Move over here close."

She scooted over by him and he put his arm around her shoulders. "Laurel," he said, "thank you for putting up with me. You've made me happier than I ever thought I would be." He looked at her with a mixture of candor and vulnerability. "And I never expected to love a woman as much as I love you."

"I know. I feel the same way about you." She put her hand on his knee and they rode along awhile in thankful silence. Harmony had been restored in their private world. And that would be a source of strength to face the larger world.

The wagon road ran for a long way between the river and the railroad. They had to raise their voices to talk above the noise of the rushing, foaming white water.

"Does that river always foam white like that?" Laurel asked.

"No, it's high now because of the spring rains."

As the river snaked back into the forest, out of sight, Laurel asked, "What is that roaring sound?"

"That's Laughing Falls. They're about seventy-five feet high, I think. They drop straight off like a curtain onto the rocks below. We'll walk around through the woods one day and see them."

"I wonder where they got that name. I like it."

"I liked it, too, 'til I heard the story about it. You see, the current runs so swiftly from the bridge up ahead to the falls, it's said you can't get out of the river, no matter what. Cherokee legend has it that Laughing Falls means that they always claim their victims. Evidently there have been people who have gone over. No one has ever survived."

"That does take some of the joy out of the name." Laurel shivered.

They rode on in silence for a few minutes, each with their own thoughts. Then Laurel saw a log bridge crossing the river to the left, leading over to the small white church.

"Is this the bridge you meant?" she asked.

"Right. And from what I hear, you wouldn't want to be in that river below the bridge."

"I wouldn't want to be in it anywhere with it raging like that," Laurel said.

"You be careful on that bridge when you go to church," he said.

He bent down and pulled a small package out from under his seat. It was wrapped in newsprint and tied with string. "I bought you a present. See if you like it."

When Laurel unwrapped it, she laughed. "Oh! A book on wildflowers! Justin, how did you know I wanted to learn about wildflowers? Hannah said she would show me some she knows and now we can look up the ones we don't know in this book." She showed him some of the pictures, talking as she flipped the pages.

"Pink Lady Slippers...Aren't they dainty?...Jack-in-the-Pulpit...Somebody named that one well. And Dutchman's Breeches...They look like little pantaloons hanging on the line to dry!"

She stopped and looked at him. "Where did you buy this?"

"From Sam. I saw them in the newspaper office last week. I know how you love your flowers, so I thought you might like it."

"Thank you!" She hugged the book to her breast and leaned over and kissed his cheek.

He was pleased by her reaction. "I know my woman pretty well, don't I?"

Chapter Eight

By Friday afternoon, Laurel believed for the first time that they might be ready to operate the camp by Monday morning. Zeke and Odell had finished the tables, benches, and shelves for the mess hall. Nora and Hannah had helped put up the supplies. Nora could not contain her joy over the new dishes. She heated a pan of water and washed them lovingly before she put them on the shelves.

The rust-colored oil cloth did wonders for the long rough tables. Laurel hesitated about showing them the curtain material. She suddenly felt that an attempt at curtains might look silly. Nora, however, took care of that. "They's probably never been such a nice mess hall in a loggin' camp before. Why, all we need is some curtains for the windows and a rug on the floor," she declared, grandly giving a sweep with her hands.

Laurel burst out laughing. "I don't have a rug, Nora, but I do have some curtain material."

She untied the paper package and laid the plaid material on the table. It was important to her that Hannah and Nora approve of the curtains.

"How pretty!" Nora exclaimed. "It matches the tablecloth and the dishes!"

"This material sure is cheerful," Hannah added. "How do you plan to make the curtains?"

Laurel told them she would just make a wide ruffle to go over the top of each window above the shutters.

Hannah nodded. "We can put them up with some straight sticks. I'll get some this afternoon. We can just drive nails into the walls to hold up the sticks."

"I'll keep the children while you sew them," Nora said.

"I'd like to make them tomorrow morning," Laurel said. "I'm glad you both think they will look all right."

"Miz Worth," Nora said softly, "you make me happy inside. We ain't never had curtains before."

As they started to leave the mess hall, Hannah said, "Alice and Tom Raines got here this mornin', Miz Worth, while you was gone. That makes all of us except the crew in the bunkhouse."

"I'll have to go over and meet them later. What are they like?"

"Tom is like an overgrown young'un. He's bigger than Jed or Mr. Worth either one. Alice is real skinny and shy. She looks kind'a peaked. I figure she might be pregnant."

"If she is that will make six children in camp," Nora said contentedly.

"Has Tom worked with Jed before?" Laurel asked.

"No, Jed says this will be his first loggin' job, but he seems mighty eager to learn."

"Logging is dangerous, isn't it, Hannah?" Laurel asked. It was more of a statement than a question.

"Yep. The men have to know what they are doing and always be on guard, watching out for each other."

"We women will have to watch after each other, too," Laurel said. "I'm glad both of you are here."

"We're glad you're here, too," Nora answered.

"I haven't seen Bess since the morning she arrived. Is she all right?"

"Bess is okay as long as she's got her chewin' gum and fingernail polish," Nora said.

"Jonah comes over and plays with the boys," Hannah added. "She's a regular tomboy. Bess don't take good care of her."

Laurel started to say something about teaching the children in camp but checked herself.

The next morning, Nora took the children over to Hannah's so Laurel could sew the curtains. The hum of the sewing machine in the quietness without the children was soothing to her. Her thoughts turned to Justin – paradoxical Justin. She thought of Curt Redmond's family and wondered how they felt when they received the food he sent. This quality of kindness and compassion in Justin had impressed her greatly while they were dating....

Justin had been hired as a photographer for the Knoxville Sentinel and started coming around regularly. When Laurel heard a horse coming she found herself hoping it was Justin instead of Evan. Papa always invited him back. They could talk non-stop about most any subject, often inviting Laurel into the conversation.

One afternoon as the three of them were talking on the porch after Laurel and Papa had come home from school, they saw Evan, in full uniform, coming in the carriage.

Justin grinned and impulsively asked, "How often does that uniform come around?"

"Who?" Papa asked. "Oh, you mean Evan? He's a habit around here, I guess. But he'll be going back to camp next week."

As Papa talked on unsuspectingly, Justin's and Laurel's eyes met and held. Each knew the other was glad Evan wouldn't be around much longer.

Evan had been a habit and a friend, Laurel thought. She had not known what it meant to love a man until she had met Justin. She had never felt any stirring of desire toward a man until Justin. Their courtship had been a time of enchantment for her.

She brought her thoughts back to the present with a guilty start at being idle while Nora had her children. She had almost finished the curtains for the mess hall and quickly decided to do the same for the two windows in the main room of their house. She used some unbleached muslin and several rows of green, yellow, and rose colored rick-rack. She made them long enough to gather nicely above the square windows. There was something about curtains that made her feel cozy and in charge of her home, like a finishing touch.

Suddenly, she felt like celebrating. She would invite the women and children over tomorrow afternoon so everybody could get better acquainted before their busy schedule started. Her Fresh Apple Cake with coffee would be good to serve the women, and she would bake sugar cookies and have lemonade for the children. They could play just outside her house, except Adam, and maybe he would go down for a nap. If not, Nora and Hannah would help with him. That baby got plenty of attention.

Laurel told Hannah and Nora about her idea as they put up the curtains in the mess hall. Nora was enthusiastic and Hannah was quietly pleased. As they stood back and looked critically at the curtains, they were happy with the result. The bright colors along with the tablecloths did cheer up the crudely built mess hall. The three of them went quickly to Laurel's shack and put up her curtains. Nora loved the rick-rack. She chattered happily while they worked.

Laurel asked her to stay with the children a little longer while she went to visit Bess and meet Alice, and to invite them to come over the next afternoon. After she passed Hannah's shack, she followed a path through the trees until she came to the stream Justin had mentioned. Someone had placed some large flat rocks in it to step on. Just a little way beyond, she could see Bess's shack. The door stood open and Laurel called, "Bess, are you there?"

"Yeah, come on in," Bess called back.

She was sitting at the table polishing her fingernails a bright red. When she saw Laurel, she stood up suddenly. "Oh, it's you! I thought you was Hannah."

"I just came by to see if you're all right. I haven't seen you since you arrived." Laurel's glance around the room took in dirty dishes on the table, dirty pots on the stove, clothes scattered on every chair, and unmade beds.

"Yeah, I'm fine," Bess said as she looked around the room as if seeing the mess for the first time. "Here, let me clean off a chair."

"I can't stay. I'm going over to meet Alice Raines. I wanted to invite you to come to my house tomorrow afternoon at three o'clock. I would like for us women to have some time together to get to know each other."

Bess looked at her, puzzled for a moment, then she answered, "Okay."

"Bring Jonah. The children can all play close by my house. I'll have some cookies for them."

"If I can find her when I come. She's out in the woods climbing trees and wading the creek most all day."

"I'll see you tomorrow, then," Laurel said as she escaped out the door.

Alice Raines saw her coming and came out to meet her. "You must be Mrs. Worth," she said.

"Yes, and I'm happy to meet you, Alice. Hannah told me about you. I'm sorry we were gone when you arrived. Are you getting settled in?"

"Yes, ma'am. Come on inside and visit a few minutes."

As she entered, Laurel saw an old cook stove, a crude homemade table, two straight back chairs, and a mattress made of shucks lying on the floor of the bedroom.

Alice, following her glance, said, "We ain't got much. Tom just set everything inside and went to find Mr. Worth and Mr. Owen. He's plumb tickled over this job."

As they sat down at the table, Laurel asked, "Where has Tom been working?"

"At the tannery. But he don't like to work inside. He says he's always wanted to be a logger. I'm glad he's going to get the chance."

Alice was not pretty with her thin, pale face and long blonde hair hanging straight down each side to her shoulders. But when she spoke about Tom, her blue eyes lit up and a half-smile hovered around her lips.

"I'm sure he'll do a good job," Laurel said kindly. "Tell me a little about yourself."

"Well, they ain't much to tell. Tom and me has been married since January first. He asked Paw for me right proper-like. Said he wanted us to start the new year out together. It'll soon be four months since we got married."

"Do your folks live near here?"

"My Paw and two brothers do. My Maw died when I was about six. I don't remember much about her."

"My mother died when I was three," Laurel said. "I don't remember her at all, but I had a good stepmother."

"Paw never did seem to want to marry again. He drinks too much so nobody would have wanted him, anyway."

Laurel didn't know how to reply to that so she said, as she stood, "Is there anything I can help you do while I'm here?"

"No. I'll have to leave my things in boxes 'til Tom builds me some shelves to put them on. He said he would build us a bed too, so we can get our mattress up off the floor."

"Good. I hope he gets it done before the job starts."

"I'm sure he can fix it up on time," Alice said with a little smile. "He's handy about fixin' things. I just know we're goin' to like it here."

As Laurel turned to go, she said, "Could you come over to my house tomorrow afternoon at three o'clock. The women are all coming for a get-acquainted time."

"Yes. I'd like that."

"I'll look for you. If you need anything before then, please let me know."

"Thank you for comin' to see me. It was neighborly of you."

As Laurel walked briskly back through the trees and across the clearing, she wondered what Alice's life had been like without a mother and with a drunken father. She also realized she was eager to meet Tom.

Laurel's get-together didn't turn out exactly as she had visualized it. Thad, Jesse, and Jonah got there first. The boys' blond hair had been wet and combed down carefully. Jonah kept brushing her bangs aside to try to see.

Laurel was ready for them. She had spread a small tablecloth on a patch of moss at the side of her house, with sugar cookies and lemonade on it. Nora held Adam.

"Jesse, you pour everybody a cup of lemonade. Thad, you hold the cups for him. Jonah, you're the oldest girl around here, so you serve the cookies after everybody sits down."

She was busy instructing the children when the women walked up. They were all happily doing as they were told until Bess's voice rang out sharply. "Jonah, are your hands clean?"

Jonah ducked her head, stood very still and didn't make a sound. Bess stridently called again, "Answer me, girl!"

Laurel took over. "Her hands are fine, Bess. She's helping me."

She put the plate of cookies in Jonah's hands and squeezed them. She then stooped to Jonah's eye level, smiled at her, and said, "Thank you for helping me."

Jonah looked at Laurel gratefully and shyly started serving the cookies.

As soon as the children were settled, Laurel turned to the women and said, "Welcome to my house. Please come in."

There was an awkward pause for a moment but Nora ended it by exclaiming, "I've just been bustin' all over for you to see how pretty Miz Worth has fixed up her shack."

Alice looked around shyly, almost wonderingly, and said, "I ain't never seen so many pretty things." She gently touched the delicate china shade on the Aladdin lamp.

Bess smacked her gum, plopped down in Justin's reading chair, looked bored but said nothing.

Hannah stood in the open door, watching the children. "I told Thad and Jesse to watch Sarah, Miz Worth. Jonah's helping, too. She's helping Sarah drink her lemonade."

"She ain't going to help nobody for long," Bess declared. "Just wait, she'll be gone into the woods again."

"Bess," Laurel asked, "how do you spell her name? I'm not sure what it is."

"It's Jonah, like Jonah in the whale. Before she was born I was a big as a whale. When she popped out I thought, *'This must be the way the whale felt when it got rid of Jonah,'* so I called her Jonah."

The four women stared at her.

"What did Bulldog say about it?" Hannah asked softly.

"Oh, Bulldog thought it was a joke at first. Then he said for me to name her what I wanted since I'm the one who had her. He knew I was mad because I didn't want a baby."

Laurel felt anger wash through her. The child would go through life with a boy's name, the butt of a cruel joke by an ignorant mother. She could hear schoolchildren at recess dancing around chanting, "Jonah in the whale, Jonah in the whale…."

"Jonah is a boy's name," Laurel protested. "I'm going to call her Joanie."

"Call her what you like," Bess said curtly, "but her name is Jonah."

Hannah broke the silence that followed. "Alice, do you need us to do anything to help you get settled in?"

"No, Tom built me some shelves in my kitchen last night. He's plannin' on buildin' us a bed frame soon."

"Jed says that Tom has the name of bein' a good worker."

"He sure ain't lazy. I'm glad Mr. Worth and Mr. Owen gave him a chance at this job."

"I'm sure he'll do fine," Hannah said kindly.

"You'uns might help another way," Alice said. "I'm expectin' and I'm real sick to my stomach every mornin'. Do you know anything I can take for it?"

"How far along are you?" Laurel asked.

"About two months. I expect it to be born in November."

"Your morning sickness should be over in about another month," Laurel said. "Meanwhile, you need to be drinking milk and eating right. Come over and get some milk from us every day until Tom can buy a cow. I'll tell you some things to eat that should be good for you and the baby."

"You sound just like a doctor, Miz Worth," Nora said.

"I went to nursing school for awhile," Laurel explained.

"You're a nurse *and* a teacher?" Nora asked.

"I didn't finish nurse's training. Papa had his heart set on me teaching school with him, so I stopped nursing school and went to Normal School for Teachers."

"Did you help deliver any babies?" Alice asked.

"No, but I studied how to do it."

"Hannah has helped deliver some babies," Nora said proudly.

Alice smiled. "Looks like I'll have plenty of help."

"You'll need all the help you can get and then some," Bess countered. "Bulldog said they could probably hear me screamin' over the next mountain. I had…."

Laurel stood up quickly and said, "Let's have some cake and coffee. Nora, let Alice hold Adam and you come and help me serve."

Nora proudly served the cake while Laurel got the drinks. There was a few minutes of quiet conversation while everyone enjoyed the cake and coffee.

"Ain't these dishes pretty with the wild roses on them?" Nora asked Hannah as she went over to point out something on the plate to her.

"Yes, and I noticed the wildflower design on your pitcher and bowl, Miz Worth."

Before Laurel could say anything, Bess blurted out, "Looks like one of her bowls is under the bed, Nora. It's even got a lid on it. Have you noticed it?"

Nora was speechless for a moment. Then she said angrily, "Bess, you ain't got no sense and no manners."

Bess laughed heartily.

"It's hard to find a pretty chamber pot with a lid anymore," Laurel said evenly. "So, I'm careful with that one."

"We just use a bucket at our house," Bess drawled. "And we call it a slop jar."

"Well, you ought to keep it covered because of flies and germs," Laurel retorted. Her annoyance showed clearly.

Hannah changed the subject. "This is good cake, Miz Worth."

"Thank you. It's easy to make. I made enough for each of you to take a piece home to your husband."

"Nora will have to get her a husband first," Bess said as she shifted in her chair. "She needs…."

Hannah was on her feet in a second. "That's enough, Bess!" Her voice was measured and hard.

Bess looked startled but closed her mouth slowly and was quiet. Nora moved to the door. "I'll go check on the children," she said, with her head down.

Hannah spoke again in the same, unmistakable tone. "Bess Aiken, you've got a mean, spiteful tongue in your head, and I'll be a thankin' you not to use it on Nora."

"I was just teasin'," Bess said flatly.

"Your teasin' is cruel. You make fun of everybody, including your own little girl, but don't ever make fun of Nora again."

Alice was sitting wide-eyed at this exchange. When Laurel got up to take Adam to the bedroom to change his diaper, Alice followed quickly. She chattered nervously. "He's such a good baby. Could I come over and help take care of him some? I ain't never even changed a baby's diaper."

"Well, here, change this one," Laurel said absently. She was still listening to Hannah and Bess.

"I didn't mean to hurt Nora's feelings, Hannah. You know I like Nora. It's *her* and *her airs* I don't like." Bess lowered her voice. "If she's so educated, why's she livin' in a place like this?"

"This is the kind of work her husband wants to do and she's trying to make the best of it. She ain't puttin' on airs, Bess. She's different from us, but we can learn a whole lot from her if we're willin'."

Laurel felt warm inside from Hannah's understanding and loyalty.

"Well, I ain't needin' to learn nothin' from her as far as I know," Bess declared stubbornly.

"Someday you might, Bess. We all need help from each other."

They were quiet as Laurel and Alice came back into the room. Alice held Adam up and said, "Look, Mrs. Owen. I pinned a diaper on him and Miz Worth says I can help take care of him some."

"You done a good job, Alice."

Laurel said, "We had better see how Nora is doing with the children. Don't forget your cake as you go."

She was suddenly tired of trying so hard. But she was mostly disgusted with Bess. She wanted all of them to go. Even Nora and Hannah. She wanted some time alone with her children before Justin got home.

That night as she told Justin about the afternoon, she summed it up by saying, "I expected too much, I guess. I thought we could enjoy some women talk and get to know each other better. Bess was bent on mischief from the beginning. Why do you think she dislikes me so much?"

Justin was relaxed in his reading chair, feeling good about the accomplishment on the job. He was in a teasing mood. "Look in the mirror, Honey. No man in his right mind would look at Bess with you around. She's probably never met anybody like you before. Come to think of it, I haven't either." He smiled at her and held out his hand. "So, come here, woman!"

"Justin!" Laurel laughed, but she was pleased. She went over and sat on his lap. Bess was forgotten for the rest of the evening.

Chapter Nine

Sunday morning dawned clear and warm. At breakfast Laurel asked, "Could you hitch up the wagon for me in a little while? I'll need to leave for church about ten o'clock."

"Just let me know when you're ready. Do you think you can manage okay?"

"Yes. It's not very far."

As she dressed herself and the children, Laurel had a sense of comfort and anticipation about going to church. It was a familiar action in the midst of too many unfamiliar ones.

Justin brought the wagon around and helped to get her and the children settled. As he handed her the reins, he said, "You should enjoy your ride. It's a fine spring day." Then he patted Tattoo's head and said, "Take care of them, Boy!"

They rode under a canopy of spring green, splattered with sunlight. Dogwoods bloomed in abundance. Sarah, on the front seat beside Laurel, chattered happily. When Adam kept fretting in his box on the floor behind Laurel's seat, she stopped and set the box up on the wagon seat behind her on the right side so he could see out and Sarah could talk to him. He sat happily now with his dark brown eyes watching his sister.

As she wondered what this new church would be like, she suddenly saw it to the right across the river. Tattoo would have to pull the wagon in a sharp right hand turn to cross the narrow log bridge. She glanced at the swirling, foaming water and, remembering Justin's words on Thursday, hesitated briefly. Then she had Tattoo swing wide to get the wagon safely on the bridge.

Just as she thought they had made it, the right back wheel went off the bridge, tilting the wagon at a crazy angle. Laurel screamed as the box with Adam in it was jolted over the side into the foaming water. Miraculously, it stayed right side up, with him still in it, but was being pounded against the rocks.

Laurel pulled Sarah into the floor of the wagon and said, "Stay here!" She climbed out of the wagon and jumped off the side of the bridge downstream from Adam. The swift water pulled at her clothes immediately and she was swept quite a way downstream. She tried to grab hold of the rocks as she went by but they were too slippery. Suddenly, there was a tree limb just above her head. She grabbed it and held on, while she got her breath and faced upstream.

The box carrying Adam was swept away from the rocks under the bridge into the mainstream. Laurel saw that she would have only one brief chance as it rushed toward her. She pulled on the limb. It was sturdy. Her feet kept slipping until she found a crevice in a rock where she pushed her left foot in tightly at an angle. It was a foothold.

She was not aware of anything else in the world except the box as it rushed toward her. She whispered, "O, God, help me!" Just as she reached for it, it careened away. Then, just as suddenly, it whirled around and was within reach. She pulled it to her with her right hand and saw that Adam was safe. The current kept grabbing at the box with tremendous force. Somehow she braced it with her body as she grabbed Adam out of it before the current tore it away toward the falls.

She clutched Adam, who was screaming heartily, to her body with her right arm as she held on with her left. She felt weak with relief for a moment. She had done it! Her baby was safe!

For the first time she looked up at the bridge. She saw several people, so she knew Sarah was safe, too. All at once she realized her left arm was going numb from holding on to the limb and her left foot was hurting from being crammed into the crevice. The water was clutching at her and Adam with tremendous force.

"Ma'am," a voice said behind her. "Hold on a minute longer. I'm coming in to help you."

Then he was there beside her, holding onto the limb and bracing against the water.

"Give me the baby, Ma'am."

She looked at him blankly.

"It's okay! See?" he said gently. He pointed to the rope around his chest and under his arms. She turned her head to see another man on the bank holding the other end of the rope.

She allowed him to take Adam and saw the man on the bank hold out a long stick for him to hold onto until he was out of the water. He handed Adam to a woman nearby, then he was back.

"Give me your hand now, Ma'am." He smiled at her as he reached out and took her right hand.

"I can't get my foot loose. It's stuck between two rocks," Laurel explained.

"Turn loose and let me hold onto you. Maybe I can help you pull."

She consciously had to will her hand to turn loose of the limb. She cried out with the pain in her foot as the water swung her around before his arm went around her waist.

"My foot is twisted. You'll have to back up and pull straight," she directed. She guided him the best she could in the swirling water until her leg was straight. Then she said, "Pull!"

Her foot came free and they both went under for a moment, but he caught hold of the limb until they got their footing again. Then he was moving her slowly to the bank. She kept slipping on the rocks but each time he hauled her back up with seeming ease. He had enough strength for both of them.

Friendly hands reached for her. He boosted her up and she was on dry land again. There was a large group of people gathered on the bank. For a moment Laurel couldn't figure out why they were there. Then she remembered church.

Laurel turned to the man who had come in after her and Adam. She held out her hand. "Thank you, Mr... ?"

"Stevens," he supplied. "Cal Stevens. I'm the pastor of the church here. And you must be from the new logging camp."

"Yes. My husband is Justin Worth."

"One of the men will go get him," the pastor said.

Laurel looked around at their kind, concerned faces and said, "Thank you, all of you, for helping me."

Then, worried suddenly, "Where is my little girl? She was in the wagon...."

The woman who had Adam said, "She's in the church. We're going to take you there right now where it's warm. Someone has gone to get dry clothes for you and the baby. Can you walk?"

Her wet clothes clung heavily around her legs, she was shivering with cold, and her left foot throbbed with pain but she and Adam were alive! With a sudden smile she said, "Yes, I can walk." But she was grateful to have someone to tell her what to do.

The men had taken care of the wagon, and Tattoo was standing under a tree beside the church. Laurel limped over to him, pulled his head down and embraced his neck. As she laid her wet head on him she said, "Dear Tattoo, you are a good friend! Thank you for taking care of Sarah!"

The woman who had taken charge was the pastor's wife, Mrs. Stevens. Laurel was soon dressed in some of her clothes and Adam was dry and warm in borrowed baby clothes. Sarah was subdued, with her face smudged from crying. As Laurel hugged and reassured her, she touched her mother's face and wet hair as if to see that she was real.

"We'll take you to our house," Mrs. Stevens told her. "It's not far. You've had a shock and you need something warm to drink, and then you need to rest. My husband has to go get into some dry clothes, too, and get back to church."

Laurel looked at her gratefully. "Thank you," she said simply.

After they left in the Stevens' wagon, with the pastor telling the people he would be back as soon as he could, everyone stood around in groups talking in hushed voices. One of the older men stood on the steps and said, "We've witnessed a miracle this morning. Let's go inside and thank God."

Just as the prayer was finished and everyone was still standing, the door of the church sprang open and Justin strode in. He looked around, searching, then asked, "My wife...and children...where are they? The woman and baby who...were in the river?"

The older man in charge said, "So you're her husband? She's a brave woman. And God just delivered her and your baby from death."

Justin looked at him with distaste for mentioning the near disaster. From the coldness within him at the mention of her possible death, he said, "From what I hear, she and some of you are responsible. Where is she now, please?"

The man stood speechless for a moment at this rebuke but another man stepped forward and said, "They've taken her to the Stevens' house. It's…."

"I know where it is," Justin said and was out the door.

As he crossed the bridge on Jed's horse, he could not bear to look at the treacherous water. Laurel had somehow won against it and saved Adam's life and her own. "Laurel," he said softly, thinking of her strength and her tenderness. He would not allow himself to think about what could have happened. If she and Adam had been killed after…after he had insisted she move here…. He shook his head to fight off the swarm of thoughts.

As he neared the Stevens' house, he willed his panic to ease off and his anger at the man's words to cool down. His reaction had been instinctive, without reason. He had not even said, "Thank you," to that group of concerned people. Well, he would think of a way to make it up to them, he thought, as he rode into the Stevens' yard.

Mrs. Stevens, a practical, motherly woman, who enjoyed telling and embellishing a good story, talked for weeks about what happened when Justin got to her house.

"I heard the horse as it come into the yard," she would say. "Then he was comin' through the door without a by-your-leave from anybody. He didn't see nothin' but her as he crossed the room and had her in his arms. Then he held back and touched her face, gentle-like, several times. They just looked at each other for a long time."

Mrs. Stevens would usually pause and look wistful, thinking of her thirty year no-nonsense marriage. "I ain't never seen nothin' like it. I felt like I was in church. They didn't know anybody else was in the world.

"Then Mrs. Worth remembered her manners. She's that kind, you know. She introduced us all proper-like. He took my husband's hand and thanked him for gettin' his wife and baby out of that river – for savin' their lives – he called it. Said he would be indebted to Cal for the rest of his life. They talked a few minutes 'til Cal had to leave again. Then he thanked me for takin' care of them. One of the men from church brought his horse and wagon into the yard. He has the bluest eyes. They're the handsomest couple I ever seen."

Laurel and Justin examined Adam carefully but could find no sign of bruises. He had nursed with his usual eagerness and had immediately gone to sleep after they arrived at Mrs. Stevens' house. Justin soon had Sarah laughing and playing again.

Laurel's left ankle was swollen badly with a blue bruise running across it. She could not bear to put any weight on it. "It's just a sprain. I know when I twisted it," she explained matter-of-factly. Nobody asked any questions.

They left after Sunday dinner with Mrs. Stevens promising to look in on them the next day. As they passed the bridge, Justin reached and took Laurel's hand, and said, "I'm glad that preacher is such a strong man." Then he added with a puzzled expression, "You know, Laurel, I like him!"

"Yes. He seemed to pluck me out of that rushing water with ease." After a moment, she added, "I picked a terrible time to sprain my ankle, with the job starting tomorrow."

He looked at her and a tender smile lit up his face. This woman, he thought, defied death today for her baby and herself...and she apologizes for a sprained ankle.

"Hannah and Nora will take over the cooking until your ankle is better."

Nora, Hannah, and Alice were waiting when they pulled into the clearing. The next half-hour was blurred to Laurel when she tried to remember it later. She remembered the kindness and concern on all their faces, the way they took care of the children, the food on the stove that they had prepared, the warmth and security of being home. Justin and Nora got her to bed with Nora clucking over her ankle.

As she sank into her feather bed she realized the nightmare was over. She could let go now. Justin's concerned face swam out of focus and she surrendered to sleep.

Justin sat on the side of her bed until her steady breathing told him she was sound asleep. When he laid his palm on her forehead and her temperature seemed normal, he knew he had to turn his thoughts to the logging crew that was gathering outside. He left quickly to look for Hannah. She, Bess, and Alice were in the mess hall cooking supper.

"Laurel's asleep and seems okay," he told them. "Hannah, would you look in on her every fifteen minutes or so? I need to help get ready to start the job in the morning."

Hannah smiled at him. "Don't worry about Laurel or the children or supper. Nora has the children at our house and we'll have supper at six o'clock like Laurel was plannin'."

Bess spoke up. "Bull and Tom has gone to mark the trees where the lead choppers need to start in the mornin'."

Hannah added, "Jed's showin' the crew the loggin' areas. I think all the crew's here."

"Good! It looks like we'll be in the loggin' business by tomorrow! Thank you ladies for all you've done and are doing," Justin said as he turned to leave.

"We're glad the job's startin'. Seems normal to be hustlin' around." Hannah followed him to the door. "Don't worry about Laurel. I'll watch after her."

He nodded his thanks and headed for the bunkhouse. He knew he and Beck Lumber Company had done a good job in constructing the camp in two weeks. The bunkhouse should be adequate. It was a long building with a row of upper and lower bunks built along each wall with windows on each side. Thirty men could sleep there if needed. He was starting out small with sixteen men in the bunkhouse and he, Jed, Bulldog, and Tom made up the rest for a crew of twenty. It was easier to add men than to take away jobs.

The bunkhouse was empty but he saw some bedrolls and clothes on several bunks. He had put straw ticks on twenty bunks and asked the men to bring their own bedrolls. *They're staking out those lower bunks*, he thought, *and I don't blame them.*

He walked on through to the lobby, a smaller room built on the end of the bunkhouse toward the forest, where the men could sit at night and talk and play checkers or cards. Jed and Tom had constructed some crude benches and tables. Justin had bought several checkerboards and checker sets and some decks of cards. A lantern was hanging in the center of the room ready to be lit.

He was glad Jed had taken the initiative to show the men the logging job while he was taking care of Laurel. The men could see what they would face tomorrow and they could get on with the job of dividing up crews and jobs tonight. During the week he had learned to trust Jed's and Bulldog's judgment. They were both seasoned loggers, and Tom was learning fast.

He was sticking to Bulldog like a cocklebur, watching and listening.

Justin knew he needed to check out the horses and equipment. The barn and shed were backed up to the edge of the forest on the other side of the clearing from the bunkhouse. He had two teams of horses, including Tattoo. He would buy another horse as soon as possible because he and Laurel needed Tattoo for personal use. When he opened the barn door, Tattoo snorted and jerked his head up and down in greeting. Justin nodded and said, "And good afternoon to you, sir!" He patted Tattoo's mane lovingly. "You sure kept your head this morning on that bridge. Another horse might have tumbled all of them into that river." He paused as he stroked the horse's side. "Tomorrow we start a new job. Do you think you can show these other horses how to snake logs out? It's going to be hard, dangerous work, Tattoo. I don't want you hurt, so be careful!"

He moved on and spoke to the other horses and examined their feet and legs. He checked the bridles and equipment for each horse. Laurel's two cows were in a stall nearest the house with a separate door. Bossy had been with them several years. Mooey, named by Sarah, had been bought recently. Laurel knew they would need more than one cow for their family plus the camp. Justin would ask Tom to help him milk them tonight after supper.

When he reached the shed where the logging equipment was stored he was pleased to see that the men had brought their own axes. A well-used crosscut saw stood over in one corner. Those were signs of experienced timber cutters. He again felt the surge of excitement this job brought to him. He was eager to get on with it!

There was still no sign of the men returning, so he turned toward Hannah's shack to check on the children, especially Adam. Nora was enjoying herself as usual. She had sent Thad, Jesse, and Jonah outside to play. Sarah held up hands white with flour. "Daddy, look! We're making cookies," Sarah said.

"Good! Save one for me and your mother. She'll be proud of you."

He looked around for Adam. Nora said, "Adam's still sleeping off that wild ride he had this mornin'." She nodded toward the bedroom door. Justin stepped to the door and looked at him anxiously. He was sound asleep and seemed to be breathing fine. He figured he would get a cold from being in that icy water.

"When he wakes up just take him on over to Laurel to nurse. I'm sure he'll be hungry. Take this punkin' over, too," he said as he tousled Sarah's hair and tried to stay away from her floury hands.

"Thank you, Nora," he said as he went out the door.

When Justin returned to check on Laurel, she was sitting up in her reading chair with her foot propped up on a kitchen chair. She still had on Mrs. Stevens' shapeless, faded cotton dress. Her hair still showed signs of her struggle in the river and she looked pale.

She smiled at him and he crossed the room quickly and hugged her close for a moment. He pushed a curl back and kissed her forehead.

"How did you get in here?"

"I hopped on one foot. I can't put my weight down on this one yet," she said, pointing to the one in the chair.

"I still think I ought to take you to the doctor to see if you have any broken bones," he said as he began unwrapping her foot.

"I don't think so. I walked on it from the river to the church. I don't think I could have done that if it was broken."

"It may have been so numb you couldn't feel it." He had the wrapping off and was moving his fingers gently over her foot. It was swollen and turning blue around the outside ankle area. There was a bad scrape and a dark purple bruise across the ankle. "Is it hurting bad?"

"It's hurting, but give me a little time. I think it's just a bad sprain. If it's worse in the morning, we'll go to the doctor. Now tell me how Adam is and about the men getting here and…"

"Whoa, Woman! Let me get a cold compress ready for your foot then I'll tell you everything."

He poured some cold water into the dishpan, dipped a towel in it, wrung it out and wrapped it carefully around her foot. Then he pulled up a chair and gave her an account of the afternoon. When she was satisfied that Adam was fine and that supper would be ready for the men, she asked, "Are you disappointed that you didn't get to show the men the logging area?"

He realized one part of him was disappointed but a bigger part was glad Jed had taken that initiative. "Jed's the foreman, so it's good for him and the men to understand each other from the beginning."

She knew in spite of his matter-of-fact answer how eager he was to be with the men on the job. "You need to go with them in the morning to start the job. Nora can help me with the children. When you come in for lunch I'll know if we need to go to the doctor."

"We'll see," he said.

"Justin, how is Bess dressed?"

He looked at her in amazement and shook his head. "Laurel, I didn't notice how Bess or anyone else was dressed."

"Well, she must look decent then."

He grinned at her. "I'll go back and look her over proper and come back and tell you."

"You will not! And you know what I mean."

"Yes, I do, but I'm not worried. Bulldog and Bess are happy together. The men will know that after being around a little while."

"I'm sorry I won't be there tonight for the first meal."

"I am, too, Honey. I'm sure the men have heard what happened this morning." He was silent a moment then went on, "Hannah has things under control. Bess and Alice seem happy to be helping."

"Could you hand me my hair brush and hand mirror? They're in the washstand drawer."

He watched her brush her hair as he said, "When Nora brings the children, be careful and don't let them hurt your foot. Nora will take care of them and someone will bring supper. You sit with your foot up or lie in bed with it propped up."

"We'll be fine," she said, touched and amused by his line-by-line instructions. "You need to go now and get ready to meet the crew. It's almost suppertime."

He brought a glass of water, lit the Aladdin lamp and checked the wet compress on her foot. "Have Nora take the compress off and put the bandage back on."

He rubbed her hair back and kissed her forehead. "Will you be okay now?"

"Yes. Nora will be here soon. Thank you for taking such good care of me."

He turned reluctantly to go. As he started to close the door behind him, he stuck his head back in. "I'll be sure to check Bess out so I can tell you...."

He closed the door quickly as he saw her raise the hairbrush. He laughed as he heard it hit the door.

Laurel laughed, too. *That's one thing about him,* she thought. *He can always make me laugh.* Her Bible and wildflower book were on the table by her chair. She picked up the wildflower book to see if she could find the picture and name of an unusual flower she had seen on the bank this morning on her way to church. Before.... She shivered slightly, laid down the book and picked up her Bible.

She knew God had delivered her and Adam from going over the falls that morning. She found the verse she was looking for in Psalms that declared, "He that is our God is a God of salvation; and to God the Lord belong the issues from death." She lingered over the verse for a few minutes, then bowed her head for a tearful thanksgiving. After awhile she dried her tears and was smiling as Nora and the children came through the door of the shack.

Justin stepped through the door of the mess hall. "Hannah, do you need any help with anything?"

"No, sir. It's ready. I'm going to take Laurel's and the children's supper to them right now before the men get here. If you see the boys and Jonah, send them in."

He heard voices and knew the crew was coming in. He headed toward the edge of the forest to meet them. As they reached the clearing Jed saw Justin. He said, "Men, here's our boss." They gathered around to shake Justin's hand. He had hired all but the last four, whom Jed had recommended and hired. To a man, they were happy to have jobs and their attitude reflected this.

Abe Johnson, a good natured, talkative giant of a man, at least six foot four, in his late thirties, pumped Justin's hand. "Jed jist showed us one of the finest stands of timber I ever seen in all my loggin' days."

Justin replied, "This forest is full of stands like this one; big, hardwood trees. I've heard it's the biggest variety in the country."

Dirk Tate, a small, dark, wiry quick-moving, quick-tempered man in his forties spoke next. "It'll be easy to get the logs out. It ain't straight up and down like some jobs I've worked."

"We'll have some like that before we're through but we thought we'd start with this level stand until we develop our teamwork," Justin said.

Jed spoke up. "Justin, Hannah's standin' in the door of the kitchen lookin' this way. I think that means supper's ready."

"Let's wash up in this stream today," Justin said. "The women have a good supper. After we eat we can talk about starting the job."

The men spread out and stooped to wash. Some washed just their hands, a few washed their faces and slicked their hair back with their wet hands. Justin noticed that three or four seemed surprised to be told to wash up. But they did. They all wiped their hands on their pants to dry them.

On their way to the kitchen, Abe said, "We heard about your wife jumpin' in the river this mornin' and gettin' your baby out. That took some courage."

A murmur of agreement ran through the group. "I'd be scared to death to be in that river where she was," said Dirk. Justin knew they all would be, including him.

"She's got plenty of spunk, as you'll find out," said Justin. "But I think she acted out of instinct to save our baby. I'm thankful that the tree limb was there and the men got her out as fast as they did."

"Is she hurt bad?" Bulldog asked. He and Tom were at the back of the group.

"Her left foot and ankle are swollen and bruised pretty bad. She thinks it's just a sprain. She'll have to be off it for a few days. She sent her apologies for not being here to meet all of you tonight."

They arrived at the mess hall and Justin introduced Hannah, Bess, and Alice. The men settled in on the benches around the two long tables. Justin saw them looking at the oilcloth, the dishes, and even glancing at the curtains. He felt a pang of pride for Laurel's way of doing things. Hannah had added her touch. On each table there was a fruit jar full of greenery and dogwood blossoms.

The women served beef stew, cornbread, and coleslaw. They also had peach cobbler and coffee for dessert. The men were subdued but there was a steady flow of talk and laughter that pleased Justin. He didn't have to be told what they thought of the food. They were putting it away fast.

Suddenly, Thad, Jesse, and Jonah burst through the door in a scuffle. They had been racing. When they saw the men they dropped their heads and backed into each other. A few of the men chuckled at the three children with tousled hair and smudged faces. Hannah edged them back out the door and spoke quietly, "All of you go to our shack and wash your face and hands good, then come back and eat."

They took off running again. She shook her head and called, "Comb your hair, too, all three of you."

Bess had joined her outside. She said, "Jonah should have been a boy. She acts like one."

"She's fine, Bess. I'm glad her and the boys play together so good."

When the children returned, the women got them settled with their food just as the men were finishing.

Justin stood and said, "Let's go over to the lobby and get things worked out for tomorrow. These ladies need us out of here." He turned to the three women. "You cooked a mighty good meal. I think you can see that by the way it disappeared." The men voiced their hearty agreement and thanks as they left.

Chapter Ten

Once the men were seated, Justin got down to business. "As you men can see, we're starting off small with a crew of twenty. We may need to add some more men before we're through. Jed and I believe you're some of the best loggers around. That's why you're here instead of a bunch of others who wanted and needed these jobs." He paused and let his steady gaze travel around the group before he continued.

"We'll be working ten-hour days during the summer. We need to be on the job at seven, knock off for dinner at twelve, back at one and work 'til six. As you know, the pay is one dollar per day plus your meals. The food will be good. No meals will be served on Friday night, Saturday, or Sunday. On Fridays we'll stop at four. You'll come by the lobby here to get paid, then you can ride the train out to get on home to your families."

He looked around, propped his foot on a bench and asked, "Any questions so far?"

The men shook their heads and remained silent.

"I have a few rules of camp, simple and short: No drinking, no gambling, no cursing. Respect the women in camp. We may have to add some more rules later, but that's it for now."

The men looked at him steadily but he sensed a tightening of their mood. He grinned and said, "I know you're no Sunday school boys and you're going to have your fun. Enjoy yourselves, but the rules stand."

A couple of the older men nodded their heads in agreement and the younger ones grinned at each other. The tension eased.

"Jed's your foreman. He's in charge on the job. I'll be working with you some but not all the time. Jed, let's get the crew set up."

Jed came around and stood by Justin. His manner conveyed a quiet confidence. He was a man who knew his job, but had patience to teach others. He spoke quietly. "Let's start with two lead choppers. Bulldog, you and Tom take that on for now. I want you to teach some of the others how to do it as soon as you can."

Jed knew the importance of this job. The lead choppers would choose the trees to cut, then would cut a lead or notch in the side of the tree to show the cutters which way they wanted it to fall. This was important for safety and for saving the younger trees that could be destroyed as a large tree fell.

"Next, we need four cutters. Abe, I noticed you brought your own crosscut saw. You choose the three men to cut with you, making two teams. You watch after that part of the operation."

Abe looked around. "I reckon Dirk and me'll team up again." He inclined his head toward Dirk who nodded. Then Abe pointed to Zeke and Odell who he knew always worked together. "You boys ready to make a little music with that old saw of yours?" They grinned and nodded.

"Four knot bumpers may be too many but let's start with four and see."

This job of cutting limbs off the trees that had been cut down required less skill than the other jobs so Jed pointed to the three youngest men on the crew.

"You boys take this on for now." He turned to Red Miller, a veteran logger. "Red, you work with them for awhile and teach them all your tricks."

One of the young men spoke up. "Will we have a chance to work the other jobs?"

Justin answered, "Every logger needs to know how to work every job. You make it your business to learn. Let Jed know and he'll put you with a more experienced man. But wait 'til we've got this job running right before you do any switching."

He laid his hand on Jed's shoulder. "Jed's got patience. He got some of mine. Swampers, next."

Three men were picked for this job of cutting out a path through the bushes and undergrowth, wide enough for a team of horses to pull logs through from the cutting area to the loading dock by the railroad.

"You're responsible for choosin' the quickest and safest way through these woods. If a spot needs slickin' down to move the logs faster, you water it down. We don't have a water jack," Jed said.

"For now, we need two teamsters. Rob, you be the head teamster with Clay handling the second team. I know both of you have the reputation of workin' good with horses." Rob and Clay nodded. Rob, a tall, handsome, black-headed man with a quick smile, seemed pleased.

"That leaves three for the loadin' crew," Jed said. He pointed individually to the three men left. "I know Frank has operated a loader before. Have you other two had experience loadin' and workin' around the train?"

They nodded to indicate they had.

"I thought so. You know what to do then. Frank, you're in charge. All of you know the dangers."

Justin spoke up. "We've all logged enough to know this is very dangerous business. We have to watch out for ourselves and each other." He paused for emphasis on every word. "We cannot be careless! We can't ever let down our guard against the dangers. That way we'll all stay alive and keep our body parts."

He shifted his foot on the chair and continued in a more conversational tone. "We'll be cutting standard sixteen-foot logs as much as possible. I know we'll have some that are twelve or fourteen foot from trees with a crook in them but keep these to a minimum. It'll be interesting to see how many flatcars we can load in a day."

He turned to Jed who said, "Tomorrow mornin' the teamsters and loadin' crew will help cut, to get some logs ahead. Bulldog and Tom have already cut some leads. After dinner we'll take in the horses and start pullin' out the logs."

Justin asked, "Any questions?"

Nobody said anything for a minute then Abe looked around and grinned. "Looks like we're ready to roll."

"That wraps it up then," said Justin. "Breakfast at six-fifteen. We'll hit the trail at six-forty-five."

When he got back to his shack, Nora had the children ready for bed. Laurel was already in bed with her foot propped up on a pillow. As Nora left, she told Justin, "I'll be here early in the mornin'." He thanked her and closed the door. It was good to be alone with his family.

The next morning was charged with excitement from the moment Justin's feet hit the floor. He was up at four-thirty and found Jed and the women already in the kitchen. By the time the men arrived for breakfast he had fed and watered the horses, milked the cows, and had his family settled with Nora in charge.

Laurel knew how much this day meant to him. She hugged him and said, "I'm happy for you. I hope the crew gets off to a good start."

As he left, Nora said, "Goodness! He's like a whirlwind this mornin'."

The men were in high spirits, too. They were on the job site a few minutes before seven. Their experience was soon evident. Justin and Jed seemed to be everywhere observing, making suggestions, giving a helping hand.

Justin worked first with the cutting crew. As Abe and his partner started to cut a large chestnut, Justin studied the surroundings for a moment, then stuck a stick in the ground where he wanted it to fall. He called, "Lay it down on this, boys."

The tree fell about two feet downhill from the stick, breaking a smaller tree on its way down. Abe frowned, "We can do better than that. We'll adjust our sights and our rhythm."

"Let's see if we can hit the bull's eye, Jed," said Justin. He drove down another stake.

The crew watched as Justin adjusted the lead a few inches and he and Jed felled a big oak on top of the stake, driving it into the ground. No smaller trees were broken. It was a clean fall.

Justin said, "Jed, tell them why we want this kind of precision."

Jed said, "It's something we learned in Forestry School." He spoke in a disarming manner, Justin thought, imparting valuable information without being a know-it-all. "We cut as clean as we can and protect the younger trees for our children to use or enjoy. We'll also do some replanting and erosion control, but we'll talk about that later. Let's get these saws to singin' right now."

The men scattered. Each team examined the lead and drove a stake into the ground. They had accepted the challenge. Some healthy competition would keep their adrenaline flowing and help the hours pass faster. Justin and Jed looked at each other with satisfaction before they went their separate ways. Jed would work with the swampers while Justin took Frank and the loading crew to look at the loader.

Eight flatbed cars, each one eighteen to twenty feet long, stretched around a curve of the logging railroad. Justin climbed up on the loader that stood by the first car. He swung the crane around in various positions, then turned it off and called down to Frank.

"There seems to be a catch in the extreme left swing. I noticed it yesterday."

He climbed down and said, "See what you think."

Frank scrambled up and started moving levers. He held his head close to hear the gears, as intent as a doctor with a patient. After awhile he switched it off and climbed down.

"That one gear is slippin' some but, with the right handlin', it should work a while longer. We won't know 'til we get a log on it. I may need to stay over on Saturday and fix it. I've worked on these things before."

"Good," Justin said with relief. "Let's get back and lay down some more of those trees."

It was a week before Laurel and Adam fully recovered. They both developed colds and Laurel couldn't put all her weight on her foot for several days. She was convinced it was not broken so she would not go to the doctor. It was, however, a very bad sprain and bruise. She knew how to take care of it and did so, with Nora's help. Hannah, Bess, and Alice carried on with the meals after Laurel and Hannah worked out the menus.

Justin was excited about the way the crew was performing. They were proving themselves. And they seemed to be working as a team with no apparent problems yet. On Thursday Justin rode into Deerbrook to give Mr. Beck a report and to get the first week's payroll. He took the wagon to bring back supplies for the next two weeks. Hannah and Laurel had worked up a supply list based on how much food it had taken the first week.

Hiram Beck was pleased and in a talkative mood. After taking care of business, he said, "I heard about your wife jumping into that white-water and saving your son."

"She was fortunate," Justin said.

"And brave," added Mr. Beck.

"Yes, that, too," Justin agreed.

"Folks around here say she's a mighty fine school teacher and you're a mighty fine photographer."

Justin wasn't sure where this was going. "She taught school several years. But she's staying home now since we've started our family."

"Do you plan to continue your photography?"

"Some. On weekends."

"Good. Could you take some pictures of the logging crew at work and let me see them?"

"Sure. In fact, I was planning to do that."

"When you get time, bring some pictures in. If I like them we might hire you as our official photographer for the industry. You'd be paid separately for that, of course."

Justin smiled. "I'll see what I can do in the next few weeks."

He rose. "And now I'd better get going. I have to buy our supplies for the next couple of weeks. Got to keep the women in camp happy." He had another reason for hurrying. He planned to take a surprise home to Laurel. He would have to hustle to get it all done.

As he watched Justin hurry away, Hiram Beck wondered what drew a man like him to do such hard work, and how well an educated, cultured young wife would adjust to life in a logging camp.

Laurel, meanwhile, was content to be alive and have Adam alive. The struggles which had seemed so monumental last week had been put in perspective. She and Justin and the children had their lives, had each other, had their health and a job. The crude shack was even losing its power to disorient and depress her.

At dusk she heard the wagon stop right in front of her shack. Suddenly, Justin was through the door, laughing. "If the lady of the house will close her eyes, her delivery man has a surprise."

She laughed at him and closed her eyes obediently. She heard him set something in front of her. "Keep them closed," he instructed as he guided her hand to touch.

"A window – with glass panes!" Her eyes flew open. "Justin, you got real windows for me!" She pulled him down and kissed him. His eyes were dancing like a child on Christmas morning.

"Three glass windows with six panes in each. Couldn't very well have those pretty curtains you made without real windows."

"I can't wait to get them in!"

"I know. Zeke and Odell will put them in early in the morning before they go to work." He couldn't have pleased her more.

The next day after the windows were in place, Nora cleaned and polished them, her pleasure lacing her bursts of speech while she worked. When she finished, Laurel asked, "Nora, can you move my chair over some? I want to be able to see out all three windows at once."

The spring sunshine poured its warmth and cheerfulness into the shack. As Laurel picked up her mending and adjusted her foot, she was content.

Quitting time at four o'clock on Friday found a crew proud but tired and ready to be off to their families. Justin and Jed met them in the lobby to congratulate them on a great week. Their teamwork was clicking along and they had cut, snaked out, loaded and shipped more logs than any of them had expected.

As Justin paid each man five dollars in cash, he knew it was the first money some of them had made for awhile. He was pleased to think of what it would mean to their families. As the train pulled out with the crew on board, he, Jed, Bulldog, and Tom were relieved. They were ready for a break and some time with their own families.

The days Laurel had to spend with her foot up were put to good use. She worked up two weeks worth of basic menus that would be alternated. She had another section in her notebook that would include in-season vegetables and fruits and meats that were available.

Breakfast would be hearty with bacon or ham, eggs, sawmill gravy, biscuits and coffee. Once or twice a week they would cook oatmeal or grits or applesauce in addition to the basics.

Lunch might be beef stew or thick vegetable soup with coleslaw and cornbread or sometimes navy or pinto beans with fat back, fried potatoes, and cornbread. They always had dessert.

Supper would be the heaviest meal with fresh meat such as beef, pork or chicken as it was available. Canned salmon for salmon patties or cured ham were favorites and could be kept on hand. Pinto beans or macaroni and cheese were used as meat substitutes when no fresh meat was available. Potatoes, sweet potatoes, and rice were good stick-to-the-ribs fillers. Vegetables, canned or fresh, when they were in season, balanced out a healthy meal.

Desserts would be apple, peach, or blackberry cobblers, cake, egg custard, gingerbread, or sugar cookies. Banana pudding was a favorite when bananas could be bought. If time ran out, they could serve canned fruit. Hannah told Laurel the men emptied the two gallon coffee pot at every meal. So coffee and water would be the standard drinks. In summer they could serve lemonade.

Laurel spent a good bit of time working on cooking shifts that would be fair. She came up with a long, ten-hour shift and a short six-hour shift per day with alternating weeks. She and Alice would work from four-thirty in the morning to two-thirty in the afternoon, cooking breakfast and lunch and cleaning up for one week. Hannah and Bess would work from two-thirty to eight-thirty in the afternoon, cooking supper and cleaning up. The next week they would switch. Nora would take care of Sarah and Adam and watch Thad, Jesse, and Jonah while their mothers were cooking. She would also help with Laurel's and Hannah's housework. Laurel would ask Nora and Alice to switch work some as Alice's pregnancy advanced. Each needed to know how to do both jobs. She would wait at least a month to give Sarah and Adam time to adjust to their new circumstances. Nora had won their hearts as well as hers. She would introduce Alice to them gradually.

Bess was another matter. She was giving Laurel a wide berth. Hannah and Alice had come by every day to see how Laurel was doing. Bess's absence was noticed in such a small group but no one said anything. Laurel knew Hannah could work with Bess and keep her in line, as she had shown at their get-together. She sure didn't want to work with Bess and she knew the feeling was mutual.

The amount of food they had bought amazed Laurel. One hundred pound bags of pinto beans, twenty-five pound bags of flour, meal and sugar. Five-gallon cans of coffee. Gallon size cans of peaches, applesauce, green beans and other vegetables. Shelves couldn't hold it all so it was stacked at the opposite end of the mess hall from the stove.

She made a section in her notebook to enter kitchen expenses. One column for the cost of groceries and one for the women's wages. Justin had told her to plan to pay the women five cents an hour, half what the men made. This would be two dollars and a half a week for the ten-hour shift and one dollar and a half a week for the six-hour shift. Eight dollars a month plus their meals. It was good pay.

Justin would receive the same weekly pay as the crew and Laurel the same as the women. They would, however, receive ten per-cent of the profit at the end of each month, which would more than double their pay. Justin would turn in a bill for the food and supplies, which he would pay the company store. Laurel was encouraged. Since they would have few personal expenses living here, they should be able to save most of what they made.

Chapter Eleven

Laurel and Alice took the six-hour supper shift for her first week of cooking. Justin had brought home some sirloin which she needed to cook on Monday. Instead of the usual beef stew, Laurel sliced the meat, beat it to tenderize it, dredged it in flour, salt and pepper, and fried it. She then cut it up and let it simmer in a pot of cream gravy. She made four pans of biscuits while Alice prepared mashed potatoes and green beans. Justin had asked her to make one of his favorite desserts.

As suppertime approached she realized she was nervous even though they had everything ready. She felt hot and sweaty from standing over the stove, so she hurried across to her shack to freshen up and check on the children. Nora had taken them on a walk or to Hannah's. Laurel sponged her face and arms, changed to a clean white blouse, and combed her hair which, when damp, insisted on framing curls around her face. Her cheeks were flushed from heat and excitement. She hurried back so Alice could take a short break.

The crew poured through the door with its usual ready-to-eat gusto. She and Alice stood across the room facing the men. She smiled and tried to look at each one directly. They reacted differently. Some spoke, some mumbled, and some ran their hand through their hair. As they sat down, they all became quiet. Justin went over, put his arm around her shoulder and said, "This is my wife, Laurel. She'll be in charge of cooking. She'll want to get to know you, so go around the tables and tell her your first names. Abe, you start."

Laurel interrupted. "I know Zeke and Odell. We wouldn't have got moved in without them." Their grins showed surprise and pleasure.

She heard the rest of their names as a litany. Abe, Dirk, Rob, Red,

Frank...then she lost track. She would make it a point to know their names by Wednesday, the same way she used to learn her student's names quickly. And Justin could fill her in about each one.

After they finished she said simply, "I'm very pleased to meet you. Justin has talked about you and bragged on you all week, so I feel like I already know you. Help me out with your names for a day or two. And now Alice and I will dish up supper for you. I know you're hungry."

Most of the men were too shy to initiate a conversation with her. Abe and Dirk didn't have that problem. After talking about her jumping in the river and pulling Adam out, Abe said, "I hear you're a school teacher."

"Yes," Laurel said as she put some more bread on the table. "I taught four years before Justin and I were married and then two afterward."

Dirk asked, "What grades?"

"First grade through seventh."

"Lots of people around here never had a school close enough to go to, so they can't read or write," Abe stated so wistfully she wondered if he was one of them.

Dirk piped up, "If you're as good a teacher as you are a cook, your students was lucky. I ain't never had such good beefsteak and gravy."

"Thank you," Laurel answered with a smile.

Justin had been quiet, watching her put the men at ease. And supper was delicious. He was proud of her. He said, "I asked her to bake us some of her special gingerbread for dessert. I think you'll like it." They did. They ate every crumb.

By the time the men were through and the women brought the children to eat, Laurel's ankle was throbbing. She sat down and put her leg up on the bench. Nora noticed first. As soon as they ate, Nora and Hannah helped Laurel home with the children. They helped Alice wash dishes in her place. Bess was friendly enough to everyone except Laurel. She acted as if Laurel wasn't there.

Routine was established by the end of the second week, and everyone seemed to know what was expected of him or her. Laurel realized Justin was pushing himself too hard when he started falling asleep in his reading chair as soon as he sat down. He was up at four-thirty in the morning and worked 'til eight-thirty or nine at night, putting in a full day with the crew besides cutting wood, carrying water and taking care of the livestock. After the third night of this, Laurel woke him up bathing his face with a warm washcloth. She told him her concerns. He agreed to work out a fair system where the men would take turns helping with the chores, morning and evening.

By the second week Hannah and Laurel had found a good spot for a community wash place at the spring close to Hannah's shack. When Justin and Jed started building their wash table one night after supper, they had more advice than they needed from the crew, so Justin put the men to work. They soon had a fire pit ringed with rocks. The huge black wash pot with its metal frame fitted over the pit.

The clothesline went up in record time after the women showed them where they wanted it at the edge of the clearing. Abe had men digging holes and finding and setting poles as soon as the words were out of their mouths. He said, "Miz Worth, I set my wife a battlin' block next to her wash pot. She likes to lift out my work clothes, beat the dirt out and put them back in the pot awhile. Would like you one?"

"I'm sure I would. How do you make a battlin' block?"

"You don't make it. You find one and shape it up. The best kind is a big flat stump." He raised his voice, "Hey, you lumberjacks, we need to find these women a big hickory stump or part of a hickory tree trunk for a battlin' block. Be on the lookout for one tomorrow."

He continued to Laurel, "We'll snake one out for you and cut and plane off a couple of battlin' sticks. They look like oars. You lift the soapy clothes on to the battlin' block and beat the dirt out with the battlin' sticks."

"Thank you, Abe, for all your help. That sounds a lot easier than scrubbing those stiff work clothes."

Justin hammered another nail, pleased the men were willing to help him. He had heard the exchange between Abe and Laurel. He saw her now talking to Dirk and Tom who were setting a clothes line post in the ground. Then the truth hit him. *They're not doing this for me. They're doing it for Laurel*. He started whistling again as he worked.

Laurel had always enjoyed abundant energy and the drive to get things done quickly. She was surprised when she felt her body was betraying her the first Monday she worked the ten-hour shift from four-thirty in the morning to two-thirty in the afternoon. She had worked steadily except when she sat down twice to nurse Adam and twice more to eat. She and Nora had planned to go straight to the wash place as soon as she finished in the kitchen. When the time came, she was so tired she felt sick at her stomach. She couldn't go.

Nora took charge. "I've already got the water boilin' and the tubs filled, so I'm goin' to start. You rest while the children take naps. Then maybe we can finish together." Laurel agreed because she knew this was their only day this week to use the wash place.

That night she went to bed when the children did, about eight o'clock, and went right to sleep. Justin followed by nine, missing their special time when he felt he had all her attention.

The next morning after breakfast dishes were washed, she and Alice were peeling potatoes for lunch when Hannah came in. She picked up a knife and started peeling, too. Before Laurel could protest, she started talking in her quiet way.

"Nora told me how tired you was yesterday. I got on to her for lettin' you help do that washin'. I could'a done it this mornin' with ours."

"No, Hannah. You're just as busy as I am."

"I'm not. I ain't nursin' no baby and I ain't got the responsibility of lookin' after everybody. So I'm goin' to look after you. If you get sick everybody feels it."

"She's right, Miz Worth," Alice added.

"But everybody's working hard," Laurel protested. "I don't want people to think I'm lazy and not doing my share." She was thinking of Bess.

"Lord-a-mercy, Laurel! You're 'bout as lazy as a whirlwind! Now here's what we want to do. Nora wants to help more in the kitchen. She likes to be in the middle of things. She can bring the children to play here some while all of you work together. She's as strong as an ox, Laurel, so she can lift and do some of the heavy work that you and Alice don't need to do." She grinned and added," And you know how she loves to talk."

Laurel hugged Hannah and agreed. She knew Hannah was right. She had never done such hard, consistent physical labor in such primitive conditions. This would give her time to adjust and improve her stamina.

By the end of the first month, Justin and Jed knew they had picked a top-notch crew. The men had worked hard, shipping out more flatcars of logs than even Justin had estimated. They also got along well with each other and observed the camp rules. Justin had been around enough logging camps to know he was very fortunate.

They were also becoming a community. It had started when they set up the wash place. Abe and Bulldog helped Tom make a bed frame. Laurel and Hannah helped Alice make some sheets and started planning some quilts. Alice only had two old faded ones. They moved Laurel's sewing machine to the mess hall where someone could sew while the others were cooking. Bess even showed an interest in learning to sew, with Hannah as her teacher.

Laurel changed the practice of having women and children wait to eat until the men were finished. It made her uncomfortable. It seemed like an effort, even here in this primitive setting, to "keep women in their place." The practical reason she used was that it took less time and the cooks could get things cleaned up faster. The women and children sat at a small table across the room. After a few days, however, the three older children ended up eating with the crew, sitting by different people. The crew enjoyed the children and the youngsters enjoyed the attention the men gave them.

One afternoon about the third week in camp, Justin came into the mess hall just before suppertime, pulled a chair near the stove where Laurel was working and opened his newspaper. He had been to Deerbrook and was anxious to share the news. Over the years he and Laurel had formed the habit of discussing issues, agreeing or disagreeing. He liked to tell her—or read to her—the news while she was cooking supper. She was amused that he thought their private ritual would work here while she was cooking for thirty people.

"You'll be interested in this, Laurel. According to this article, public opinion in the United States is growing against joining the League of Nations. President Wilson must be disappointed. He's spent so much time on it since the war."

"The League of Nations seems to be a good idea on the surface. We can't ignore Europe, as the war just showed us," Laurel said as she took two iron skillets of cornbread out of the oven. Alice was setting the table. Abe and Dirk came and slipped quietly on to the bench.

Justin continued. "Isolationism is always a temptation for Americans. The war has turned the public against joining up with Europe on anything." He turned the page. "It goes on to say that people are calling for a return to normalcy and seem to think the man to lead us is Warren G. Harding."

Laurel dished up two bowls of pinto beans. "You'd like that, wouldn't you?"

"Of course. He's a Republican. But you know I think Woodrow Wilson is a fine man. He's had a rough presidency with the war and the aftermath."

"Anything about the Nineteenth Amendment – women getting the right to vote?"

"Oh, yes! Congress will vote on Women's Suffrage in the summer session. And the suffragettes are marching on Washington next week – a parade! You want to go?" he teased.

"No, I don't need to go to Washington to march," she answered on her way to put the corn bread on the table. "But I do plan to encourage the women in Wildwood County to fight for the right to vote."

"I know you do. What are you and Mrs. Sargent up to now?"

"We're putting articles in the paper to encourage women to vote. We're also planning a rally as soon as Congress gives us the right to vote."

"And you'll be the speaker?"

"Yes. I've been asked."

Laurel and Alice finished getting the meal on the table as the crew trooped in with the women and children following.

After they had eaten awhile with their usual mealtime gusto, Abe Johnson spoke up. "Justin, why don't you tell us that news you and Miz Worth was talkin' about before supper."

Justin looked around to see if the men agreed. Several nodded their heads and they all looked interested. After Justin shared what he and Laurel had discussed, Abe asked, "Miz Worth, what kind of speech you goin' to make?"

"I'm hoping to speak in August to a group of women about why we need to vote." She laughed. "I may practice on all of you. Then you can go home and tell your wives why they need to vote."

She had been teasing, but Abe answered seriously, "We'd be mighty pleased if you would speak it to us first." He looked around the table for support. The men agreed.

Laurel looked at Justin who inclined his head slightly. His smile was encouraging but amused. She could almost hear him thinking, *You put your foot in it this time, Mrs. Worth.*

She looked around. "Thank you. When the time comes, I'll speak it to you first and you can tell me if it's okay."

"What else is in the news?" Jed asked.

Justin opened the paper again. "The Boston Red Sox have traded Babe Ruth to the New York Yankees for one hundred twenty-five thousand dollars. He plans to give up pitching and play the outfield." He passed the paper around to show the picture of George Herman Ruth at bat. So, one more unusual custom was established that night at the Worth Logging Camp, as it came to be known. The men expected, and received an update on world, national, and local news and sports every time Justin took a trip to town.

The women had established that each one had the same wash day each week. Monday was Laurel's; Tuesday, Hannah's; Wednesday, Bess's; and Thursday, Alice's. One morning in May, Laurel and Nora were washing. It was a glorious day that seemed bursting with new life

Laurel's senses were again caressed by the smell and sights and sounds of the forest. Sarah played with Adam who stood in his box, holding on. He soon would be walking.

They worked together, with Laurel scrubbing the children's clothes and Nora using the battling stick on Justin's clothes. Laurel straightened a minute, flexed her back, and looked at the woods surrounding them.

"Nora, let's mark off boundaries and explore these woods around camp. I would love to know what's out there. We could start behind our house and work our way around camp."

"I'd love it," said Nora enthusiastically. "Alice could keep Sarah and Adam. Hannah would like to go, too. She loves to look for wild flowers."

"We'll try to have a once-a-week adventure until we're all the way around," Laurel said. "Maybe on Sunday afternoons."

"There's one section behind the men's bunkhouse where we better not go. We won't let the boys and Jonah play there." Nora said.

"Why not?"

"That's where the men go to the woods, Miz Worth." Nora was embarrassed.

"What do you mean?"

"That's where they go to…to…." Nora searched for a polite word.

"To their outhouses?" Laurel helped her.

"They ain't got no outhouses. They just go to the woods."

Laurel stared at her. Since their outhouse stood primly hidden by trees not far behind their shack, she had assumed there were outhouses for everybody in camp, concealed by trees.

She stood straight and pushed her hair off her forehead, leaving a blob of glistening suds perched on top of her head. She felt contaminated. And angry. At Justin and all the men. Nora saw her expression and ducked her head.

Laurel said, "I'll talk to Justin about that!"

And she did. That night. As soon as they were alone.

Justin protested, "Laurel, be reasonable. Logging camps don't have outhouses."

Laurel had thought about it all afternoon, and knew she needed to confront Justin without anger. But every instinct in her rose up in defiance.

"Do you have any idea of all the sicknesses we can get from flies carrying germs to our food from – from human excrement? And our water supply may already be contaminated from seepage and runoff."

Justin was exasperated. *If it isn't teacher talk, it's nurse talk,* he thought.

"These loggers would laugh at me if I asked them to build outhouses for everybody, Laurel. I would bet that many of them don't even have them at home."

"Then we'll have to figure out a way to convince them," she said.

"Let's figure it out another day. The loader is giving us problems. I've got to get it fixed tomorrow to keep us on schedule. That means pulling Tattoo off the job for a trip to town, which causes other problems."

Laurel knew when to back away. But she pulled her medical book off the shelf and settled in her chair to check on some things. She made occasional notes in a lined writing tablet. Justin, taking refuge from his problems a little while in a Zane Gray western, did not want to know what she was doing.

The next day while Justin was gone, Laurel asked Hannah, Jed, Abe, and Dirk to meet with her for a few minutes after lunch. She knew too much to allow the health threat to continue.

"Justin has too many other problems to deal with this one right now, so I'm bringing it directly to you for help. The men respect you and will listen to you."

She talked to them earnestly for a few minutes and showed them a couple of pictures in her medical book. She told them what she would like to do and asked them to think about it and give her their opinion after work. They agreed and left looking sober.

Laurel had experience in the power of persuasion. It helped to give people the facts and encourage them to use their own judgment and make their own decisions, based on the facts. The results were usually twofold: accomplishment of the task at hand, plus a proud group of people who had taken the responsibility. She had never been disappointed yet.

She spent some time getting the facts together and deciding how to present them. She remembered asking Papa once how he got people to cooperate so well in getting things done. She remembered some of his words, "Never talk down to people. They sense condescension even if it's unspoken. Respect them and expect the best from them. Remember, you can learn something from everybody no matter how little schooling he's had."

She got the go-ahead from her four allies: Jed, Hannah, Abe and Dirk. Justin wasn't home yet but she felt she would be doing him a favor. As soon as supper was over, Jed said, "Mrs. Worth has some things to say that we all need to hear."

She stood and talked as she had in town meetings in the past. "We have a problem which we need to take care of. We could be in danger of typhoid fever right now."

Alice gasped. "Why?" She unconsciously placed a protective hand on her stomach. The men looked at Laurel, startled. She had their attention. Only Bess looked bored as she chewed her gum.

"The typhoid germ lives and grows in waste from the human body. The germs can infect the water supply if water runs over the waste where humans have relieved themselves outside like we are doing here. Or from outhouses built over streams like many people have. Also, flies carry the germs from human waste directly to food and drink. The sickness sometimes kills a person outright or goes into meningitis, which almost always kills you."

She paused and looked around the room. Silence and waiting…Bess had stopped chewing. Laurel continued speaking in elementary terms, avoiding medical jargon. "Another disease we can get from human waste lying around is hookworm. The tiny larvae burrow through the skin, usually through bare feet, get in the blood stream where they suck out the iron and end up in the intestines where they suck out all the nutrients. This leaves a person pale and weak. A child can be pasty-looking with a large stomach and sometimes have dropsy in the legs. Hookworm disease stunts growth and causes people to become mentally slow."

She passed her book around. "Here's an enlarged picture of the hookworm."

A painful awareness had passed over some faces and Laurel knew they recognized the symptoms in someone they cared about. Their children, maybe. Hannah and Bess looked at their children's bare feet.

"If you know anyone you think has hookworm please talk to me later. You can get rid of it with the right medicine, and stay rid of it by knowing what causes it. Right now we need to prevent these diseases in our camp. What do you think we can do about it?"

"The first thing we need to do is build some outhouses," Abe said.

"Yeah, as soon as we can," Tom said. "I seen a friend of mine die with meningitis."

Then they were all talking at once. It was their problem now. She nodded to Jed and sat down with the women. Adam reached for her and she took him on her lap.

After the initial noisy reaction, things settled down a little and Jed, in his easy way, said, "We need to decide how many outhouses, where to build 'em and when."

"We need to build them well away from the stream," Bulldog said. "We can go look for places now."

They decided to build two outhouses for the men in the bunkhouse. Another one would be shared by Bulldog's and Tom's families.

Just as Jed started to summarize what they had decided, Justin walked in. He stopped and was quiet when he realized he was interrupting Jed and some kind of meeting.

Jed finished. "It looks like we've decided to build three outhouses as soon as possible, beginning tomorrow afternoon. We need to go find the best places before dark." He looked at Justin. "Glad you're back. What's the news about the loader?"

"They'll be here to fix it first thing in the morning. Maybe we can catch up and get back on schedule in a couple of days."

"Good," Jed said. Then he grinned. "You want to come with us to help decide where to build some outhouses?"

"No. I'm hungry and I believe you Paul Bunyans can handle it." His blue eyes were amused as they traveled around the room and settled on his demure wife, who was suddenly busy with Adam.

That evening after the children were asleep and they sat down to relax a few minutes, Justin said, "Well, Mrs. Worth, are you going to tell me voluntarily or do I turn you over my knees?"

She tilted her head. "Tell you what, Mr. Worth?"

"Just how it is that nineteen men eagerly—yes, eagerly—ran off to the woods to find places to build three outhouses. They couldn't even stop to give me a decent howdy. What in the world did you do?"

"Why do you think I did something?"

He leaned toward her, lowered his head, looked her straight in the eyes and said softly, "Laurel…."

She looked straight back and raised her chin: the teacher look. "Justin, I told them the dangers of typhoid fever and hookworm that come from exposed human waste."

"Tell me what you told them and how you told them. Everything."

She did. Even how she remembered Papa's words. She repeated how the diseases are spread.

His expression grew soft as she talked and when she finished he said, "Come here." He settled back in his chair and spread his arms. She settled into his lap and snuggled her face against his. They were quiet awhile savoring each other's touch. The old magic was still there.

Then she felt Justin's stomach muscles ripple just before he burst out laughing.

She sat up as he said, "Laurel, Honey, you've scared those men so bad they may not—as you say—relieve themselves again until the outhouses are built. If they do have to go, they'll probably feel obliged to travel to the next county."

She laughed, then whispered, "So, you're not mad at me?"

"No. But you're a dangerous woman. I'm going to try to keep you on my side."

The outhouses were ready in four days. This was record time considering they had to work after hours before dark. Justin worked with them and reported progress each night. The night they finished, Justin came in highly amused over something. She waited as she did some mending.

After he took his boots off, he approached her slowly, bowing, and asked, "Does Mrs. Worth think she could arrange to inspect three outhouses tomorrow after supper?"

She laughed. "Of course not! An outhouse is an outhouse."

"Oh, no, Ma'am!" He said as he kept his humble position. "These are three works of art done to please the lady who inspired them. They even have lids for the seats."

"Really?" So they had heard and had taken responsibility. She stood up and hugged Justin. "And the men are pleased with their work?"

He turned serious. "Yes, m'dear. And they have asked for your inspection. They seem eager to please you."

She was very pleased and plainly told them so the following evening. When she was through, they felt they had personally averted a typhoid epidemic. She finished by saying, "If anybody wants to know about that hookworm medicine, please talk to me about it."

The following week three of the men approached her alone and at different times. Each asked shyly about the medicine and how to give it to their families. Hannah decided to give Thad and Jesse a run of the medicine just in case, and talked Bess into giving some to Jonah.

The weather was getting warmer and they needed spring boxes for their milk and butter and meats. The women were using their round tin washtubs to keep the food cool. They would place two tubs in the stream by the wash place, secured by rocks, put the food in them, and cap larger tubs down over them. It was a good temporary measure and Laurel hesitated to bring up building spring boxes because the men were working so hard. And they had already built the outhouses and the wash place. She didn't want to nag. The matter, however, was taken out of her hands.

One night the whole camp was suddenly brought awake. The clanging and clanking brought the men out of bed fumbling to light the lanterns. It sounded like an invading army coming from the wash place. The crew, half running, stopped in their tracks. The full moon silhouetted a mother bear and two cubs at the stream. She was after the food and was making progress. It looked like food from one tub was scattered on the bank and the cubs were eating. The mother bear saw the men and stood facing them. There she was, hundreds of pounds of brute strength, fiercely protective of her cubs. The men knew how dangerous she could be. They were hardly breathing.

Justin spoke quietly, "We don't want to rile her. Let's back up slowly and turn the lanterns off." His rifle glinted in the moonlight. The bears kept eating with the mother raising her head every minute or so, as if to remind the humans she knew they were there.

"I'm going to shoot into the air," Justin said. "Maybe it will scare her off. But get ready to run."

The crack of the rifle through the silence did the job. For a moment she lowered her head and swung it back and forth like she was going to charge. Then she loped off into the woods behind her cubs.

The men relit their lanterns and examined the damage. Broken milk jugs, trampled butter, eggshells, a large dirty slab of bacon and pieces of bananas littered the bank.

"There's our breakfast," Bulldog spoke for all of them. "And our banana pudding."

"They must've smelled the bananas," Abe said.

Justin had brought in a supply of groceries that day. He always tried to buy enough bananas for a banana pudding.

"I'm glad she didn't get into the other tub. It has our fresh meat in it. We don't need a bear around that has tasted blood," Justin said. "Let's put some heavy rock on that tub and clean this place up, so maybe she won't come back."

Abe and Dirk brought shovels and dug a hole across the branch at the edge of the woods. The others put the broken glass and food scraps in it. When they had buried it deep, they went back to bed.

Breakfast the next morning was sawmill gravy, grits and biscuits without butter. Warm milk straight from the cow to cream their coffee. No bacon and eggs. Hot sweet applesauce helped some.

"Wonder where that fierce black mama is this mornin'," Abe said. Jed told Hannah to keep the boys and Jonah close to camp for a day or two. Justin told the men to take their rifles to the job.

"You know as well as I do that bears sense us first and try to avoid us. But a mother bear can be extremely dangerous if she thinks her cubs are threatened. I know you won't shoot unless you have to. Be careful and keep a good lookout."

That night at supper Justin brought up the subject Laurel had delayed. "The women have been making do without proper places to store our perishable food. We saw what happened to it last night. We need to build some spring boxes."

After a general discussion, Abe said, "Miz Worth, you and the women draw us off a picture and tell us how many. We'll try to build 'em bear-proof."

They built three sturdy, rectangular spring boxes with holes cut in each end for the cool water to run through. The milk and fresh meat would sit in containers down in the water. A shelf was built in the end of each one for butter, eggs, leftovers, and other perishables. The latches were metal, with a bar securing them. Hopefully, only humans could open them. One was left at the wash place. The other two were placed near the cooler spring with denser foliage near the kitchen and Justin's shack.

Justin felt he needed to make atonement someway to Rev. Stevens and the others for Laurel's and Adam's lives. On his trips back and forth from town he had examined the bridge to the church and checked with the proper authorities about widening the entrance. Since any wagon approaching the bridge from either direction had to make a sharp right-angle turn, the bank needed shoring up and rounding off on both sides of the bridge, widening the turning space. He experimented with Tattoo pulling the wagon onto the bridge from the left and the right. It was very close. When he figured out what he needed to do, he put it to the men one night in the lobby.

"If anybody wants to make a little extra money, I'll personally pay you to help me fix the turn-in to the bridge where…," he paused and was quiet a moment before he continued, "…the bridge to the church, before somebody else goes in that river and over the falls. Think about it. You can let me know tomorrow and we'll look it over and try to start after supper. We'll have enough daylight to work awhile."

Nobody said anything the next day until supper. When they were about finished, Abe said, "Justin, I guess every one of us jackleg engineers is goin' to help fix that bridge."

Justin stood, looked around the tables, and propped his foot on the bench. "I thank you all. But I have a problem. I'm paying for this work out of my own pocket and I can't afford all of you."

Abe stood and looked at him. "You ain't payin' nobody nothin'. We talked it over last night. You and Miz Worth's runnin' the best loggin' camp we've ever been in." He looked across the room at Laurel. "Miz Worth, we're doin' this for you, too. We figure you'll be goin' to church and we don't want you jumpin' in that river no more."

Laurel saw Justin swallow and knew he didn't know what to say. She came over and put her arm through his. "Thank you – from both of us. One of the reasons this is a good logging camp is because of you men. Justin says you're a top-notch crew and I say you are helping to make this place into a community instead of just a place where a group of people happen to work together."

They were embarrassed by her praise, but they were also pleased. Jed rose and said, "Let's be goin' and see what we can do before dark."

It was the middle of the next week before they finished, working every night until dark forced them to quit. When Laurel went to church on Sunday she couldn't believe the difference. A horse could now pull a wagon easily and safely on to the bridge from either direction. They had even put up rails. She knew she was safe, but her hands got clammy and she refused to look at the water.

Rev. Stevens and the congregation were all agog over the changes. "It looks like we've had a crew of engineers in here," the pastor said from the pulpit. "Mrs. Worth, tell your husband and his crew how much we appreciate this. It was mighty nice of them to do this for the church."

The congregation agreed and she graciously accepted their thanks. But she knew he hadn't done it for them. He had done it for her. She thought momentarily of his sharp words to her about asking for God's help with their lives; then all this hard work and effort to make it possible for her to come to church. She didn't understand that part of him but she knew the work had been done because he loved her and the children and wanted them safe. She treasured the thought and allowed the warmth of it to fill her as she brought her mind back to the sermon.

The congregation fervently sang the words she knew so well:

"O, come to the church in the wildwood, O, come to the church in the dell,

No spot is so dear to my childhood, As the little brown church in the vale."

For a moment she imagined Papa in his pew at the little Methodist church where she had grown up. She would write him this afternoon and tell him about life in a logging camp. She would also ask Madeleine to send her some recipes that could be stretched to serve a logging crew. Madeleine was the favorite cook for church suppers and community events.

The old well-known hymns comforted Laurel. She needed something of her old life to hang on to. Everything about this life was foreign. At times she felt she had crossed the Rubicon – like Julius Caesar when he crossed with his men to fight for the leadership of Rome – and like his, her life would never fit into its former familiar dimensions again.

After church the congregation gathered around to ask if she and Adam were over their river ride and if she was settled in at the camp. She was warmed by their friendliness. Mrs. Stevens, proprietary toward Laurel and the children, said, "I hope we can be good neighbors. I know you're awful busy but I do love a little woman company every now and then." Laurel invited her to visit whenever she had time.

On her way home she thought of the children she had counted in church. Five girls and four boys, probably under twelve years old. They needed a Sunday school class. And Jesse, Thad, and Jonah needed to be in it. She would think about it.

Chapter Twelve

Justin leaned forward in the saddle, he and Tattoo working as one, as they made their way up the mountain where their next tract of timber lay. At Justin's request, Hiram Beck had provided another horse for the crew after seeing the first month's profits. This freed Tattoo for Justin's personal use. He had decided to push the crew to cut further away from camp on the steep mountain slope during summer and fall, saving the closer, easier tracts for the hard winter months. He would look it over and make some estimates, then ride over it again with Jed for his suggestions.

The dogwoods were still in bloom and the buds on the laurel and rhododendron were opening, ready to burst into flowers. The sunshine, threading its way through the trees, dappled the floor of the forest with patches of light.

Justin was happy. *Yes,* he thought, *that's the right word. I am beyond content.* Happiness must be contentment plus joy. All the separate components of his life were working together smoothly, like the gears meshing again on the repaired loader. He was doing the work he enjoyed in the forest he loved, with the woman he loved helping him. His pride was satisfied because of the accomplishments on the job and because he was making money for his family's future. He and Laurel had gone to the bank last week after they had received their first monthly percentage pay and had opened a savings account toward the purchase of a home.

This morning he had watched and listened, on his way through the logging area, to the sounds of sawing and chopping, to the yell of "Timber!" and falling trees, to the calling out to the horses and each other, to banter and laughter. The men, intent on their individual tasks, were always aware of what everyone around them was doing and where the dangers were.

He was the boss, as Jed called him; not the water jack, nor the lobby hog – the errand boy for camp – nor any of the others. But he had done them all; had worked his way up. He had been destined to someday be where he was today: The man in charge.

He had been fourteen when he'd left home to live in his first logging camp. His father had been surprisingly agreeable about it. Justin wondered if his father guessed how much he despised his stepmother. No words had ever passed between them on the subject.

He found a home, rough as it was, and grew up quickly in the primitive, exacting, but not unkind atmosphere of the logging camp. The crew liked him. He was never sure just why. As he progressed in learning one job after another, starting with lobby hog and water jack, one logger after another took pride in trying to make him the best lead chopper or cutter or knot bumper or swamper or loader. He was a willing pupil, ready to be told and shown. He took their advice and their teasing. He learned how to argue after awhile with reason instead of temper. He learned gradually how to stand his ground, with confidence instead of cockiness, when he knew he was right. He learned to fight – even how to box. He learned the power of humor. He learned the beginnings of how to be a man among men.

It may have been the determination to learn to box that initially earned him the crew's liking. He liked to read and was often asked to read aloud the occasional newspaper that was brought into camp. He read aloud several accounts about Jack Dempsey, the boy boxing wonder from Colorado known as Kid Blackie. Detailed descriptions of his boxing style fired the loggers' imagination. Dempsey, the paper read, bobbed up and down, moved from side to side; crouching, delivering blows at a blinding speed. Always on the offensive, his speed and constant movement made up his defense.

Mr. Winston, supervisor of the logging camp, came in one day with two pairs of boxing gloves. The crew went crazy. Who would be Kid Blackie in this crowd?

They asked Justin to read—over and over—the description of Dempsey's boxing style and each tried to emulate it. After several days of watching the others, Justin stepped forward and said, "I want to try it."

"Son," said Mr. Winston, "you could get hurt. All these men are considerably bigger than you."

"I still want to try," Justin said.

The first two bouts were disastrous. He found himself on the floor most of the time, nose bleeding, hurting from the punches. In the third bout, he started getting his boxing legs and staying upright, but still took a lot of punishment. His progress was slow but he gradually learned to use his small size to his advantage. He learned to bob and weave around the larger, clumsier men and actually land some punches.

The hardened crew watched his progress with satisfaction. One day in the midst of a bout, he heard them yelling, "Come on, Kid, come on." He took it to mean Kid Blackie and flew into his opponent raining blows on the side of his head, stunning him. He had found his own boxing style. The crew loved it. He wasn't the best boxer in camp, but being the youngest and smallest, he had become a worthy opponent. He would use those skills the rest of his life.

Most of the loggers could not read or write. He sometimes did their figuring for them on paper, and even wrote letters for them. He was thankful for all the years he had stayed in school in spite of his stepmother nagging for him to "quit that foolishness" and pull his own weight in the family. He knew he already pulled his weight, getting up early, working late and on Saturdays.

His two sisters had gone to school for five years and his two brothers had gone about three or four years. He was the only one who went the full six years, all that was offered in the remote mountain community of Tennessee where he lived.

The schoolmaster, a stern but fair man, was challenged by Justin's quick, analytical mind. He introduced him to algebra and geometry. He also urged him to find a boarding school and to further his education. He had broken his own rule and had loaned Justin his personal books. Among them were Homer's *Illiad* and *Odyssey*, Bunyan's *Pilgrim's Progress*, Hugo's *Les Miserables*, and Stowe's *Uncle Tom's Cabin*. It was, however, in reading the history of America, including The Mayflower Compact, The Declaration of Independence, The Constitution, The Bill of Rights, and Lincoln's Gettysburg Address that Justin's imagination was captured and his spirit soared with pride. A love of his country was kindled that burned bright at the center of his being. After reading the history of the Civil War, he knew he would have fought to save the Union. Lincoln, the first president elected by the Republican Party, was a hero to one more young boy who read by lamplight or firelight late into the night. Justin became a Republican long before he was old enough to vote.

Mr. Winston, boss of the logging crew, had come to depend on Justin's quick way with figures to help with his accounts. He taught Justin how to estimate the board feet of timber in a single tree or in a given tract of trees. After taking him along the first time, he never did another stand without him. After a few months, Justin did the estimating and Mr. Winston checked his figures. He had a knack for it.

Mr. Winston was the one who told Justin, rather unhappily, about the boarding school near Asheville, North Carolina where he needed to go to finish his education. After three years in the camp, which had given him an education not to be found in books, Justin left to seek to further his learning.

About a week before he planned to leave, Justin asked Mr. Winston if he could buy Sterling, the horse he had named, ridden, worked, and taken care of for two years. He and the crew called him "Stir" most of the time. Mr. Winston refused, saying Sterling was too well trained as a logging horse to give up. Justin fought hard to hide his disappointment.

The night before he planned to ride out on the logging train, the crew of forty men became quiet as they finished supper. The cooks stopped work and leaned against the wall.

Mr. Winston stood at the head of the table and said, "Justin, come here, son."

As Justin walked up, the boss reached down, brought out a saddle and bridle and laid them on the table.

"You've helped us all in one way or another while you've been here. We don't want you to forget us when you get all that learnin'. This here's to help you remember us."

Justin rubbed the saddle and lifted it up and looked it over. It was beautiful. He swallowed hard and blinked his eyes, struggling for control.

"I thank you and I can't forget you—ever! You've been my family and taught me all your tricks about logging. I'll be back to visit as soon as I can." He grinned. "I'll have to get me a horse somewhere to put this saddle on."

A voice behind him asked, "Would this one do?"

Someone had led Sterling up to the open door of the mess hall. He stood there looking solemnly at Justin and flicking his mane.

Justin looked back and forth from Mr. Winston to Sterling, puzzled. The boss said, "He's yours, son. You're the only lumberjack that's ever left here to – to further his education. We couldn't let you walk, could we? Everybody in this room had part in it."

Justin looked around the table at their roughened, weather-hewn faces. He reached deep inside himself for his response.

"I came here as a kid, wet behind the ears. You took me in and put up with my ignorance and taught me how to be a good logger. But you taught me more than that. I've started learning how to be a man from you! That's your best gift to me forever."

Then his exuberance broke free. He laughed. "And now you're giving me Sterling and my own saddle. My own! I never owned nothin' but my britches before! I'm rich! Thank you! Thank you!"

Everybody started laughing. This was more like Justin. They had been worried there for a minute that he was going to make them wipe a tear.

He went to the door and rubbed the horse's forehead with the tips of his fingers. "I'll take good care of him," he said quietly.

"We know," one of the men said. "You done been doin' that for two years."

He rode out the next morning before the crew left for the woods. He knew they wanted to see him off. He stopped once and turned Sterling full around to face them. He touched his forehead with the tips of fingers and slowly drew an arc through the air. A salute of respect and gratitude.

The crew, as one, returned his message solemnly. Mr. Winston said simply, "We'll miss him. Every man jack among us would like to claim him as a son."

As he rode out of sight through the trees the crew turned to face another day of their circumscribed world. Justin's gift to them was a glimpse into another world where dreams were permitted…where boundaries were extended…where courage and determination had been repeatedly defined by a young boy who had pitted himself against difficult tasks and had refused to give up until he had won. They knew he would win the next one…and they would have been a part of it. They walked tall into the woods. Maybe they weren't just plodders or drudges after all. Maybe they were part of a bigger scheme.

For all his manly leavetaking, Justin had a lump in his throat and a weight in his chest. He had talked big, but he was scared. He fought the urge to turn Sterling around and go back—to the familiar—to the place where he was accepted. But he knew he had to go on. He knew instinctively that he had to do it for that rough crew of men as well as for himself. He couldn't dash their hope and pride that somehow rode with him.

He leaned forward and rubbed Sterling's neck. Then the full realization swept over him. Sterling was his horse! He stopped, slipped off and pulled Sterling's head down to look him in the eyes. "It's just you and me now, Boy. We'll have to take care of each other." He gave the horse an exuberant hug. Enjoying the heady feeling of ownership, he made his way around Sterling, looking him over and checking his feet like a veteran horseman. Then he fingered his saddle. It was far better than anything he could have bought. This horse, saddle and bridle must have cost each man two days' wages. He knew how hard that money was to come by and how much they needed it for other things.

He felt of the small buckskin pouch hanging under his left arm against his skin. All the money he had saved was there. He had sent money home regularly until his father had told him on one of his rare visits home to save his money and to go on to school somewhere. He had also helped through the years in camp, many of the crew who had family sickness or death and had to have extra money. He would be careful with the money he had left and spread it out over a period of time.

As the sun warmed his back and Sterling's stride lengthened the distance between him and camp, he tried to think about where he was going instead of where he was leaving. It was, however, the unknown. He wasn't even sure he could get in the school. Then what?

With the sun directly overhead, he stopped by a stream. After he watered the horse he opened the lunch the cooks had fixed for him. A small covered lard bucket was almost filled with fried chicken and biscuits and corn on the cob. A tomato and apple sat on top. In a separate waxed package were six fried apple pies. Six! He had never had all the fried apple pies he wanted at once.

"Stir, Old Boy, you'll have to watch me. I may get foundered on all these pies."

He actually ate about half the contents of the pail and two pies. He would have plenty for supper. He fed the apple to Stir.

Then he completed his ritual. He cut a branchlet off a dogwood tree, splayed the ends, and brushed his teeth, dipping water from the stream. He had taken considerable teasing about his habits of cleanliness in camp, but he had kept them up.

He spread his bedroll that night beside a log that was softened by age using his saddle as a pillow. Sterling stood a few feet away from his head, hitched to a tree. The next morning, after boiling some coffee and finishing the last of the chicken and apple pies, he turned his face toward Asheville and the future.

Tattoo brought Justin to the crest of the ridge and stopped. Justin had become so bemused by his memories he sat still a moment, not quite wanting to let go of that young man and the first horse he had loved. The present, however, has a way of putting the past in its place. Soon he was the expert timber man again, eyeing his domain with total concentration. After he studied the possibilities and wrote some figures in his pocket notebook, he directed Tattoo along the ridge line until he knew he had an ample tract to cut. He swung off Tattoo and notched a distinctive birch tree for his corner boundary. He then fastened the bridle tightly to the saddle horn, patted Tattoo, and said, "Find the best way down, Tattoo."

He had learned some time ago to trust Tattoo's judgment in the woods. As Tattoo picked and angled his way down the steep, dense slope, Justin followed obediently on foot. After he mounted Tattoo and started back to camp, Justin picked up his thread of memory again ...

His adjustment from logging camp life to boarding school life went smoother than he had expected. Perhaps any life would seem easy after logging camp. He did have a few bouts of homesickness for the men. He had two basic fears the day he rode into the small mountain town of Mars Hill, looking for the school. He was afraid he couldn't pay his way and he wouldn't be smart enough to pass the required school work.

The tuition was one dollar a month for lower classes and four dollars per month for college classes. Room and board was six dollars a month and he could get his laundry done for fifty cents a month. He had to get a job.

He kept his eyes and ears open the first few days seeking an opportunity to work to pay his way. By the end of the first week he had a plan. When he found out the president was in charge of the school finances, he went straight to him. He walked into Dr. Alastair's office, over to his desk, extended his hand and said, 'Hello, Dr. Alastair. I'm Justin Worth."

Dr. Alastair rose and shook Justin's hand. "You're new here, aren't you?"

"Yes, sir. I've been here one week. Came from East Tennessee near Newport."

"Are you settled in all right?"

"Yes, sir. I came to see you because I have a plan for working my way that I need to ask you about."

Dr. Alastair, somewhat wary, said, "Go ahead."

Justin took a deep breath and made his proposal. "I will provide all the stove wood needed for cooking, including cutting down the trees, trimming the limbs and snaking them out. Then I will cut the logs up and chop and stack the wood under the shed by the kitchen. I will need a crosscut saw, three axes, a chain and J grab for pulling out the logs – and two part-time helpers."

Dr. Alastair's eyes sparked with interest. "Do you know how to do all this without killing yourself? And how do you plan to snake the logs out?"

"I've lived and worked in a logging camp for three years – since I was fourteen. I left there and came straight here to try to finish my education. I brought my horse, Sterling, with me, sir. One of the farmers near here is letting me leave him there a few days in return for some work I'll do for him."

Dr. Alastair asked, "If we agree on this, what do you need in return for your work?"

"My room, board, tuition and laundry – and a stall and food for my horse. There's an empty stall in the barn on the edge of the campus."

Dr. Alastair rubbed his chin. One of his chronic mundane problems was keeping an adequate supply of stove wood. He knew how much it took to keep those cook stoves going for three meals a day. But he had the feeling this boy could handle it. He held out his hand. "I agree to the deal. Let's try it for two weeks and see how it goes."

"Thank you, sir. And you'll need to show me where to cut the trees."

"We can do that tomorrow just after classes. Do you want to pick out your helpers?"

"My roommate said he needs some work. Maybe you know someone else."

"Send your roommate to see me in the morning."

"Yes, sir!" Justin turned to go.

Dr. Alastair spoke softly, "Would you like to bring your horse over this evening? I'll see that some food is made available for him."

"Yes, sir!" Justin repeated happily and was out the door and on his way to get Sterling.

The cooks were soon spoiled by Justin's constant supply of wood cut just the right size – and even pine kindling! They spoiled him in return with leftovers and fried apple pies.

The course of study was a challenge. When the results of his entrance exams were in, he was told, to his surprise, to sign up for the college classes. He had evidently learned more than he realized from reading his teacher's books and from life in the logging camp. He found he had a bent for algebra, geometry, and trigonometry. He had already used some of the formulas and basics in real life when he figured the board feet in a log by knowing the diameter and length. Greek was not his favorite. Latin interested him because of its influence on subsequent languages. It was in his senior year that he found himself in his academic element: political science, philosophy, orations, essays, debates. He had a way with words and a passion in his arguments – spoken and written – that earned his professors' recommendation that he go on to law school.

Mrs. Alistair, the president's wife, became the model he had never found before for his own wife. She was a primal force at the college, overseeing everything from cooking to canning to laundry, to seeing that the dorms were kept clean. She taught them manners by example and opportunity. She was not beautiful, but attractive, with a grace and kindness that leavened the students' lives.

His memory pulled up another picture that made him smile. The first Halloween at Mars Hill, he and his roommate took two sheets to the graveyard to scare some couples returning from a party. A girl he liked had gone with a boy he didn't like. When the two of them walked back past the cemetery, Justin rose slowly from behind a large tombstone, fluttering his sheet and moaning. The boy ran, leaving the girl to face the ghost alone.

Justin quickly wadded up his sheet, handed it to his roommate behind another tombstone and ran to be hero to the abandoned girl. She never suspected, and the result was gratifying. She quickly switched her affections to Justin.

Since Mars Hill was a Christian school, Justin was immersed in Christian teachings and ethics. He studied the Bible, treating it as history and literature instead of the basis for a set of beliefs. He admired Dr. and Mrs. Alistair and knew they would always serve as examples to him in their morals, especially in their kindness to others. But he never attributed their lifestyle to the Christian ethic. He believed they were simply good, kind, educated people who spent their lives helping others.

So Justin, in the very midst of the sanctuary, managed to steer clear of God.

As he rode Tattoo into camp that afternoon in time to see the crew off for the weekend, Justin thought his eyes were deceiving him. He had left the weekly payroll with Jed, instructing him to pay the men if Justin was delayed.

A group of Indians, in feather head-dress, stood in the center of the clearing, talking to Laurel. The men, women, and children from camp stood around in a semi-circle. Nora was holding Adam, and Hannah had Sarah's hand. Justin slipped off Tattoo and led him toward the group.

"Here's my husband now!" Laurel said, her relief apparent. "Justin, this is Chief Lion Heart from the Cherokee Indian Reservation. Chief, meet my husband, Justin Worth."

The two men measured each other and each knew the other was a man of authority.

Justin inclined his head. "It's a great honor to meet you and your people, Chief. Welcome to our home." He nodded to the three men and three women.

"Chief, could you start over, please, and tell my husband why you are here?"

Chief Lion Heart was not a large man, matching Justin's height of five feet, eight inches. His dark hair was gathered into two long braids which hung down across his chest. He had an angular face and dark brown eyes. His aura of power came partly from his dignity and partly from his voice. Its resonance and cadence included and captured each person as he began.

"One week ago the story reached us of a young red-haired woman who defied Laughing Falls and was given her baby's life as a trophy for her courage. The Great Spirit prompted me to seek her out and honor her and the baby with the Victory Dance. With your permission and hers, of course."

Justin looked at Laurel. "Do you agree to this?"

"Yes. I would be honored, and I would like it for Adam's sake, too."

Justin smiled at her.

"Please allow me a moment, Chief." His eyes swept the crew and he turned to Jed. "What about the men catching the train? Did you pay them?"

"Yes. I paid them, but they sent word for the train to wait." He grinned. "They didn't want to…to miss anything."

Justin understood. They had stayed to protect the camp. They stood now, most of them, with folded arms, squared shoulders and guarded expressions. Justin was grateful for their loyalty but he knew they needed to relax. The atmosphere was strained.

"Chief, could you tell us the meaning of the Victory Dance before you start?"

"Yes. It began as a celebration of victory in battle. Each brave would hold a wand of eagle feathers in one hand and evidence of victory in the other as he told and acted out his exploits. We have enlarged it to celebrate other types of victories in our lives, such as an unusual accomplishment or an escape from death. The wands of eagle feathers are symbols of courage and victory. Your wife and son battled the river and were victorious in their escape from death."

He motioned for the Indian men and women to get in position. "We will start the ceremony now." The three men made an outer circle with the three women making a smaller circle, one step inside and at alternating positions so they could move in opposite circular directions. Two men had rattles and feather wands like the three women. The third man was the drummer. "This ceremony can only be performed in our native language, but I will translate its meaning for you after we finish."

The drummer set a low, slow pace and the dancers moved to the rhythm, their wands of eagle feathers speaking eloquently as they wove a story through the air in keeping with the chanting of the chief. After several minutes, Chief Lion Heart drew Laurel, with Adam in her arms, inside the moving circle. All was done with grace and rhythm. With exaggerated movements, he removed a leather water pouch from his shoulder and handed it to Laurel, telling her what to do. As she held it high and poured a stream of water on the ground, the dancers suddenly became still and bowed their heads. The eagle feather wands, however, were lifted high and tilted forward, forming a canopy over the chief and Laurel and Adam. The chief then put the water pouch in Adam's hand and helped him pour until the pouch was empty. Everyone, including Adam, seemed mesmerized. To Laurel's surprise and relief, Adam had shown no fear, but his big brown eyes missed nothing.

After the silence Chief Lion Heart began to speak. "The Wands of Eagle Feathers have spoken. They have told the story of a young woman whose courage, strength of heart, and love for her son triumphed over Laughing Falls." His voice took on a lyrical quality, building a bridge of understanding and communication, one sentence after the other. "The Great Spirit was pleased with her and guided her son's little boat into her arms. He instructed the tree to reach down for her. He guided the people there to lift her and her baby to safety. He smiled on the little brown-eyed warrior and gave him back his life."

He turned to Laurel and Adam. "The water you poured on the ground came from Laughing Falls. I dipped it out of the river on my way here. Because you defeated Laughing Falls, you will both take the name. I name you, Laurel, to be Laughing Strong Heart; and you, Adam, Laughing Brave Heart. You both are now accepted as one with my people." Seven hands reached out and touched her head and shoulders, then moved on to Adam. Laurel felt tears prick her eyes. She wished Papa was present. The chief's dignity reminded her of him.

Justin saw Laurel's emotions and realized the ceremony was over. He stepped forward and he and the chief looked at each other a moment with mutual respect. He then took Adam and put his other arm around Laurel.

"It was a beautiful ceremony, Chief," including the entire party in his glance. "Thank you for this honor to our family."

He turned to the crew, who was reluctant to leave. "Thank you for staying. It meant more to us, having you here to share it. And, now, I know you need to go. Have a good weekend with your families." They headed toward the waiting train, talking quietly.

Justin turned back to the group and said, "We will be honored if you will have supper with us."

The chief nodded. "Thank you." They took off their headdresses and carefully wrapped them and the feather wands together in buckskin and laid them near their horses.

The chief asked to see their logging site and was pleased to see their conservation efforts in protecting the under-story trees and bushes. Jed told them the crew would plant seedlings when they finished each tract to prevent erosion and provide trees for the next generation.

Meanwhile, Laurel, Hannah and Bess led the women to the mess hall to visit while they cooked supper. Wise Owl was the oldest and had obvious respect from Wild Turkey, who was some years younger, and Red Bird, who was still a maiden. Their black hair was straight and their dark eyes, which had been inscrutable during the dance, were now alive with enjoyment and warmth. Laurel felt especially drawn to Wise Owl.

"I wish you could be here long enough to teach us about plants that can be used as medicine."

"I can tell you some now."

Laurel said, "Wait. I want to write it down." She ran to her shack and came back with a notebook and pencil.

"Blackwort or comfrey is important because it heals and knits the edges of wounds," Wise Owl said. She looked at Alice. "It also helps heal when applied after childbirth." She described it, told where to look for it and how to use it.

The next hour went fast as they discussed using catnip for fever, horsemint for burns and sumac for dysentery. Alum-root tea mixed with honey was good to cure thrush, or "thrash", in children. Wise Owl told where the plants would likely be found and how to prepare and use them. Laurel would have become hopelessly confused about where to look for the plants, but Hannah understood and explained in a way that Laurel could write it down. They would refer to it later.

Wise Owl went on to tell how to use puffball for nosebleed, dandelion for women problems and tansy for sore throat and ears.

"You may want to know how we treat broken bones. You may need it with the dangerous work the men do," Wise Owl said, as they were putting the finishing touches on supper.

"Yes, please," Laurel answered, grabbing her pencil and paper again.

"We use birch bark. Skin the bark off a small sapling, splitting it down one side only. We soak it and cut it to fit the arm or leg. After setting the arm or leg, we apply grease, then wrap the bark around it and tie it on. It hardens, keeping the leg straight."

"That sounds like it works better than a splint. And, now, I hear the men coming. We can dish up the food."

The men were obviously engrossed in their own conversation during supper, so the women carried on their intense gathering of information. Hannah told Wise Owl about the wild flowers she had found nearby: Jack-in-the-Pulpit, Dutchman's Breeches, and Violets. "Do you know of others that are likely to grow in this environment?"

"You should find Lady's Slippers or Pink Moccasin Flowers. A rare find is an Indian Pipe. It's found in decaying leaves under the trees. It's grayish-white."

Wise Owl finished by saying, "Gather some of the medicinal plants and have them ready. They will serve you well, as they have our people."

After supper Laurel asked Justin if she might talk to the chief alone. Justin understood instinctively that she was thinking of Papa. He and Hannah kept the children. As she and the chief walked into the clearing in front of the shacks, Laurel said, "I'm honored to be accepted among your people, but there's an even greater tie. My paternal grandfather was Cherokee."

They both stopped. He looked at her with a smile in his eyes. "I guessed. I knew you were one of us when our Great Spirit spoke to me to come to you. I didn't know if you would tell me that you had Cherokee blood or not."

"My grandfather, Forest Kingsley, was full Cherokee. Have you heard of him?"

"Oh, yes! We all know about Forest Kingsley! And now I understand more why you are truly Laughing Strong Heart. Your grandfather was a brave and wise man. He chose the ways of the white people but, by his life, he brought great respect and better understanding for our people."

"I never knew him," Laurel said, "but I have an idea of what he was like because of Papa. My father is Professor Hunter Kingsley. You remind me of him. I hope you can meet him someday. He lives in Knoxville where he still teaches school."

"I'm sure that's a great compliment that I am like him. Perhaps soon I shall visit him and bring him word of how his daughter is thriving in her natural habitat."

She looked at him sharply. "What do you mean?"

He stopped and looked at her solemnly. "You are hardy…and beautiful…like the Mountain Laurel for which you are named. You are having a hard time coming to terms with your circumstances right now, but you will."

He saw her resistance to his words in her eyes, but he continued. "Let me tell you about the Mountain Laurel. It is one of the hardiest and most beautiful shrubs, or small trees, native to this land. It flourishes where weaker shrubs don't have a chance. It thrives in circumstances that discourage and destroy more fragile plants. I have seen Mountain Laurel grow to thirty feet high. And laurel thickets are well known for their toughness.

"Mountain Laurel has even developed its own protection in the harsh winter. When you see laurel or rhododendron leaves rolled up like a cigar, you know the winter is cold enough to kill. But these plants endure and, come spring, the blossoms seem more glorious because of the hardness of the winter."

She had heard him out, but she was angry. "You call this my natural habitat?" She waved her hand back toward camp. "The primitive living conditions, the never-ending hard work. You don't know my background at all."

He was totally unperturbed by her outburst. "I do know you aren't a fragile flower, needing coddling and pampering. You have staying qualities. You make things happen. You think more about giving than receiving. But out of your giving, you receive nurture and fulfillment."

By now they had walked to the edge of the clearing and had stopped. Laurel looked at him searchingly. "That's true. I've never had it put into words before. How do you know these things about me?"

"I know. How I know is not important. This region – this forest – has been the home of your people for thousands of years. You are beginning to feel its call to you. It frightens you, along with your living conditions, because you are resisting it. But someday you will know it's your natural environment."

"I didn't choose it," she said stubbornly. "I was thrust into it!"

"We often don't have the luxury of choosing our circumstances. The test of character is how we respond to our circumstances, the choices we make within our relentless boundaries." He stopped and drew a circle in the sand with the toe of his shoe. "Stop fighting, Laurel. Save your energy. Accept the things you can't change. Settle in. Put your roots down and draw up nourishment. Open yourself to your surroundings and survive, and grow, and flourish."

He was sorting out and putting words to her jumbled thoughts and struggles. He was telling her to go beyond mere grudging acceptance, to choose these circumstances, which would free her creativity to work. He was telling her the same thing that Papa's Serenity Prayer was telling her.

"Do you think I can?" she asked, her voice soft and uncertain.

"I'm absolutely sure," he answered. "Your grandfather loved his way of life with his people, but he chose the white man's ways to promote understanding between us. Do you think he had some adjustments?"

She looked at him for a long, measuring moment. "You came for more than the ceremony, didn't you? You came because I needed help." Her eyes held his.

"Yes." His dark eyes regarded her gently but firmly. No explanations this time. "But the ceremony was important, too. Surviving that river and bringing Adam out safely tells me that you will survive and flourish in difficult – even dangerous – times, and others will survive because of you."

She heard the prophecy in his voice but she had one more protest. "But I'm not a heroine. I jumped into that river to save my baby, but the rest was done for me. I can't take the credit. I was only an instrument."

He looked as if she had presented him with a gift. "Understanding that advances you considerably toward your destiny, Laughing Strong Heart. When you commit yourself totally—jump in—to life, to your goals, then the Great Spirit marshals His forces to do the part you can't do, to insure your success. We are always only instruments."

His smile had a trace of mischief as he continued, "'For it is God who worketh in you, both to will and to do of His good pleasure.' Saint Paul from your Bible tells us that."

Laurel's face lit up. "So your Great Spirit is the God of the Bible?"

"Mine, yes. I chose the Christian God when I was young. I don't consider myself wise enough to speak for all Indians and their Great Spirit. I do believe that most of us try to box God in and limit Him to our understanding. He transcends our efforts to know Him completely, but He does allow us to know Him well enough to live our lives accordingly. And for the true seekers, He reveals much more of Himself."

Laurel's last line of resistance collapsed. She knew that this wise man had been sent to her. God had responded to her need in a dramatic way. She was not alone.

She held out her hand. "Thank you, Chief Lion Heart, and your name fits. You are like the regal mountain lions that roam these lands. And you have given me the strength to go on!"

"No," he protested, as he took her hand. "It is God who does that!"

Laurel asked, "Will you come again? You are part of my destiny, you know!"

He laughed. "Yes. I hope I can. And I will go to visit your father."

They walked in companionable silence on their way back to camp. Their business was concluded. When they arrived back to camp, Justin asked, "Could you and your party spend the night? We'll send you on your way after a good breakfast."

"Thank you for the invitation, but we must leave soon. We must travel awhile tonight in order to reach tomorrow's destination."

His party saddled the horses and soon they were ready to go. After a brief farewell, the camp families watched them ride out of sight. Chief Lion Heart stopped once, turned his horse around and raised his hand as in a final blessing.

152

Justin saw Laurel's eyes fill with tears as she raised her hand in the same manner. He put his arm around her shoulders and held tightly. As the others moved back toward camp ahead of them, she said quietly, "The Great Spirit sent him to help me, Justin, and he did."

Justin said, "I know." He was wise enough not to ask any questions.

Spring evolved into summer, the tender young green unfolding into the lush green which the mountains chose for their summer wardrobe. June found the camp in a comfortable routine that pleased everybody. They figured they'd had enough excitement for awhile. The long days and good weather allowed a little leisure, for the men more than the women. Usually after supper the quietness was punctured by the clank of horseshoes hitting the metal stakes, accompanied by yells and laughter.

The men drew off and cleaned up an area for a baseball field in the center of the clearing. Everybody seemed to enjoy the games. One evening as Laurel watched them play in the heat, she went to the kitchen and made a small tin tub of lemonade, using cold water right out of the spring. When Justin and Abe carried it out to the field, the men gathered around and drank it like they were dying of thirst.

"Better'n moonshine," Dirk said, smacking his lips.

"And better for you, too," said Laurel, laughing.

So the tradition of "Laurel's Moonshine" was born. The weekly supply list grew to include several dozen lemons and an extra bag of sugar.

Even as Justin played ball and enjoyed the fun, his mind was full of the next phase of the job: moving to the steep slope. It would require more time and work for everybody, including the women. He might as well get on with it.

After the game was over, he asked the men to meet in the lobby of the bunkhouse. He, Jed, and Bulldog had discussed the move and the changes it would require. He felt they were ready to talk to the crew.

As soon as everybody was seated, Justin began, "Three months ago we were an untried group taking on difficult and dangerous challenges. Most of you are away from your families. The work is hard with long hours. The evenings can be boring. These conditions often lead to problems."

He paused and propped his foot on the bench in front of him as he continued. "In three months we've become a team – a precision team. You've switched jobs and learned the things you needed to know. We've met our goal of finishing this tract on time with more board feet than I estimated.

"You've taken on the other difficulties of living in a logging camp with the same success you've shown on the job. As Laurel says, 'You've helped make a community here.' I'm mighty proud to be working with you. And, now, I'll stop my speech making and ask Jed to tell us the practicals about moving the job."

For the next hour they discussed the demands and dangers of logging a steep slope. They would have a half-hour walk to get there, which meant a longer day. They would have to take their lunch and eat on the job. It would also take longer to get the logs to the boxcars so their production would be cut accordingly.

The steep-slope schedule also meant several changes for the women. They would need to be in the kitchen at four o'clock in the morning to have breakfast by six and finish packing the men's lunches, most of which would have been prepared the day before. Lunch would usually be beef stew or thick vegetable soup with coleslaw and cornbread or sometimes pinto beans with potatoes and cornbread. Dessert always finished off their meal, with plenty of coffee.

The difference was that the men had to transport the food and heat it on the job. Zeke and Odell rigged up a couple of contraptions to set across the horses' backs to hold the containers of food and utensils. Justin and Laurel made a quick trip to town to buy covered metal containers that could be placed on an open fire. As they walked through the company store, Justin teased, "I know you want to pick out the tin plates and cups."

Laurel nodded. "I will. I think they're necessary for the woods but not for the table."

"You've got these loggers so spoiled they'll never adjust to another camp."

"They've spoiled me, too. They're all so good-hearted. I'd like some day to meet their wives and children. They must have it hard."

"I'm sure they do. But, at least they have money coming in regularly. Lots of people don't."

The first few days on the steep slope took some adjustments, but the crew responded to the demands. The first day Justin built a fire, heated lunch and made coffee. He almost scorched the stew, which brought forth unfavorable comparisons between his and Laurel's cooking. The men enjoyed a short rest time after eating rather than having to walk back to work.

Abe leaned back against a tree and rubbed his full stomach. "A man could get fat and lazy layin' around like this." Everybody laughed. Abe was never still nor quiet for more than a minute.

"Okay," Justin said. "Who thinks he can warm up lunch tomorrow without burning it? We'll take turns. Maybe two would be better and quicker."

Bulldog said, "Me and Tom'll try it."

"Good," said Justin. "Let's have volunteers for a few days. Then if somebody decides that's his calling, we'll talk about it."

After Zeke and Odell had their turn, everybody realized they were good cooks. They took on the job for the duration.

After two near accidents in two weeks, Justin and Jed realized they had to build a chute – a dry flume – down the mountainside to get the logs safely to the loading dock. They also had to pick up production, which had fallen drastically.

Snaking out the logs, which was usually a routine job on level ground, became a dangerous, even deadly, task on a steep slope – especially for the teamster and the horses. One morning after a week of slow going, Rob, the head teamster, chained six big logs together, end to end. He hitched them to the horse with a "J-grab", a hook that could quickly be released if the logs started to run too fast. A few minutes after the horse started pulling them downhill, the logs picked up a momentum of their own. Rob quickly pulled the horse to the side, unhooked the J-grab and watched the train of logs rush down the mountainside. This technique was standard. After the logs settled, the teamster would go hitch up the horse and start pulling again.

This morning, however, the logs jumped the trail and headed straight toward the swampers. The two men scrambled to safety behind a huge hemlock while the logs bounced and kept going. They came to rest against some sturdy trees at the foot of the slope.

The next week, Clay, the younger teamster, hooked up four large logs and headed down the mountain. This time when he turned the logs loose, they hit a tree, which changed their direction and sent them flying over a cliff into an ivy slick where they could not be retrieved. Several hundred board feet of timber was lost. Clay was ashamed of himself. This wasn't supposed to happen to a good teamster.

Jed said, "At least they didn't take you and the horses with them." Privately, he was worried about safety and production.

Building the chute took almost a week. It was a V-shaped trough going down the mountainside, built of small logs and boards. The teamster on the mountain pulled the logs to the edge of the chute and turned them loose. Then the loaders at the bottom of the chute had the biggest worry. They had to watch out for flying logs. Sometimes a log would hit a bump in the chute and fly thirty or forty feet from the bottom of the chute.

The crew had been on edge. Now they could settle down to their steady, normal teamwork. Production was soon climbing and danger was reduced to its customary level.

The women all worked together the first week to prepare the men's lunch for the next day and put it in the spring boxes. They decided to keep their original ten hour and six hour schedule. They had become accustomed to the demands of the hard week and enjoyed the in-between weeks of six hours a day when they could get other things done.

Laurel's sewing machine, which she moved to the mess hall, became the focal point of social life for the women. One day about a week after the men started taking their lunch, Laurel asked Alice to meet her in the mess hall about ten o'clock. Hannah and Bess were cooking and Nora came to watch the children.

They were all there when Laurel handed Alice a package wrapped with brown paper and string. Alice pulled the string off and unfolded the paper. Beautiful, sky blue cotton material with tiny white flowers lay in her hands.

She looked at Laurel. "This is for me?"

"Yes. It's a new dress. Hold it up to your face. That color is good with your eyes and hair."

"It's beautiful!" She hugged it to her. "But, I can't sew!"

"Would you like to learn?"

"Oh, yes, ma'am!"

"Then we'll make this dress together and maybe you can make the next one. It's time you got into maternity clothes."

"Thank goodness," Bess drawled. "I've been waitin' for them seams to start bustin' all week."

Alice blushed and moved her hands over her rounded stomach. "I felt the baby move yesterday. I guess it's time. I'm gettin' big."

Laurel sketched off a loose fitting dress with a large pleat in front. She asked Alice if she liked it. She then measured and cut a pattern out of newspaper. Hannah helped her make sure it was right. They spread out the material on one of the long tables, pinned the pattern to it and started cutting. Bess and Alice followed every move as if Hannah and Laurel were performing magic tricks. After they finished and Hannah and Bess moved back to the stove to check the food, Laurel heard Bess ask quietly, "Do you think I could learn how to sew?"

"Sure," Hannah replied. "We'll teach you along with Alice." Laurel waited for Bess's objection to getting help from her, but it never came.

The next two days were exciting as the dress came together under four pairs of hands. Alice and Bess took turns sewing with the supervision of Laurel and Hannah.

When Alice slipped the dress on and turned around, everybody clapped.

"Alice, you look plumb pretty," Nora said softly.

Bess looked her up and down with half-closed eyes. "Yeah! We're gonna knock Tom's eyes out. You got to let me cut your hair a little shorter and show you how to make it wave around your face. I've got some bobby pins. I'll even wash it for you."

Alice put her hand over her mouth and looked nervously at Laurel.

"I think that's a good idea. But, first, climb up here and let's turn up your hem."

That night when the men trouped in for supper, Tom stopped in his tracks. Alice stood in her new blue dress near the stove with a potholder in her hand. Her blond hair was waved and held back loosely with barrettes. Her cheeks were flushed, but she looked steadily at Tom.

He crossed the room and stood in front of her. "Alice, you look so...so pretty! Where'd you get that dress?"

"Laurel and Hannah and Bess helped me make it. I was gettin' too big for my other clothes. I'm glad you like it."

"Your hair looks pretty like that."

"Bess done that. She cut it and waved it."

"I like it, Honey."

He had spoken softly but his words were heard around the room. Everybody was seated and waiting for the food to be served. Tom sat down between Jed and Bulldog. After the usual noisy conversation started again, Jed leaned over to Tom and said quietly, "You done good, son. We won't have no lynchin' tonight."

"What're you talkin' about?"

"Them women. If you hadn't acted right toward Alice…"

Tom chewed, swallowed, and grinned. "Oh! Well, she is pretty, ain't she?"

"Shore is," Bulldog said with a twinkle in his eyes.

Chapter Thirteen

Summer was picture-taking time. Justin was invited to family reunions, church homecomings, and baptisms – more events than he could attend. Anyone who wanted pictures taken left a message at the office of The Wildwood Journal. Sam Parker, in self-defense, put a box on his desk with Justin's name on it. He also left instructions for people to write out their requests with places, dates, and times. He did it for those who couldn't read and write. Justin checked in with Sam every week when he came in for payroll and supplies.

"Laurel," Justin said. It was Saturday morning and they were enjoying a second cup of coffee together. "I want you and the children to go with me tomorrow. I miss being with you on Sundays."

She started to speak but he held up his hand. "Hear me out first. For the past two Sundays, everywhere I've gone the people have asked about you. The people whose children you taught, the children themselves, the women who heard you speak at the temperance rally, the ones from your church in Deerbrook…I'm going to start introducing myself as Laurel Worth's husband."

She laughed. "Justin, are you making all this up just to convince me to go with you?"

"No, ma'am. People are going to think I've tied you to a tree in the woods if you don't start showing your face in town."

"It's hard with the children to be gone all day on Sunday with no rest. Then I start my cooking schedule again on Monday."

"I know you can't go every Sunday, but I want you to go as often as you can."

She sat quietly, toying with her coffee cup, not looking at him. After a moment, he said, "I know your other reason is your little church."

"Yes. I just talked to Rev. Stevens about starting a class for the children. I hope to take all the children in camp with me."

He felt his old resentment stir inside him, but deliberately sat back and waited.

"But I would enjoy going with you and seeing some of my friends. Will you promise to get us home as early as you can?"

He nodded.

"I can wait a little while to start the Sunday school class. The children and I need some time with you."

He stood up, pulled her to him and held her close.

"My real reason is I want you with me. I'm proud of you."

She returned his hug. "I love you, you rascal. Even when I'm aware you're charming me into doing what you want."

"Isn't it what you want, too?"

"Yes, it's what I want for now." She lifted her head and kissed him.

The next day they arrived at Beulah Baptist Church just as the preaching service began. Justin told Laurel to go on in and he would come as soon as he took care of Tattoo and the wagon. He also needed to check his camera and equipment. She sat toward the back so Justin could join her without disturbing the service. She knew he would delay coming in because of his discomfort in church. He was here for business only.

She looked around at the congregation. Several people nodded and smiled. Some of her former students pointed and whispered. She smiled at them and turned her thoughts to the sermon.

After awhile Justin slipped in beside her and took Adam to give her a rest. Sarah immediately claimed her daddy's attention and Laurel relaxed. At the end of the service, the pastor gave instructions about the meal to follow. Then he said, "We're happy to have Mr. and Mrs. Justin Worth with us today. Mr. Worth will be taking pictures of our homecoming and of any family groups who request his services. I think all of you know him."

The congregation looked back, nodded and smiled. The pastor continued, "Many of you know Mrs. Worth from her teaching and speaking."

He paused and looked at Laurel. "Mrs. Worth, I heard you recite a poem once that I would like for our congregation to hear. It's about how brief our life is. Would you do us the honor of sharing it with us today?"

Laurel gave a quick glance at Justin, whose grin said, "I told you so!" She stood, smoothed her skirt where Adam had wrinkled it, and walked to the pulpit. She looked over the congregation and smiled. "The title of the poem is 'Why Should the Spirit of Mortal be Proud!' by William Knox. It was President Lincoln's favorite poem. It sounds sad at first, but the message I get from it is that we live such a short time, at best, that we should make our lives count for something in the time we have."

She was still for a moment and the congregation grew quiet. Then her clear voice reached all around the room. "Oh, why should the spirit of mortal be proud! Like a swift fleeting meteor, a fast flying cloud; A flash of the lightning, a break of the wave; He passes from life to his rest in the grave.... ."

As she continued through the poem, Justin looked around. She had them with her, in the palm of her hand, even though some of the subject matter was difficult to understand. Justin thought, *I guess that's called charisma.*

Laurel enjoyed seeing her students and their parents again. Justin stayed busy as she knew he would, but she had a good time visiting. About the middle of the afternoon she went to the wagon, nursed Adam and put him in his box to take a nap. She was sitting nearby visiting with a friend from Deerbrook Church when Justin walked up. She couldn't quite read his expression. He seemed to be fighting amusement and concern at the same time.

He spoke to her friend, then held his hand down to pull her up.

"Laurel, I think I just got you in trouble." Then he grinned and angled his head. "But it's not all my fault. I can't help it if people think you're the prettiest woman here."

"Justin, what are you talking about?"

He scratched his head as she and her friend looked at him. "Sol, the retarded son of Tom Ogle, kept following me around wanting me to take his picture. To get rid of him, I told him to go find the prettiest woman here and I would take his picture with her. I didn't think he would really do it!" He looked at her humbly, but she could see the laughter banked in his eyes.

"Go on," she said.

"He picked you. He wants his picture made with you."

"Where is he?"

"He's waiting over by the camera."

Sol was a mongoloid, probably in his forties. He had on overalls with a nail stuck in one of the top straps to hold it up. The overalls were too big and he stood with his thumbs hooked in the sides where the bib started. When he smiled, Laurel saw that his two front teeth were missing.

Laurel knew she was dealing with a child in a man's body. That soothed her.

"Sol, I'm pleased to have my picture taken with you. Which side do you want me on?"

He smiled again and nodded his head to the right.

"Okay, let's ask Justin to tell us where to stand." Justin got them posed and snapped their picture.

Laurel turned to Sol. "Justin has to develop the pictures at home. Then he'll bring one to your house in a week or two."

Sol blinked his eyes and held out his hand. She shook it and turned to go. Sol's mother stepped up to her and said, "Thank you for being so kind to him. He understands more than we think. He'll be lookin' for that picture."

Justin gave Sol a piece of candy and squeezed Laurel's arm.

"Thank you, Honey." He was sobered by the respect she had shown Sol.

On the way home Sarah and Adam played while Laurel and Justin talked. After he talked to her some about logging the steep slope, he asked, "How are things going with the cooking?"

"Fine. Everybody's doing her share and getting along well."

"How's Bess doing?"

"She's coming around a little. We're teaching her how to sew. And I hope she'll agree to cut Sarah's hair and maybe Joanie's." She paused and said pointedly, "You know I told Bess I refused to call her Jonah. That's a boy's name. So, I'm calling her Joanie!"

Justin was startled, but asked quietly, "What did Bess say to that?"

"Oh, she didn't like it. But Jonah is Joanie to me!"

Justin didn't have anything else to say, and Laurel continued, "Anyway, to get back to Bess, she did a good job with Alice's hair. She needs to learn to do some things so she'll feel better about herself."

He thought that over a little, knowing how Bess treated Laurel. "You're good with people, you know that? You respect them. Old, young, people with problems like Nora and Bess—and Sol today. Where did you learn that?"

She sat with a puzzled look on her face. "I don't know. From Papa, I guess. I always want people to believe in their own worth, in any set of circumstances."

"You help them to believe in themselves by the way you treat them. You help them gain self-respect, and they love you for it. Alice, for example."

"Alice is a motherless girl. Has been for years. Maybe I can be a mother substitute and make her life a little easier."

The next week Laurel invited Alice to go to town with her and Justin when they went for supplies. While Justin was getting the payroll and checking at *The Wildwood Journal* office about his photography, Laurel and Alice went shopping.

"You need to pick out fabric for another dress. Then we'll look for material for baby clothes," Laurel told her. Alice's eyes were shining as they picked out flannel for baby blankets and soft cotton for gowns and shirts. She bought needles, thread, measuring tape, and scissors like a seamstress.

Every woman got involved with sewing baby clothes. Laurel was touched as she watched Nora's big hands sew a little gown and embroider tiny flowers around the neck. And Bess! Bess couldn't learn fast enough! She went from sewing on the machine to hand sewing to embroidery to buttonholes. After watching her awhile, Laurel said, "Bess, if you keep going like this, you'll be the best seamstress in camp."

Bess became totally still. Then she narrowed her eyes and asked, "Are you makin' fun of me?"

Laurel looked at her with astonishment. The woman wanted to fight over a compliment! Laurel's temper drove her to her feet. Just as she stood, Hannah said, "Bess, Laurel's telling you the truth. You've got the knack. You need to tell Bulldog you want a sewing machine."

Bess stared at Hannah, then at Laurel. "I ain't never been able to do nothin' right," she said, shaking her head. "Bull ain't goin' to believe me."

"He will when we show him what you've been doin'," Hannah said.

"You and Alice almost made her second maternity dress by yourselves and look at these baby clothes!"

Bess was still skeptical but excited. "Okay! I'll tell him tonight. Y'all be ready to show him our sewin'."

Bulldog agreed quickly to buy a sewing machine. He told Jed later, "Them women! A feller better watch out when they all get excited over somethin'."

Jed just grinned in sympathy. Secretly, Bulldog was very pleased over the changes in Bess.

A few days later, the women were all in the mess hall cooking and sewing when they heard a commotion outside. They rushed to the door to see Justin riding bareback, holding Tom on the horse in front of him.

He yelled, "Laurel, Tom's snake-bit! Help me get him inside! Bulldog's gone for the doctor."

Nora ran to the horse. "I can carry him!"

They were a strange sight. Justin's left sleeve was cut off at the shoulder. Tom's right pants leg was split up beyond his knee. A tourniquet – Justin's sleeve – was tied just below his knee. His right shoe was off.

Justin slid off and pulled Tom down slowly. "You can't walk, son."

Nora lifted him like he was a baby and Justin steadied his feet and legs. They laid him on one of the tables. Laurel said, "He has to sit up. His heart needs to be above the bite. Nora and Bess, go get some pillows quick!" They held him in a sitting position as they looked at the bite. They saw two small cross-like cuts that had been bleeding about half-way between the knee and ankle on the outside. His leg was beginning to swell and turn blue. Tom was sweating heavily and breathing hard.

"I cut both the fang marks and sucked the blood out," Justin said. "I hope I got most of the poison."

Laurel checked to make sure the tourniquet was not too tight. She washed his face and gave him a drink of water,

"He needs to stay as still as possible," Justin said.

Nora and Bess came in with the pillows. Laurel stacked some behind him and put a small one under his knees. He leaned back and closed his eyes. A sob, more like a moan, broke through the activity. Alice was sitting at the end of the room, with her hands over her face. Her whole body was shaking. "He's goin' to die! My baby...."

Hannah reached her first. "Alice, hush! You've got to be strong for Tom." She pulled her apron off and wiped Alice's face. Alice hiccupped and stopped crying.

Hannah continued just above a whisper, "Now, pull yourself together and go tell Tom he's goin' to be all right."

Tom looked around slowly, "Where's Alice?"

"She's coming," Laurel said. They all moved away from the table. Alice stood, drew a deep breath and walked over to Tom. She leaned down and kissed his forehead. He opened his eyes.

"Alice, I'm sorry. I should'a been more careful. It was a copperhead in some rocks by the trail."

Alice's voice was strong. "Tom, you're gonna be all right! You're strong as a horse! You've got to be okay for me and this baby!"

She took his open hand and laid it on her stomach for a moment. His eyes widened. "He—he moved! I think he kicked my hand!"

"He's tellin' you they ain't no snake gonna win a fight with his daddy!"

Tom gave a weak smile and closed his eyes again.

Justin and Laurel had stepped outside. Laurel put her hand on his arm. "Justin, are you sure none of the poison got in you? What did you do?"

"I was really careful. As far as I know, I don't have any bad teeth. I kept the blood in the front of my mouth. I know I didn't swallow any."

"Did you wash your mouth out?"

"Yes. I've done this before, Honey. I keep a bottle of moonshine on the job to pour on cuts." His grin was lopsided. "I washed my mouth out with it. I doubt if even snake venom can stand up to that."

"What are Tom's chances?"

"I don't know. It was a big copperhead, about three and a half to four feet long. Bulldog killed it."

She put her hand over her mouth and closed her eyes as Justin continued, "Tom's real strong. He's young and healthy. We'll have to fight to save his leg, if he lives. I guess it mostly depends on Dr. Leighton. If he has some anti-venom we have better than a fifty-fifty chance"

The next hour passed agonizingly slow. Tom's leg kept swelling and turning blue. Angry red and purple streaks appeared. His face was flushed and sweat poured off him. His labored breathing made everybody take deep breaths, trying to breathe for him.

Alice stood by him talking, washing his face and occasionally kissing his forehead. Laurel adjusted the tourniquet as needed.

His eyes became glazed and he seemed to have trouble focusing. He suddenly yelled, "Watch out, Bulldog! That tree ain't fallin' right! Move!"

He thrashed about until Justin calmed him. "Bulldog's okay, Tom. He got out of the way."

He tried to look around. "Alice…Alice, where are you?"

"I'm right here, Tom, holdin' your hand."

He stared at her. "You ain't Alice."

She dropped his hand and ran to Laurel. "What can we do?"

Laurel took her outside and hugged her close until she calmed down. "Alice, I'm proud of you! You're acting like a strong woman, but you have to think about the baby as well as Tom. I'll get Nora to bring you a chair. You need to sit down awhile and eat something. You've had a shock."

A little while later, Bulldog and Dr. Leighton rode into the yard at a full gallop. Dr. Leighton was off his horse before it came to a full stop, with his bag in his hand.

"I've got some anti-venom. Mrs. Worth, help me here," he said as he walked up to Tom. Laurel sponged Tom's right arm with alcohol and Dr. Leighton plunged the needle in.

He looked at Tom's eyes, listened to his heart, examined the bite wound, and checked the tourniquet, while Tom talked nonsense the whole time. When he finished, he jerked his head toward the door. "Mr. Worth, Mrs. Worth, come with me."

Laurel said, "Alice, come with us. You need to hear what the doctor says."

Justin called Bulldog over. He knew how anxious he was.

Dr. Leighton said, "It'll be touch and go for awhile but I believe we've got to him in time. His heart is beating very fast but it's not out of rhythm. That's the best news we can have."

He turned to Alice. "Mrs…. ?"

"Alice Raines," she supplied.

"Mrs. Raines, your husband is fortunate he had these people around who knew what to do and," he stopped and looked at Bulldog, "a man who was determined I was going to get here fast. I don't know when I've ridden a horse so hard."

Bulldog grinned. "You're a good rider, doctor. We sure do thank you for hurrying!"

The doctor looked at Justin. "So, you used the suck and spit method to get the poison out?"

"Yes. I'm still spitting. Every time I think about it."

"It's a little late, but move over here and let me check out your mouth." He shone his light and probed until he was satisfied. "Did you wash your mouth out with anything?"

"Moonshine."

The doctor laughed. "Fight poison with poison. That ought to do it."

The crew was subdued as they walked into camp. Bulldog had ridden over to the worksite earlier to let them know Tom was still alive. One of a logger's worst fears is a snake bite. It could have been any of them.

Hannah and Bess had been preparing dinner. Nobody seemed hungry, but Laurel had the men serve their own plates and go outside to eat. Tom was completely out of his head and Alice needed to be away from him a little while. Laurel coaxed her outside where she finally drank some milk to please Laurel. She knew she couldn't swallow solid food.

About the middle of the afternoon, Tom quit muttering and thrashing about. He slept fitfully. His foot and leg, meanwhile, kept swelling and turning purple. His toes were distended and looked like they would burst.

After Dr. Leighton checked him again, he smiled at Alice. "The medicine's working. His heart rate is slowing down. I think he's going to make it."

Alice's tears streamed down her cheeks. "Thank you, Doctor." She put her hands on her stomach. "We both need him."

His eyes were kind. "I know you do."

As Alice went outside to get her tears under control, he called Justin and Laurel over and said, "Now we have to work to save his leg. Let's lower his body a little at a time over the next couple of hours. Then we need to keep his leg level with his body for good circulation." He looked around. "Can you make a stretcher and get him to bed? Somebody needs to watch him tonight. He'll have to use a jar to urinate. He can't put any pressure on that leg."

Bulldog and Justin carried him to his shack on a stretcher made of two-by-fours and a heavy quilt. Laurel and Justin would stay with him and Alice until midnight. Then Bulldog and Bess would take a shift. Nora would keep the children.

Dr. Leighton left reluctantly after giving Laurel some medication for Tom if his leg hurt unbearably. "I'll be back to check on him in the morning. He's still a very sick man."

"Youth and strength and good health tells," Laurel said, when Tom woke up in his right mind and hungry the next morning.

"And prayer," said Alice.

"Yes. And prayer," repeated Laurel. "I think lots of people were praying last night."

Tom had been restless all night and his leg and foot were grotesque. Laurel knew the pain must be intense but Tom bore it stoically.

Dr. Leighton came riding in early with some medicine. "This is a diuretic," he told Laurel.

Then he turned to Tom. "This is to help the swelling go down in your leg. It will make you urinate often. So keep your jar handy."

Jed and the crew kept the job running. Hannah, Bess and Nora kept the kitchen going and took care of the children. Everybody wanted Justin and Laurel to stay close to Tom and Alice.

It was two more days before Dr. Leighton felt they were going to save Tom's leg. The swelling gradually decreased and Tom had to start moving it to increase the circulation.

The night the crew trouped in and found Tom sitting at the mess hall table, there was a happy hullabaloo. When they quieted down, Tom said, "I'm thankful to be alive and have both legs." He held up a crutch. "As soon as I can get rid of these, I'll be back on the job. But I'm goin' to buy me some knee boots like Justin's before I go in the woods again."

Chapter Fourteen

Justin returned earlier than usual on Friday with the payroll and supplies. He came through the door waving the newspaper. "Laurel, here's the news you've been waiting for! The states ratified the Nineteenth Amendment! It's now lawful for women to vote!"

Laurel stopped peeling potatoes. She jumped up and threw her arms around him. "Oh, I'm so glad!"

"Come take a walk with me," he said gently, as he led her out the door.

As they walked away from the mess hall, she said, "Don't you see, Justin? This is a wonderful victory for women! It's a victory that has taken at least fifty years of struggle against ignorance and bigotry! I wish Susan B. Anthony was alive to see the date – August 26, 1920. I'll mark it on the calendar when we get back."

She stopped and looked at him. "The right to vote is the key to other rights for women! We women have had about the same legal rights as idiots and lunatics!"

"I know you have," he said. "So, right now, take time to enjoy this victory."

"I am enjoying it! I wish we could have a celebration! I can't just go back to peeling potatoes this very minute."

Justin looked at her. "There's a place I've been wanting to take you. Let's go! I'll get the women to finish what you were doing and to take care of Sarah and Adam."

In a little while they were riding double on Tattoo toward Justin's destination, Laurel in the saddle with Justin behind her, his arms around her holding the reins.

"I saw Mrs. Sargent at the bank this morning. She recognized me as your husband and asked if you could come to her house soon to finalize plans for the women's rally now that the amendment has passed."

"Yes, we need to get right on it!" Her voice was charged with excitement. "Tomorrow would be a good day for me. Could I have Tattoo for awhile?"

"Sure. I'm planning to be here."

"I'm glad I've been thinking about my speech even if I wasn't sure I would ever get to give it."

"You've had plenty to do besides preparing a speech."

"I jot down notes as I'm working. It keeps my mind busy while I'm doing routine work."

"Honey," he said, tightening his arms around her, "I'm glad you're…you're just the way you are. That woman…Sargent is a totally inadequate name. I would call her Mrs. General. She needs four stars pinned on that…that formidable front!"

Laurel laughed but twisted sideways and asked, "Justin, were you polite to her?"

"Yes, Ma'am," he said, grinning. "You would'a been proud of me. Besides, her husband is president of the bank that handles the Beck Lumber Company accounts and our savings."

Tattoo was steadily climbing. They had turned off the wagon road and were headed up a gap where it was not so steep and the undergrowth not so dense. On each side rose the oaks and maples and chestnuts – the hardwoods – and the evergreens. Rhododendron and laurel flourished underneath the tall trees. They rode under a canopy that admitted sunlight only in patches. Yet, when she looked up a shimmering haze enwrapped the mountainside. The beauty was beyond telling. Joy struck her. She felt a sense of belonging that brought the sting of tears. Was this the call of the mountains on her soul? No words were spoken during the climb. They both felt transported from their mundane concerns.

Then they arrived at the top. Before them stretched endless mountain ranges, swathed in the mystical blue haze. An occasional wispy cloud tugged at a peak and moved on. Others nestled between the peaks. When Laurel realized she was holding her breath, it escaped with an, "Oh-h-h…."

They dismounted but still stood close together. "Eternity," she whispered. "It's like looking at eternity and steadfastness and endurance."

Justin was quiet. She turned to him. "You don't need words, do you? You just let it fill you up."

He nodded. "It does work its magic on you. I knew you'd love it."

They stood awhile, apart, each with private thoughts, absorbing peace and strength and perspective. Before they left, they held each other in a satisfying embrace. They knew they held happiness in their hands. Elusive, but nonetheless real.

On the way down, Justin walked to lessen the chance of Tattoo losing his footing on the steep terrain. When they reached level ground and Justin was behind her again, she leaned against him and said, "For all their grandeur, these mountains are friendly. I felt…enfolded."

He laughed. "You do have a way with words, Mrs. Worth."

"Today, elusive words like eternity and steadfastness and serenity took on a form I could see and feel. That is very satisfying."

"I know," he said, nodding. "Do you feel better?"

"Yes. That was the best gift you could have given me. Thank you." She pulled his hands with the reins into her lap and nestled hers inside them.

Carried on her wave of excitement over women's right to vote, Laurel made her plans. She needed a new outfit for the rally. She knew that if she knew she looked good, she could forget about her appearance and focus on her speech. That night she rummaged in her trunk and found a piece of Shantung fabric Madeleine had given her in April. It was a slubbed rayon, a deep sea-foam green. She would make a skirt. And she would buy a new blouse. Her two white Sunday blouses were showing their age.

The next morning she rode out of camp to visit the real world again. Or was the logging camp becoming her real world? She thought of Chief Lion Heart's words about her being in her natural habitat. They still prickled. But yesterday she had felt such a belonging! And she was happier in camp than she ever thought she would be.

To her delight she found a Gibson Girl blouse just a shade lighter than her skirt fabric. A soft, restful sea-foam that complimented her hair, eyes, and skin tone. It was just right, fashionable but not overdone. She would wear her round gold watch on a long chain and her wide gold bangle bracelet. After a little more shopping, she rode out to Mrs. Sargent's home.

"My dear girl," Mrs. Sargent exclaimed, surprised and pleased. "Do come in! Your husband gave you my message?"

"Yes. I hope I'm not intruding, coming unannounced."

"No, no, I'm so glad you came. Isn't it wonderful to have the right to vote? Have a seat and I'll have the maid fix us a cup of tea."

Laurel looked around at the Victorian furniture, the fringed rug, the paintings. She felt a yearning to return to this gracious type of living… a homesickness crowded in on her. *Chief Lion Heart*, she thought, *you're wrong this time.*

When Mrs. Sargent bustled in, Laurel said, "I'm enjoying your beautiful room. It's quite different from our logging camp."

"My dear, is it just horrible living there? I've thought about you often, you know, just buried up there in the woods."

"It's hard work and the living conditions are crude. But we're happy. We have good people working for us—with us."

"Well, that helps. And your husband is such a charming man."

Tea was served with scones and strawberry jam. It was refreshing to Laurel's body and spirit. Then the two women got down to business to finalize their plans for the rally.

"We hope to have twice as many women as we had for the temperance rally. Sam will give us good coverage in *The Wildwood Journal*. We'll put posters in places of business where women shop. We'll also ask the churches to announce it."

Laurel was impressed with the plans already underway. "Good. I'm looking forward to it. I'm polishing my speech."

"I'm sure you'll convince them. You're a great motivator."

As Laurel later rode home, she reasoned that she could be a citizen of both her worlds and didn't have to choose which one she really belonged to. But a niggling little voice seemed determined to raise doubts.

True to her word, Laurel practiced her speech on the crew a few days before the rally. They listened with total attention and she sold them. Every one of them went home to tell his wife she needed to go hear Laurel's speech, and to vote in November. They would take them to both events.

The rally was scheduled for two o'clock on Saturday afternoon, the last week in August. Hannah and Alice were going. Nora was going to keep the children and Bess was not about to go. Justin drove Laurel to the Sargent house where she would change clothes and ride to the rally with Mrs. Sargent in her carriage.

"What will you be doing while I'm here?" she asked.

"Oh, I have plenty of things to see about." He walked her to the door and knocked. The door opened and Mrs. Sargent descended upon them. "Laurel…and Mr. Worth! How nice to see you! Can you come in?"

"No, thank you. I'm just the driver for the speaker today." He smiled. "I know you've done a lot of work planning this rally, Mrs. Sargent, and I hope it's a great success. Do you think I might masquerade as a woman and attend?"

Mr. Sargent looked him up and down and coyly replied, "I doubt it."

He laughed and turned to Laurel. "You'll do a good job, Honey. I predict Wildwood County will have a stampede of women voters come November."

He kissed her and walked to the wagon. Mrs Sargent looked after him. "He has such good manners. And you do realize how good-looking he is?"

Laurel laughed. "Yes. I realize all of it."

Mrs. Sargent suddenly reached out and hugged Laurel. "And our big day is here! Come in and let's get ready to go!"

Mr. Sargent, himself, drove them to the church to a side door. Women were gathering from different directions. A group of men, ragged and dirty, called out insults to the women.

"Goodness, Henry," Mrs. Sargent turned to her husband. "I didn't expect this. Can you do something?"

"Hecklers," he said calmly. "Yes, dear, we'll clear them out."

He turned to Laurel. "Harriet tells me you're a good speaker. I wish you well today. You both are to be commended for fighting for this good cause."

Laurel liked him. She extended her hand. "Thank you, Mr. Sargent. It's a pleasure to meet you."

He saw them through the door and drove away quickly to find Justin Worth.

As they walked into the front of the church, Mrs. Sargent exclaimed, "They've come! The church is full! Now, let's convince them to go to the polls in November."

"We will!" declared Laurel. She was sure of it. The preliminaries were soon over and Mrs. Sargent was introducing her.

She walked to the lectern. She paused and smiled as she swept her eyes across the audience, taking in the corners and the rows from front to back, including them all, gathering them to her. Then her clear voice carried throughout the church.

"A woman is one of God's most magnificent creations, and most practical. He created this beautiful earth, all the animals and man. Then His last and ultimate creature—*woman...you*—came forth from His hands. Even God didn't want a world without a woman in it!

"Look at your hands. If they're like mine they're work-worn from peeling potatoes to washing dishes to changing diapers to washing clothes. You name a few things – aloud – that your hands do."

She listened to the hubbub of sound with occasional laughter. Some women were holding their hands up, looking at them.

"Now," she called them back to her, "can you imagine how bleak, how comfortless, how dismal, how hopeless your home and family would be without the touch of your hands – without all the physical things you do for them?

"God made us to 'look well to the ways of our households,' but we're made for much more. In cooperation with God, we are the givers of life. And with that great privilege comes responsibility. We are responsible to nourish those of our household, and not just physically. Mental, emotional, and spiritual nourishment come from women who love, who care for, who have faith in, who encourage and who want a better world for their children.

"And that is why our vote is so important! Along with our hands, we have a brain – a mind – in which we have stored experience and knowledge. This results in common sense, opinions, beliefs, and wisdom.

"Our society, our political system, our government, our world – the one we leave to our children – needs our touch, our influence, as much as our home and family needs our physical touch.

"We can have a say in our children's futures and our children's children's futures. We can influence, for good, the kind of country and world they inherit from us. Our influence is needed beyond the wash pot and the cook stove and the dishpan. Those are necessary and we do them gladly, most of the time. But we must look at our inner strengths and extend our influence beyond the walls of our home.

"We are here today with the legal right to vote because of women whose influence was felt outside their homes. I'll name four but there were many others. Susan B. Anthony, Elizabeth Stanton, Lucy Stone, and Lucretia Mott challenged public opinion, confronted ignorance and exposed powerful people whose small minds could only produce cramped ideas, mean thoughts, and narrow views that 'women must be kept in their place.'

"These women have cut out a path, a road right through the jungle of opposition to give us the right to vote." She paused and emphasized every word of her next sentence. *"But we must get out of our houses and get on that road and walk!"*

Her voice became the instrument that imparted information, pride, courage, dignity. The women instinctively shifted and sat straighter, prouder.

"Some of you here probably have husbands who don't want you to vote. Now I'm starting to meddle. *Proverbs*, the book of wisdom in the *Old Testament*, says that the price of a good woman is far above rubies; that the heart of her husband doth safely trust in her; that she will do him good…all the days of her life.

"One good thing you can do for your husband is to stand tall as a person in your own right, with freedom to think and to express yourself. No man is blessed who has a wife who depends on him to do her thinking. Find that inner strength that has been inherent in women since time began. Stand tall and apart and see how your husband draws strength from you. Don't be a leaner or a clinger. Know who you are!"

She finished by making her last appeal. "Use your hard earned liberty. Let's do our part to make this a great nation under God! Let's go vote in November for the candidate of our choice."

As if on cue, the door to the left of the pulpit burst open. A large bull of a man, in dirty overalls, with matted hair, lurched in. The women sat stunned as he turned to Laurel.

"You're a troublemaker," he yelled, swaying as he talked. His finger pointed to Laurel, punctuating his words. "Women ain't got enough sense to vote. Women's good for one thing," he sneered. "Yeah, mostly one thing…"

Fury possessed Laurel. "What is your name?" she demanded.

He blinked. He wasn't used to women talking back. "Roscoe Werner," he muttered.

Laurel moved from behind the lectern and leaned slightly toward him. She spoke slowly, deliberately. "Mr. Werner, a fine gentleman like you wouldn't stoop to having a *woman* as your *mother*." She drew a deep breath. "So, tell us how you were born! How did you get into this world?"

The entire church full of women was on its feet, clapping and laughing. It penetrated his brain that they were laughing at *him*. He lowered his head like an angry bull and moved toward her. "Why, you red-headed...."

Suddenly, Justin and Henry Sargent were there. They manhandled him through the side door.

Laurel gathered her composure and walked back to the lectern. "Thank you, each one of you, for being with me all the way today. Please be seated."

She nodded to Mrs. Sargent and sat down. She was trembling.

Mrs. Sargent's remarks were brief. "We have been informed and inspired. And this is just the beginning. Thank you, Mrs. Worth."

The women were on their feet again clapping. After a moment, Mrs. Sargent said, "I know you'll get on that road and go to the polls in November. Thank you for coming. You're dismissed."

Laurel was besieged by women who wanted to shake her hand, ask her a question, or tell her how she had made them feel. Mrs. Sargent brought a small, well dressed lady to Laurel. "I want you to meet Letitia Beck, Laurel. I believe your husbands work together."

Laurel smiled and shook hands. "It's a pleasure to meet you. My husband enjoys working for your husband. They seem to think alike."

"Yes. Hiram is very pleased to have someone like your husband to supervise the work."

She had a gracious manner and an easy smile. "Thank you for your challenge to us today. I promise to vote."

Looking over her shoulder, Laurel's eye caught a group of women standing over by the side door. Hannah and Alice were with them and they were waiting patiently. Their appearance tugged at her heart – faded dresses, work-worn faces. She knew immediately they were the wives of the logging crew. The men had brought them to hear her!

She finished shaking hands with the women in line in front of her and said, "Mrs. Sargent and Mrs. Beck, excuse me. I see some people I need to meet. I believe they're the wives of our crew."

Mrs. Beck and Mrs. Sargent turned to look. "Oh, yes," Mrs. Sargent said. "Go right ahead."

Hannah smiled as Laurel approached. She had known she would come as soon as she saw them. "Laurel." She hugged her. "I'm so proud of you! And the crew brought their wives!" She rushed on, "Here's Abe's wife, Margie, and Dirk's wife, Helen, Zeke's wife, Marie, and Odell's wife, Betty." They were all there but three.

"We thank you for the speech," Abe's wife said. "You made us feel important."

The others nodded.

Zeke's wife said, "Our men folks talk a heap about you and Mr. Worth. Zeke and Odell tore down our old outhouses over the creek and built new ones."

"Thank you for sending the run of worm medicine. Our Jimmy is doing better," said Odell's wife.

"I'm glad. If you ever need my help in any way, just send word," Laurel said. "Thank you for coming today." She lowered her voice. "I'm so happy to meet you and I'm happier to see you here than anybody. Tell your husbands I said that."

Alice came around and hugged her. "I guess we'll all be votin'."

"I guess we will," agreed Laurel.

She made her way back to Mrs. Sargent and Mrs. Beck. They made plans to meet again in October. Laurel would "come out of the woods," as Mrs. Sargent put it, and they would confer on any practical things they needed to do before the election.

As she and Justin rode home, she asked, "How did you get there so fast to get Roscoe Werner out?"

"Henry and I were in the foyer of the church with the doors partly open. We didn't tell you but we expected trouble. Hiram Beck, Henry Sargent and I persuaded that group of men on the corner to leave, but Werner sneaked around back and got in without us seeing him."

She shivered as she remembered him threatening her.

"Laurel, I'm sorry you tangled with him. He's mean and he won't forget. We'll have to be careful."

"You mean …?"

"Yes. He may try to attack you if he ever gets a chance. I don't like to have to tell you this but I've got to warn you."

"I'll watch out for him." She put her hand over his. "Thank you for being there."

"You're welcome, Honey." He squeezed her hand. "Your speech was great. I heard it all. You gave them a sense of dignity and pride. They'll vote."

"Do you really think so?"

He laughed. "God help the husbands who try to stop 'em!"

Laurel was glad to have life simplified back to the logging camp routine, which wasn't simple at all. But she didn't feel pulled in so many directions.

On Monday at supper everybody discussed the rally. Laurel thanked the crew for bringing their wives.

"We've been wantin' them to meet you for a long time," Abe said.

"Yeah," Odell added, "they was glad to git to come."

After that the men often asked Laurel's advice on something their wives wanted to know. Or sometimes they would bring her word from them about a certain plant that had medicinal properties.

Jonah was eight years old and had never been to school a day. Jesse and Thad had gone sporadically, learning their ABC's and how to count, but they couldn't read. Laurel couldn't leave it alone. She knew the kind of life they would be condemned to live.

She had visited the county school office one day while she and Justin were in town and picked up four *McGuffey Readers* for first grade. These books enabled the teacher to use the phonic method, the word method or the ABC method in teaching reading, or to combine all three. Children who weren't auditory learners – learning by sound – could learn by sight, and vice versa. In the hands of a good teacher, the little books worked miracles. There was a lot of repetition, with six new words introduced in each lesson. Laurel believed she could teach the three children to read and write and do simple arithmetic in a minimum amount of time.

She talked to Hannah about it first. Hannah talked with Jed and they were happy for the opportunity for their boys. Hannah said, "The only way we'll agree to this is if I do some of your kitchen work while you're teaching them." They agreed that she would help Alice wash dishes and clean up on the days Laurel taught the boys.

Bess was defiant in her refusal to allow Laurel to teach Jonah. "I can't read and write and I don't see no sense in it," she said, raging to Bulldog.

He surprised her with his firm answer. "Bess, I want Jonah to learn to read and write and do arithmetic. Maybe she can have a better life than we have."

"Bull, I don't want to be beholden to – to that woman for anything!"

"We already are beholden, Bess! You know they're good to us!" He stood and looked at her. When he spoke, his tone was flat and intractable.

"Bess, you've got a spiteful streak that I don't like. It seems that Laurel sets if off. I ain't said nothin' because I hoped you'd work through it. But, I won't let you keep Jonah from getting' some schoolin' when she has the chance!"

He paused. "I want you to tell Laurel she can teach Jonah and I want you to help do some of her work while she's doin' it. Just like Hannah's doin'."

He turned and walked out the door. Bess stared after him. He was angry with her and it was Laurel's fault. She would have to do what he said, but she didn't have to like it...or kow-tow to Her Highness for her favors!

Laurel spent some time with Jonah first, teaching her the ABC's and how to count. Jonah—Laurel stubbornly called her Joanie—learned fast. She enjoyed being with Laurel, so she was always eager to do her lessons. She would count and say her ABC's to her daddy at night and he would brag on her. Bess never paid her recitals any attention.

When Jonah was ready, Laurel started teaching her and Thad and Jesse together. They did reading, writing, and arithmetic every day. She had bought all of them some pencils and lined tablets for doing their work. They also used a small chalkboard that she had borrowed from the county office. They all learned fast and soon were reading haltingly. They even read to the men around the table after supper. As Laurel worked with them and saw their progress she felt she was doing something of lasting value. Justin understood and held his peace.

Chapter Fifteen

One hot, still afternoon toward the end of September, all the women went to their shacks to rest awhile before starting supper. The men were all on the job. Laurel had put Sarah and Adam down for their naps with the windows and door of the shack open. She was sitting at her desk doing accounts when suddenly a figure loomed up behind her and a smelly hand went over her mouth. A voice that chilled her to the core whispered. "I told you I'd gitcha'!"

It was Roscoe Werner. He had caught her here alone with her children.

"You made fun of me and made ever'body laughed at me. But, ain't nobody gonna be laughin' now, Miss High and Mighty!"

Her heart was thudding, but she sat a moment without struggling, praying, "Oh, God, protect me and my children."

"So you ain't goin' to fight!" He stuck his fingers into her hair on top of her head and pulled her to her feet. Then he turned her around to face him. "Look at me good," he ordered. "You're gonna remember me a long time."

Then she was on him. Scratching, kicking, screaming for Nora, but his bull-like strength was too much for her. His fist crashed into her face, stunning her. Her vision dimmed and she tasted blood.

She heard Adam crying and Sarah screaming, "Mama, Mama." Werner ignored them. He threw Laurel to the floor. The back of her head hit solid. Everything turned black for a moment as a pain ripped across her forehead. He straddled her on his knees, ripped her dress down the front and started fumbling to get her skirt up.

She was addled from the two blows but she still struggled. "No! No! My children!" She had to protect them from seeing this.

Then with blurred vision she saw Nora coming through the door behind

Werner. As if in slow motion, Laurel saw Nora's hands fasten around Werner's neck. Nora hauled him back off Laurel toward the cook stove, choking him. Then she held him with one hand while she picked up a hot flat iron with the other. She swung it wide and crashed it into his skull. He fell and lay still.

Laurel passed out. Nora picked her up and carried her to the bed. The children were still screaming. Nora grabbed a diaper from a stack, wiped their faces, and picked up Adam. "Sarah, your mama will be okay. You need to go get Hannah. Run as fast as you can."

As Sarah went out the door, Nora turned to Laurel. Her face crumpled for a moment and tears rolled down her cheeks, then she got herself under control. Still carrying Adam who was now hiccupping, she walked around Werner and poured some warm water in a pan. She went back and began washing Laurel's bloody face. Laurel moaned and started shaking uncontrollably.

Hannah came running in and took it all in with one sweeping glance.

"Oh, Hannah, he attacked Laurel. She's shakin' all over and her face is white as a sheet."

Hannah said, "She's in shock. Help me rub her to get her circulation goin'." They worked with her a few minutes while the children watched wide-eyed. Hannah covered Laurel with a warm quilt. Then she rolled the hot flat irons that were sitting on the stove in towels and put them to her feet and back.

"Hannah, who is he and why did he do this?"

"He interrupted the rally when Laurel was speaking. Laurel said something to him that made everybody laugh. He threatened her. Now, go call the boys and Jonah. Tell them to get Bess and Alice here as fast as they can. You'll have to find some rope or chain and tie him up. He may come to any time."

The children answered Nora's call. She yelled, "Go git Bess and Alice. Tell 'em to come quick!"

They were off like a streak and Nora ran to the barn. She found some rope. Then she saw a harness. She came hurrying back with both.

When Bess and Alice and the children came running, Nora was dragging Werner out the door. Alice stopped, her eyes wide. Bess said, "I'll help her,

Alice. You need to go in and set down. You shouldn't have run."

Without a word, Bess and the boys helped drag Werner out behind the shack to a sturdy pine tree. "He sneaked in here and attacked Laurel. I knocked him out," Nora said.

Jesse and Thad looked at the huge man on the ground, then looked at each other. "How?" croaked Jesse.

"I hit him with a flat iron. Now hush and help me tie him to this tree."

They worked together harnessing him to the tree, his head lolling. They tied his hands together, then his feet. He wouldn't be going anywhere.

Hannah called, "Boys, go bring Tattoo and his saddle. Bess, you need to ride to the job and get Justin and Jed. Make sure Jed comes, too."

In a few minutes, Bess was off. Laurel's color was returning, but she still had trouble focusing. Alice took care of Adam and Sarah and anxiously watched Laurel.

Laurel mumbled, "Children…?"

"They're fine. They're right here," Alice said.

"Justin…?" she asked, blinking.

Hannah said, "Bess has gone to get Justin. We're all safe. Nora has Werner trussed up to a tree. He'll keep 'til Justin gets here."

Awareness struck Laurel…with fear of what Justin would do.

"Hannah," she whispered, "you and Alice help me get some more clothes on and my hair fixed. Justin must not see me like this."

Outside, Werner groaned, jerked his head, then shook it. He opened his eyes and saw his predicament. He slowly lifted his head and his eyes traveled from Nora to the boys and Jonah and back to Nora.

"You _____," he growled a rude word.

"Jesse," Nora said. "Go get me a flatiron off the stove."

She and Werner stared at each other. He drew back his head and spit at her.

Jesse handed her the iron with a potholder. It was hot. She held it up.

"I done knocked you out with this once. If you say one more word, I'll do it again. Mr. Worth is on his way to take care of you."

A flicker of fear mixed with the anger in his eyes. He was quiet.

When Justin and Jed rode in, Laurel was sitting up, dressed with her hair combed, trying to look normal. But nobody could hide her swollen face and split lip.

As Justin came through the door, Nora and Hannah took the children outside.

"Laurel," he said, kneeling by her chair and touching his fingers to her face. "What did he do to you?"

"He didn't hurt me bad. When I fought him, he hit me in the face."

"I see he did," he said, his voice clipped. He looked at her searchingly. "He didn't...?"

"No" she said with a suppressed shudder. "Nora came and...and knocked him out."

She gave a weak smile.

"Why are you blinking?"

"I hit the back of my head on the floor when I fell."

He pushed her hair back and kissed her forehead. "Do you think you need to see a doctor?"

"No. I'm dizzy and my head hurts, but I think I'll be okay after I rest awhile." She reached out her hand and took his. "What are you going to do?"

"I don't know yet. But this is between me and him now."

She sat still, afraid. As he went out the door he said, "You should lie down. I'll send Nora in to stay with you."

The women had taken the children to the camp kitchen and closed the door. Justin called Nora and asked her to put Laurel to bed. Then he walked around to find Werner. Jed was there, leaning against a tree.

Justin looked Werner over without a word. "Let's untie him and take him out behind the barn." Werner looked from one grim face to the other and was quiet. He ran his tongue over his lips. When they had the ropes and harness off, Justin said, "Get up and walk. The barn's that way." He pointed across the clearing.

When they were out of sight of the shacks, Justin clipped, "Turn around and look at me."

Werner did. His hands were opening and closing slowly as he glared at Justin.

Justin's voice was low but his eyes were a cold blue. "You're good at beating up women and children, Werner. Everybody knows you abuse your wife and family. But you hit the wrong woman this time."

Justin hit him square in the face with his fist. Werner swung back but Justin sidestepped and hit him under the ribs, winding him. Werner's full strength was hampered by clumsiness. He couldn't connect with Justin or get hold of him. Justin landed a few more punches, moving from side to side, pleased that his boxing skills from that early logging camp were still with him.

Suddenly, Jed yelled, "He's got a knife!"

Justin backed away as Werner lunged. He saw the knife flash and felt a sting on his left arm as he dropped and rolled to the right. Werner's momentum carried him forward and the knife stuck in the side of the barn. Justin moved in and hammered the side of Werner's head with his fist. As Werner fell, Jed grabbed the knife out of the wall.

Blood was running down Justin's left arm and dripping off his hand. He and Jed examined the cut. His arm was sliced to the bone. He pulled a handkerchief out of his pocket and pressed it to the wound.

Jed said, "You need to get the blood stopped. Go get Hannah to help you. I'll take care of him. Tell Jesse and Thad to bring me the rope and harness. We'll use 'em again."

As Justin walked around the barn, Werner stirred and looked at Jed.

"Scoot over and set up with your back against the barn," Jed ordered. Werner did as he was told, his eyes following the length of a pitchfork in Jed's hand.

"You try anything and I'll pin you to the barn wall."

When Jesse and Thad came running around the barn, Jed told them what to do. In a little while Werner was tied fast to a hitching post beside the barn.

"Where'd you hide your horse?"

Werner nodded his head toward the woods behind the barn.

"Boys," Jed said, "go find his horse and bring him here. He'll be needin' him."

Meanwhile, Hannah worked on Justin's arm. They didn't want Laurel to see it, but soon realized they had to have her help. They couldn't get the bleeding stopped. Laurel was sitting in her reading chair when they came in. She was too keyed up to stay in bed. When she saw the cut, she instantly responded as a nurse.

"Sit down here at the table. Hold your arm up straight, as high as you can. Hannah, can you get some of your comfrey powder while I hold this wound closed?"

As Hannah left, Laurel asked, "You've bled a good bit, haven't you?"

"Some," he answered.

"Enough to cleanse the wound, you think?"

"Yes."

She paused. "Where is he?"

"Behind the barn with Jed."

"And…?"

"I knocked him out after he cut me. We'll take him in and turn him over to the sheriff."

"You'll have to get stitches in your arm, Justin, or it will take a long time to heal and leave a bad scar. You can't ride anywhere. The doctor will have to come here."

He started to object and she continued, "He can check me, too. I may have a slight concussion. My vision's still blurred and I have a headache."

"Okay. I'll have Jed and some of the crew to take him in. They can ask the doc to come. We seem to be keeping him busy lately."

When Hannah came in with the comfrey, Laurel had Justin lie down on the bed. She opened the cut enough for Hannah to sprinkle the powder inside. Then she closed and taped it.

"You'll need to lie here with your arm on a pillow until the bleeding stops. The comfrey should help."

"I have to get up and talk to the men."

"I know. This won't take long. Then we'll put your arm in a sling."

Bulldog brought the crew in early. When the word spread about Roscoe Werner attacking Laurel, they were ready to get to camp. Jed corralled them into the lobby so Justin could talk to them.

"How is Laurel?" Abe voiced every man's fears.

"She's okay. Been doctoring me," Justin said. "Werner hit her in the face with his fist. When she fought him he knocked her down. Her head hit the floor pretty hard. Nora got to him before he…before he did any more damage."

The men understood what he was saying and were greatly relieved. But Justin read their mood. Werner was in danger of never making it to jail.

Bulldog broke the silence. "What happened to your arm?"

"Werner and I were fist fighting. He came at me with a knife. Jed yelled at me but I didn't quite get out of the way."

He paused and added briskly, "Here's what I want us to do. Jed, Bulldog, Tom and Abe, you need to take Werner to Deerbrook and swear out a warrant for his arrest. I want him put in jail tonight. I'll write out a statement for you to give to the sheriff. Tell him I'll be in to see him tomorrow. You also need to send Dr. Leighton out to check if Laurel has a concussion and to stitch up my arm."

"Where's Werner now?" Dirk asked.

"He's trussed up to a post out behind the barn," Jed answered.

Justin spoke again with emphasis. "Men, I know what you would like to do to Werner. So would I! But we're not going to! We'll obey the law."

He turned to Jed. "Do you have anything to say?"

"The women have supper ready," Jed said. "Let's go eat. Then we'll get on our way with Werner."

He paused. "It won't hurt none for you to see Werner and let him know he better never show his face around here again and," he grinned, "see how Justin worked him over in a fair fight 'til he pulled his knife."

Supper was subdued. The crew could tell Justin was in pain and Laurel was too dizzy to come to the mess hall. Each man was busy with his own thoughts. They would respect Justin's request to obey the law. But that shouldn't keep them from putting the fear of God in Mr. Werner before he left camp.

Justin sat down in his reading chair and rested his arm on a pillow. It eased the burning pain. Laurel sat in the other chair, unable to focus enough to read or sew.

They looked at each other and started laughing. "We make a lively pair," Justin said. "Want to do the polka with me?"

"All I could do is go around in circles," Laurel said. Then she grew serious. "Before Nora brings the children back, I need to know what's going on."

As Justin was reassuring her that Werner was going to jail, the men were mounting their own plans.

Roscoe Werner, like most bullies, was a coward. The crew had moved in on him. Dirk walked over to him and slipped a noose over his head, adjusting the knot and muttering about the right size. Abe, in a conversational tone, reasoned that it would be better to lynch him out of sight of camp. That he knew a place just around the bend that had a good hanging tree.

His eyes wide and his throat working convulsively, Werner screamed, "You can't do that! Lynchin's against the law!"

They looked at him with contempt. Tom continued as if Werner hadn't spoken. "What do we do with the body once he's dead?"

Bulldog answered, "Oh, we'll toss him over the falls. Everybody'll think he was drunk and had an accident when his horse wanders in without him."

"Good riddance," somebody mumbled.

"Yeah, we'd be doin' his family a favor."

Werner begged, "I'll do anything you want me to do. Just don't hang me." His voice rose, "Don't hang me!"

"Bring his horse and the rope and let's get on with it," Bulldog said.

They got him, kicking and fighting, on his horse and led him down the road to the hanging tree. Jed, meanwhile, had been getting instructions and a statement for the sheriff from Justin. He rode up just as the men were positioning Werner under the tree with the noose around his neck. He waited until they threw the other end of the rope over the sturdy limb of a giant oak. Then he steered his horse around so he could face the terrified Werner.

"Any last words, Werner?"

Werner's body was trembling and his eyes were rolling. Saliva ran down his chin as he rocked and babbled, "Don't hang me. I'll leave the county...."

"You'll what?" Jed snapped.

"I'll leave the county. You'll never see me again," he jabbered.

"Boys, come gather 'round so he can see you," Jed said.

As they all grouped near his horse, Jed continued, "Werner, you're goin' to jail. We ain't goin' to hang you right now, but you're a marked man. If you come near here again or touch Laurel or Justin Worth again, you'll be swingin' from a tree. That's a promise from all of us. Look at us good so you'll remember! Do you understand?"

"Yes, yes! Thank you!"

"Don't thank us. Thank the man whose wife you attacked; the man you tried to kill with a knife. He says we obey the law and we respect him enough to do it—this time! Next time we'll make our own laws and rid the world of a varmint." His measured, level tone carried a certainty that no one wanted to contest.

He turned to the crew. "Watch after Justin and Laurel. We'll send the doc as soon as we can." He took the reins of Werner's horse and motioned for Bulldog, Abe, and Tom to follow.

It took about a week for the camp to return to routine. Dr. Leighton sewed up Justin's arm and advised him to keep it in a sling for at least a week. His diagnosis for Laurel was a concussion and his remedy was a few days of bed rest. She wasn't in a position to argue. Her head hurt abominably, and when she stood up, dizziness made her nauseated.

Werner stayed in jail a few days on assault charges but his real punishment came after he was released. As he walked toward the Beck Company Store one of the men in a group near the door called out, "Hey, Werner, I hear you got ironed and tied up by a bunch of women."

"Yeah," another voice yelled above the laughter. "Maybe you're losin' your touch in beatin' up women."

He adjusted his direction and kept walking past the store as the ridicule poured over him. The last thing he heard was, "We hear Justin Worth knocked you out flat, even after you sliced his arm open with that knife o' yourn."

A couple of weeks later Justin, with his general news summary at supper after going into town, said, "I heard today that Roscoe Werner has left the county. He talked some nonsense about bein' scared of a lynchin' party." He looked around the table. The crew looked back innocently.

"Anyway, his family seems relieved he's gone. His wife got a job at the Central Hotel and Sam Parker's paying his boy to deliver some papers. They'll be better off without him."

Later that night Laurel asked, "How did you know about Werner's wife and son working?"

"I checked."

She hugged him close, knowing full well he had checked to see if they had food.

Laurel's few days alone in bed turned out to be a blessing in disguise. As her dizziness and headache gradually eased, she had time to think. One morning as she was working through some problems and plans in her mind without interruptions, she realized that time alone had gradually been erased from her life in the past few months. No wonder she was feeling pulled in all directions! She couldn't totally give herself to one task without feeling that she needed to be doing another. It was a scattered way of thinking and foreign to her normal way of managing her life.

Community living had its good points and she enjoyed working with the other women, but she knew she had to take time to plan ahead. And she had to have some time alone just to *be*, to gather strength to meet life's demands.

The memory of hers and Justin's trip to the mountain top tantalized her. The next Sunday afternoon while Justin was gone to do his photography – she didn't plan to show her face in town until her bruises were gone – she asked Nora to stay with Sarah and Adam during their nap while she took a walk and had some thinking time.

With Nora's admonition to watch out for snakes and bears still ringing in her ears, she set out. She knew she had to be careful not to get lost but she intended to climb up the side of one of the mountains to try to find a view, where she could look across or down instead of up. Noticing certain landmarks, she found a place not far from camp to start climbing. Pine needles had discouraged the usual dense undergrowth. She slipped and slid, holding on to bushes and trees to pull herself up the steep slope. Her long skirt caught on briars, and twigs tugged at her hair. She was soon breathing hard. She tied a white strip of cloth on a low limb every now and then, like Hansel and Gretel, she thought, to lead her back home.

Her efforts paid off. She came out on a rocky ridge with a limited view, but still a view. She looked around for snakes with some trepidation before she chose a place to sit. She pulled out her round gold watch on a long chain which she had tucked inside her blouse. After checking the time, her hand closed over the watch and she held it up to her chest. It was one of her treasures. Justin had given it to her soon after they were married, after she borrowed his a few times to take to school with her. She was rarely without it.

And now, she would take an hour or two to *be*. No demands from anybody. With her back against a birch tree, she gave herself up to the mountains. She looked at the mountainside facing her, varying shades of green made visible by the bright sunlight, sculpted by wind, deceptively smooth as a carpet one could walk on except for an occasional tree rising well above the rest. As she considered the relentless weathering – the forces – that had produced such beauty, clouds moved in and cast huge shadows on her perfect landscape. Shadows that moved, changed shapes, darkened, diminished the brightness, cast gloom. Capricious! Irritating!

After awhile they dissolved or moved on and she had her mountain back just as magnificent and constant as it had been before, absolutely unimpressed by the transient shadows. Laurel laughed. Her pleasure seemed to reach her toes.

With a contented sigh, she leaned her head against her tree and closed her eyes. After a few moments she became aware of the silence…stillness…the absence of noise.

Her eyes flew open. When had she ever known such soothing silence? She sat a long while, considering her life and the turn it had taken. She would never have imagined herself in this setting, doing what she was now doing. Yet, she was learning to cope and was even challenged by it. In the quietude she asked God for perspective, for the ability to keep the important things in their lives in spite of where they lived. His answer seemed to be an inner voice that urged her to absorb the serenity and constancy of the mountains. *Then* she would find the perspective and strength she was looking for.

A breeze whispered through the trees, teasing the leaves into a graceful dance. A rustle nearby brought her fully back from her reverie. Two squirrels were playing chase. Reluctantly, she checked her watch and saw that it was time to go.

On her way down she removed the white strips of cloth. She didn't want any signs of her intrusion to mar the beauty of her mountainside. As she neared camp, she felt as if she had been put back together again. Her scattered feeling was gone. She could again deal with the threatening shadows that seemed to move regularly across the landscape of her life.

Even the sight of the crude camp failed to induce her usual inner cringe.

That night when she and Justin went over their day together, she shared about her venture and told him she had found a place to be alone. She didn't share the feelings the mountains had evoked. They were too personal. He warned her, in an absentminded sort of way, about getting lost. His mind was already on tomorrow's job with its problems.

The next Sunday Laurel started again to the little church across the river. She explained to Justin that she had enjoyed going with him on his photography rounds, but she and the children needed their own church, a place where they belonged.

He had responded simply, "I understand."

The second Sunday she started a class for the children. This time when she left camp, Jonah, Thad and Jesse were in the wagon with her and Sarah and Adam. All of them were spiffed up for church. She knew Bulldog had put his foot down in order for Jonah to go. Bess's mean streak would be operating for the next few days. *It's worth it,* she thought, *if Joanie can have a better life.* Nora, Laurel's guardian angel, was going with her to help with the children.

The class was a success from the beginning with about ten children ranging in age from three to twelve years. Laurel's expertise from classroom days helped her span the wide range of ages and interest levels.

Mrs. Stevens, the pastor's wife who had taken Laurel home with her after Laurel had been fished out of the river, invited them all home with her the second week for Sunday dinner. The afternoon left Laurel comforted and warmed, and Nora relaxed and enjoyed herself. It would have been hard not to. Mrs. Stevens was the mothering sort, and mothered everybody no matter their age or size or status. It was good to have her so near.

Besides church, Laurel came to look forward to her Sunday afternoon trips to her mountain top. If she was awed by the beauty of summer in the mountains, the splendor of October took her breath away. From her now familiar vantage point, the lush greens of the facing mountainside had turned to a vast range of colors – yellow, orange, red, bronze, and gold – contrasting with the evergreens always nearby.

One night she asked Justin, "Why is the sky bluer now than in summer?"

"Probably the colder weather."

"It's the most beautiful blue there is, the same color as your eyes."

He was pleased. "Describe it to me."

She looked searchingly into his eyes. "Well, it's intensely blue, crisp, definite – banked with sunlight – happy, perfect…."

He smiled and drew her to him.

She leaned back a little. "I was going to ask you which trees are which, according to the color. Like which is red or yellow, or…?"

He put his finger on her lips, pulled her tighter, and said, "That'll wait."

America, Wildwood County, and the Worth Logging Camp moved inexorably toward election day, November 2, 1920. The country's mood called for a return to normalcy, rejecting President Wilson's involvement in the League of Nations.

"The World War and Kaiser Bill have made their mark on America, and it's not a good one," Justin observed one night at supper.

"What do you mean?" Abe asked.

"America has enjoyed and treasured independency from Europe ever since we became a nation. It scares us to get involved again, which is what the League of Nations will require."

"Are you in favor of the League of Nations?" Jed asked.

"I think it's necessary for nations to stand together for the common good against aggressors like Wilhelm Kaiser ll, but we don't seem to be ready for it. Wilson may be pushing us too hard. We seem to need a healing time. Maybe that's what people mean by a 'return to normalcy.'"

"Do you think Warren G. Harding can give us that?" Dirk inquired.

"I hope so, Dirk. I hope so."

The women, meanwhile, had their own reasons to celebrate. They were going to vote! No more formal meetings or rallies were held, but according to the time-honored, word-of-mouth grape vine, the women of Wildwood County would be at the polls come election day.

The day arrived, with a wet, cold whirling wind busily stripping the last stubborn leaves off the hardwood trees. But the gray day brightened for Laurel when she and Nora drove into the school yard where they would vote. Justin was already there, serving as watchman over the ballot boxes for the Republican Party.

"Look at all the women, Nora! They've come!"

"I know," Nora answered forlornly. "I'm here, too!"

Laurel laughed and patted Nora's shoulder. "Nora, we've gone over this a hundred times. You're one of the most wonderful people in this whole wide world and you can't keep hiding yourself away."

Nora was quiet. No need to argue with Laurel. One part of her did desire to get out and be with people, even knowing the stares and whispers that were ahead. But, she was doing this for Laurel. Laurel made her feel normal.

The women in camp had arranged to come in shifts to vote. Hannah and Alice would come after Laurel and Nora got home. Bess wouldn't vote simply because she knew Laurel wanted her to. The crew had a day off to go to their different precincts to vote. They knew Justin Worth's loggers had better vote.

The schoolyard was full of people milling around despite the weather. As Laurel and Nora approached to get in line, several women joined them.

"We're here, Miz Worth!" one woman announced. "They's as many women as men, I believe!"

Laurel smiled. "I'm so glad you came."

For the next few minutes, women were talking to her from all directions.

"We feel mighty proud getting' to vote. You made us feel like we had to."

"We heard what Roscoe Werner done to you."

"Yeah. We heard what happened to him, too."

They turned to Nora.

"Are you the one who hit him with a flat iron and tied him up?"

Nora blushed. "Yes."

They gathered around laughing and hugging Nora.

"Every woman in this county owes you a debt. You got rid of a snake. We're mighty proud of you!"

Nora smiled uncertainly and looked at Laurel whose eyes said, "I told you so!"

Most of the men spoke to Laurel and Nora, showing their respect and commenting on women voting and, humorously, on Roscoe Werner leaving the county.

As they entered the building, Laurel looked around with a momentary wistfulness tugging at her heart. Schoolrooms always evoked memories of Papa. And a yearning to teach again.

Her full attention was claimed, however, by the history being written before her eyes. Women voting with the men for the first time! Justin and a man she didn't know, a Democrat, were sitting on each side of the ballot box which was on the opposite side of the room. Two men sat behind a long table explaining to the voters how to mark their ballots. As the line moved around the table, there was a good natured teasing about the women voting.

As Laurel and Nora dropped in their ballots, Justin motioned for them to wait behind him until he could talk to them. The congenial atmosphere was suddenly shattered. Three men burst into the room, seemingly on a strong gust of wind that sent ballots whirling and people scrambling after them.

Justin was on his feet instantly. One of the men, Curt Redmon, staggered over to him, followed by his two friends. All three were drunk.

"I figured you'd be here, Justin. Where do we vote?"

"Curt, you don't vote here. You're supposed to vote at the Oakdale Precinct."

"What do you mean? You can't tell me where to vote."

"Let me look over the list to make sure," Justin said as he turned and leaned over the end of the table to look at the list of voters for this precinct.

Curt picked up a piece of wood near the pot bellied stove and swung it to hit Justin in the back of the head. Laurel grabbed the back of his shirt and jerked. The wood clattered to the floor and Laurel looked with dismay at the piece of faded, threadbare cloth in her hand. She had ripped the back out of Curt Redmon's shirt.

He turned and reached for her, but Justin grabbed him and wrestled him out the door. Nora stepped forward, turned both of Curt's friends in their tracks, and propelled them out the door behind Curt.

Everything was quiet for a stunned moment, then one of the women burst out laughing. "I don't know how you men ever run an election without us!"

Everybody was laughing when Justin and Nora came back in. Justin knew Laurel was mortified by the way she stood with the hunk of shirt still in her hand. He took it from her and threw it in a trashcan.

"Good thing Curt put on his long johns this morning. They'll keep him covered 'til he gets home."

Excitement was still running high that night at supper, with opinions flying about the outcome of the election. After some serious talk, Justin sat back and in a sober tone asked, "What would you men think about a woman, who, on her first trip to vote, tore the shirt off a man who was trying to vote?"

Laurel glared at him and blushed. Before she could protest, a hubbub rose.

"Oh, law!"

"You don't say!"

"Huh-uh!"

"Who done a thing like that?"

"Laurel did."

He walked over and put his arm around her. "I'm right proud of her. She kept me from getting clobbered in the back of the head with a stick of stove wood."

"Tell us," Abe said.

When Justin had finished about Laurel, he told how Nora helped the two drunk gentlemen leave the voting premises. He was a good storyteller and, by the time he was through, everybody was in an uproar.

He added, "The men agreed that the women did add some flavor and spice. We didn't know what we've been missing all these years."

Laurel and Nora laughed with them. Laurel said, "If you repeat that story, tell all of it and tell it right. I just gave a little yank!"

That set them off again. The party atmosphere kept everybody up talking long past their usual bedtime. Early next morning Justin rode Tattoo into Deerbrook to get the news. Warren G. Harding had been elected as the nation's twenty-ninth president.

In early December, cold weather settled over the mountains and invaded the logging shacks. Laurel bundled Sarah and Adam in so many clothes,

Justin called them his Eskimos.

Alice's baby chose the first snowy night of the year to make his appearance. The camp sprang to life just as everybody was in their first doze, when a frightened Tom cut a swath, yelling and banging on every door except the bunkhouse.

Laurel and Justin dressed quickly; Nora came to stay with Sarah and Adam; Hannah and Bess met Laurel at Alice's shack. Bulldog rode for Dr. Leighton. Laurel called after him to send Mrs. Stevens. Justin and Jed chunked up the fire in the cook stove and the little black heater in Alice's shack. They carried in two pails of water and put them on the stove. Tom wasn't much help. He was, in Jed's words, "like a chicken with its head cut off."

Alice's contractions were about five minutes apart. This gave Laurel hope that Dr. Leighton would get there in time. She was scared. For all her book learning, she had never actually delivered a baby. Two lives were at stake. But Hannah—calm, constant, practical Hannah—was a balm to her fears. Hannah had done this before, so Laurel followed her lead. They changed Alice's bed where her water had broken and put heavy pads under her. Bess sat by Alice, sponging her face and talking to her. She combed her hair and put in enough bobby pins to keep it out of her face.

The men were happy to escape to the mess hall. They would rather face a she-bear with cubs than to deal with the birth ritual. Justin and Jed felt for Tom. They both knew the feeling of helplessness and dread. They had just got the fire going well and had put on some coffee when the door opened to admit a whirl of snow along with Abe, Dirk, Odell and Zeke.

Abe came in talking. "Why are babies always born in the middle of the night in the worst weather?" It wasn't a question that needed an answer. Soon they had Tom grinning at their teasing. Justin was proud of his men.

Rev. Stevens brought his wife, wrapped up against the storm. They were greeted heartily as their wagon pulled in front of the mess hall.

Tom took Mrs. Stevens to his shack and she came through the door taking off her wraps. She crossed the room to Alice.

"Ain't you glad your time is here, Honey? Don't have to push that big belly around no more. And gonna soon have a fine baby to show for all your trouble!"

She turned to Hannah and Laurel. "Everything ready?"

They had scissors and a knife sterilizing in a pan of boiling water, for cutting the umbilical cord. They had twine for tying it off. And the baby clothes were ready.

Alice groaned and rolled as a pain hit her. Mrs. Stevens took one of her hands and told Laurel to take the other one.

"Pull hard on our hands and push down as hard as you can! That pain is tryin' to push that little rascal out. You help! Ride that pain out like you're on a buckin' bronco!"

After they had all ridden it out, Mrs. Stevens looked at the cook stove. "Where's the coffee? We can't birth a baby without coffee!"

Laurel soon had it brewing. She realized Mrs. Stevens had not only dispelled the strained atmosphere. She had introduced an air of festivity.

Tom came from time to time to check on Alice. He would give a timid knock on the door and one of the women would assure him she was okay. Then he would go back to the mess hall.

When Bulldog rode in with word that Dr. Leighton couldn't come—he was in bed with flu—Tom went white to the gills.

Rev. Stevens spoke slowly. "Son, don't you worry none. My wife knows what she's about. She's delivered many a baby. Never lost a mama or a baby!"

Jed had his say. "Hannah's done this before, too. And Laurel's there. Heck, Tom, them women don't need no help. If the doc came, they'd probably shoo him out the door with the rest of us men."

Justin studied Rev. Stevens. He hadn't known many preachers, but he liked this husky, outdoorsman. He was a man's man. *I'd like to have him as a friend,* Justin thought. *But I'd better remember that he's a preacher.*

The night wore on as Alice fought the age-old, universal, yet private struggle, unique to women, to bring forth a new life. Even with the care and concern of the other women, the pain was hers alone.

It was about four o'clock when Mrs. Stevens declared the baby was coming. Its head could be seen. Laurel held the lamp while Mrs. Stevens quickly cut a gash, giving the necessary room for the baby to come out.

Suddenly, everything happened at once. On the wave of a giant contraction, the baby burst forth streaked with blood. As Hannah caught the baby, Laurel crumpled to the floor in a faint. Mrs. Stevens caught the lamp as she fell.

"Bess," she said, without missing a beat, "pull her out of the way and hold this lamp!"

Bess dragged Laurel from under their feet and dumped her by the door. So Miss High and Mighty couldn't take it! Bess felt gratified as she hurried to take the lamp. Hannah held the slippery baby, who gave several cries of protest, as Mrs. Stevens cut the cord and tied it. Then, Hannah wrapped the baby in a blanket and held it close as Mrs. Stevens massaged Alice's stomach, coaxing her body to expel the afterbirth. With one more contraction, it came and was dropped into a bucket at the foot of the bed. Mrs. Stevens finished her ministrations, which included an application of comfrey to the cut she had made.

Alice, free from heavy pain at last, said, "Can I see my baby?"

Hannah laid the bundle in her arms. She unwrapped it and smiled. "Bess, go tell Tom to come and see his son. But, first, help me comb my hair and wash my face."

Hannah, meanwhile, had put a pillow under Laurel's head, and was washing her face, trying to bring her around. "Tell Justin to come, too."

Tom heard his son's cries before he got to the shack. His heart and steps quickened and he was soon on his knees beside the bed, his face alight with something akin to reverence.

When Justin followed Tom through the door and saw Laurel on the floor, he dropped beside her, alarmed.

Hannah explained. "She fainted when the baby come, Justin. She'll be okay. Put her to bed for awhile."

He picked her up, let Hannah wrap a quilt around her, and carried her to their shack. The cold helped to bring her around.

"Alice...the baby?" she asked.

"They're both fine. It's a boy!"

"Oh...good."

He tucked her in bed and she was soon asleep.

Zeke and Odell fixed breakfast with Abe and Dirk setting the table. They simplified bread making, mixing a stiff dough and dumping it into several greased skillets. They let the cakes of bread, called hoe cakes, cook on top of the stove, flapping them over when they were about half done so they cooked through and browned on both sides. The bread, along with the rest of breakfast, was tasty. The women bragged on it. Mrs. Stevens brought her air of celebration to the mess hall. Laughter soon replaced the tension. The mother, baby, and daddy had all survived.

Before she left camp about mid-morning, Mrs. Stevens went to visit Laurel, who was up but still looking peaked.

"I wasn't much help, was I?" Laurel said, embarrassed.

"Lord, Honey, the first time I helped deliver a baby, I about threwed up my guts. Just as the baby come out, I had to run outside. I was sick all day."

Laurel, who still felt queasy, was relieved.

"I never just passed out like that before in my life. The smells, the heat from the stoves, the baby popping out streaked with blood, Alice worn out…."

"It's a shock to your system. Ain't nothin' pretty about it for sure. You'll do better next time, now that you know what to expect."

Laurel refused to think about the next time.

They named the baby Thomas Justin Raines. He would be called Tommy. Justin was honored and pleased.

"A new baby brings its own magic," Laurel said to Alice one night at supper about two weeks later. Tommy was lying on a pillow in his box, one similar to Sarah's and Adam's, on the table in the mess hall. The men took turns talking to him or adjusting his clothes. Everybody felt proprietary about this baby. They all had lived through the pregnancy and birth.

A beautiful snow made Christmas become real as they decorated the fir tree in the mess hall. Abe and Dirk had brought it in and set it up. The children worked excitedly for several days under Laurel's and Hannah's directions, stringing popcorn and making paper chains out of colored paper—red, green, yellow, blue. They even cut out a chain of paper dolls. A cardboard star covered with yellow paper adorned the top of the tree.

On Christmas morning the families who lived in the camp gathered in the mess hall for the children to find their gifts from Santa. Sarah and Jonah each found a baby doll and a tea set. Laurel had determined that Jonah would get something appropriate for a girl. She had bought the gifts, then showed them to Bess and Bulldog, together, and asked if they would like to give them to Jonah from Santa. "If you don't like them, I can return them," she assured them.

Bess had surprised Laurel. She had looked at the doll wistfully. "I ain't never had a doll. I'd like for Jonah to have one—and the tea set, too."

Jonah's pleasure was evident. She helped Sarah set up the tea sets on a bench, while holding her doll with a definite maternal air. Every now and then, she would rock it back and forth in her arms and croon to it.

Watching her, Hannah said, "There's been a little girl there all the time in tomboy clothes."

Adam's favorite gift was a small wooden horse and wagon. He pounced on it, calling it Tattoo, and spent the morning rolling it on the benches around the table, making appropriate boy noises. He pulled Justin over to play with him.

Thad and Jesse received a ball and bat they would share and each received his own pocketknife. A pocketknife showed that they were growing up. They were soon out the door with Jed and Bulldog to find some whittlin' wood. They wanted to make some whistles.

Tommy got some baby rattles and new clothes.

Each of the older children, including Sarah, received a school tablet, some pencils and their own box of crayons.

Soon after breakfast, they could smell the wild turkey which had been popped into the oven as soon as the biscuits were out. The turkey was Bulldog's contribution, bagged one day after he heard Laurel wishing they had one for Christmas dinner.

Laurel had bought some white muslin material that could be used as tablecloths. She gave the older children the job of gathering galax leaves, turkey brush, and holly. They now importantly carried out the job of decorating the table. It was simple and beautiful when they finished adorning the center, all the way from end to end, with the beautiful natural offerings from the woods around them.

By mid-afternoon, after a hearty Christmas dinner, everybody was filled and ready to go to his and her own shacks to rest awhile or be alone with their families.

While Sarah and Adam watched, Justin and Laurel exchanged gifts. He gave her a longer gold chain for her round watch which she wore around her neck every day. And she gave him a longer gold chain for his round pocket watch which he was never without. They laughed so hard, Laurel ended up in his lap with her face nestled against his. They sat in silence, savoring the touch, until they realized Sarah were silently studying them from across the room. They also had books for each other. She gave him four Zane Grey westerns and he gave her a book by Helen Keller and one by Susan B. Anthony, *Failure Is Impossible*.

After Sarah and Adam went down for a nap and Justin settled down to read awhile, Laurel asked, "Do you mind if I take a walk?"

"No. Go ahead. But bundle up carefully."

"I won't go far."

The blanket of snow, at least six inches deep, glistened in the afternoon sun. The hardwood trees, barren of leaves, were now highlighted with white frosting on the branches and the evergreens were borne down with it. She laughed with pleasure when she passed a hitching post with a deep plop of snow on top, like a tall winter toboggan.

Then she allowed herself to think of Papa. Would she ever grow beyond being homesick for him? It would hit her at the strangest times. She had wanted desperately to talk over her suffrage speech with him. She wondered if Chief Lion Heart had visited him. She knew, of course, that Papa missed her as much as she missed him and felt a twinge of guilt.

"Papa," she said aloud, "I think you would be proud of me. We are happy in this primitive logging camp."

Justin, meanwhile, had put down his book and was watching her through the window. Sometimes he had a passing whisper of anxiety that Laurel didn't need him as much as he needed her. He had listened as she had urged the women not to be clingers or leaners, but equal pillars of support in the home.

He thought irritably, *Something in me wants her to lean on me, and occasionally she does, but she sure stands upright and apart most of the time. Self-sufficient woman!*

But as she went out of sight, a shaft of truth hit him. He could never endure a clinging woman!

Sunlight on the snow reflected light into the shabby room. He looked around him and thought, *Happiness sometimes comes wrapped in a rough-hewn lumber shack.*

Chapter Sixteen

No bells rang-in the Year of Our Lord, 1921, in the sequestered community of Worth Logging Camp. It came softly over the snow-draped mountains. Its coming was dignified by the white carpet spread to welcome it, a new slate on which to write.

Justin and Laurel stayed up to welcome the new year, as they had every year since they had been married. Laurel teased him about his way of looking so intently into the darkened sky on the stroke of midnight. "It's as if you actually expect to see some manifestation of the New Year, like a message of things to come."

He laughed at her fancies but then grew solemn. "Well, 1920 has been a historic year. The Eighteenth Amendment declared Prohibition of the use of alcoholic drinks; the Nineteenth Amendment gave women the right to vote – and *you, Mrs. Worth*, gave the women in Wildwood County the courage to vote! A tired, sick, disenchanted Democratic President is waiting to leave office and a Republican is waiting to be sworn in. We always hope the new administration will do better than the last…Oh, and we have lived eight months in a logging camp."

The problems of the world seemed far removed. The snowy grandeur surrounding them gave a sense of peace and promise. "We're wrapped in our own cocoon," Laurel said softly. There was no premonition of what was ahead.

By mid-January, the winter, bitter-cold and relentless, gripped the mountains and wreaked misery on the camp. Frigid air poured through the cracks in the walls and floors. There was no escape from it. Even in bed, the cold and dampness swirled around their heads. Laurel found herself tired and aching from always bracing against the cold.

She couldn't imagine why she had ever thought the mountains were friendly. They were her enemy, slowly freezing not only her body but her soul and will as well. One day she noticed the laurel leaves curled into thin cylinders, and remembered Chief Lion Heart's words about protecting themselves. She understood and emotionally rolled herself into an uncommunicative and unreachable coil, laced around with a feeling of helplessness. The whole camp was affected by her withdrawal. She was no longer with them, except in body.

Even Justin's unfailing good humor didn't compensate. He was worried but had his own problems. The freezing weather had played havoc on the job. Their normal routine was shot. Some days were so cold the trees were frozen and their crosscut saws simply would not cut them. These same days, however, were great for snaking out logs because the ground was frozen hard and the logs slid easily. The crew learned to fell as many trees as it could on warmer days and then to snake them out on colder days.

It was anger that brought Laurel out of her emotional hibernation. When Adam and Sarah came down with such bad colds that she feared pneumonia, anger and fear made her start looking for some solutions. Nora was happy to have her back, even angry. They were in Laurel's shack, taking care of the sick children, and had just tacked quilts around the walls of the bedroom at the heads and sides of the beds. The constant cold draft was stopped in the bedroom and now they were surveying the walls in the main room of the shack.

"Wallpaper would cover those cracks," Laurel said, "But that would be a joke. Wallpaper in this…this…."

"Couldn't we just use old newspapers?" Nora asked.

Laurel looked at a pile of newspapers by Justin's chair and was on her feet. "Nora, Nora, what would I do without you! Let's try it!"

She mixed flour and water for paste. They glued two sheets together for thickness, then glued them on the wall, starting in Laurel's and Justin's reading corner. In a little while they had papered the corner to the top of the window.

"We'll only go that high for now," Laurel said.

Sarah and Adam, in bed to stay warm, wanted to see what they were doing. Laurel brought them, blankets and all, and tucked them into the reading chairs. Then she and Nora moved to the other side and papered the wall beside the table all the way to the door.

"I can tell a difference, except for the air coming through the cracks in the floor," Nora said. "One time me and Hannah nailed pieces of cardboard on the floor."

"Of course, that's the answer!"

"I'll go bring some of them boxes from the mess hall. I'll have to empty out the canned stuff and supplies."

"It's okay. Bring all the boxes you can find. Just stack the supplies against the wall."

They covered half the floor of the main room of the shack, the side where their reading chairs were, before they ran out of cardboard. It wasn't exactly cozy yet, but the cold draft was gone.

When Justin came in that afternoon, he looked around surprised. "Who did all this?"

"Nora helped me. Something had to be done…if we expect our children to survive living here."

"Laurel," he said, trying not to strike back at her anger. "I would have done it…."

She didn't let him finish. "Well, you didn't, so I did! It's called survival in a cruel land, Justin! Nothing more! Just survival!"

She grabbed up his work jacket and jerked it on. "Watch the children a few minutes. I'm going for a walk."

He sat, startled, with Adam on his lap and Sarah in Laurel's chair. So, she had moved from unapproachable to angry. He couldn't decide which he disliked the most.

Sarah observed, "Mama's mad."

"Your mama's tired, Sarah. She works too hard."

"She fixed it warm for us."

He patted his knee. "Come here. I need two bear cubs on my lap instead of just one."

"I keep telling you we ain't—we're not—bear cubs," she scolded, scrambling onto his lap beside Adam and snuggling against him.

Justin sat looking at the door Laurel had slammed. He knew he was more to blame than she was. He had been so wrapped up in the job, he had left Laurel to cope with things that were his responsibility. He had not provided a warm place. Everybody else in camp had lived through winters before and had just accepted the misery. He, again, had failed to remember how absolutely different Laurel's life had been and had failed to appreciate her constant struggle to adapt. That night in bed he wanted to draw her into his arms, but she still held herself so far away from him, he might as well have been alone.

On Friday, on his weekly trip into town, he brought back some boxes and finished covering the floor of their shack. He also brought a stack of old newspapers and some sheets of gray-white newsprint. "A gift from Sam," he explained. "When I told him what you were doing, he kept bringing paper to the wagon."

The next week Zeke and Odell helped Justin finish papering around the cook stove part of the room—the lower part. Then they papered the upper part, all around the room. Laurel felt, at last, that she and the children had a haven from the cold, and she could turn loose of her anger. They still spent much of their waking hours in the drafty mess hall, but the knowledge that there was some place where they could get warm appeased her.

When she brought the other women to feel the difference in her shack, and urged them to do the same, everybody else got to work on what Bulldog called "a paperin' and cardboardin' binge." It made for a more contented community, and fewer colds.

She gradually adjusted to winter in a logging camp. Things no longer seemed out of control, no longer totally overwhelming. Then she smiled at her thoughts. The creeks and springs were frozen over. They had to break the ice to get water. On a rocky bank near the spring, icicles hung as tall as a man and as big around. Snow and ice encased the camp. They now washed, only what they had to, indoors. Clotheslines were strung behind the cook stove in all their shacks and the mess hall.

In spite of all this, her natural optimism returned. Winter was not going to win. They weren't just eking out a miserable existence. They were making a living and helping to provide a living for others. They were saving to buy a home. Three children were learning to read, write and do arithmetic. And she had returned to Justin's embrace.

Everyone was relieved—even Bess—when Laurel, in Bess's words, started up with "her everlastin' ideas" again. This time she wanted quilting frames put up in the mess hall, hung down from the rafters over one of the tables. They could roll them up during the meals.

"Let's try to do four quilts this winter. One for each family here," she said. When they drew straws to see whose would be first, Bess's straw was longest. Happy as a child with a present, she asked Hannah to go to town with her to pick out quilting material to do the Dresden Plate pattern. The quilting was a social time, which took them for awhile each day off the endless treadmill of work.

Thad and Jesse still played out in the coldest weather. Sometimes, when Hannah made them come in, they would practice their whittling or try to play a game of checkers. But Jonah had defected from her tomboy role. She and Sarah played dolls and had tea parties. Laurel made each of them a doll bed out of shoe boxes, with some squares for blankets, and they played house for days in the corner of the room. When Thad and Jesse teased them, Hannah ran them off.

Then there was their schoolwork. With a little time each day, Laurel kept them going in reading, writing and arithmetic, and she always gave them homework. They all were improving. Sarah was learning her ABC's from just being there. Laurel used some of the white newsprint for art paper, asking the children to draw their ABC's, then decorate around them, or write from one to one hundred, or as far as they wanted to count. She tacked their work on the wall.

Adam was a busy one-and-a-half year old, getting into everything and in everybody's way. He loved to run under the quilt, push it up with his head and wait for someone to thump him on the head with a thimble. He was developing a stubborn, show-off streak. Laurel thought she knew why. The men picked at him and laughed at everything he did. When the crew was around, he was always riding on somebody's shoulders.

And Tommy was everybody's baby. The women took turns cuddling him. "Do you think he's gonna know who his mama is?" Alice fretted to Tom one evening. As Tom watched him nurse with gusto, he replied, "Ain't much danger in him gettin' that mixed up. Little pig knows who gives him his dinner."

So their first logging camp winter spent its full measure of the year and grudgingly bowed to spring. April was glorious! Dogwoods dotted the new green of the woods and birdsong floated on the air. Everybody felt new life rising in them to match the sap rising in the trees. One night at supper Laurel said, "I read something last night that describes April. I think you'll like it." She read, "For, lo, the winter is past; the rain is over and gone; the flowers appear on the earth; the time of the singing of birds is come, and the voice of the turtle is heard in the land."

"Who wrote that?" Abe asked. "Somebody from the mountains, I bet."

"No, it's from the Song of Solomon in the Bible," Laurel said.

"Is he that wise man?" Dirk asked.

"Sounds like he was wise enough to appreciate his surroundings," Justin observed.

Laurel and Bess made Easter dresses for Sarah and Jonah. Bess was becoming quite a seamstress, keeping her new sewing machine busy. She offered to sew most of Sarah's dress along with Jonah's.

On Easter morning when the girls put on their new dresses and new white sandals, everyone bragged about how pretty they were. The boys weren't left out. Uncomfortable and awkward in new clothes, complete with parted and slicked down hair, they sure didn't want to be told how pretty they were.

All the women in camp except Bess were now going to church with Laurel and the children. They helped her with her Sunday school class when she needed them. Today, after church, they would have an egg hunt and a picnic. Jonah was becoming a wonderful helper. She was always by Laurel's side.

Chapter Seventeen

Summer presented herself almost suddenly and moved on in a hurry. The crew was pleased with its output and the women had honed their cooking skills to record time. Horseshoe and baseball games were back. The hard winter made everyone appreciate these days.

The first Sunday in July dawned without a cloud in the sky. Laurel was looking forward to church. Justin had Tattoo and the wagon ready, and she knew the women and children would be around soon. Jonah was supposed to recite the books of the New Testament today to the whole church. She had already done the Old Testament. Laurel had just finished dressing Sarah and Adam and she was starting to change her own clothes when they heard Bulldog call, "Justin, Laurel!"

Justin went to the door and Bulldog said, "Can Laurel come quick? Jonah's real sick. We don't know what's the matter with her."

Laurel left the children with Justin and went with Bulldog. When she entered their shack, the mess disgusted her and the smell of the open slop jar almost made her gag.

Bess looked scared but didn't say a word. Laurel asked, "How long has she been sick?

"She ain't wanted to do much for two or three days. Said her throat was sore."

Jonah's breathing was raspy. Laurel laid her hand on her forehead. She was burning with fever.

Laurel said, "Joanie, I'm sorry you're sick. We're going to try to make you feel better." Jonah's eyes lit up briefly when she realized Laurel was there.

Laurel thought it might be pneumonia until she saw Jonah's swollen neck.

Her fingers traced the swelling and her heart gave a lurch. She whispered, "Oh, no! No! Bull Neck!" It was one of the symptoms of diphtheria.

When she had finished examining Jonah, she asked Bess and Bulldog to go outside with her. Her face told them it was bad before she spoke.

"I believe Joanie has diphtheria. I've seen it before."

"I don't believe you!" Bess's voice rose angrily. "You're not a doctor! Bull, I want a doctor to come!"

"Be quiet, Bess! Jonah will hear you!" His tone didn't encourage argument.

He turned to Laurel. "What should we do?"

"I think we need a doctor, too. I'll write down her symptoms and you need to ask Jed or Justin to go for him as soon as possible. Bess, do you have a paper and pencil?"

Bess, scared and sullen, went inside and brought out Jonah's lined school tablet and a stubby pencil.

"First, I need to wash my hands good with soap," Laurel said. "Both of you need to, also."

Bulldog brought her the wash pan with water, soap, and a towel. The towel was so dirty Laurel dried her hands on her skirt. Then she sat down on a log and wrote for a few minutes. Bulldog went inside to stay with Jonah but Bess watched Laurel intently as if she were performing a mystical ritual. When Laurel finished she asked Bess to get Bulldog.

"You both need to hear this. Diphtheria is very contagious. That means it's catching. We all have been exposed to it, so we can't get close to anybody else or they might catch it from us. I'll stay here until…until she gets better."

Neither of them spoke, so she went on. "Bulldog, you go only as far as the branch over there and leave the note on the ground. Call Jed to come and get it." Her voice trailed off in uncertainty and she was quiet for a moment.

"No," she said suddenly. "I'm afraid to send a note. Nobody should touch anything from this house."

They looked at her with dread as she continued.

"Let's do it this way. Bulldog, you go to the branch and call Jed. Warn him not to come close because we think Joanie has diphtheria. Ask him to go get Justin. I'll tell him her symptoms and have him go for the doctor."

Her voice got quiet as she added. "And tell Jed to ask Nora to go...take care of Sarah and Adam."

As Bulldog turned away, Laurel fought the urge to run...away from this sullen, ignorant woman...away from the filth and smell of the shack...away from Joanie...away from...death. She could ask Justin to bring her a complete set of clothes. She could bathe carefully outside the shack, burn the clothes she had on and...go home to Justin and the children. Bess and Bulldog would just have to take care of Jonah. She had to think about her own children. She could just leave...but Jonah would die.

She walked away from the shack – and Bess – into the woods. Pictures flashed through her mind. Jonah climbing trees, playing with her doll and tea set, eagerly learning to read, doing extra school work to please Laurel. Just last week she had shyly brought Laurel some violets pressed in her tablet when she came for her lessons. No, of course she couldn't leave her.

As she entered the shack, Bess was sitting at the table looking at Jonah. The stench of the place hit Laurel again. It made her angry.

"Get up, Bess," she ordered, "and empty that...that slop jar. Then put some water on the stove. We need to clean up this shack."

Bess bristled. "You ain't got no right to order me around in my own place!"

Laurel glanced across at Jonah, then said quietly, "We have to work together to try to save Joanie's life. Cleaning up is part of it. Now, please, take that slop jar out and empty it in the outhouse."

Bess turned reluctantly and did as she was told.

Bulldog appeared at the door. "Justin's here, waitin' across the branch like you said."

When Laurel saw him, she fought the impulse to run to him. They looked at each other across the space. They didn't need words to communicate their fears.

Laurel took a deep breath and got right to the point. "Did Jed tell you I think she has diphtheria?"

"Are you sure? Couldn't it be something else?"

"I'm almost certain. You need to go for Dr. Leighton. He should come as soon as possible." She told him Jonah's symptoms.

"I'll have to stay here, Justin. If I come home I might bring it with me to you and the children."

"I know. Nora is going to stay with the children. She and Hannah will take care of things."

"Justin, watch the children closely. If one of them starts feeling bad I want to know."

"I think our children will be all right. They haven't lived like Jonah's had to live." After a moment he added, "How long do you think you'll have to stay?"

"Til she gets better and isn't contagious…or else…."

"Laurel, will you please be careful?"

She shook her head. "Yes, I will. And I almost forgot: ask Hannah to send us some lye soap. One of the boys can leave it on that stump. Bess and I are going to clean up and wash everything."

That information seemed to improve Justin's spirits. He grinned and shook his head. "I see I don't need to worry about you. But I might need to worry about Bess."

She laughed with him as he turned to go for the doctor.

Bess was putting a kettle of water on the cook stove when Laurel came back in. Bulldog was sitting by Jonah's cot, looking helpless.

"Bess, do you have a clean glass? I'm going to see if she can swallow a little water. Then I'll need some warm water and soap and a clean cloth."

Bess brought a glass of water and followed Laurel over to Jonah's cot. Laurel put one hand under Jonah's head and raised it slightly. Jonah swallowed one sip but the second sip caused a coughing fit that racked her whole body.

After she was still again, Laurel said, "We're going to bathe you and change your bed. Maybe that will make you feel better."

The only response Jonah made was to open her eyes briefly and close them again.

Laurel asked Bess for some clean sheets and a clean gown, then turned to Bulldog.

"Could you build a fire outside and heat some water in your tin tub? We need to wash these sheets and the clothes all of you are wearing. Hannah is sending some lye soap."

213

Bulldog nodded, took a worried look at Jonah, and went out. Bess and Laurel worked together silently, bathing Jonah and changing her bed.

Laurel was thinking as they worked. She had never seen Bess show any tenderness or sign of affection for Jonah. She had only seen criticism and neglect. She wanted so much for Jonah to feel something from her mother so she said, "Bess, why don't you comb her hair."

Bess crossed the room, picked up a dirty comb and thrust it at Laurel. "*You* comb it!" Her tone left no doubt as to who was giving orders this time.

As Laurel combed Jonah's hair she remembered the first time she had seen her peeking through long dirty bangs…how shy she had been…the lessons they had started…Jonah's eagerness and intelligence gradually overcoming her shyness.

The teacher part of Laurel had been challenged and intrigued to see what she could do with a child like this. Now, as she watched Jonah struggle to breathe, she realized her pity and curiosity had somehow, somewhere turned to love.

She loved this child.

She impulsively reached out and rubbed the problem bangs back from Jonah's forehead.

"I love you, Joanie. I'm so proud of the way you're learning to read and write. And you're really good at arithmetic."

Jonah opened her eyes, looked intently at Laurel and reached out her hand. Laurel took it and Jonah closed her eyes again.

Bess had watched this exchange. A soft, yearning expression touched her face briefly. Then, suddenly, she turned and went out the door.

After a few moments Jonah's breathing became more regular and Laurel knew she was asleep. Laurel gently withdrew her hand, washed her hands thoroughly with soap and went outside.

Bulldog had a good fire going under the tub and was filling it up with water. Bess was helping him. Laurel saw at once that Bess had been crying.

"She's asleep," Laurel said. "Maybe it won't be long 'til the doctor gets here." They looked at her as she continued. "There are several things we need to do for protection. First, let's clean up the shack, including washing and scalding all the dishes, and sweeping and scrubbing the floors. We'll wash the bed clothes in lye soap."

Bess started to interrupt but Bulldog said, "Be quiet, Bess."

"After we've got everything clean, we'll bathe and put on clean clothes. Last, we'll wash these clothes we have on. Our best defense is to keep everything and ourselves as clean as possible. We need to wash our hands with soap each time after we have touched Joanie."

Bulldog said, "I'll wash the clothes while you work in the shack. I know you need to be with Jonah." Bess picked up the bucket and went to the spring for more water.

Laurel was putting another stick of wood on the fire when she heard Hannah call her from across the branch by the stump. "I decided to bring this lye soap myself and see how Jonah is."

Laurel went a little closer so they could talk. "She's real sick, Hannah. I'm anxious for the doctor to get here."

"Jed said you had to stay here. I don't want you worryin' none about your children or the cookin'. Nora is takin' care of the children, and me and Alice'll do the cookin'."

Laurel felt the tightness inside her begin to unwind. Hannah, with her common sense and kindness, always had this effect on her. She felt tears sting the back of her eyes.

"I'm glad you're my friend, Hannah."

Hannah smiled and echoed, "And I'm glad you're mine"

"You and Nora and Alice need to watch all the children to see if they start feeling bad. I've been trying to figure out how long it's been since they played with Joanie. She's not been to the mess hall for two or three days. I asked about her every day and Bess always said she had a cold. Do you remember before that?"

"She's not been outside playin' for awhile. It rained several days last week and I don't remember her and the boys playin' together durin' that time."

"She missed her lessons…I don't believe our children have been exposed."

"We'll keep a real good watch on all of 'em."

"Hannah, have Nora send me a complete change of clothes."

As Bess emptied another bucket of water into the tub, Hannah called to her. "Bess, I'm sorry Jonah's sick."

Bess answered. "She's real bad, Hannah."

Laurel knew Bess would feel freer to talk to Hannah if she left, so she took the bucket and went to the spring.

"Hannah," Bess blurted out, "you know about me. You know I ain't fit to be a mother. And now I've let Jonah git diphtheria and I'm afraid she's goin' to die."

"Bess, anybody can get diphtheria no matter who their mother is."

"I ain't never knowed how to treat her like you and *her* treat your children." She nodded her head in the direction Laurel had gone.

Hannah knew this was true but she said, "Jonah's been happy here, Bess. She loves her doll and tea set but she still loves to play in the woods. And she's real smart in her school work."

"That's because of *her!* Jonah loves her."

"Jonah loves you, too, Bess. And I know you love her. And, Bess, if you really want what's best for Jonah, listen to Laurel. Work with her, not against her."

Bulldog came out the door. He called, "Bess, Jonah's wakin' up!"

Hannah said, "I'll be back this afternoon and bring some supper. I'm cookin' enough for you'ns, too."

Bess said, "Thank you, Hannah." She hurried inside. Bulldog walked a little nearer to Hannah. "Jonah's awful sick. It hurts me to look at her."

"I'm terrible sorry, Bulldog. I'm thankful Laurel is here."

"Yes. Maybe Jonah will have a chance with her here."

"I'm goin' to leave the lye soap on this stump. Laurel sent for it. And now I need to git back before the beans burn."

After Hannah's visit they all felt a little better. Bulldog put the dirty bedclothes in the tub. Bess and Laurel started cleaning the shack, with Laurel stopping every few minutes to check on Jonah or to comfort her. After Laurel washed a dishpan full of dirty dishes, she poured scalding rinse water over them. She saw Bess watching her and said, "This boiling water kills the germs, Bess. We need to do this every time we eat."

Bess said grudgingly, "It ain't right for you to have to clean up my shack. If you'll sit down, I'll do it."

It was one of the first civil things Bess had ever said to her. She replied carefully, "Since I'll be here awhile I'd rather be busy. We'll have to work together to try to get Joanie well again."

They had just finished scrubbing the rough wooden floor when Bulldog came to the door and said Justin was back. They all went to the branch to talk to him.

His news was not good. "Dr. Leighton can't come. There are several cases of diphtheria in town. When I told him Jonah's symptoms, he said he was sure it's diphtheria. I told him what you are doing, Laurel, and he said you're doing the right things. He said for all of you to stay quarantined. He also said for you to tie a cloth over your nose and mouth when you're working close to Jonah. He thinks the germs are air-borne and this will give you more protection."

They all looked at Laurel, expecting a reply. Her disappointment and fear kept her silent for a moment. Then, taking a deep breath, she said to Bulldog and Bess, "Well, I guess it's up to us."

Justin spoke again, "I'm going to check on the children and Nora. Please, be careful. And, Laurel, try to get some rest when you can. I'll be back after while ."

Now that they knew the worst, all three were quiet. Laurel checked Jonah while they watched her. After a time she went over and talked to them in a low voice, telling them some things to expect and how to deal with it.

"One of the dangers is choking to death on what she coughs up. We'll need to take turns staying close by her bed. And she may have spasms if she gets worse."

"I'll sit with her awhile," Bess said hesitantly.

"I'll go check on the clothes," Bulldog said. "Why don't you rest awhile like Justin said?"

"Bess and I need to take a bath and wash the clothes we have on. Then we'll take turns resting." For the first time, they were functioning as a team and were settled into a routine.

The next morning they all knew Jonah was worse but didn't want to say it aloud. Laurel noticed Bess touching Jonah more and speaking to her gently. She hoped Jonah was able to understand it was her mother.

After they had finished their breakfast, Bulldog said, "I've got to get out and clear my head. I'm goin' over to look at our next section of trees to log.

It'll take me about two or three hours. Will that be okay?"

Bess and Laurel both nodded to him. "Go on, Bull," Bess said, "You'll be like a caged animal if you stay in here all day. We'll take care of her."

"Just stay away from everybody," Laurel added.

After he left, they rubbed Jonah with alcohol again to try to get her fever down. When they finished Bess said suddenly, "If she dies it'll be my fault."

"No, Bess. Diphtheria can strike anybody."

"Yeah…but it'll be my punishment. I always knowed I'd git punished."

"What do you mean?"

"Can Jonah hear us if we talk over there across the room?"

"No, she won't hear us."

They sat down in two straight-back chairs.

Bess spoke quietly but with urgency. "I ain't never told nobody this but I've got to tell somebody. I ain't treated you right, but you've loved Jonah anyway. And I think you'll be fair even when you know the worst. I…I guess I want you to understand why I am the way I am."

Laurel was still as Bess closed her eyes as if to think how to start. Then she began slowly. "My mama died when I was fourteen. She hadn't been right for a long time. My daddy beat her so much when he was drunk I think it touched her mind. She just give up, I reckon. Not long after she died, my daddy was drunk and he come to my bed and…and forced hisself on me. After that he'd come regular, just like I was his wife. I couldn't fight him off. If I tried he'd hit me with his fist 'til I was still. I couldn't git away from him."

Bess's voice was without emotion and that made the horror more real. Laurel knew that the tears had stopped for Bess a long time ago. Laurel sat without moving or scarcely breathing as the words poured out.

"When I was sixteen I run off with the first man who looked at me. I knowed if I stayed I would kill my daddy. I had already loaded the shotgun twice and then was too scared."

"The man I left with was a drunk, too. He beat me and it was like my daddy all over again. I figured I was ruint anyway, so I left him and went to the red light district."

She looked beyond Laurel as if seeing it all again.

"I had been there about a year when I met Bulldog. He was one of my customers, but he was different. I liked him and I knew he liked me. One day out of the blue he said, "Bess, when are you goin' to marry me and git away from this here place?"

A smile lit up her face. "I couldn't believe it! He actually wanted to marry me! I told him 'no,' that he would always remember what I was and would throw it up to me. He said 'no,' he wouldn't ever mention it to me and never wanted me to mention it to him. And he ain't never shamed me about it to this day."

Water started to boil out of the spout of the teakettle and sizzle on the stove. Bess got up and moved it to the cool side of the stove.

"But there's a deep, deep shame down inside of me because of what my daddy done to me. It's all mixed up with hate. I wish I could take a knife and cut it out, then maybe I could be more like…like…Hannah…or you."

The only sound in the shack was Jonah's struggle to breathe. Both women looked over at her.

Laurel spoke slowly, "Bess, I'm so sorry." She wasn't even aware that tears were rolling down her cheeks. "You've started getting rid of that shame and hate and anger by telling me. You couldn't help what your daddy did to you, Bess. It wasn't your fault. You were only a child."

"If Jonah dies, I think it will be God punishin' me for…for what I've done."

"Oh, no, Bess, no! God is not like that! He doesn't punish people for something they can't help. I believe it was God who sent Bulldog to take you out of that kind of life."

Bess was wide-eyed. "You do?"

"Yes, I do!"

"But I ain't nothin' to God. Why would he help me out?"

"You *are* something to him. He loves you just as much as he loves the most important person in the world, no matter what you've done."

"How do you know that?" Bess challenged.

"I've been taught that all my life. It's in the Bible."

"Well, I ain't never heard it before. Does he love me as much as he loves you?"

"Of course he does! And I believe he feels more tender toward a person who needs him more, like we feel toward a child who especially needs us."

Bess's eyes showed a fleeting hope, then Jonah started coughing and they both went to her. After she settled down again Bess said, "You won't tell nobody what I told you about my daddy?"

"No. I won't even tell Justin, Bess. I promise."

"Can we talk some more about that other stuff…that's in the Bible?"

"Yes. We'll talk whenever you want to."

They heard someone calling. Laurel opened the door and saw Justin standing across the branch. The sight of him chased away the ugliness and horror of what she had just heard. It was as if she had awakened from a nightmare and found all was well. Justin represented decency and security and true love of a man for a woman. She wanted to run to him and feel his arms around her.

"How's Jonah this morning?" he asked as she came a little closer.

"She's worse. I don't know anything else to do for her."

"I'm sorry, Honey. Did you get any sleep last night?"

"Not much. I tried, but she needed help all through the night. How are our children?"

"They're fine. They miss you, but you know how happy they are with Nora." Then he added, "Hannah and Alice will do the cooking this week."

"You didn't go out with the men this morning?"

"No. Jed will take care of things on the job today. I was afraid you might need me. Besides, there're plenty of things around camp to be done."

"I'm glad you'll be close."

"How are Bess and Bulldog taking this?"

"Bulldog had to get out this morning. Said he was going to look over your next section of trees to log."

"Good…and Bess?"

"Bess is helping take care of Joanie. She's…we're…talking."

Justin raised his eyebrows. He had been worried about Laurel having to deal with Bess while trying to save Jonah's life.

"Get out of the shack some, Honey, and get some fresh air. And promise me you'll try to rest some."

"I promise. Please tell the children I'll be home soon, and give them a hug and kiss for me."

She turned to go, then turned back and said, "Justin, I love you!"

"I know." His smile was tender. "I love you, too, and I'm proud of you!"

After she and Bess bathed and changed Jonah, Laurel slept awhile then insisted that Bess sleep. They struggled through three more days and nights, fighting for Jonah's life, knowing she was getting worse.

The whole camp revolved around the little shack. Justin, Hannah, Nora, or Alice came to the branch regularly to check on things and to bring food.

One night Laurel heard voices. Across the branch some of the logging crew were seated talking quietly around a campfire.

"Bulldog, what are they doing?"

"They've decided they're going to take shifts stayin' close by in case we need them. Somebody will be there all night from now on. They told me they had seen Justin's lantern comin' back and forth the last two nights. So, he's been out there at night."

This news brought the tears Laurel had felt close to the surface for two days.

"Bulldog, we're not going to be able to save her. She's too far gone."

"I know. Bess knows, too… But it ain't your fault. You've fought hard to save her."

Laurel's soft crying brought Bess over from Jonah's bed. "You're plumb wore out," she said softly. "Go lay down and sleep awhile. We'll call you if there's a change."

Laurel did as she was told. Bess went back to Jonah's side. And Bulldog sat wondering about the change in Bess.

For the rest of Laurel's life, the smell of a campfire and the call of an owl would remind her of the night Jonah died. Bess and Bulldog slept while Laurel took her turn beside Jonah's cot. It was not an easy task. Besides her painful effort to breathe, Jonah had developed the diphtheria stare that sometimes occurred in the last stages. Laurel knew she could not close her eyes because her eyelids were paralyzed. She also knew Jonah was unconscious, but the stare was disconcerting.

Around four o'clock Laurel realized Jonah's pulse was steadily weakening. She called Bulldog and Bess because she knew it couldn't be much longer. They were around her as she breathed her final breath.

"She's gone," Laurel said. "Her suffering is over."

Laurel worked quickly to close Jonah's eyes. She asked Bulldog to lay some coins on them while she held them closed. She ran a cloth under

Jonah's chin, pulled it tight, and tied it on top of her head to keep her mouth closed. Then she covered her face with a sheet.

"I'm sorry," she said. "I wanted her to live. She was so eager to learn."

It was Bess who comforted her. "You done everything in your power to save her. Maybe if I had told you sooner that she was sick…." She stopped, her eyes filling with tears.

Bulldog said, "No, Bess. It ain't your fault either. Diphtheria usually kills people no matter what you do. And, now, I'll tell the men across the branch."

As Bulldog approached the group of men around the campfire, Justin stood up and went toward the branch.

"She's gone, Justin. Our little girl's gone."

"I'm sorry, Bulldog. I'm as sorry as I can be."

The men gathered around Justin. They removed their caps and twisted them in their hands as they murmured their sympathy, feeling helpless and awkward.

"She suffered awful. I'm glad she ain't sufferin' no more."

"There's not many people who survive diphtheria, even with good care," Justin said.

"She had good care," Bulldog said. "Laurel seen to that."

"Are they okay? Bess and Laurel, I mean."

"Yes. They're really tuckered, but they ain't sick."

"Could you ask Laurel to come out and speak to me a minute? Then we'll talk again about burial arrangements."

When Laurel came out to talk to Justin the men sat back down around the campfire and left them to talk privately. Justin could tell by her halting manner that she was totally exhausted.

"I'm so sorry, Honey. You did everything possible to save her."

"I'm numb right now, Justin. I don't feel anything except relief that she's through her suffering. It was bad."

"I know it must have been. Will you be able to rest awhile?"

"Yes. I know I have to rest a little while."

"The men and I will build the coffin and dig the grave. I'll work out the details with Bulldog."

"She needs to be buried today. Somebody should go to see Dr. Leighton and ask him to sign a death certificate. The time of death was about four fifteen. Bess said she would like Mr. Stevens, the preacher, to say a few words at her graveside."

"We'll take care of it. When you wake up we'll finish making plans. Now, go rest!"

She turned and went back inside the shack.

Laurel's memories of the rest of that day were mercifully blurred. Her chief concern was to give Jonah a decent Christian burial without exposing the whole camp to diphtheria. Justin and the men followed her instructions.

The men brought the pine coffin and set it in the yard on some logs, then left. Laurel, Bess, and Bulldog put a quilt in the bottom, dressed Jonah in her Easter dress and wrapped her body in another quilt and placed her inside the coffin. They each dealt with their own private emotions as Bulldog nailed the top securely on the coffin. The waiting men carried the coffin and put it on the wagon. Tattoo would take Jonah's body to be buried in the graveyard behind their little church.

Bulldog, Bess, and Laurel, after bathing carefully and putting on clean clothes, rode on the wagon with Jonah. Everyone else kept their distance. They did not come close, even at the graveside. Not even Justin. Laurel would take no chances.

The preacher's words were appropriate and comforting. Something he said made Laurel reach and take Bess's hand and whisper, "I hope there are trees to climb in heaven. Joanie loved them so."

Bess and Bulldog looked at her with questioning eyes that gradually softened. Bulldog noticed that Bess held on to Laurel's hand for the rest of the service.

Laurel told Justin she felt it would be safe for her to come home the next day. She was afraid today would be too soon.

When they returned from the burial, they burned the straw mattress from Jonah's cot, put all bedclothes and clothes they had worn in the tub and boiled them, using lye soap. They aired the shack and scrubbed the floors.

They were too exhausted for heavy conversation so they talked about everyday things. Bulldog even talked some about logging. Hannah brought them a good supper.

The next morning Laurel shampooed, bathed and put on clean clothes that Justin brought her. She left her other clothes for Bess to wash. Only then did she feel safe enough to go back to Justin and the children.

Justin waited for her as she hugged Bess and said quietly, "We'll talk some more when you're ready."

Tears came to Bess's eyes. She hugged Laurel, swallowed and nodded her head, unable to speak.

Bulldog shook Laurel's hand. "Thank you for…for everything you've done."

"You're welcome. You and Bess will be okay. You're both strong people."

Laurel's homecoming was a celebration. The children were delighted to have their mama home. Nora hugged Laurel fiercely. "I'm so glad you're home with your family again."

"Thank you, Nora. I didn't worry one minute about my children because I know how happy they are with you."

"And I'm happy with them. Now you rest some today and just enjoy being home. I've done cooked dinner."

"She baked a cake," said Sarah. "The kind you like."

"Your one-egg cake with orange flavoring," Nora said as she went out the door.

Laurel, Justin, and the children savored the feeling of being a family again. The children played close by, never getting far from her side, while she and Justin talked. Then she listened carefully to their tales about how Nora played with them.

That night after they went to bed she did talk some about Jonah. Then she surprised Justin. "Bess asked me today if I would teach her to read and write. She never went to school."

Justin started to object. She already had too many things to do, but he didn't say a word. He pulled her closer and listened for her breathing to tell him she was asleep. Just before sleep claimed him, he thought, *I'm blessed. I'm married to a good woman.*

The camp folks reeled for a time under the shock of Jonah's death. They had somehow grown to feel insulated from the problems of the rest of the world. But death had found one of them. Sarah was confused and cried for Jonah. Thad and Jesse seemed angry and scared.

Bulldog and Bess picked up their lives the day after the funeral, keeping to their regular schedule. When Justin objected, they insisted this was the best way for them. The change in Bess was dramatic. Her attitude toward Laurel had moved from hate to love. No in-between. Her eagerness to be near Laurel was almost too big a switch for Laurel to take. Laurel needed her own space to grieve but Bess always seemed to be in it. She even started going to church with Laurel. She wanted to hear more about this God that Laurel talked about.

Jonah's death had left Laurel disoriented and angry. Her grief contained the frustration of unfinished plans, of interrupted dreams.... If Jonah had changed so much in one year, what could she have accomplished in a lifetime? Laurel grieved over what might have been. She railed inwardly against the dreadful finality. Jonah wouldn't be coming through the door for her lessons. She wouldn't be shadowing Laurel to help, to seek approval and a hug.

"God," she breathed repeatedly, as she hung out clothes or washed dishes, "how could you do this to her…to us? Why?"

One Sunday morning as they were driving to church several weeks after Jonah's death, Bess said, "Bulldog wants us to meet him at Joanie's grave after church." She could barely conceal her excitement. Laurel had noticed Bess saying "Joanie" recently instead of "Jonah," but didn't want to comment on it.

As they approached the cemetery now she saw a long, thin rectangular rock with a rounded top standing upright at the head of the grave. Bulldog was waiting. Bess stepped beside him and they watched as Laurel went closer. Chiseled on the homemade tombstone were the words: JOANIE AIKEN. Below were the dates: 1912-1921

Laurel traced the crude etching with the tips of her fingers, hesitantly…lovingly.

In a low voice, she said, "You let her be Joanie."

Bess stepped forward, her tears flowing, too. "She became Joanie. You helped her be Joanie. We're proud of how smart she was."

Bulldog stood, twisting his cap in his hands.

"How – and when – did you do this?" Laurel asked.

"You know I can't read nor write, so I asked Justin to help me. He printed her name and the dates on a piece of paper and I copied it. I worked on it at night." He stopped and swallowed. "It was somethin' I could do for her."

Laurel put an arm around each of them. They stood in silence, bound in their love and grief for a little girl, forever named Joanie.

One Friday, a few weeks after Joanie's death, Justin brought a letter from Papa with exciting news. He was coming to visit! Laurel's joy was tempered with her desire to make everything look as good as it could. She flew into cleaning the shack. She pulled the dirty cardboard off the floor and scrubbed the wood. She polished the cook stove and her furniture. Her childlike excitement was contagious and the women helped clean the mess hall. The crew helped Justin clean the clearing. Everybody instinctively wanted to make a good impression on Laurel's papa.

Justin, Laurel and the children met him at the train depot. Laurel hugged him, stood back and looked him over and hugged him again. She finally allowed him to greet Justin and the children.

He was interested in everybody and everything. Laurel was made aware again of his rare ability to focus, with genuine interest, on the person he was talking with, drawing him or her out, making everyone feel important. The crew and the women in camp were soon under his spell, calling him "Professor" as Justin did. And, after he told a ghost story one night, Thad and Jesse asked him to teach them their lessons. He challenged them to memorize their multiplication tables through the fives while he was there. They worked at them so diligently, Hannah and Laurel were surprised. When Laurel commented on it, Papa said, "This is between us men." Thad and Jesse gave her a superior grin. They had a secret. The professor had promised each of them a harmonica as a reward.

Sarah took charge of Papa every chance she got, to take a walk or even have a tea party. Adam climbed on him every time he sat down. Papa let him listen to his watch tick, and opened it to let him see the tiny wheels turning.

But the professor was the learner the day he spent with the crew on the job. That night at supper he said, "It's a good thing I'm not a logger. I couldn't do what you men are doing. I'd get killed or kill somebody. I hope you realize you are experts doing a difficult and dangerous job. I wish some of the people I work with could see your teamwork." The crew enjoyed the compliments. He made them feel like kids with A's on their report cards.

He and Justin enjoyed their usual stimulating exchange over politics and national events. The highlight of his trip, however, was the day he and Laurel climbed up the mountainside to her aerie to enjoy some private time together. After his gratifying response to the view, they settled down with their backs against two birch trees and looked at each other.

"So what do you think of our way of life?" she asked.

He smiled. "I see you still know how to get straight to the point."

"Well…?"

"It's hard. But you've adapted. In fact, you've more than adapted. Life here is inevitably pressing you into its mold. But you're pressing right back. You're pressing this life into your mold."

She studied him seriously. "Tell me what you see."

"You can't escape the primitive conditions and the isolation, but you and Justin are bringing a higher quality of life to these people than they've ever known…cleanliness, nutritional meals, a properly set table with manners observed…education for the children… help with family sicknesses…even sewing and quilting…And, then there's church. They wouldn't be in church without you.

"And these men are absorbing more than logging skills from Justin…self respect, respect for each other…a genuine concern for each other…a comradeship. Justin seems to be in his element with this group of men. They recognize him as boss, yet he's one of them. This ease and ability must come from those early years he spent in a logging camp."

"Papa, you always help me with the big picture. I'm usually too busy or too tired to see anything but segments."

"You have reason to be tired. You work many hours in the mess hall. Then you have to keep up with the other parts of your life."

"It took my body awhile to adjust to the constant, hard work. My mind still objects that my total being is used up – consumed – doing the same mundane things over and over."

He could offer no solution and knew she wasn't asking for sympathy. He said, "Talk to me about Joanie."

"Yes. I need you to help me. I'm in a quagmire, mental and emotional, over her death. She was very important to me, Papa. I came to love her. Every new achievement of hers was a fulfillment for me. I wanted so much for her, and she had taken my challenge and was running with it."

Laurel toyed with two acorns, putting their caps on and off as she sought words to communicate. "And, now, Joanie's gone, with all my dreams for her. I think part of my grief and anger is for that lost purpose and fulfillment. So I'm grieving for myself, too. Is that selfish?"

"Grief always has a selfish element. But it's perfectly human and healthy. That is, if we work through it and learn from it and go on. That's what you're doing."

She looked at him, soaking up his words like parched ground soaks up the rain.

"Now," he said, "tell me the rest of it." He sat perfectly still, listening, absorbing willing her to go on, to voice it all, drawing it from her.

The words slowly emerged, picking their way carefully through her mental roadblocks and confusion. Painful. Very personal. But the listener was Papa. Personal was safe with him.

"I think I had worked it out in my mind that Joanie was one of the main reasons I was in this camp. Perhaps, she was God's purpose for me here. If I could snatch her from the clutches of ignorance and poverty, my time of drudgery would be redeemed. Something of lasting value would be achieved. But now both – she and my purpose – are dead. Buried."

He still didn't move. Laurel's eyes, unseeing, scanned the horizon as she asked, "What do you do when life thrusts you back on the treadmill with your lofty purpose gone? What do you do when a dream dies, leaving you with a vague, hovering dread?"

She looked at him, wanting an answer, wanting him to fix it as he had when she was a child. But his words brought them back to the present and gave it back to her to fix.

"You need to identify your dread – your fear – and name it. Once you name it, you can figure out what to do about it. To name it is to gain power over it."

She realized the simplicity and profoundness of his answer. She sat awhile turning it over in her mind before she moved. Then she looked at him and smiled.

"Of course! That's sensible. Otherwise, the fear has the upper hand."

As they got to their feet, Laurel laughed. "And, as usual, sir, you've given me my homework!"

He was serious for a moment. "You're going through a hard time, but you'll come out of it with the right answers. My daughter is a strong lady!"

On the train going home, Papa was not so philosophical. His erect posture belied the slumped spirit within him. Laurel's primitive living conditions and the regimen of never-ending work appalled him. Laurel, his most capable and dynamic daughter, was working as a drudge. How long could her creativity and vitality survive in these conditions? He felt a rush of anger toward Justin. Could he not see what a price Laurel was paying?

Laurel, meanwhile, had followed Papa's advice. She had summoned enough courage to look the nameless dread in the face and put words to it. "Is this the beginning of death to who I really am, if I continue to live in a logging camp?"

Chapter Eighteen

Two years to the day of Joanie's death, Worth Logging Camp moved. Not toward civilization; further away from it. Beck Lumber Company had extended the logging railroad several miles further into Pisgah Forest into a tract of virgin hardwood timber where Justin and Jed had estimated an unusually high figure of board feet. Their production should be better than average. Many of the trees were five feet or more in diameter.

Their shack, this time, had wheels. It was built on a flatbed railroad car, extending several feet wider and longer than the standard rail coach. The whole community – four shacks, the mess hall and bunkhouse – were in a line on the track. They would be hooked up as soon as everyone was moved in. Their destination was a switchback section of railroad, built especially to accommodate the camp. It was a good idea. When this tract of timber was cut, the train would simply hook onto the flatbeds with the shacks aboard and pull them to the new location. This eliminated the necessity of building a whole new camp every year or two.

Laurel now stood for the last time in the shack that had been her home for more than three years. She had just directed the careful handling of her three glass windows. They were going into the new shack.

She couldn't do her usual amount of work during this move because she was heavily pregnant. She figured her baby was due in about six weeks. With Sarah six and Adam just turned four, it was past time for a new baby. She had realized last December that she was pregnant when she awoke one morning and the smell of coffee made her nauseous. After the first few weeks of adjustment, however, she was one of those few fortunate women who actually felt more energized and happier during pregnancy. The other women watched her with a mixture of confusion and concern. Bess finally summed up their feelings. "You know she's happiest when she's workin' on a project. Well, she's workin' on a good one now."

A smile tugged at Laurel's lips as she thought about how everybody tried to take care of her. If she happened to mention she would like a certain food, Hannah somehow got it. One afternoon Laurel said, "I'm going to ask Justin to catch some rainbow trout. I can already taste them"

The next day at supper a pan of trout was waiting for her, fried golden brown. Zeke and Odell had gone fishing. She ate four.

Another day it was rabbit. Abe heard that she liked fried rabbit with gravy and biscuits. He took a detour on his way in from work and bagged two young rabbits. And so it went. Nora wouldn't let her lift. Alice, who remembered how tired she was when she was pregnant, kept telling her to rest. Bess was the prime mover this time in getting maternity dresses made and in getting everybody working on baby clothes again. She even made a soft pad and a fancy ruffled cover to line and hang over Sarah's old box.

"I'm bettin' on a girl," Bess explained, as if reading Laurel's mind. "But, if it ain't, I'll make another one."

Justin appeared at the door and called her back from her reminiscing to the task at hand. "You coming, Honey? We're ready to move out."

The switchback, with the logging camp now on it, was built on a large, flat, meadow-like area with a small creek running through it. Laurel stood facing the line of buildings on the tracks, taking in her surroundings. Behind the camp and across the regular logging railroad which ran almost parallel to the switchback, a bare granite-like rock face towered straight up at least two hundred feet. The steep wooded inclines on each side of it and a few hardy gnarled pine trees on top softened the starkness. She stood staring. It was permanence, durability, security, stability. She liked it.

She turned to look at the mountain across the meadow, the one facing camp. Its tree-covered gradual incline was a friendly contrast to the monolith behind camp. This was a mountain she could climb. Her eyes were then drawn to the railroad. It disappeared both ways into the woods along a divide, a gap, through the inflexible, insistent rises on each side. She wondered how much further the rails cut into this ageless, ever-new, ever-bearing, awesome land. Was the railroad like a wound? And how did the mountains feel as the trees were removed? She shook her head to clear away her whimsies, caressed her rounded stomach, and turned practical again.

The meadow in front of their shacks was thickly covered with small bushes. The crew set to work. The men organized into teams and in two days they had cleared the meadow from the shacks to the creek, leaving a mossy, grass like covering. They built two outhouses with the promise of two more; set up the wash place and the spring boxes; and got a good start on the barn. They also built steps higher than usual for each building on a flatbed. Zeke and Odell put in Laurel's glass windows.

The women worked just as hard at their tasks and felt gratified when the crew trouped off to work on the third morning on schedule. They were working close enough to come in for lunch, so the women were plunged into their original routine again.

Laurel was aware on some level that this move signified major changes in their life style. The railroad – and the climax engine – was their umbilical cord to the outside world. No wagon roads nor beaten horse trails existed this far into the forest. She was sure Justin would soon change the status of the horse trails. However, as far as these problems were concerned right now, she felt the lassitude of a woman whose entire being was currently consumed with getting ready to deliver a new life. Her focus was primal and instinctive.

They had been in the new camp a month when her time came. It was just dark when Justin, with light from the full moon, rode hard for Dr. Leighton, stopping by on his way to send Mrs. Stevens. Rev. Stevens, a veteran woodsman, would bring her. Hannah was with Laurel. He hated to leave her during labor, but he was the only one who knew the trail. He would guide the doctor here.

Dr. Leighton followed him. Even by the light of the moon, it seemed to the doctor they were lost most of the time. But Justin, keeping them at a fast pace, seemed sure of his direction.

He heard the doctor mumbling once and yelled, "What did you say?"

"I said I don't understand why you have to live out of civilization!"

Justin grinned at the doctor's tone and well spaced words. He was used to the reaction.

"It grows on you," he called back

Mrs. Stevens and Hannah had things ready when Justin and the doctor arrived about midnight. Bulldog and Tom met them and took the two horses for a rubdown. After Justin checked on Laurel and was assured she was progressing normally, he checked on Sarah and Adam. Nora had them in Hannah's shack, asleep. Bess and Alice were there. Everybody was waiting. When he got to the mess hall, the whole crew, it seemed, was there, plus Rev. Stevens. They were glad to see him.

"We've had some anxious minutes wonderin' if you'd get the doctor lost, since it's dark," Jed said.

"Tattoo wouldn't allow that," Justin answered. He was touched by their concern. "Got any coffee?"

Zeke brought him a cup and a couple of pieces of gingerbread. His stomach felt a little better after he ate and drank, but nothing could help his anxiety until….

"Anybody plannin' to get any sleep?" he asked, looking around the room. They all kept talking or playing cards or checkers.

"Don't look like it," Abe answered.

His fear and misery drove him out the door again. Jed laid down his hand of cards and said, "Tom, take over. I'll go keep him company."

Justin was standing with his hands in his pockets, looking at the shack, listening, willing it to be over. Jed walked up and stood beside him.

"Were you scared sick when Hannah had your boys?" Justin's voice was tired.

"Scared out of my wits…and guilty for puttin' her through it."

"Yeah, that, too," Justin said.

After a few moments of companionable silence, Jed asked, "How did you find your way in the dark without a trail?"

"I've ridden in and out several times so I have some landmarks and a sort of a trail by now. I'm just glad the moon's full or I would've needed a lantern. Almost did a couple of times, anyway."

"You made good time."

"The doc didn't waste any time starting, and Tattoo seemed to know his way. I believe he could've brought the doctor without me."

Jed knew better. Justin had an almost unerring sense of direction in the woods.

"Well, if I'm ever lost in these mountains, be sure you come with Tattoo to find me."

Laurel gave birth to a girl just as dawn streaked the sky. Justin now sat by her bed, washing her face and rubbing her hair back from her forehead. The smell of sweat and blood still lingered around them. Hannah laid the warm bundle of life in his arms and followed Dr. Leighton and Mrs. Stevens out the door toward the mess hall.

While Laurel dozed in the tranquil state her body and mind demanded after her travail, Justin examined his daughter, perfection in miniature. Gratitude and happiness rose in him and sought expression.

At a sound like a sob, Laurel opened her eyes. He said, "I'm so relieved you both are okay. And she's beautiful! Thank you, Darling."

Laurel looked at him a long time. She said gently, "I didn't do it by myself, Justin. You need to thank God." Then she was asleep again. He felt like a pin had pricked his balloon. Of course, he couldn't thank God. They weren't on speaking terms.

The camp drew a collective breath. An air of festivity leavened their preparations for work. After a hearty breakfast of bacon, eggs, sawmill gravy, biscuits and coffee, Dr. Leighton said, "I see why you men are ready to get going. You have to work off all this food these cooks stuff you with."

"This is a lumberjack breakfast," Abe said. "Real food."

"So real I might fall off my horse, asleep, before I get home," the doctor replied. He and the Stevenses said their goodbyes. If Rev. Stevens would lead him as far as his place, the doc could make it on in. The preacher, like Justin, didn't fear getting lost.

They named the baby Madeleine Caroline. Sarah, all of six years, immediately claimed her. Bess, to everyone's surprise, gave Sarah serious competition. Adam, who at four dogged Thad's and Jesse's footsteps, followed their lead and showed only fleeting moments of interest.

Justin's weekly news report was all about President Warren G. Harding's death. He had become ill while on a speaking tour and had died in Seattle, after a bout with pneumonia. Vice President Calvin Coolidge was sworn in to finish the term.

Caroline was a good baby and Laurel was soon back to her normal routine, carrying her fair share of the work. It was a demanding time. A new baby, with all the accompanying joys, siphoned off a major amount of her energy. Night feedings, diapers to change, stomach upsets…Adam's and Sarah's needs…and Justin's…she felt like she was a machine with no cut-off switch. She fell into bed, woke for the feeding, and woke with Justin shaking her to get up and go again. The women, concerned, tried to get her to rest some, but she stubbornly refused to let them coddle her. She would do her part, especially since Alice was pregnant again and not doing well.

However, when her weight loss was apparent, her eyes showed a dazed, even hurt look, and she began, in small ways, to neglect her appearance, Hannah went to Justin. Together, they told her she had to cut back her hours for a few weeks. The other women in camp would take up the slack. She was glad to be told what to do. She no longer felt capable of making a decision.

She rested more and slowly regained her energy. With time, she began to feel in control again, but the unbidden awareness of their isolation crept upon her slowly. There were no wagon roads. She couldn't hitch up the wagon and go to town. Their only way, in or out, was on the logging train during its regular run on workdays. She hadn't gone often, but the knowledge she couldn't go perversely made her think of many reasons why she needed to go. She even wished she could go spend the day with Mrs. Sargent.

There was no church. The train didn't run on Sundays except to bring in the crew late Sunday afternoon. All the women and children missed church; with Bess being the most vocal about it. The children missed their Sunday school class. They were all out-of-pocket on Sunday morning.

There was no school. And Sarah, her firstborn, was of school age. She was more than ready for first grade. She knew her ABC's and could count to one hundred. She should have started in August, two months ago. Laurel probed the hurt within herself as one would probe a tooth that was aching. She knew she had agreed to teach Sarah at home one more year, but the necessity to do so, to deprive her of a normal school experience, festered into resentment against Justin.

However, Justin had never been happier. These were the best and biggest trees and production was the best ever. His obvious pleasure grated against her efforts to cope with this isolated, unreasonable lifestyle. He was bothered by her distance from him, but he put it down to the demands of a new baby.

One day in October, when Caroline was a little more than two months old, Laurel, on impulse, decided to walk the railroad tracks that led further into the mountains. The trees had donned their extravagant autumn wardrobe. She loved to be in the middle of it.

Around a few bends from camp, she came upon a trestle. Surprised, she ventured out a few steps and peered down into a deep gorge. She walked on, her knees weak, knowing the crossties were too close for her to fall through. Yet, the fear was there. It wasn't far across and she was relieved to set foot on solid ground again. She kept walking, stepping on the crossties. Her next surprise was a boxcar, all closed up, pulled off the mainline onto a small switchback. She walked around it, wondering what it was for.

After a while she found a spot of afternoon sun and sat down on a log. It was time to examine her problems with isolation and see what could be done. A person could only ruminate on a problem so long. She was not going to be like a cow chewing its cud any longer. The thought of the cow regurgitating and re-chewing its food made her shudder, but that's what she had been doing mentally.

So, what could she change and what would she need to accept? "God," she said softly, "give me the wisdom to know the difference." It was the same prayer she had prayed when initiated into logging camp living, three and one-half years ago.

The dirt was soft and sandy under her feet. She picked up a stick and absently drew two straight columns. She put a plus sign at the top of one and a minus sign at the top of the other. Next, under the plus sign, she printed "Town". She would figure out a way to go to town, on the train and on Tattoo. She would work out the details with Justin.

Next, "Church". She couldn't change the facts about church. Five women and six children, one an infant, couldn't ride horses through the woods four of five miles to church, then back. Hesitantly, she printed "Church" under the minus sign. She had to accept that for now, but it rankled.

School was next. She couldn't get Sarah to school but she could bring the school to Sarah. She would compromise this year, teaching Sarah the first grade curriculum and then later seeing about entering her into second grade next August. Somehow, Sarah would go to a regular school next August. She printed "School" under the plus sign. Two out of three wasn't bad.

That night Justin sensed a change in her before she started talking. "I saw that boxcar across the trestle today. What's it for?"

"It's empty. It'll stay there for whatever we might need it for. Why?"

"I just wondered…and, Justin …"

"Yes?"

"I want to know how I can get to town when I need to—on the train and on Tattoo. Tell me about the train first."

"The train doesn't have a regular schedule except Friday evening and Sunday evening when the crew leaves and returns. The rest of the time it goes when it has a full load of logs and returns as soon as they're unloaded."

"So if I wanted to go?"

"You'd need to tell the loading crew. They could send for you when the train is almost loaded. Once you get to town, you have to wait 'til the train is ready to return. Usually several hours. Sometimes all day."

"Sounds frustrating."

"Well, it's not a passenger train."

"How about me riding to town on Tattoo?"

"It's a long way with no marked trail. I'd be afraid you'd get lost."

"You could ride with me a couple of times and even mark a trail for me."

"I still don't want you to do it, Laurel. Most of the crew would hesitate to try to find their way out on horseback."

She stood in defiance. "Justin, I'm not going to be a prisoner here, not to distance or to fear or to you!"

His voice was low, but charged with anger. "I didn't know you felt like a prisoner!"

"Of course, you wouldn't know! You come and go as you please! And you think this is normal or above normal! No roads! No church! No school! No civilization!"

He stood. "Laurel, on Saturday we'll ride the horses to town and back. You make plans about the children. Next week, plan to go one day on the train. I'll speak to the loaders. You'll have to work out the cooking schedule."

He got up and went out, closing the door quietly behind him.

She hated it when they had a fight, but, if that's what it took, so be it. She hadn't been out of camp—out of this blasted forest—for almost six months. And winter was ahead.

The next day she boiled some cow's milk and tried to tease Caroline into taking a little out of a bottle. At first the baby refused, pushing the strange nipple out with her tongue. After a couple of days and several tries, however, she clamped down and took the milk. Bess was happy when Laurel let her give a bottle to Caroline. She crooned, "Now we can get rid of your mama sometimes and you can be *my* baby." That suited Laurel just fine. She would plan to give Caroline an occasional bottle from now on, so she could leave her for a few hours.

On Saturday, with some last minute misgivings about leaving the baby, she and Justin rode out of camp about mid-morning. Coolness still lay between them. It was a glorious day, however, not one to waste on pettiness toward each other. And he took his job seriously. He had asked for some white strips of rags and he had a small bundle of poles tied beside his saddle.

She followed him on Tattoo. He was a good guide, showing her landmarks, making her listen for the river even when she couldn't see it, leading her for a long while beside a high bank which ran like a shelf just higher than their heads. He tied cloths on limbs, and every time they changed direction he put up a pole with a cloth on it, explaining that this turned east or west or north or south.

When she asked how he knew that, he explained. "There are always signs. See how the moss grows on one side of the trees? That's the north side where the sun doesn't reach. Moss grows better without sun."

After she looked for moss awhile, she said, "So, if that's north, we must be riding west."

"Good! Now, look at the tree branches. They grow thicker and larger on the south side. We'll watch for them as we go. Right now look at the tops of those pines. Do you see they are leaning to one side?" She looked straight up and saw what he meant.

"Yes."

"They lean toward the rising of the sun. So, if you're ever lost there are some signs. I'll show you some more later."

238

She warmed toward him. How could she not? His knowledge and intentness and attention and charm—and the glory of October—all worked to enchant her.

"This is fun, Justin. I feel like a kid skipping school."

"And I'm happy to have some time alone with you."

In Deerbrook they ate lunch at the Central Hotel. It was wonderful to have a good meal she hadn't prepared, in nice surroundings, with Justin at his charming best. They enjoyed some leisurely talk time without the children or crew. Neither wanted to get up and go do what they came to town to do. Finally, she went shopping while he checked with Sam on his photography and took care of some business.

She felt hesitant and disoriented in the stores at first. Then she got going. She bought herself underwear and two gowns, two everyday blouses and material for two work skirts. She found fabric to make Sarah some dresses and Adam some shirts. They were outgrowing everything. Then she turned to other not-so-essential purchases.

Justin laughed when he saw her packages and her face. "Good thing we've got saddlebags or we might have to buy a sled." He stuffed the four saddlebags full and helped her into the saddle.

When they arrived at the edge of the forest, he pulled back and said, "You lead us home." She hesitated, then tugged at Tattoo's reins, guiding him onto the narrow, almost concealed trail. They rode awhile single-file, Laurel feeling clever, until she drew Tattoo up short in a small clearing, having no idea where to go from here. Justin hadn't marked this place. He had run out of white strips of cloth. He now waited for her to choose.

"It all looks the same to me, Justin."

"Look closely and try to find some sign of the way we came this morning."

She knew how serious this was if she wanted some freedom to come and go, so she slipped off Tattoo and walked around, looking at the ground. Finally, she found some leaves and twigs that looked as if they had been disturbed by horse hooves.

"I believe this is it."

"Good! Any other clues? Listen."

"The river!" she said. "It's on our right, where it's supposed to be on our way back."

239

And so it went, all the way back to camp. She was touched by his serious urging to notice this and that, but was ready for the lessons to be over well before they got back to camp. She wouldn't tell Justin but she knew she would have been hopelessly lost without the white strips of cloth. Justin knew, of course, and was determined it would be a long while, if ever, before he turned her loose in these woods.

She was refreshed in spirit, if tired in body, when they arrived. Caroline was asleep. Bess reported, "She took her bottle fine and talked to me awhile before she went back to sleep. Said she'd be my baby any time."

Laurel hugged Bess. Maybe Caroline was easing the empty spot in Bess's heart.

Then, in a party atmosphere, she and Justin gave the children the toys they had brought. Sarah got paper dolls and her own special pair of scissors. Adam was hypnotized by a bright colored spinning top. Tommy's red rubber ball, soon bouncing all over the place, almost ended up in the stew. Thad and Jesse eagerly fingered the hooks and line Justin had brought them. They had become serious fishermen and couldn't wait to tease those trout.

Then she surprised the women. For each of them she had a bottle of lotion and a bar of scented, feminine soap. They set up a hubbub, as excited as the children, smelling all the fragrances.

"Goodbye, Octagon Soap," Bess said. "I'll be smellin' so good Bull will have to open up the windows."

For the next two weeks, the women sewed in all their spare moments. Laurel had not realized how much she needed new work clothes. Her others had become faded and stained. She felt more like herself in the fresh, new skirts and blouses. Then came the children's clothes. When Sarah tried on her new dress, she rubbed her hands over it, delighted, and said, "I'll wear this to church."

Perhaps her look and longing planted the seed for Laurel's next inspiration. The following Monday morning at the washtub, the idea came to her full-blown. She was so startled by it, she stopped scrubbing Justin's shirt, and just stood there, looking into the distance. Nora, who was using the battling stick on Justin's pants, stopped, too, and looked at Laurel.

"Nora, we're going to have church."

"Where?"

"There's a boxcar across a trestle just around a few bends in that direction." She pointed. "It's just been sitting there waiting for us. It's going to be our church."

With that pronouncement, she fell to washing with such vigor, Nora shook her head and smiled. Laurel sure kept things stirred up. And a hubbub it was that night when Laurel brought it up at supper. "Justin, could we have church in that empty boxcar?"

"Church?" Justin questioned, as if he hadn't heard right.

"Church?" Several voices echoed his.

"Yes." She had their attention. "With a little work it would make a good church. Some benches and a set of steps."

"Who's goin' to be the preacher?" Nora asked. She'd been wondering that since this morning at the wash place.

"We can get a circuit rider to come about once a month. Rev. Stevens will help us find one. The other Sundays, I'll teach Sunday school to...to whoever wants to come."

The women and children were excited. Even Thad and Jesse looked pleased. They enjoyed Mrs. Worth's stories.

Dirk broke the men's silence. "First, outhouses. Then school. Now a church. We might get us a courthouse next." Everybody laughed and shifted around, talking.

Abe spoke. "I ain't here on Sundays but I think it's awful good of Laurel to offer to teach Sunday school. It'll take a good bit of her time. If I'm ever here on Sunday, can I come?"

"Yes," Laurel answered solemnly. "Everybody will be invited." She could have hugged Abe.

"Justin?" she prompted.

"We would have to do some work. This church business is a little different from the other things you men have helped build. If you don't want...."

Zeke, shy Zeke, interrupted. "But we do want!"

Jed got Justin off the hook. "Tomorrow we'll open it up and see how many benches and how long they need to be." He looked at Laurel. "I think we can have it ready by Sunday."

"Thank you," she said. "It'll make life seem more normal to have church."

But getting to church on Sunday was more challenging than Laurel had anticipated. The boxcar was ready, cleaned up, with steps and rough benches in place. Abe had even built a stand for her, or the preacher, to use to lay a Bible or book on. The women and children, dressed in their Sunday best, left the camp together. The four men, content that they had pleased the women, sat drinking coffee and talking in the mess hall. Sunday was a day of rest when the demands of life were suspended.

The trestle brought the happy pilgrimage to a halt. They all had been to the trestle that week. Laurel, Bess, and Hannah had crossed it several times. Thad and Jesse had been shooed off it several times.

It was Nora who balked. When they came to the edge, Nora bowed up like a mule. "I…I can't!" Alice lined up beside her. "I'm scared, too." No amount of prodding would budge them.

Laurel said, "Thad, go get the men." At their look of alarm, she explained. "I just realized we need them to help us carry the children across. We'll go on and start. If you want them to, they'll walk you across, but you decide."

So the tranquil morning for the men came to a quick end. Soon the children were squealing with half-scared delight as they were carried across "the railroad in the sky," as Sarah called it. Adam rode on Bulldog's shoulders, Sarah on Jed's, Tommy on Tom's. Thad and Jesse skipped across, showing off for the younger children. Justin carried Caroline, the precious bundle small enough to fall through.

Before she started across, Laurel said quietly to Nora and Alice, "Take your time, but try to come on. You both are too brave to let a trestle stop you."

The men deposited their cargo on the other side and started back to help the two scared women. "Be patient with them," Laurel instructed.

Justin's reasoning and humor won them over. He held on to Nora's arm and Tom held on to Alice as they stepped out. When Nora stumbled, Justin saw that her eyes were tightly closed. He laughed. "Nora, open your eyes. Look! See how close the ties are. You can't fall through."

Alice was mechanically matching her steps to Tom's. Slowly, they made their way across the chasm. They both sat down suddenly on the solid ground on the other side. "My knees are like jelly," Nora said. "They have to firm up before I can take another step."

"You both did fine," Justin said. "I'm proud of you."

"Yeah," Tom added. "Everybody's a little afraid of a trestle. It ain't natural to see all that space under your feet."

"We'll be back after church to help everybody get home. Send Thad and Jesse for us when you're ready."

The two women nodded miserably. They had to go back across! But they refused to think about that now. After a little while, they got up and headed toward the boxcar.

Laurel wanted church to be church. Not just playing at it because it was just them and in a makeshift building. She looked at the windowless, solid rough box that enclosed them. The huge door stood open a few inches for light and air – cold as it was. Two lanterns helped give light.

They sang a few well known choruses. Then the women and children gave their full attention as she skillfully told how Jesus walked among the people meeting their needs, healing, feeding, loving them, giving them purpose.

Tommy squirmed and moved around the benches and Caroline, in Bess's lap, made baby noises, but nobody noticed them. For a little while on Sunday morning the women were transported out of their daily grind, elevated beyond survival to inspiration, even purpose. And the children, through good stories, were learning values that would be with them through life. Laurel knew this instinctively and it was like flowers blooming in the garden of her soul.

Chapter Nineteen

Autumn's flamboyance turned quickly to winter's stark beauty. Frost, wind and rain worked together efficiently to accomplish the task. The exposed lay of the land, with the undergrowth gone, and the pattern of barren dark limbs against the crisp, blue sky was satisfying to Laurel. When she explained this to Justin, he said, "They say it takes a real lover of the mountains to see their beauty in winter. Most people only see the deadness and barrenness of the trees."

"But they're not dead and barren at all!" She was definite. "They are resting and receiving and waiting."

He looked at her for a suspended moment, then gathered her in a tight embrace. "I've never heard it said better." He was smiling.

But anybody should see that, she thought, *mountain lover or not*.

Darkness came earlier now and Justin was caught in it one night on his way home from Deerbrook. Hog killing time had come and gone. He had taken time to ride out to a farm and pick up a ham a farmer had promised him to pay for some pictures Justin had taken of his family. Now he was drawing on his and Tattoo's instincts to wind his way through the forest. The moon was hidden tonight by clouds, peeping out only occasionally. The white rag strips he had hung for Laurel helped guide him a few times. The ham rode behind the saddle, wrapped in curing spices and cheesecloth, then some newspaper and twine, and finally in a burlap sack which he had tied to the saddle. It smelled rank and strong.

When he first realized Tattoo was nervous, he put it down to his own anxiety about finding his way. Tattoo was sensitive to his moods. But when they entered a particularly dense patch of woods with large overhanging branches, Tattoo lifted his head and shook it from side to side. A shudder passed through him as if he were trying to control his fear. Justin understood as clearly as if Tattoo had spoken.

Something was stalking them, a natural enemy, something big enough to spook Tattoo. Justin leaned over and rubbed Tattoo's shoulders and neck, speaking softly, "I understand, Boy. It must be a cat. I haven't heard a sound." He kept talking to Tattoo while he felt in his saddlebag for his thirty-eight. He transferred it to his pocket. Tattoo was suddenly moving too fast for the terrain. Limbs pulled at Justin and scratched his face. One large, low limb slammed into his forehead and jerked his head back. For a moment he was stunned, then they cleared the density and were running close beside the river. He leaned low in the saddle, keeping one hand moving on Tattoo's neck. At least they weren't lost. He knew where they were and what was ahead.

"Tattoo, we're coming up on that stretch by that high bank. That's where he'll try to jump us."

He tensed as the bank loomed beside them. He took the pistol in his right hand, and pressed his legs into Tattoo's ribs. Tattoo tore up ground.

The panther was air borne before Justin saw it. Tattoo veered and rammed sideways into the bank as Justin flattened himself. An overhang spoiled the big cat's aim and he sailed over them. Justin felt a hind paw graze his back. He shot his pistol into the air. The tawny cat left country in one direction as they took the other. It was a wild ride. No doubt now that Tattoo knew his way home. He barely touched ground getting there.

The crew was still in the mess hall when they heard Justin ride up at a fast gallop. Something was wrong. They stood up almost as a unit.

When Jed opened the door with Laurel behind him, Justin was off Tattoo, talking to him, rubbing the sweat off the horse's face with his handkerchief. "Good boy, Tattoo! Good boy! We outmaneuvered him!"

He turned and Laurel gasped. His forehead glistened red in the light that spilled out of the mess hall door. Streaks of blood crisscrossed his cheeks. Dirt sprinkled his hair and was caked on his right side from shoulder to toe. She ran to him as the crew poured out the door.

"You're hurt," Laurel said, pushing his hair off his forehead. "What happened?"

245

"A panther stalked us and jumped us."

"Did he scratch your face?"

"No. He didn't get that close. Tattoo was too smart for him."

"Then why is your face so scratched and bloody?"

He felt of his face and looked at the blood on his hand as if puzzled for a moment. "Oh! That was limbs. I couldn't dodge all the limbs." The crew could picture the chase and attack.

Justin turned back to the horse. "I need to rub Tattoo down and put a blanket on him. He's lathered and winded."

Bulldog took Tattoo's reins. "I'll take care of Tattoo. You go get rubbed down yourself. You're lathered and winded, and bloodied to boot."

Tattoo's breathing was easing and the wild look was leaving his eyes. Justin pulled his head down and rubbed his forehead. "You're one smart horse. Thank you! Now go get some rest." He turned to go with Laurel.

Bulldog saw the sack behind the saddle, untied it and handed it to Abe. As he led Tattoo toward the barn, he called back. "Don't tell your story 'til I get back."

They all smiled at that and went into the mess hall. Hannah had already cleaned up the wash pan and filled it with hot water. She sent Thad to their shack for some ointment.

The crew went back to their supper and Justin obediently sat down by the stove to let Laurel clean up his face. He had just become aware of how bad it was stinging. And there was a throbbing pain between his eyes.

Laurel knew he didn't want to be fussed over in front of the crew, so she was the nurse instead of the wife. She combed the dirt out of his hair and wiped it off his right shoulder before starting on his face.

"Something took the skin off your forehead, and a blue bruise is forming."

"It was a big limb."

She held a warm cloth on his cheeks to absorb the blood. "These scratches aren't deep, but they'll scab over. I'm going to put some ointment all over your face. You'll feel greasy."

"It already feels better. Some of the stinging has stopped."

When she had finished, she couldn't be calm and collected any longer. As she looked at his torn face with concern, he closed his right eye in a flirting, mischievous wink. She smiled back. He was still in there under all the dirt and scratches and bruises.

"Do you think you can eat?"

"Of course. It's your country steak and gravy."

Bulldog came back in and everybody waited for him and Justin to finish eating. Then Abe said, "Tell us about it."

Justin knew they loved a good story, so he spun it out, describing the darkness and how he was so intent on finding his way he missed Tattoo's first messages.

"Tattoo told me more than once that something was stalking us, but I didn't pick up on it."

"And," Dirk interrupted, "was Tattoo speaking English when he told you?"

The crew grinned. They kept continual jokes running about how Justin thought Tattoo was human.

"No," Justin said, grinning. "He was speaking Horse. But I usually understand Horse and he understands English, so we get along."

"And...?" Abe prompted.

So, Justin told them the rest. "That was the biggest cat I've ever seen. He must have been hungry to take on a horse and rider. He was after the ham." He looked around. "By the way, where is it?"

"Is that what's smelling funny in that toe sack?" Jed asked, nodding toward the bundle by the door.

"Sure is. Somebody paid me a picture debt with a ham. We'll let it cure awhile longer and one fine day these ladies will cook it, complete with red eye gravy and biscuits and grits."

"Why didn't you just throw him the ham?" someone asked.

"After all that hard work I did for it? I couldn't let him win that easy."

The crew knew that was true. To Justin a scuffed up face was a reasonable price to pay for winning.

"Let's watch out for the kids and livestock, and each other, for a few days," he warned as he turned to Bulldog.

"Was Tattoo okay when you left him?"

"Yeah. I rubbed him down and put a blanket over him. Gave him just a little water. He has a scratch on his left haunch – not deep, but I put some carbolic acid on it."

"Thanks. I'll go check him out. He may have saved my life tonight."

Jed got up. Justin would take care of Tattoo and Jed would watch after Justin. "I'll bring him home in a little while, Laurel."

She nodded as they went out the door. She thought, *That man and his horse.*

That night in bed, Justin admitted his fear to Laurel. "I didn't know when he might jump us."

"Tell me about the bank again where he did jump you."

"It had an overhang – a perfect shelter – right there, just as he jumped."

She was quiet. She knew God had protected him. And he knew what she was thinking. But neither put words to it. She held him close 'til his body went slack with sleep.

The panther attack brought a halt to Laurel's plans for riding to town on Tattoo. About a month later, she took the logging train to Deerbrook. She enjoyed her time, but it turned out to be a very long day. When she got home, she realized the trip had cost too high a price to happen often. Caroline rebelled against too many bottles, Laurel's breasts ached with too much milk, and the cooking schedule was upset.

So, her flare of rebellion against isolation fizzled and she stomped out the embers. Right now she had no time to *be*. She only had time to *do*, but she would change that as she could. She made a deliberate choice to enjoy her children. A baby was a baby for such a short while.

This time their shacks were fortified against the cold beforehand. Everybody knew her expectations and met them. Nora, Justin, Zeke and Odell helped her paste the newspapers on the walls and tack down cardboard on the floor of her shack. Her glass windows extended her emotional living space, inviting the outside in. The front window looked out over the meadow and the friendly mountain beyond that beckoned Laurel now more than in summer. She would enjoy climbing that slope for her quiet times. The back window faced the sheer rock face which she found comforting. It represented boundaries and security. The bedroom window faced the solid end of the mess hall which was lined up on the track next to them, but it still let in daylight. It was a cozy burrow set in the midst of the harsh beauty surrounding them.

One Sunday morning about a month after they started meeting for church, Laurel pushed the boxcar door open and stepped inside to feel the comfort of warm air embracing her. Confused, she looked and found a small black heater in the back right corner. A stovepipe, with an elbow, stuck through a neat round hole cut in the side of the boxcar near the roof. She took this in with a glance and turned to Justin who had followed her in, helping with the children.

"Who ...?"

"All of us. Jed, Bulldog, Tom, and me. We figured if our women and children were determined to meet here even in the cold, we'd better get some heat for you."

Everybody else came trouping in, excited over the warmth and the light. A lantern was placed in each of the four corners. The dark, windowless interior was well lit.

"We ordered the stove the first week," Bulldog said, "but it just come in a few days ago." The four men were hugged and thanked and told they were clever. They had totally surprised their families and made them happy.

After that first fearsome winter, Laurel never allowed the cold and privation to control her again. She now understood her need for emotional survival and worked hard to meet it. Was she learning the lessons of the mountains? That winter was a time of slowing down, burrowing, absorbing, waiting....

Teaching Sarah first grade lessons was as good for her as for Sarah in spite of the time crunch. Sarah was a quick student and worked well independently. Thad and Jesse, at thirteen and eleven, were reading and doing simple arithmetic, but they had to be pushed. Laurel turned to Justin to motivate them in long multiplication and division. Bess was making progress in reading and writing. It had been slow at first, but Bess's humor and determination had kept Laurel going. She sent Justin, with a letter, to the county school office for some more readers, spellers, and arithmetic books, grades one through six.

The quilting frames went up again in the mess hall. This time Laurel asked for something she had wanted since she had first set foot in Hannah's shack nearly four years ago: a Stained Glass Window Quilt. As the quilt started coming together under five pairs of practiced fingers, Laurel felt as if she was preserving their personal history. She had gathered some memories in the form of clothing. The green velvet skirt she had worn the night she met Justin; the gray coat from Justin's wedding suit; Sarah's red wool coat with a black velvet collar; Adam's first long pants of brown wool; Caroline's turquoise sacque of sateen which Madeleine had sent.

When Laurel asked Bess for something of Joanie's, Bess didn't question why she wanted to include Joanie in her family quilt. After looking at the other heavy material that was making up the quilt, she brought the only nice winter coat Joanie had ever owned. It was a cheerful red, green, and blue wool plaid.

"I can't take this, Bess. It's the only thing you have left except her red dress we made like Sarah's, and her overalls." They had buried her in her Easter dress.

"Yes, you will take it, too. This is so much better than it being hidden away in a drawer or trunk. You loved Joanie and when you see the quilt you will remember."

"She's right, Laurel," Nora said. "My quilt holds such dear memories of Mama and Daddy. Don't it, Hannah?"

"Yes. Every piece can bring back a story," Hannah answered.

Laurel, unconsciously holding the coat close to her with both hands, decided. "I'll take some material from the coat but you must keep some, Bess. We'll make you a quilt next. This way we can both have our memories."

Bess looked at her a moment, then enveloped her in a hug with the coat still between them. Tears glistened in the eyes of all the women, both for Joanie and for the miracle of the change in Bess.

When Alice's time to deliver came on a freezing February night, Laurel redeemed herself from her failure in being of any help with Tommy's birth. Nobody was available to help. Hannah and Mrs. Stevens both had flu. Dr. Leighton was delivering another baby. Laurel and Bess delivered a girl, without a great deal of fuss and bother. Alice named her Laurel Elizabeth, after her two best friends, Laurel and Bess. Telling Bulldog about it later, Bess said, "Bull, I ain't the same woman I was when I come here. I even have a beautiful baby girl named after me." Her eyes filled. "Who would'a thought it a few years ago?"

"You've been a good friend to Alice, Bess. I'm proud of you."

Later, when Justin asked Laurel if she had been scared during the delivery, she answered. "Yes. But I remembered my training and what Mrs. Stevens and Hannah did when Tommy was born. It was a challenge. I'm glad to know I can do it!"

Production on the logging job was good. The crew members had worked together enough winters now to know what to expect from each other. The train and railroad figured more prominently in their lives now, since they lived on the sidetrack. Because the current job was on the side of the camp toward Deerbrook, the camp was spared the loaded train rattling by daily almost close enough to their buildings to reach out and touch. That was yet to come. However, the Climax engine, with one or two flatcars attached, ran past the camp to the end of the line two or three times a week to, in Justin's words, keep the track and trestle seasoned out for safe usage in the future.

This event brought great excitement to brown-eyed, four year old Adam. The first time the women heard the whistle signaling the train was coming, they rushed out to make sure the children were off the tracks. When the engine clanged and clamored through camp, Adam jumped up and down yelling, "Train coming! Train coming!"

The engineer, Mr. Hayes, a grandfather with a head of white hair and a round figure like Santa Claus, put on the brakes. Hissing and protesting, the train stopped. Mr. Hayes leaned out the window, smiled and doffed his striped cap to the women.

"Howdy, Ma'am," he spoke to Laurel. "I need me a helper. Think that little one could ride on my knee to the end and back?"

"Adam," Laurel said, "he means you. Can you help him drive the train?"

Adam stood wide-eyed and speechless, but his eyes sparkled as he nodded his head. Laurel helped him climb up into the cab and Mr. Hayes pulled him onto his knee. He put his striped cap on Adam's head and said, "I'm shore glad to have me a helper." With a glance at Laurel, they pulled away.

That night at supper, Adam told his daddy about his adventure, emphasizing it with body motions. His excited voice carried over the other conversations and soon everybody was watching and listening. He even imitated the train whistle. After Adam settled down to eat, Abe said to Dirk, "Sounds like Adam may have that charmin' gift of gab like his daddy."

The train rides became a ritual. Mr. Hayes would blow his whistle to let them know he was coming. Sometimes Thad and Jesse would go, too. Sarah went a few times. Adam went almost every time. He never willingly missed a ride.

Chapter Twenty

In August, 1924, they celebrated Caroline's first birthday. Later that evening in their shack, Laurel voiced her maternal thoughts to Justin.

"Caroline has been a wonderful baby. Of course, she has so many mamas, she never gets the chance to fret. And Adam is all boy! He's five and he can't be still long enough to learn to count to ten, but he can help drive a train."

Justin laughed. "He'll learn to count soon enough. He's a smart boy."

Her voice rich with enthusiasm, Laurel continued, "And Sarah. I'm so glad she'll be starting school soon. I'm sure she's ready for second grade and I can't wait for her to be with some children her own age on a regular basis. I'm making her some school dresses."

"Laurel, I've been wanting to talk to you about her school. She's doing so well, I don't see why she needs to go to school. Couldn't you teach her for another year?"

Laurel went perfectly still. He wasn't even sure she was breathing as she stared at him.

"I didn't mean to knock the breath out of you," he said lightly. "It's the logical thing in our circumstances. By the time I take her to school and go back to get her in the afternoon, it'll really cut into my work schedule. It'll tie me down. My whole life will have to revolve around being at that schoolhouse twice a day."

Laurel heard him trying to talk his way out of a promise he had made to her a year ago. It seemed to be the first time he had counted the cost in practical, everyday terms. And he didn't want to pay the price. The betrayal swept through her, sucking out her enthusiasm and energy of a few moments before, leaving her in thrall to a sudden overwhelming weariness. She closed her eyes to shut out the sight of him.

Justin had expected a fight. He knew it was important to Laurel for Sarah to go to school. But it would cut into his work schedule, and it would be confining to be tied to that school house every day, when Laurel could teach Sarah as well or better than the teacher at school. He was perplexed by Laurel's reaction.

"Well, what do you think?" he asked.

She stood up. "I think I'll go to bed."

"So you aren't going to talk to me about it!"

"No," she answered flatly, "not tonight."

He sat awhile after she was in bed, wondering what next. For some unaccountable reason he was irritated with Laurel because she had not fought him on this. He didn't recognize it as guilt.

The next morning Laurel woke under the same cloud that had hovered last night. Disappointment, weariness, helplessness, disillusionment with Justin, all flew in her face like a swarm of gnats. She went about her work mechanically, quietly. She had no energy to be or do anything above the minimal because of the pain she was carrying. Everyone was aware that she was dealing with something important and respected her space.

In the afternoon of the second day, after working from four in the morning to two in the afternoon, she arranged for Nora to keep the children while she took a walk across the trestle to a secluded spot. She sat down on a root and leaned back on a rock, a makeshift, sunlit seat on the bank beside the railroad. She was back to her chronic dilemma. Should she accept this or try to change it? She breathed a prayer for wisdom and guidance.

Earlier that morning while she was peeling potatoes, she had suddenly tossed her head and swept her hand over her hair as if to brush away her plague of thoughts. She didn't like the direction in which they were carrying her. She wasn't helpless. She still had the ability to make a choice. With that ray of truth piercing her gloom, she had put her energy into seeking a solution rather than wallowing in self pity.

It was no longer a contest between her and Justin alone. Her child's future was involved. She faced with irony the fact that Sarah, Laurel Kingsley's daughter and Professor Hunter Kingsley's granddaughter, was being denied the right to go to school. She was being denied her birthright.

Laurel stood up. Her flame of purpose was ignited again. Now she must decide her course of action. She walked the track further into the forest, precisely matching her steps to the cross ties as she planned the steps she must take for Sarah to start school two weeks from today.

That night she told Justin she wanted to go into Deerbrook on the train the next day.

"Do you want to talk about what's bothering you?"

"No. Not yet."

The next day when she arrived in Deerbrook, she went straight to the county school office to talk to the superintendent, Mr. Mahaffey. He was surprised and pleased to see her. She was one of the best teachers he knew.

"What brings you to see me?" he asked, smiling. "I couldn't interest you in teaching this year, could I?"

"Do you have a position open?"

"I could have."

"What do you mean?"

"I still need a teacher for the Dodd School. I have someone coming in tomorrow to see about the position, but I haven't made any commitments. You know I would like to have you if I could get you out of that logging camp. I don't want to pry, but are you planning to move back to town?"

His respect and words were like a balm to her wounded spirit and a lifeline to her plans. She hesitated, then was talking to him easily. "We have to make some kind of decision. Sarah, our oldest, is seven. I have taught her first grade but I'm not willing for her to continue to miss going to school with other children. My husband could take her to the Westberry Elementary by horseback every morning and go back in the afternoon for her, or I could move to town with the children and teach this year and take her to school with me."

"I see. And your husband would remain in the logging camp?"

"Yes. He could be with us on weekends." She paused, then went on. "Could you hold this position for me until tomorrow afternoon? My husband and I will need to discuss it."

"Yes. Why don't we say day after tomorrow? That way I can talk with the woman who is coming and tell her the position might be taken. That will give you more time to work through your decision."

She left with the aura of his respect and esteem for her as a teacher clinging about her as a cloak. She felt she would need it for what lay ahead.

That night after the children were in bed, she said, "I'm ready to talk now about Sarah's schooling."

Justin laid down his book and looked at her. She got straight to the point.

"The way I see it, we have two choices. You could take Sarah to school and pick her up daily as we had agreed or I can move into town with the children and teach this year. I went to see Mr. Mahaffey today. I have a job if I want it at Dodd Elementary. That way I can take Sarah with me to school."

"And what about Adam and Caroline?"

"I'll get someone to keep them during the day. I may ask Nora to go with me."

"I see. And what about your responsibilities here?"

"You can hire a cook."

"And you think that's all you are here? A cook?" His tone was incredulous.

"Justin, don't!" Her voice rose then became matter-of-fact. "I trusted you and your promises about Sarah's school. No matter how much I give up of what is important to me, you want more! You expect me, Laurel Kingsley, to deny my daughter the right to go to school because it will tie you down. It will be inconvenient!"

She had never spoken to him in such a scathing tone. Her contempt cut him to the quick. He checked his impulse to retaliate and said, "I know you're angry."

"No! I'm beyond angry. I've lost some confidence and respect for my husband. You expect your family to pay a high price in order for you to do the work you choose. This time you raised the price above what I'm willing to pay!"

No man would have dared talk to him the way Laurel was talking. He struggled to keep control. He realized he had blurted out the easiest solution for him without thinking about its effect on Sarah or Laurel.

"I honestly didn't think it through. Of course, I'll take her to school. I'll work it out with the crew."

"And hate every minute of it, I'm sure!"

He rose as if in slow motion and looked at her squarely. A muscle jerked at the right corner of his mouth. He spoke slowly. "Laurel, I'm tired of you throwing up to me the fact that I'm keeping you from being who you really are! Who are you? Who do you want to be? You've done things in this logging camp nobody's ever done in one before. These people would die for you. They love you that much! Yet you constantly chafe under this life!"

He was quiet for a moment but his eyes showed confusion and misery. "I think you married the wrong man." He held his arms out, palms up. "This is who I am and what I do. I've carried guilt with me over ruining your life ever since we moved here. Yet, we have had all the things that really matter."

"Justin," she began....

"I'm not finished. I think it may be best, for you, if you do move to town with the children. I don't want that and I don't think it's best for the children. But, I repeat, I believe it may be best for you!"

She looked at him, stricken silent, as he continued, "You make the choice. I'll help you find a place and move you, if that's your desire. If you choose to stay, I'll take Sarah to school."

He turned his back, lit the lantern by the door and went out into the darkness.

Laurel sat still in the pool of lamplight. The wave of indignation that had carried her on its crest now dashed her back to shore. Justin's words were unfair. She hated the portrait he had drawn of her. She had worked hard to make his logging camp a success. She had no idea he saw her in the way he had just described. She felt more demeaned by his words than by anything that had happened to her in the logging camp. They hurt deeply. But she didn't have time to lick her wounds. She had a decision to make. Utterly weary, she realized tomorrow would have to suffice. She left the lamp burning and went to bed.

The next morning after breakfast she sent for Hannah. As they worked together, she told Hannah the problem and the choices. She didn't mention their quarrel.

Hannah asked, "Do you want to move back to Deerbrook for reasons other than Sarah's school?"

Laurel frowned slightly, thinking as she continued washing the breakfast dishes. "No. I don't think so. There's a part of me that is pulled toward teaching again and I'm naturally pleased to be offered a job. But I know the children would be unhappy without their daddy and the rest of you. Everybody here is like their family—mine, too. My home is here now, with all of you."

Hannah smiled. "I didn't want to say this before to try to influence you against your choice, but I can say it now. If you left us, you would take the heart right out of this camp. Justin is the head, but you're the heart." She stopped, her voice faltering, her eyes filling.

Laurel's hands went still in the dishwater. "What do you mean?"

"You keep us all going. Even Justin. Everybody knows it. I ain't sure what it is except we know you care about us." She wiped her eyes with the corner of the dishtowel. "You would do anything for us, but you won't let us get by with nothin'. Look what's happened to Bess. She keeps her house clean and she's learnin' to read. Nora believes she's somebody important because you treat her that way. You've taught the children and we have church...." Her words trailed off.

Laurel thought back to Justin's words the night before. '*And you think that's all you are here? A cook?*' And she had cut him off.

"Laurel," Hannah said softly, hesitating. "I think it's love. I think you love us and we love you."

Laurel threw her arms, soapsuds and all, around Hannah. They stood hugging for a moment. Then Laurel started laughing. "Lord, Hannah, I'm never going to get in an argument with you!"

Hannah laughed. "I meant every word I said."

"I know. Those were some of the kindest words anybody has ever spoken about me."

"And they're true."

As Laurel attacked the dishes again, she declared, "Well, Ma'am, since that decision is made, we can get on with our lives."

That night she asked Justin, "Are you sure you can work it out to take Sarah to school?"

"Yes. I told you I would."

"Then my choice is to stay here."

"Are you sure? I don't want you to stay against your will, just for my sake."

"I'm not staying just for you. This has been my home and the children's home for four years. These are my people now. I'm staying for them, too."

He was greatly relieved and knew he should be happy, but he felt like he had been diminished in her eyes. They both knew they should talk and work out an understanding, but the hurt they had inflicted on each other was a wall too high to be easily or quickly breached.

The next day she went back to Deerbrook to tell Mr. Mahaffey her decision.

"I'm disappointed but not surprised. You have a busy life in your forest community."

"Yes. I do."

"Haven't you been teaching the children in your camp? Seems like someone told me you or your husband came to pick up books all along."

"Yes. Three children and one adult. I wish I could teach the whole crew, but there's not time."

"So, your husband will take your daughter on horseback each morning and go get her each afternoon?"

"Yes."

"He's a rare man around here. Most don't value education that much. I'd like to meet him when he comes in again for books."

"I'll tell him." She stood to go.

He walked her to the door. "You're my kind of teacher, so don't give up on us totally. I hope to have you back in the classroom someday."

She offered her hand. "Thank you for considering me for this job. I'll stay in touch with you."

The next two weeks went by quickly. Laurel and Bess finished Sarah's dresses. Laurel had bought her some new shoes and socks and a sweater. She also had a covered lunch pail, a tablet, pencils and crayons. Bess cut her hair in a Dutch Boy bob. She looked so grown up it pricked Justin's heart. That night at supper he stood before her with a puzzled look and solemnly asked, "Ma'am, have you seen my little girl named Sarah? She was here this morning but I can't find her now."

"Daddy! Daddy!" she said, half laughing and half scared. "I'm Sarah!"

"You're Sarah? How did you grow up so much in one day/"

"Well," she said, touching her hair and dress, "Bess cut my hair and Mama made my dress and…and…you and Tattoo are going to take me to school."

He hugged her to him. "Yes, we are, Punkin'. We sure are" And for the first time his heart warmed to the task.

Hannah and Jed talked to Laurel about Thad and Jesse going to school with Justin and Sarah. They could ride another horse. But Thad, at fourteen, was gangling, awkward and shy. Jesse, twelve, was more sociable but was large for his age. Laurel felt it was too late to expect them to fit in. Most of the children would be younger and smaller. They were doing well. Laurel and Justin would continue to teach them at home.

Justin talked to the crew about his plan to take Sarah to school and go back and get her. He told them the two choices and that Laurel had chosen to stay in camp.

Abe spoke up. "We'd rather have you gone part of the time than Laurel gone all the time."

"Yep," said Zeke. "Wouldn't be the same with Laurel and the young'uns gone."

The rest of the crew agreed.

"I reckon it's normal for Laurel to want Sarah to go to school," Bulldog allowed, "with her bein' a teacher and all." The men shook their heads again.

"I figured you'd understand and I thank you," Justin finished. On his way back to his shack, Justin thought, *Whatever Laurel wants…if Laurel wanted to go to the moon, these men would just shake their heads and agree.*

The big day arrived! Justin hoisted Sarah into the saddle and swung up behind her. Lunch and book satchel were in the saddlebags. Laurel smiled and waved goodbye. Her firstborn was on her way to school. Papa would be pleased.

Laurel was surprised how much she missed Sarah's companionship and her quickness in learning. Sarah had also become like a little mother to Caroline and could ride herd on Adam when he needed it. They missed her, too.

Laurel and Justin had distanced themselves from each other over Sarah's schooling. She realized that in her desperation for Sarah to go to school, she had said and done some things that had hurt him. He realized that his suggested practical solution was not thought out and was seen by her as a betrayal, as a solemn promise he wanted to break. He resented her forcing his hand in the manner she had chosen. She resented him putting her in a position where she had to force his hand. They both were tired of the demands each made on the other, disillusioned with each other. Each one kept busy. Neither had the inclination to start the peace process. They each wrapped a self-justifying cloak about themselves and went on with their lives, taking care of everybody except each other.

The women noticed the change first, then the crew. They reacted like children whose parents are fighting. They pretended it wasn't happening. Then they did subtle things to try to fix it. Laurel and Justin didn't respond. They were at an impasse. They didn't even seem to like each other anymore. They found nothing to talk about when they were alone, so it was a strain to be together, but neither could garner a desire to fix it. They slept as far apart as the bed would allow.

To Justin's surprise, taking Sarah to school became a pleasure instead of a chore. Holding her in front of him in the saddle, listening to her chatter and laughter, naming the trees at her request, identifying the birds by their song, all released for a little while each day the tightened spring of responsibility that was always within him, for the job and his family and his people. He longed to tell Laurel his thoughts and that she had been right, but he and Laurel were polite strangers. Their closeness and companionship that had fueled their demanding life was gone. It had also been a security and pleasure to the families and crew. Everything was thrown off balance without it, and the very light seemed to have gone out of their lives.

After two weeks of misery, Hannah asked Laurel to take a walk with her. She got right to the point. "You need a vacation from all this. Why don't you take the children and go visit your papa for a week or two?"

Laurel stopped in her tracks. "Oh, Hannah, do you think I could?"

"Yes. I think you could and should. They've never even seen Caroline. And Sarah and Adam have grown up a lot since the professor was here."

"Do you think you can manage with the cooking?"

"Sure. There's four of us women. Thad and Jesse will help with the errands."

That night Laurel said, in the flat tone they had adopted for each other, "Justin, I would like to take the children to visit Papa for awhile. Caroline is more than one year old and they've never seen her."

Justin felt his gut tighten up. Was she leaving him? "When do you want to go?"

"As soon as we can arrange it. I'll have to write Sarah's teacher a note. She'll send me her books so I can keep her up in her work. Hannah and I will talk about the cooking. The four women can handle it, I'm sure."

"I have to go to town tomorrow. I'll buy your tickets if you know when you're going."

"I can be ready by day after tomorrow."

"Do you want me to buy return tickets?"

"No. I'm not sure how long I'll stay."

Silence fell between them again.

Laurel's homecoming brought joy and a flurry of excitement to the professor's house. Soon after she and the children arrived, she made a request.

"I've been out of touch with styles and fashion. Before anybody sees me, I'd love to buy a couple of dresses and get my hair cut. The children need some new outfits, too."

That night Papa said to Madeleine, "She needs time to adjust. She's skittish...and exhausted, I think."

Madeleine replied, "Hunter, did you notice her hands? They're red and chapped so bad they're cracked in places. After she was in bed, I went in and we talked awhile. I rubbed some of my greasy, homemade lotion on her hands. After a couple of nights of that stuff, they'll be better."

The next day Laurel tackled her appearance with single mindedness. She enjoyed looking at the new styles and bought a burgundy dress with soft flattering lines. The color highlighted her auburn hair and set off her fair skin. Her second purchase was a forest green jacket with a matching green, burgundy and gold skirt. She found a pair of burgundy shoes that matched both outfits.

She even had her hair styled. Bess had trimmed it for years and Laurel had kept it the same, namely a pouf around her face with it pinned up in a twist at the back. She was definitely out of style for 1924! Plucking up her courage, she went to a beauty salon and asked for a shorter style. Not a bob and not mannish, just shorter.

The result delighted her and the stylist. When her hair was set free from the length and the pins, it fell into natural waves and curls. She knew it made her look younger. And she felt younger! She could feel it bounce when she walked.

After buying each of the children a couple of outfits, she felt ready to face her family and friends. Papa and Mama let them settle in for a couple of days. Madeleine Caroline became Madeleine's baby. Adam was Papa's shadow. Sarah, wide-eyed, was everywhere, loving everything. She whispered to Laurel the second day, "Is Papa rich?"

"No."

"But this house is so big!"

"Sarah, most people like us live in bigger houses than we do. The logging shacks are a temporary way for us to live."

"What does temporary mean?"

"It means for a little while."

"But we've lived there ever since I was little."

She thought, *Will Sarah grow up to think a logging shack is the normal way to live?* But she said, "I know we've lived there a long time, but we'll have a normal house someday."

Laurel put her feelings about Justin on hold and, even with the ache in her heart, allowed herself to be taken care of and to soak up the atmosphere of her childhood home. Linen tablecloths, china, silver, educated tones and topics. This was her natural habitat. She returned to it as a fish would to water. For the next few days the house seemed full of people…her sisters and their families, cousins playing, women catching up….

On Saturday afternoon a family picnic turned into a community gathering, as often happened at Papa's house. Isabel, Laurel's best friend from childhood, came with her husband and children. After the meal was over, the women gathered on the front porch to visit while they watched their little ones play.

Isabel, always seeking center stage, had been loud and restless during the picnic. Now she turned her curiosity loose on Laurel.

"Are you still living in the backwoods?"

"Yes," Laurel answered, "only more so."

"Tell us about it."

"Our logging camp is located in Pisgah Forest. The only way in and out is by train or by horseback. There aren't any roads. Four families live in camp and sixteen men live in the bunkhouse during the week. We women do the cooking and the men log the timber and send it out by train. That's the bare bones of it."

Isabel stared at her in horror. "But…but how often do you get out and…go and do things?"

"It's an effort to get out at all. This past year since Caroline was born, I've been out of the camp only three or four times."

They all were looking at her now with unbelief, and sympathy.

She didn't want their sympathy, so she tried to explain. "It's not as bad as it sounds. The camp is like a community in the woods. We've worked together four years, so we're like family. And we have to stay busy to get all the work done."

Isabel wouldn't leave it alone. "But those *people*, Laurel. What are they like?" The sneer was barely disguised.

Laurel stood, her temper barely in check. "They're mountain people, Isabel. They're good and kind and decent. They don't have a formal education but they have learned the major lessons of life. They're at peace with who they are and what they have. They go to great lengths to help each other."

She stopped a minute and looked into space as if she were seeing them, then she continued, "They're not in a hurry. In fact, I've just realized they've absorbed some wonderful qualities from the mountains—patience, serenity, courage, a sense of timelessness."

She paused again, then said with obvious emotion. "I would trust them with my life and everything I hold precious. I hope someday I'll be more like them in terms of simple goodness and kindness."

She opened the screen door and stepped inside, closing it gently, leaving a stunned group behind her.

Isabel looked around, "I didn't mean to...."

"Yes, you did, Isabel," Madeleine said, who had been dealing with her since she was a child. "Did you get the answer you were looking for?"

"I'm sorry, Mrs. Kingsley. Could I go and apologize?"

"No. Laurel doesn't need to have to deal with you anymore today. Maybe you'll have another chance to see each other."

Laurel, meanwhile, had gone up to her bedroom to check on Caroline who was taking a nap. She stood at the window, looking out across the yard. She had been surprised at her words and emotions, but they had revealed her dilemma. She loved this kind of life but the logging camp had become her home. The people had become her people, closer to her than anyone here except Papa and Mama. She suddenly longed to be there. She longed for Justin. What was he doing? What was he thinking? Was he wishing she would come back? Could they work it out? Hope dared to course through the maze of her emotions for the first time since her arrival.

Papa knew, of course, that she was dealing with a sizable problem. He also knew she would talk when she was ready. The next day after lunch, she and Papa lingered over coffee and fried apple pies.

"Madeleine told me what you said to Isabel last night."

"Yes. She was so snobbish and disparaging in her attitude toward our people. Isabel has become brittle and waspish. She's unhappy, I think." She paused a minute and played with her fork. "With all her education, station in life, and material goods, she doesn't come close to being the person Hannah is, or Nora, either. Yet, she calls them 'backwoods' in a derogatory tone. I'm upset with her."

Papa said, "She knows it. She asked if she could come back and apologize."

"I'll talk to her but I won't have her insulting my friends or feeling sorry for me for my chosen way of life."

Papa, with a straight face, said, "I believe she understands that. And you just answered a question before I asked it."

"What question?"

"I was going to ask if you feel primarily a victim to Justin's chosen way of life, or has it become your choice, too?"

"And I answered that already?"

265

"You just said 'my chosen way of life.'"

"Papa!" she scolded. "You know what I mean! I have chosen what my husband has chosen, of necessity, if we're to have a decent marriage. But choosing doesn't make it 'happy-ever-after.' I'm still me and he is still he…but, no, I don't feel like a victim. Sometimes, I still recoil from the primitive conditions and physical demands, but a bigger part of me responds to the challenge. The logging camp is home and the people are like family."

Her voice trailed off. Then she asked, "Can we talk this afternoon while Caroline takes her nap?"

Later, on the swing in the arbor, she blurted out, "Papa, Justin and I had a quarrel about a month ago. We hurt each other pretty bad. We haven't even wanted to make it up, but we're both miserable apart. I guess we think that's better than keeping on hurting each other."

Papa stayed silent, waiting.

"So I came home. Hannah told me to come. I needed to see you and hear you and know you were near." She blinked back tears. "Papa, do you know how much I love you?"

"I believe so," he said. "Because of how much I love you."

They sat, savoring the rare moment. Then Laurel said, "I needed distance from Justin and the camp, to heal and to think through what's important to me. My words to Isabel surprised me. The logging camp is home – not forever – but for awhile. And Justin is my true love, Papa. He's a stubborn, impulsive lumberjack but he's the best man I know, besides you."

"Good! I'm glad you can still reason your way out of a dilemma. And I'm glad you listen to your heart as well as your head. But, does this mean you'll be making plans to leave soon?"

"I want to stay at least another week. I'm enjoying myself too much to leave. And the children think they've arrived in heaven." Her voice quietened, "And Justin needs some time, too. Do you think he'll want me back?"

Papa shook his head in wonder at the vagaries of love. "Justin's not a fool. He's probably having a harder time dealing with this than you are."

Laurel said, "I hope so!"

They laughed together and went inside.

Papa was right. Justin was pretty deep in misery and the camp wasn't far behind. Everybody tried to put a good face on it, but just keeping the camp running was uphill sledding. On Saturday the loneliness drove Justin to town on Tattoo. He picked up his camera from Sam and went to eat supper at the local cafe. He knew everybody there. Laz—short for Lazarus—Logdon, a bootlegger, scooted onto the stool beside Justin. The smell of liquor that emanated from Laz gave Justin an idea. He was tired of being miserable. He'd get a little booze to help him through the weekend. The deal was made. Justin met Laz at his wagon a little later and bought two pint jars of whiskey. Laz fished them out of a bale of hay. Justin put one jar in his saddle bag and the other in his camera case, a good, accessible hiding place. His camera and tripods were tied behind the saddle.

On his way out of town, Justin stopped by the company store to get a couple of items Hannah had requested. When he came out with his purchases, a young boy ran up to him through the crowd of men. "Mr. Worth, Mr. Worth, your camera's leakin'!"

"My what?"

"Your camera."

Sure enough, there was a steady drip from his camera case that had jolted onto its side. Several curious men were eyeing it and wondering.

"Didn't know a camera had anything to leak," one said.

Justin knew if he pulled out that pint of whiskey, half the men around would recognize it was Laz's brew. He stepped into the stirrup, reached inside the case and tightened the lid on his pint, hoping he had saved some of his whiskey.

"Developing fluid," he said easily as he swung into the saddle and rode out of town.

Justin hadn't been drunk since he married. He had learned to drink when he was young, but he didn't like the stuff and it didn't like him. It didn't take much to get him falling-down drunk. He prided himself in knowing when to stop. The other reason he didn't drink was he knew Laurel wouldn't stand for it. Her and her Prohibition speeches! Well, she was gone and he would do as he pleased! He reached around, found the pint jar and took a swig.

By ten o'clock that night when Justin hadn't arrived, Jed told Hannah, "I'm going to look for him. I can't just go to bed and wonder."

The horse trail had been traveled enough to be recognized as a trail now, and fortunately, the moon was bright. Jed found him on the riverbank, passed out, stone drunk. Tattoo stood guard over him. It took some doing for Jed to get Justin's limp form into the saddle. He tied his horse's reins to Tattoo's saddle horn and climbed up behind Justin. Jed held him upright, his head lolling, and Tattoo took them home.

Jed got Justin to bed and went to tell Hannah he was back and would stay the night in Justin's shack. He was worried and checked Justin's pulse occasionally. The only remedy Jed knew was to let him sleep it off. But Jed didn't sleep. He even worried if Justin had got hold of some poison liquor.

It was dawn before Justin stirred. Jed was ready for him, armed with cold water and hot, black coffee. After dousing his head in a pan of cold water, with Jed's help, and drinking two cups of strong coffee, with Jed's help, Justin's brain seemed to connect with the rest of him. He looked at Jed across the table.

"What happened?"

Jed told him. "I never saw anybody so soused. How much did you drink? A gallon?"

"Less than a pint, I think. I don't remember anything after hitting the trail at the edge of the forest."

"I think you fell off Tattoo. Do you feel like anything's hurt?"

"No, nothing but my pride. Anybody besides you see me drunk?"

"No. And ain't nobody goin' to know about it unless you tell 'em."

"Hannah?"

"No. She knows I went to look for you and knows we got home, that's all."

"Thank you, Jed. I let it all get me down. Laurel gone with the kids…." Justin put his head in his hands again.

"When are you goin' to get her?"

Justin's head came out of his hands. "What do you mean?"

"I mean, when are you goin' to get her?"

"I'm not. She needs to decide for herself." Something in Jed's expression made him blurt out, "Besides, I'm afraid she won't come back with me."

"She will."

Justin stared at him. "How do you know?"

"Hannah."

Justin stood up too suddenly, grabbed his head with both hands, then exploded. "Jed, can't you say but one word at a time? Hannah what?"

Jed, totally unperturbed by Justin's outburst, said, "Hannah says Laurel's waitin' for you to come and get her."

Justin eased back into his chair. "How does Hannah know that?"

"She just knows. Women knows things like that." Jed got up and poured them both another cup of coffee. "Crew's waitin', too."

"The crew? What's the crew got to do with it?" He was careful not to make any more sudden moves.

"They ain't said much, but they want you to do right by her."

"What have they said?"

"Justin, we all know somethin' happened between you'ns. It was plain as day. You need to go set it straight. You ain't never been one to run from a problem or act like it ain't there."

Justin was irritated. "So everybody's made this their business?"

Jed stood and looked at him straight. "It *is* our business. You and Laurel's been takin' on all our problems for years. We can't just set here and ignore this. The camp ain't the same with Laurel gone. And you…you ain't been worth chicken squat since she left."

Justin studied Jed's face a long time. Then he grinned. "I guess I ain't."

Jed headed for the door. "I'm sure Hannah's fixin' breakfast by now. I'll yell when it's ready."

"I'll get myself cleaned up before I come. And, Jed, thanks."

His head felt like a freight train was running through it, and when he walked, he felt like a new calf trying out its legs. But he was the happiest he'd been for a month or more. He knew now what he was going to do.

Three days later in the afternoon, Justin walked up to the front door of Hunter Kingsley's house. The door was ajar and Justin gave it a push. Laurel was standing halfway up on the foyer stairs, her back to the door, listening to Caroline's sleepy murmurings.

An expression of love and yearning crossed Justin's face. He stepped inside as Laurel turned. They looked at each other. She was more beautiful than he remembered. He was more handsome than she remembered. The old magic and longing hovered between them.

"Laurel," Justin said, "I love you and I'm sorry. I've been acting like a fool."

"I love you. And I'm sorry, too."

Then she was in his arms.

The professor heard voices and looked in the foyer. He turned away, smiling.

On Saturday night before Laurel and Justin would leave on Sunday, Madeleine planned a dinner party. The family liked Justin immensely but rarely saw him. They wanted some time with him, and Isabel somehow inveigled an invitation from Madeleine.

Dinner was for adults only, with a neighborhood girl taking care of the children. The professor guided the conversation through political, social and educational issues. Justin's knowledge and insight about national affairs impressed him.

"Sounds like you have a good source of national news," he observed.

"Oh, yes," Justin agreed. "Sam Parker, editor of *The Wildwood Journal*, is a real news hound."

Laurel spoke. "And Justin is used to digesting and simplifying it. He reports the news to the crew and families at suppertime every time he returns from town."

Isabel had to have her say; avid, in spite of herself, for some further tidbits about Laurel's life that she could pass on, in mock concern, to their mutual acquaintances.

"Laurel told us a little about life in the camp, how far back you are and that she and the women cook for the crew."

Justin recognized the comment for what it was. He set his glass down and faced Isabel.

"Did Laurel tell you what else she does besides cook? Did she tell you that she is teaching children and one adult their three R's? That, because of her, the children are free from hookworm and typhoid and other diseases. They're healthier because they eat better. They have medicine when they're sick. She saved a man's life after a four foot copperhead bit him, quarantined herself with a little girl she loved who had diphtheria, and kept the rest of us from getting it."

"Justin," Laurel interrupted, embarrassed.

"No, Laurel, I'm not finished. Your family – and Isabel – needs to know that you're more than a cook in a logging camp."

He looked around the table and continued in a quieter tone. "She has church on Sundays in an abandoned boxcar. A preacher comes once a month, but Laurel's Bible lessons are what the women and children remember and are learning to live by."

Nobody around the table moved. The professor's heart swelled with emotion.

Justin took a drink of water and continued in a lighter tone. Laurel stopped staring into her water glass and was looking at him.

"She rallied the women of Wildwood County to vote in the last election and I'm sure they're geared up to vote again. A man who attacked Laurel over her speech had to leave the county for good. He was afraid of a lynching party. She was asked to teach school again this year. She chose to stay in camp. Our people in camp like me fine, but they love your daughter, Professor. Any one of them would die for her."

He looked at Laurel and laughed. "My own foreman told me – and I'm the man who pays his wages – that I wasn't worth…that I didn't amount to much without Laurel."

Laurel laughed in spite of herself. She could picture it. "Jed said that?"

"Yes. Only he put it in words not fit for this fine company."

Everybody laughed, trying to imagine what the man must have said. "I could keep going but that gives you an idea of how Laurel Kingsley Worth spends her time."

Papa had got his emotions under control. "Thank you, Justin. You answered some questions and laid some concerns to rest." He raised his water goblet. "A toast to Justin and Laurel – our pioneers."

Madeleine served dessert and coffee and the conversation settled into mundane channels, a necessary release from the pent-up emotions Justin's words had evoked. A chastened Isabel was quiet. Laurel had succeeded in difficult circumstances while she, Isabel, had grown bored and empty in privileged circumstances. She couldn't think why. She wished her husband would look at her the way Justin looked at Laurel. Gracious! He was handsome!

Later, Papa took a walk under the stars. He laid down the burden he had been carrying about Laurel's circumstances, and his resentment toward Justin for creating the circumstances. Their lives were rich and full of purpose. He would never have expected a speech like that from Justin. He obviously adored Laurel, and Laurel's love for him was evident. Papa was content. He whispered, "She's your daughter, Alexis."

Their homecoming was celebrated with unabashed joy. It was a family reunion. The women hugged Laurel until she was breathless. The crew all talked at once to get her attention.

That night in the bunkhouse, Zeke said, "I'm proud of Justin. He went and got his woman, like any self-respectin' mountain man."

"Yeah," Abe said. "Only this woman wouldn't have come back 'til she made up her own mind."

Dirk put in, "But he done right, goin' after her."

Odell closed it down. "Yeah. For a man with all that education, Justin's right smart."

They all chuckled over that bit of wisdom, and went to sleep feeling good. Their world had been set right again.

Chapter Twenty-one

About two weeks later Laurel and Bess were in the mess hall cooking lunch when they heard a knock on the door. No one ever knocked on the mess hall door since it was considered a common building. Laurel glanced at Bess and crossed to open the door.

A tall young man with blond hair stood on the steps. His blue eyes, close to the color of Justin's, looked at her without wavering. He was pale and thin to the point of being emaciated. His clothes were threadbare and wrinkled but clean. He had a bundle that looked like a rolled up toe sack under his arm.

"Ma'am, is this here the Worth Logging Camp?"

"Yes. Are you looking for someone?"

"No, Ma'am. I'm lookin' for a job."

"Oh! Come in. The men are on the job right now but they'll be in for lunch in a little while."

"My name is Ethan Stewart." He smiled at her as he came in. She held out her hand. "I'm Laurel Worth and this is Bess Aiken. We're cooking lunch for the crew. Just have a seat."

As his eyes fell on a plate of left-over biscuits on the side of the stove, he worked his mouth and swallowed hard. Laurel turned to the stove so he couldn't see her expression, as he sat down on a bench.

"Bess, pour us all a cup of coffee and I'll get the left-over biscuits and bacon. It's time for our morning snack. Maybe Ethan will join us."

Bess looked at Laurel and frowned. They never had a morning snack. Before she could blurt that out, Laurel continued, "I'm sure you can eat a little since you probably walked from Deerbrook"

"Yes, Ma'am." His eyes didn't leave the plate of biscuits.

Laurel put plates and food on the table, including jelly and butter. Then she and Bess sat down with him.

"Please, go right ahead and eat. I think I'll have a biscuit and butter with my coffee." Bess did the same.

She knew he was starved, but he touched her by eating slowly and trying to show good manners. After three biscuits with bacon and jelly and butter, he stopped eating and finished drinking his coffee.

He sat still for a moment, then said, "Thank you, Ma'am. Now I'd like to do some work for you to pay for my food."

"No. You just rest awhile from that long walk."

"I'm used to workin' for my food, Ma'am, and I…I can't eat no more unless you let me work."

She wanted him to go lie down and rest awhile until she could feed him again. She wanted to erase the unmistakable stamp of hunger. But, she couldn't ride roughshod over his pride, which was keeping him upright.

"Okay. We do need some water from the spring. Bess, will you go show him where it is? Then you could carry in some stove wood."

When he carried in the second load of wood and bent to put it on the stack, he staggered and almost pitched forward. He looked up quickly to see if she noticed but she carefully kept her eyes on the beans she was stirring. She had to find something he could do sitting down.

"That's plenty of water and wood. Could I get you to shuck some corn? You can sit on the bench outside. Bess, let's go to the supply room."

Bess had been unusually quiet since he arrived. Now, out of earshot, she whispered, "He's so pale, you can about see right through his skin. And he's hollow-eyed, too."

"Yes. He's about past going. He's been without food for awhile."

They carried a tin washtub full of corn and placed it beside the bench. Bess brought a dishpan for the corn and a basket for the shucks. He doggedly set to work and the women went back to the kitchen.

When he heard the crew coming for lunch, he quickly washed his hands and stood to face them. Justin and Jed, in front, stopped and looked at him for a minute. He stepped closer, held out his hand and said, "I'm Ethan Stewart and I'm looking for Mr. Worth."

Justin shook his hand. "I'm Justin Worth and this is Jed Owen. What can we do for you?"

"I'm needin' some work."

"Looks like you found it," Justin said, nodding toward the corn.

"Yes, sir. Your wife gave me some breakfast and I told her I needed to work for it."

His appearance touched Justin. "Well, you've paid for breakfast for sure, son. Now, let's go eat lunch."

Something in Justin's manner warned the crew to go easy on the boy, and leave him to eat without questions or banter. Again, he ate slowly and stopped before the others.

After lunch, Justin stayed behind so he and Laurel could talk to the boy. Justin got right to the point. "How old are you, son?"

"Sixteen."

"Where's your family?"

"Me and my pa's been livin' together since my mother died two years ago. Now, he's gone. Been gone about a month."

"Gone?" Justin asked. "You mean he died?"

"He disappeared. And I ain't been able to find him."

They looked at him bewildered and he looked from Justin to Laurel and back to Justin. Then he seemed to make a decision. He straightened his shoulders and said, "My pa's a bootlegger, Mr. Worth. He left home one evenin' to deliver some 'shine and never come back. I believe he's been killed. His...his daddy and brother before him was shot and killed."

"Where do you live?"

"Near Gatlinburg, Tennessee."

"And you walked from there?"

"Yes."

"Do you have any other family?"

"No. Me and my daddy worked the still together. He was a hard man but he wouldn'a just walked off and left me. I went out every day lookin' for him, but never found no signs of him. Then my food run out and I knowed I had to get out and find a job."

"Why did you come this way instead of toward Knoxville?"

"Pa told me sometime back if anything ever happened to him for me to walk the old mail trail over the mountain to Asheville."

"Who told you about us?" Laurel asked.

"An Indian."

They looked surprised. But he continued. "He was cookin' a rabbit on a spit when I come up on him. I was scared at first but he offered me some of his food. He's been here. Said you know him. He said to tell you he sent me."

"Chief Lion Heart," said Laurel, under her breath. Justin nodded.

"Could you give me a job? I think I can learn fast."

"I'm sure you can, son." Justin's voice was kind. "We're going to have to get some food in you for a few days. You've not had enough to eat for awhile."

Ethan sat with his shoulders straight and met Justin's eyes.

"No, sir, but I'll be okay," he said with dignity.

Laurel's heart ached. "Ethan, your body has used up all its reserves. You must eat and rest for a few days or you'll be sick. You're going on willpower and pride."

"She's right, Ethan. You have a home here for now. We'll talk about work when you're able. Now you have to rest. Come with me."

They stood and went to the bunkhouse. When Justin told him to lie down on a bunk, he did so reluctantly, but his body went slack immediately and his eyes closed. Then they flew open again.

"Could somebody wake me up before the crew comes in? I don't want to be asleep when they get here."

"Yes. I understand. I promise somebody will wake you."

"Thank you, Mr. Worth."

Justin hesitated then plunged ahead. "Ethan, I left home and went to live in a logging camp when I was younger than you."

"You did?"

"Yes. It was one of the best things that ever happened to me."

Ethan looked at Justin. "Mr. Worth, when…when I'm able I'll have to go back for awhile and try to find out about my pa."

"I know. Did you tell anybody he was missing?"

"No. They's some people who would take over Pa's still if they knowed he was gone, and we ain't friendly with no sheriffs. So, I didn't want nobody to know."

"You did right, son. Rest now. We'll take one thing at a time."

Ethan closed his eyes and let go.

Justin went back by the mess hall and told Laurel to have someone call Ethan by five o'clock, in time for him to wash up and be moving around before the men came in.

"We'll talk about him tonight. I've got to get back to the job now."

As he walked through the woods toward the sounds of axes and shouts and falling timber, he knew he was going to give the boy a job. He didn't need to think about it nor figure how much it would cost him. He couldn't do otherwise and remain true to the memory of that other young boy who had been befriended so many years ago. Perhaps this was his chance to pay back a debt.

For the next few days, Ethan followed Justin's and Laurel's advice. He ate small amounts at every meal and snacks in between. "Your stomach has shrunk," she told him. "You'll have to get it stretched again before you can eat a man-sized meal."

Because they insisted, he rested awhile every morning and afternoon. Soon his youth and resilience caught up with his willpower and he was ready to work. He helped around camp for two more weeks with the endless chores. When Justin thought Ethan was strong enough, he talked it over with Jed and they told the men they wanted them to make a logger out of Ethan. He would work his way up, starting as water jack and swamper.

Meanwhile, Justin told Ethan it would be better to let the law look for his daddy. The revenuers would get in on it and destroy the still, but they would have the best chance to find his daddy. When Ethan agreed, Justin went to see the sheriff of Wildwood County and told him Ethan's story. He asked him to send a telegram to the sheriff in Tennessee.

"I'll make a deal with you," he told the sheriff. "I'll give you the general directions to the still if you'll leave the boy alone. He's working for me and I'll take responsibility for him. Pass that on to the sheriff in Tennessee."

It was agreed and the wheels were set in motion. About two weeks later, when the train returned from taking a load of logs to Deerbrook, the sheriff swung out of the cab and headed for the logging job. The swampers saw him first and took him to Justin.

"I got a telegram from Tennessee. They think they've found your man. It looks like he was shot in the back. His body's in bad shape. What do you want to do?"

"Let's go talk it over with the boy," Justin said.

They found Ethan with the teamsters, learning to snake out logs. Ethan looked so alarmed at the sight of the sheriff, Justin put his hand on his shoulder and said, "It's okay, son. Come with us where we can talk."

They stopped as soon as the noise level dropped and Justin said, "Ethan, the sheriff got a telegram this morning." Then he told him the rest as kindly as he could. "I'm sorry, son."

Ethan listened politely, swallowed hard, and walked away a few steps. After a moment, he said, "Mr. Worth, I need to know if it really is Pa. And I need to go bury him if it is."

"I know you do, and they need you to identify the body. I'll go with you tomorrow. We'll ask the sheriff to send them a telegram so they can meet us."

The sheriff had stayed quiet, noting Justin's kindness to the bootlegger's son. He now said, "Justin, if your engineer can uncouple them flat cars I'll get him to run me back to Deerbrook. I'll send the telegram that you are leaving on the nine o'clock train for Knoxville in the morning. They'll know when to meet you in Pigeon Forge. I think it's about an hour this side of Knoxville. Is that right?"

"Yes," Justin said absently. He had just looked at his watch. "Let's hurry. I have to go get my daughter at school."

"I'll get back to work," said Ethan as he walked away.

"His life has been hell, Sheriff, but I believe he's come out of it a decent kid."

"That happens sometimes," the sheriff said politely. But he had his doubts. He'd seen a lot of what the seamy side of life did to children.

Justin arranged to be gone two or three days. At supper he said, "I need one of you to take Sarah to school and back while I'm gone." While the crew thought over who could best be spared, Sarah spoke up, "I want Uncle Bull to take me."

Bulldog looked at Jed who sat considering the matter for a moment, then nodded his head. "We'll work it out."

Bulldog was pleased. Since Joanie had died, he and Bess had spent a lot of time with Sarah and Adam and Caroline.

Justin's respect for the young man grew during the next few days. When they arrived in Pigeon Forge, the sheriff had horses ready for them to ride.

"We found him in a creek that runs through an ivy slick. Because of the condition of the body," he explained to Ethan, "we've covered it and left it on the creek bank near where we found it."

When they arrived, after riding steady for two hours, the sheriff said, "You'll need to keep a handkerchief over your nose."

Justin wanted somehow to protect Ethan from the worst. "Son," he said, "let's have them keep the face covered. You can tell by the clothes if it's your daddy."

Ethan was pale and tense, but he said, "Mr. Worth, I have to look at his face. He'd expect me to. It's showin' respect. And I need to know for sure."

"Okay. I'll be with you."

When they got to the covered body, Justin said, "Show us the clothes first."

Ethan said, "Yes, them's his clothes. I've washed 'em enough to know 'em." He looked at Justin who nodded for the men to uncover the face. It was bloated and discolored ... and obscene. Ethan jerked and groaned as if he had been struck. "O-o-oh, Pa!" The pain in his voice made Justin wince. When he took hold of Ethan's arm, he felt tremors running through the boy's thin body. Then Ethan turned and ran behind a laurel bush, throwing up until he ended with dry heaves.

The sheriff's men covered the body again and moved away quickly. Justin moved away from the body, and dipped a handkerchief in the creek. He waited for Ethan to come out when he was able.

After Ethan appeared and washed his face with the handkerchief, he said, "I need to bury him"

"Do you want me to build a coffin or do you want to wrap him and bury him as he is?"

"You'd build a coffin for him?"

"Yes, if that's what you want."

"How long would it take?"

"We'd have to go to town to get some lumber. I could have it ready by tomorrow afternoon."

Ethan said, "Let me get my head clear and think about what he would want." He half-walked, half-slid down the bank to the creek and stood a few minutes with his head turned sideways as if listening.

The sheriff came over and stood by Justin. Their silence was a tribute to the boy's struggle. When Ethan turned around and climbed the bank, his movements were more decisive. He said, "My Pa was a bootlegger, but he was a proud man. He would hate to know he was layin' here stinkin'. He'd want me to bury him as fast as I could."

His eyes sought Justin's response. "I think you're right, son. I'd feel the same way."

Justin turned, "Sheriff...?"

"We can wrap him in that tarp that's covering him. If you'll pick out a burial spot, we'll start digging."

Ethan, with Justin's help, chose a spot a small distance from the ivy slick, under a large hemlock. "A peaceful spot and one I can find. I know where we are."

The sheriff's men started digging. After a little while, Ethan stepped up and said, "I thank you, sir, but this is my job."

He attacked the ground with such a vengeance, Justin knew he couldn't last long. When he saw him tiring, he said, "Let me spell you awhile." After that, they took turns; Ethan, then Justin, then the men.

When the grave was ready, the sheriff's men brought the shrouded body. They all worked together to lower it into the grave with ropes. Ethan sprinkled the first shovel full of dirt gently over his pa. It was a loving gesture, and whatever the sheriff and his men thought of the bootlegger and his boy, they were touched.

After the task was finished, Ethan asked, "Could one of you say a few words from the Bible over my pa?"

Everybody looked at Justin. But Justin looked at the sheriff and shook his head. The sheriff wet his lips and looked at his men. It seemed nobody would.

Ethan stepped up to the grave. "Pa, I'd like to give you a Christian burial but I don't know the words. Before Ma died, she told me that God loves us and He sent Jesus to show us He does. You never spoke to me about God, Pa, so I don't know if you knew He loved you."

He stopped and swallowed. "You was good to me, Pa, in your way, and I miss you terrible."

He was quiet again for a few minutes. The men stood back a ways, with their heads bowed. Ethan seemed to forget them. "I think you expected this because of the way you talked to me lately. I done what you said, Pa, when I couldn't find you. I left. Mr. Worth here give me a job in his loggin' camp. I'm learnin' to be a logger. You always told me to do the best job I could with whatever I was doin'. I'd want you to be proud of me, Pa, so I'm workin' hard."

He stooped and laid his hand, palm flat, at the head of the grave. "Bye, Pa. I loved you."

He stood and the men followed him to the creek to wash up. Ethan asked, "Mr. Worth, could you help me place one of these flat rocks on Pa's grave?" They found a large, oblong stone, polished by the elements. They carried it between them and laid it down.

Justin asked, "Would you like to stand it up? It wouldn't take but a few minutes."

"Like a tombstone, you mean? Yes, yes, I would! That would be good!"

Justin worked with him silently, leaving him to his thoughts until they finished.

Later, when they got to the horses, the sheriff asked, "Do you have any notion about who shot your pa?"

Ethan looked at him squarely. "No. I couldn't finger nobody. They's been some fuedin' among the moonshiners, but Pa and me kept to ourselves."

As they rode toward Ethan's house the sheriff said, "The revenuers destroyed your pa's still yesterday."

After looking at him sharply, Ethan rode in silence awhile before he replied, "It's just as well. My pa's daddy and his brother and now pa, hisself, has all been murdered because of bootleg liquor."

Justin spoke quietly to the sheriff. "If you and your men want to go on, I'll stay with him 'til he says his goodbyes."

The old log cabin was standing so close to the sheer mountainside, it almost seemed a part of it. Justin wondered if a desire for protection had put it there. If so, it hadn't worked.

Ethan opened the door. "Me and my pa just batched here after Ma died." Bleakness and poverty was pervasive but the cabin was clean. Justin knew Ethan was responsible for that. After Ethan had walked around the room aimlessly, he said, "Let's go see what they done to the still."

He led Justin through the woods on a round-about trail until they came upon it. "They did wreck it," Ethan said as they looked around. He walked around touching the smashed parts.

"Pa told me over and over, 'Be good at whatever you do.' And he made good whiskey. He'd run off the singlin's to get rid of water and rank oils. When he got that run off, he'd double the liquor back. He called it 'doublin's.' When it come out the last time, it was clear, pure whiskey."

"How did he filter out the oils?" Justin asked, genuinely interested.

"He used a big funnel with charcoal in it. He'd put a clean, white wool sock over the funnel, coverin' the top and bottom. When he got through runnin' it, little wads of verdigrease would be all over that sock. Verdigrease was poison, so Pa got the reputation of makin' whiskey that wouldn't poison you."

He finished his farewell ritual and took one more sweeping glance before he said, "I'm ready to go."

When they got back to the house, Ethan looked around as he had at the still. Justin was "I'm not sad to leave here, Mr. Worth. My pa wanted me to leave. This is a house of death."

On the way out, Ethan showed Justin a steep mountain trail. "From the time I was about ten, I'd carry whiskey up that mountain and hide it where Pa's customers could find it. It was all I could do to get a two gallon keg up that ridge."

Justin recognized Ethan's need to talk as a way of dealing with his grief.

His next bit of news surprised Justin. As they neared a small community, he said, "I went to school here awhile. Ma stood up to Pa about me goin' to school. I walked this trail twice a day. Pa said the school was about three or four miles from our house. It seemed further. I asked Pa once if them three miles counted all the straight up ridges I had to climb, or if it was figured as the crow flies.

"He laughed and said, 'Since you can't fly, boy, you'll just have to walk whatever distance it is.' Ma and him seemed proud when I learned to read and write and do arithmetic. I used to read to Ma before she died." On that he fell silent awhile.

When they got to town, they checked with the sheriff to see about the death certificate. Justin spoke to the sheriff privately, offering to pay any fees, but was told there weren't any.

"I want to thank you and your men for helping bury the boy's daddy."

"We was just doin' our job, Mr. Worth. I'm glad the boy's gettin' out. He comes from a rough tribe, and he'd be marked if he stayed. Maybe he'll have a chance somewhere away from here."

Chapter Twenty-two

Justin was thankful to get home. Ethan was subdued but relieved. He still had times when he had to get alone to grieve for his pa, but the dreadful uncertainty about him was over. And Ethan was thankful to have a job and a place to live. Since he had nowhere to go, he stayed in camp on weekends. He was welcome at any of the four shacks for meals. Everybody enjoyed having him. He became friends with Thad and Jesse, who took him fishing. The crew took him under its wing, and he learned fast. He shadowed the loggers on the job, absorbing like a sponge. But Justin was his hero. Justin could do no wrong.

Only in one area did Ethan vary from Justin's example. On the first Sunday morning he was in camp, he helped the men carry the children across the trestle to church. When the men turned back to camp, he went with them. On the Sunday after burying his daddy, he asked Justin, "Would I be allowed to go to church? I ain't never been."

Justin said, "Of course you can go. They'll be glad to have you."

Justin called Thad and Jesse and told them to take Ethan with them.

Laurel was inspired by Ethan's intense interest and found herself preparing her future lessons with him in mind. Since he had no knowledge of the Bible, he was a challenge for Laurel. His enthusiastic and sometimes confused response was refreshing and amusing to the whole group.

Laurel continued with reading and writing classes for Thad, Jesse, and Bess. Justin worked with the boys on arithmetic at night as he had time. Ethan was soon in on these sessions.

Life hurried on and the next August Adam joined Justin and Sarah on their way to school each day. The first day they rode off with Sarah behind

284

Justin and Adam in front, Laurel happily waved goodbye. Adam would love school and do well. He never met a stranger. Growing up among the crew had planted a belief in his very being that everybody was his friend. In spite of her rational thinking, Laurel suddenly felt tears. Her son, irrepressible and mischievous and a delight to her heart, from this day forward would grow away from her. She knew in her head that this was right – was as it should be – but her heart would have to be brought around to accept. it. And she had plenty to think about besides Adam. Caroline, at two, consumed much of her energy and patience. A sunny, laughing child, Caroline took life as it came and was rarely cross. It was her constant movement that kept Laurel on the run.

Meanwhile, Sarah's and Adam's education was being expanded way beyond the three R's, by their daddy, traveling to and from school. Justin had the quality of being able to give himself to – and usually enjoy – any situation he was in, and he was enjoying his time with his children in the forest.

One day Justin, thinking aloud, said of a large oak, "That tree should have over two hundred board feet of lumber in it."

Adam asked, "What's a board foot?"

Justin explained, "It's one square foot of wood, one inch thick."

"How do you know how many are in a tree?" Sarah asked.

After Justin explained, Adam asked, "Daddy, do you feel sad, cutting the trees down?"

""Yes, in one way I do, Adam. The tree I dread cutting the most is the monarch, the biggest tree in any stand of timber. We usually leave it 'til last out of respect."

He continued, pleased with their interest. "We use the methods from the forestry school Uncle Jed attended. We're careful not to destroy the smaller trees and bushes and we set out seedlings where we've cut. We want you and your children to have some trees to enjoy."

The forest was a treasure trove of discoveries, never two days the same. One day they came upon a large owl on a low limb near their path. It sat totally still, totally unruffled, its round yellow eyes upon them. They stopped, silenced by the sight. Tawny striped feathers, a snowy white bib and a tuft of feathers sticking up on each side of its head, the owl blinked slowly. They felt as if royalty had just granted them safe passage through his kingdom. Justin touched Tattoo's neck and he moved on. After a respectful distance, Justin said, "That was a Great Horned Owl. The second one I've seen in my life."

Some days they just had fun. Justin taught them a song he had learned at his first logging camp. The men used to sing it tramping in and out to work. It took several days to learn it because it made no sense. It ran:

"Kitty mo, kime-o, dow-wow; wid a hi, wid a ho; wid a rumpa, stumpa, rutabaga; nip at cat-a-winka; sing some kitty wants a kime-e-o." When they finally learned it and sang it together, the kids laughed so hard they almost fell off Tattoo.

He taught them a chant-like song to sing with him to their mother, standing formally with hands folded. "My Clementine, my Timontine; my tar heel and turpentine. You came down below your station; so I could ask you to become my relation; so as to increase the population, in this great nation."

When the laughter subsided, Adam wanted to know, "Daddy, how do you and Mama increase the population?"

"I'll tell you that another day."

He scared them silly on Halloween with a tale of Raw Head and Bloody Bones, a fearsome creature without skin on its bloody head or body. He told them he'd heard about it all his life. But they didn't need to worry. It only stalked bad people.

Winter again brought its own problems and joys. The snowy days were like magic to Sarah and Adam, and Justin, as they rode to school. Wrapped in blankets, snuggled against their daddy, the two children would absorb, with near reverence, the beauty and the silence.

"It's like everything's asleep," Adam whispered.

"And covered with a white blanket," Sarah added. "I love it, Daddy. I can't decide which I love best, winter or spring or summer or fall."

"You don't have to love one best. Love them all," Justin answered.

"That's what I do," she said, solemnly.

"Me, too," Adam vowed. "Can we live here always, Daddy?"

"No, son. We'll have to move someday. But we're lucky to be here now."

They knew they were lucky. Did any other children have a forest for a playground, or at least a good section of it? Justin had walked off a boundary with them around camp and told them to stay within it. He impressed upon them the dangers of getting lost, or of meeting a bear or panther or copperhead.

Most days, as soon as they were in from school and had their snack, Adam was off to play on the sloping mountainside until time to do his chores. Sometimes Sarah went; Adam went every day.

One afternoon he was sitting near the top of an oak tree in a comfortable perch made by a huge limb, surveying his realm. Suddenly, an object hurtled through the air and landed on the limb about a foot away from Adam. It was a baby flying squirrel. Its big eyes blinked at Adam and Adam blinked back, not daring even to breathe. It was a moment of joy, crystalized in its clarity. He slipped it into his memory box among the treasures he was accumulating.

Later he told Laurel, "Mama, it was close enough to touch. We just looked at each other. I could see its…its heart beating in its chest. Then it jumped or sort of flew to another limb." His brown eyes were shining. "It wasn't even scared of me."

His hide-out was under the spreading branches of a hemlock tree. The long bottom branches grew straight out for several feet, then drooped to the ground. This created a space around the base of the tree about eight feet in diameter and four feet high. It was a hidden, dry, wonderful magic room full of filtered light. He could look through the green curtain but no one could see in. Adam's gregarious soul began to learn the joys of occasional solitude.

He and Sarah learned how to leap out of a tree and catch near the top of a sapling, which would obligingly and gracefully swing them to the ground. Tall sturdy ivy and laurel bushes lined the creek near camp. They would challenge each other to see how far they could travel through the branches without touching ground.

One day after sharing their feats with Justin, he said, "Adam, come here."

He felt of Adam's shoulders and shook his head. "What're you doing?" Adam asked.

Justin said, "Feeling for nubs. Seeing if your wings have started growing yet. You're off the ground half the time." They grinned at each other, sharing their love for the woods.

In February, 1927, Laurel knew she was pregnant again. This set her off thinking about all the children in camp and their ages. Caroline was three and a half, Adam, eight and Sarah, almost ten. Tommy, Alice's and Tom's son, had turned six in December. Their daughter, Elizabeth, was three. Jesse was now fourteen and Thad, sixteen. Joanie had been dead five and a half years.

It was on Sarah's tenth birthday that Justin broke his news. He and his family would be moving out of Pisgah Forest. They had been here seven years. He gave his reasons to the crew, covering the bases thoroughly but quickly. "Whoever continues this operation will have to move further into the forest to log tracts that may take two more years. Sarah and Adam have to get to school. This move would make that impossible.

"I have talked to Hiram Beck, at length. Your jobs, every one of them, are secure. You've done a good job for him all these years. You'll have a new supervisor and foreman and some new men to work with."

"Where you goin'?" one of the crew interrupted.

"I'll still be working for Beck Lumber Company at a smaller job. It's in Locust Hollow, a community where there's a school and a church and a store…don't know how we'll handle so much civilization.

"I'll need a smaller crew. Jed, Bulldog, and Tom plan to move their families out with me. Ethan will go, of course. As far as I know there won't be any families at the next camp here. Only men in bunkhouses.

"Now, men, hear me straight on this. You know we've become like a family. All of you and your wives and children are important to Laurel and me. We hope that your friendship will be there for the rest of our lives. There will be some changes, of course, but if you ever need us we'll be there.

"Here comes the hard part. I asked Hiram Beck for four more of you to move with me. Since our crew will be so small, Jed and I picked the men most skilled in the jobs we need. We're asking Abe and Dirk and Zeke and Odell to go. This was a hard decision because all of you are top-notch timber men and you know I'd be proud to have any of you."

Two months later, as soon as school was out, Worth Logging Camp in

Pisgah Forest changed hands. The crew staying behind hugged Justin and Laurel, admonishing Laurel to take good care of herself and get that young'un here okay. Justin promised to let them know when the baby came. In spite of valiant efforts, it was like a funeral. The group that was leaving and the group that was staying had shared life and death, work and play, laughter and tears for seven years. It was the end of an era.

The train pulled out, with a special request from Laurel to stop by the church. The entire group walked over to Joanie's grave to say goodbye. Then the train took the shacks to the edge of the forest where the families' belongings would be loaded on trucks, not wagons, to be taken to their new camp. During their sojourn in Pisgah Forest, the country and Wildwood County had entered the motor-car age. Horse and buggy days were almost gone.

The twelve men who were left to work with the new crew coming in were thankful Justin had secured their jobs for them. They knew that many times a new supervisor insisted on bringing his own men. They would show him what Justin Worth's loggers could do.

Locust Hollow was a small community that was on the western end of the county, actually further in miles from the town of Deerbrook than their camp had been, but there were roads. There was a school and church and store and neighbors and cleared fields and space. The mountains were around them but at a distance. Laurel confessed one night to Justin, "I feel strange…almost adrift…with all this space. I grew used to the mountains being so close they…embraced me."

She looked so forlorn, he hugged her. "We're all a little homesick for Pisgah Forest."

But Locust Hollow was the right place for their family. And they had a house, not a shack. It was a crude log cabin with the kitchen and living room together. The difference was two bedrooms plus a loft that Sarah and Adam loved. Scampering up and down the ladder like squirrels up and down a tree, they staked out their claim at each end. All the space made them feel like they were in a palace.

The three other families were in lumber shacks close by and the five crewmen, including Ethan, were in a much smaller bunkhouse. With the crew cut to nine men in all, less than half what it had been, Hannah and Bess insisted that they and Nora and Alice do the cooking during Laurel's pregnancy. She didn't have her usual energy this time. They were all still adjusting to the fact that the rest of the crew would not be coming in, stomping the woods dirt off, slicking back their hair and laughing as they sat down to eat.

The congregation of Locust Hollow Baptist Church swelled considerably the next Sunday, by five women, three young men, and five children. The pastor and people were gratified to find out that the logging camp people were churchgoing folks. Mrs. Gertrude Quattlebaum, the most vocal of the church members, had expressed concern that with the coming of the logging crew, riffraff might be living among them.

The next week when a few of the women gathered to clean the church, one of them said, "The people from that logging camp surprised me. Did you notice how well they were dressed? Even those young men and the children."

Gertrude Quattlebaum said, "That's their way of trying to show they're as good as the rest of us. But, of course, they're not quite normal."

Belle, another talker, ventured the opinion, "They seemed normal to me. That Mrs. Worth—I talked with her—was real nice. I hope to get to know her better."

Gertrude's mouth pulled into a straight line. "Belle, you always get carried away. We need to be careful around these people. I'm sure there's something about them we aren't going like." And having laid down her edict, she handed out dustcloths. They dusted the church in silence.

After hearing the preacher, whose specialty was hell fire and brimstone, for three Sundays, Thad, Jesse and Ethan faced Hannah over Sunday dinner.

"Mama," Thad urged, "we want Mrs. Worth to keep on teachin' us. We ain't getting' much out of what the preacher's sayin'."

Ethan spoke up. "His God don't even sound like Mrs. Worth's God."

Jesse added, "We was learning stuff about how to be a Christian and live right and treat other people right from Mrs. Worth. The preacher mostly tells us how God's goin' to punish us if we foul up."

"Yeah," Ethan said. "I'm gettin' confused."

Hannah and Jed were astonished – at the boys' eagerness to keep learning and how they had sorted out the two types of teaching. Hannah looked at Jed. He raised his eyebrows. This was her territory.

"I think it's a good idea for Laurel to teach a Sunday School class," she said. "I'll speak to her and the preacher about it."

Hannah told Laurel about the boys' conversation and that the women from camp agreed. She added, "I'm afraid the boys will stop goin' to church, Laurel, and they're so eager to learn." She paused and added, "Do you feel like there's something special about Ethan?"

Laurel nodded. "Yes. I wondered if it was just me."

"He's a good influence on my boys. I never saw a young man so interested in God."

Hannah's next step was to talk to the preacher. He was delighted. His wife had been planning to start a class for the children.

"Mrs. Worth could have her class of young people and adults while my wife has the children's class just before the preaching service."

Two weeks later, the classes began. Laurel found it easier than what she had done in the box car for two reasons. First, she wasn't cooking for the crew and had more time to prepare. Second, it was easier without trying to cover such a wide age range. She could speak in adult language.

At first just the boys and women from camp came, plus a few mothers who had brought their children to Sunday school. Then one morning the preacher scooted in on the back row. Laurel was teaching a series of lessons from the Old Testament. She told how God led His chosen people, the nation of Israel, out of slavery in Egypt to the land He had given to Abraham, their forefather, several hundred years before. After she detailed God's loving kindness in meeting their needs, she explained how He does the same with His children today.

The preacher was as enthralled as Ethan. He started getting glimpses of God he had never had before. He encouraged the congregation to come, and he never missed a lesson himself. The class grew to include almost the whole congregation – except Gertrude Quattlebaum and her group of followers. She insisted that something was strange about that Worth woman. "If she's as smart as they say, what's she doing in a loggin' camp? Just wait! We'll find out something that will reveal these people for who they really are. Any pregnant woman with a proper sense of modesty wouldn't stand before a group, including men. It's not decent. And where's her husband? I don't see him at church listening to her."

Minnie, one of Gertrude's group, had been with her husband to hear Laurel's lesson on Sunday morning. She gathered her courage and spoke, "Gertrude, she stands behind the pulpit, so you can't see her stomach. Anyway, her dress is made so it hangs loose. She's very stylish. Besides, the men ought to know what causes a woman to be pregnant."

"Minnie!" Gertrude stormed in a scandalized tone. "You are offensive."

"No, Gertrude. You're offensive," the brave little woman retaliated. "I'm planning to go with my husband to hear her lessons on Sunday morning. I never heard anybody make the Bible come alive the way she does." She turned and walked away. The first of Gertrude's inner circle had defected.

Justin, meanwhile, was adjusting to the changes and demands of a new job. He and Jed estimated that their production should be about half what it was in the forest in an average week. The wages and food costs, however, were cut to less than half. The crew would be making the same. Justin would be making less on percentage because production was less, but they were still making a good living and saving for their farm.

One big adjustment was in hauling out the logs. Beck Lumber Company had provided Justin with two logging trucks. As Hiram Beck said, it was a good sight cheaper than building a railroad. Justin and Jed learned to drive the trucks first, then taught Bulldog and Tom. Eventually, all the men learned to drive them except Zeke and Odell. They wouldn't touch them. Ethan turned into an excellent driver, with Thad right on his heels. Jed made Jesse wait until he was older. Horseless carriages – Model T's and some Chevrolets – cluttered the dirt roads of Deerbrook. It was hard for a horse and wagon to get through anymore.

In the dog days of August, Sarah entered fifth grade and Adam entered third. They were close enough to the school to walk. One part of Justin was happy he no longer had to take them; but, another part was sad. He was needed full-time on the job now. Laurel felt quite civilized as she watched them walk off to school in the mornings with their books and lunch pails. They took Tommy, Alice's son, with them to start first grade on time at six years of age.

Caroline was so impressed she begged for her own lunch pail. Laurel washed out a lard bucket and put a butter and jelly biscuit in it. With a book under one arm and her pail in the other, Caroline pretended she was going to school, too.

Laurel felt her first labor pain on a September afternoon after canning apples all day. Justin went for Dr. Leighton. Hannah and Bess stayed with Laurel and made preparations. They missed Mrs. Stevens. She was at the other end of the county and out of reach.

Dr. Leighton, riding in Justin's Model T Ford over the dusty roads, commented, "I'm glad to see you're not hibernating anymore."

"I still prefer that to this, but my children have to go to school."

"How do you like your car?"

"I like the time it saves. But, again, it's not quite as satisfying as having a living horse under you, especially one you...you care about."

"Yeah," Dr. Leighton allowed. "A car is just a machine."

After a sleepless night for everyone, just before dawn broke, and as a nearby rooster started his wake-up calls, Laurel delivered a boy. She was thirty-six and this labor and delivery had been her hardest yet.

Dr. Leighton congratulated Justin. "You have two of each now. Most people can't arrange that. She had a hard time."

Justin read correctly that he was saying: "This is enough." And, at the moment, Justin agreed with him. They named the baby David Hunter Worth.

Sam Parker at *The Wildwood Journal* was the first to inform Justin that he had moved his family into rough country. "That corner of the county is nesting ground for bootleggers and outlaws."

"But Locust Hollow is a nice community," Justin protested.

"I know it is," Sam answered. "But the territory surrounding it is occupied by some rough customers."

"What do you mean by outlaws?"

"That area of the county has some caves that are almost inaccessible. The land around them is mostly vertical instead of horizontal. Outlaws can hole up indefinitely."

"Sam, say right out what you're skirtin' around."

"Okay. Do you carry-in the payroll for your crew?"

"Yes. On Fridays. In cash."

"Can you change that?"

Justin stared at him. He was serious.

"I guess so. They'd have to come into town to pick up their pay at the office."

"I'd advise it. And let the word out. The crew needs to do some belly achin' around the community that they have to go all the way to Deerbrook to get paid."

Justin held out his hand. "Thank you, Sam. I'll arrange it."

Chapter Twenty-three

About two months later on a clear November Saturday, Justin, Laurel, Nora, and the children came face to face with some of those rough customers. Justin had talked Laurel into going to Deerbrook and taking the children, with Nora going along to help. Sarah and Adam had never been to town much. Justin enjoyed showing them around, and showing off his family.

On the way back home, Justin slowed the car to a creeping pace to negotiate a hair pin curve on a steep uphill grade. Suddenly, the road in front of them was full of men with kerchiefs covering their faces to their eyes. There were six of them. Two had rifles which were pointed lazily to the ground.

Everybody in the car was struck dumb.

As the leader approached, Justin rolled down his window.

"Are you Justin Worth?"

"I am."

"You have your camera with you?"

"My camera?" Justin asked, astonished.

"Yes, your camera," he repeated.

Justin opened the car door. The masked man stepped back to let him out. They moved away from the car. One of the riflemen came to stand with them.

"What would you do with a camera?" Justin asked, trying to figure this out.

"We wouldn't do nothin' with it, but you would."

"Tell me what you want! You're scaring my family." Justin's voice was hard.

"We want you to take some pictures of our still."

"Where is your still?"

"Oh, now I can't tell you that. We're goin' to blindfold you and lead you in. You take the pictures. Then we blindfold you again and lead you out."

"What about my wife and children?"

"They'll have to wait for you. We didn't expect your wife and young'uns to be with you."

"How're you going to get the pictures after I take them? Hold me up again?"

"We'll talk about that on the way. Just get your camera and let's get movin'."

"Just a minute. I want to move my car out of this curve and onto level ground. It's blocking the road."

"Okay. You follow my boys 'til they say stop. They'll find you a place to pull off the road. If you try anything funny they'll shoot your tires down."

Justin got in the car. He told Laurel and the others what he had to do. Then he shifted into low gear and followed four of the men around the curve. The two with the rifles came along behind. Soon after the road leveled out, the men motioned for Justin to pull off on a grassy spot on the right side.

Laurel took his hand, her face pale. "Please be careful. Don't make them mad."

"They won't harm me. They want pictures of their still and they need me for that."

He turned to the children. "Sarah and Adam, don't be afraid. I'm going to take some pictures and I'll be back. Help your mama."

As he got out of the car, he said, "Nora, take care of them."

"I will," Nora said confidently.

Adam rolled down the window to try to stay close to his dad a little longer. As soon as Justin pulled his camera and tripods from the trunk, one of the men took them out of his hands as the man in charge stepped up to blindfold him. Justin held up his hand. "Wait!" He didn't want his family to see him led away blindfolded.

"No!" the man yelled. "We do it this way!"

Before anybody could react, Adam was out of the car and had launched himself at the man's mid-section, beating him and screaming, "You do what my daddy says!"

Sarah followed Adam and jerked the blindfold from the startled man's hand. "My daddy will tell you when you can blindfold him."

Justin grabbed Adam and Sarah and froze. Laurel and Nora held their breath. No one moved or made a sound. Then somebody snickered, and then somebody else. Soon all the men were laughing, including the one who had been attacked. His eyes were merry above the kerchief. "You carry your own bodyguards, I see."

"Looks like it," Justin said. He squatted down on the ground and looked Adam and Sarah in the eyes. "I'll be okay. It's safer for everybody if they blindfold me. But we'll wait 'til we're out of sight." He stuck the wadded up blindfold in his pocket.

"Now, go on and take care of your mama and the little ones."

As he passed the car, he grinned at Laurel and winked. Then they were gone out of sight. Before they blindfolded him Justin said, "Be careful with my camera and tripods."

It was an unusual journey but not as uncomfortable as he thought it would be, blindfolded. His captors had relaxed after the laughter over the children. The one in charge held him by the arm. After a few awkward minutes of trying to match steps, Justin said, "Let me follow you. It'll be easier." He had slipped the blindfold up on his nose 'til he could see straight down, where he was stepping. And his woods sense gave him confidence.

After a little way, the leader asked, "What are them young'uns names?"

"Sarah and Adam."

"Tell me about 'em."

"They both love the woods. And…and the three of us are real close. I think it's because I've spent so much time with them."

"Doin' what?"

"Before we moved here, we lived so far back in Pisgah Forest I had to take them to school on horseback. We had more than two hours a day together."

"Why'd you go to all that trouble just for them to go to school?"

"My wife's a school teacher and she would've moved out to town with them if I hadn't taken 'em."

"So your wife's a fighter, too!"

"She fights for what she believes is important." Then he added, "And she's usually right."

"I'd like to know my young'uns would fight for me like that."

"Mine surprised me," Justin admitted.

It was a big still and they were obviously proud of it. Justin worked as carefully and professionally as if he were photographing a church group. He studied the rays of the sun that filtered through the trees and caught the still from several sides. The men, faces still covered, watched respectfully as if he were a magician. He well might have been, covering his head with a black cloth to focus and click.

"Why don't you get in this last one?" he called out.

"With our faces covered?" asked one of the men.

"Sure. You'll know who you are," Justin said, laughing.

So they gathered round with some self-consciousness and teasing. Someone said, "This is the way to git your picture took. Cover the ugly part."

On the way back with just four men, the one in charge told Justin to send the pictures to a post office box just across the state line in South Carolina. It was not as far away as Deerbrook. Justin admired their caution, but he knew caution and fear were their daily rations.

"How do I get paid?" he asked.

"I thought you might want to be paid," the man said easily. "How much will it be?"

Justin told him a sum. He peeled off some bills. "Here's half of it. After we get our pictures, I'll get the other half to you." Justin didn't ask any details. Somehow he trusted them.

They had been climbing quite awhile when the men stopped and told Justin to remove his blindfold. "Just go straight up that holler and you'll find your car and family. Don't talk about this to anybody and warn your family not to. Tell them kids I was afeared to come back. Afeared they'd jump me again." Everybody laughed and Justin moved off, carrying his equipment.

It had been an anxious time for Laurel, Nora, Sarah and Adam. They had passed the time the best way they could. Sarah and Adam played in the woods. Nora took care of Caroline and Laurel watched over David, who slept the afternoon away. Fortunately, no other vehicle passed so they didn't have to try to explain their situation.

Laurel's heart quickened when she heard Adam and Sarah yelling, "Daddy! Daddy! Here we are!"

Justin stowed his camera and tripod in the trunk and submitted to hugs and kisses all around.

"Are you okay?" Laurel looked him over.

"Yes, I'm fine. How about you?"

"We're fine, now that you're back."

While he had their full attention, he said, "We can't tell anybody about what happened here today. Sarah, Adam, do you hear me? You can't talk about this to anybody. You have a secret now that you have to keep."

"Why?" asked Adam.

"If we talk, the sheriff and revenuers may come and want me to direct them to the still."

"And you wouldn't?" Sarah asked.

"I wouldn't want to get in the middle, between the law and the bootleggers. It could get dangerous for our family. Besides, I don't know where the still is. I was blindfolded."

Laurel knew this wasn't the exact truth. Justin was a natural pathfinder.

He hunkered down to the children's level and held out his hands palms up. "I want you both to give me your word, your solemn promise, that you won't tell anybody."

"Adam?"

Adam took his daddy's hand. "I promise."

"Sarah?"

Sarah took her daddy's hand. "I promise."

"Your word is your bond," Justin continued.

"What does that mean?" Adam asked.

"It means that you've given me your word of honor, your oath, your pledge. And I can trust you to keep it."

They nodded, impressed by his serious manner. They each straightened their shoulders and each said, "You can trust me, Daddy."

Laurel looked on in approval. Justin had his own effective method of teaching.

Justin kept his part of the bargain. The pictures turned out well. He mailed them as instructed. About a month later as he brought the car around the same difficult curve, a man, face covered, jumped off the bank and waved him down. Justin rolled down his window and recognized the leader of the bootlegging crew.

"So we meet again," he said.

"We liked the pictures. My pa…he ain't well… jists sets and looks at 'em over and over. But you sent more pictures than we asked for. I can't pay you for all of 'em."

"I don't expect you to. You boys worked so hard for those pictures, I thought all six of you needed one. The extras are free."

"We thank you, then." The bootlegger handed him a wad of dirty bills. "We've had a lot of laughs over your young'uns jumpin' me. The boys has told it over and over…I brung the kids a present."

He fished in his pocket and laid a large tooth in Justin's hand. "This here's a bear tooth. In our clan, a boy starts wearing it when he thinks he's ready to fight. Your Adam's ready. See that hole drilled through it? Put it on a leather thong for him."

Next, he reached inside his shirt and brought out a large feather. "This here's an eagle feather." Something in Justin's reaction made him stop. They looked at each other.

"No," he said. "We didn't kill no eagle. We wouldn't do that. My daughter found this feather. She liked the story about Sarah and sent it to her."

"Thank you. They'll be happy over these gifts."

"Thank you for the pictures and for not sendin' in the sheriff."

Justin looked at him in surprise. "How could I do that when I went in and out blindfolded?"

"A little birdie told me you could find your way back to our still without much bother. You're at home in the woods."

The masked man knew Justin could walk right in on them anytime. And Justin knew he knew. There was a lot at stake for both of them. They looked at each other. A message of mutual trust was passed. As Justin shifted into low gear he said, "If you ever need us, you know where we live. My wife is pretty good at helping with sickness." He held out his hand. The bootlegger shook it.

"I'll remember." And he was gone before the wheels kicked gravel.

Justin had no way of knowing that his encounter with the bootleggers would one day save his life.

On a cold, snowy night in early February, a heavy knock on the door woke Justin and Laurel. Justin lit the lamp, pulled on his pants and went to the door. A stranger stood looking at him.

"Mr. Worth, I come to git your wife. My wife's havin' trouble birthin' our baby."

"Oh," Justin said, laughing, recognizing the voice. "I didn't know you without your kerchief over your face." It was the leader of the bootlegger gang. He didn't even smile at Justin's joke.

"I'm real worried about my wife and baby. She's in a bad way."

Justin knew desperation when he heard it. He went into action.

"Come in and get warm. We'll be ready as soon as we can."

He called Laurel, explaining quickly. Then he went to get Nora to stay with the children and Hannah to go with them. He came back by the porch. "Come help me saddle the horses. One of the women in camp has delivered a lot of babies. She'll go with us."

They were ready to ride in a short time. As they mounted, Justin said, "This is my wife, Laurel, and Hannah Owen."

The man answered, "I'm Abner and my wife's Rosalee."

Laurel sat in the saddle with Justin behind her. They filed out of the yard.

The baby was in a breach position—buttocks first. And Rosalee was a small woman. She had already been in labor about fifteen hours and was almost lifeless with exhaustion. She was hardly aware of their presence. Laurel and Hannah realized they could easily lose the baby and the mother. The elderly woman in attendance, Abner's mother, looked utterly beaten. The shack was sickeningly hot and smelly.

Laurel remembered Mrs. Stevens. What would she do in this situation? Laurel crossed the room and opened the door wide.

"We need some fresh air. And I need some cold water and a cloth."

Hannah said, "Wait. Here comes another pain." Rosalee groaned and writhed as the contraction ripped through her. It was pain beyond endurance, and useless. Her body could not give birth as things were.

Hannah and Laurel looked at each other. "Sometimes it helps to rotate the baby slightly," Laurel remembered from her training. "It helps to clear the blockage."

"We'll have to cut her before we can get hold of the baby," Hannah said.

Rosalee gave a sigh. Her eyes rolled back. Laurel grabbed her wrist and felt her pulse. It was weak and…and her heart was out of rhythm. They were losing her…They had to call her back.

Laurel said, "Hannah, wash her face and body with cold water." To Abner's mother she said, "Rub her arms and legs. Get the circulation going."

She never knew what made her do what she did next. Anger? Helplessness? The atmosphere of death? She wouldn't just accept it.

She could hear the men talking in low tones. She ran out the door and commanded, "Justin, Abner, I want some fiddle music and some singing out here. Abner," she looked at him, "call her back to you. Play some music she likes."

Justin heard the terror in her voice. "We'll do it, Honey." Abner was already running to get the men and their fiddles.

The cold air and cold water and the rubbing seemed to revive Rosalee somewhat. She was still dazed and too exhausted to lift her hand. Suddenly, music filled the air…fiddle music…mountain music…heavenly music. Rosalee roused and looked around, confused. "Ab?"

Laurel rubbed her face gently with the cold wet cloth. "Abner and the men are playing some music just for you. This baby's going to be born listening to mountain music."

She gave Laurel a desperate look. "I ain't got no strength left," she whispered.

"We're going to help you," Laurel said. "We'll do it together."

"Laurel," Hannah said, "let's do it before the next pain hits."

They washed their hands and arms well with soap. Abner's mother poured warm water over them to rinse. Hannah handed the knife to Laurel. Laurel closed her eyes a moment and said, "God, help me." Just as she cut, as if on cue, the male voices struck up, "I love you in the mornin', I love you late at night, I love you in the evenin' when the moon is shinin' bright…."

Rosalee's eyes flew open. "Ab's singin' my favorite song."

"Now!" said Hannah.

302

Laurel could touch the baby's buttock with her fingers. She felt and probed as Hannah was holding a cloth as tightly as she could on the long cut. Laurel found the blockage and gave a twist with her wrist. The baby moved! Then moved again by itself!

The contraction was moving relentlessly down Rosalee's body. "Let her hold your hands," she said to Hannah and Abner's mother.

"Push, Rosalee! Push hard!" she called. Rosalee summoned strength she thought she didn't have, strength from this determined red-haired woman, strength from Ab's singing voice, strength from God.

With a supreme effort she pushed the baby out into Laurel's waiting hands, with blood streaming from the cut. Blue from being confined in the birth canal so long, the baby needed oxygen. Laurel laid it over her arm and smacked its bottom. It caught its breath and cried. She wrapped the baby in a flannel blanket and laid it down on the bed. Hannah cut the cord and tied it off.

Laurel was working with Rosalee, who lay totally spent. Her sweeping motions on Rosalee's abdomen helped bring the afterbirth. Laurel had to stop the bleeding from the cut. She sprinkled powdered comfrey in it and sewed it together quickly with cat gut. Rosalee was beyond feeling pain. She was close to unconsciousness.

"Get Abner," Laurel said to his mother.

When he came in, Laurel said, "You've got a boy. But we have to work with your wife now. Talk to her. Rub her face. Keep her conscious."

He sat down beside her and rubbed her hair back. He kissed her forehead. "Rosalee...Honey," he said. "It's over. We've got us a boy."

She opened her eyes and looked at him strangely for a moment. Then her mouth worked trying to get the right message from her brain. She repeated, "A boy?" Her eyes showed understanding before they closed again.

Laurel was feeling for her pulse again. It was weak and fluttery.

"Abner, help me set her up. Wash her face and talk to her. Hannah, rub her arms and legs. I want her pulse steady before we let her go to sleep."

Abner did as he was told. "Rosalee...Honey...We've got a boy. He's lookin' for his mama. You wanta see him?" He washed her face again.

She roused and murmured, "Ab, I dreamed you was singin'."

"It wasn't no dream. I really was singin'."

"You was? Why?"

"Because this woman…," he said as he looked at Laurel, then back at Rosalee, "because I…I love you."

"I love you, too."

The boy child decided it was time to be noticed and set up a healthy cry. Abner reached and picked him up.

Rosalee's eyes registered alertness for the first time. "Let me hold him."

Abner laid him on her chest. She rubbed her hand over him, feeling of him, until weariness overtook her.

Laurel said, "Let his daddy show him off while you sleep awhile."

Rosalee slept.

Laurel and Hannah looked at each other. "God was with us," Laurel said.

"That He was," added Abner's mother.

Dawn had brought a cold, snowy day. Abner's brother and his wife, who lived close, invited them to eat a breakfast of cornbread fritters, molasses and coffee. It was good, and filling.

After looking in on Rosalee and the baby, giving some instructions and promising to be back in a day or two, Laurel and Hannah were ready to go home.

Abner thanked them with sincerity and dignity. He grinned at Justin. "I take it that you can find your way home."

"I'll risk it," Justin said, returning his grin.

When they returned two days later, they carried two little warm flannel gowns with drawstrings that Bess had made.

Rosalee, with her color returning, was a pretty woman. "Ab and his mama says you saved our lives," she said. "I thank you."

"God saved your lives. He let us help. We're glad you're both okay," Laurel said.

"Let us look that boy over," Hannah said.

On their way home, through the woods, Laurel felt a sense of destiny. If she and Hannah hadn't been there….

Later at home, Laurel said, "Justin, you're trying to protect everybody but I know who Abner is."

"I figured you did. I know how you hate liquor…with your prohibition speeches and all…It seems strange for you to be helping a bootlegger's family."

"I may hate what they *do*, but I don't hate *them*. In fact, I like them. We can't refuse help to people because of what they do." She looked at him. "I've seen you turn around and help somebody who has done you wrong."

He turned the focus back on her. "Most people can't make the distinction between the person and the wrongdoing, the way you do. I admire that."

Word got around about Laurel and Hannah delivering a breach baby and even about the fiddle music. People in the community started coming to them for ills, ranging from burns and cuts to childhood illnesses such as thrush—"thrash," they called it—and mumps and measles. Their natural remedies from the forest plus Laurel's training and their combined experience usually made for success. Bess even got in on some of the doctoring. Her humor usually had people laughing before they left. Justin and his men helped with any community needs, such as repairing a bridge or patching a roof.

The people in Locust Hollow felt blessed to have the Worth Logging Camp among them. Except for Gertrude, of course. "That story about playin' fiddle music and singin' while a baby's being born just goes to show that Laurel Worth is more witch than nurse," she confided to her diminishing group. Two more women left on that statement. They knew better. Laurel had successfully treated their sick children. But a small group still stuck with Gertrude.

Chapter Twenty-four

Justin was riding Tattoo home from town one Friday afternoon in autumn when the outlaws made their move on him. Jed had borrowed the car to take Hannah and Nora to see their daddy who was sick. Justin was enjoying being in the woods on Tattoo again. The Model T and dusty roads saved time but couldn't compare with the enjoyment he felt in the woods with Tattoo's companionship. The narrow trail led for awhile between two high banks. As he rounded a curve, two masked men on horses faced him with pistols leveled. He knew these were not Abner's men. They were dirty and tattered with long tangled hair. There was tension in their stance. He felt the fingers of fear touch his gut as he drew Tattoo to a stop.

"Hand over your payroll," one demanded.

"Not even a 'howdy.' Just orders," Justin said.

"I said we want your payroll."

"I don't have a payroll. My men go to Deerbrook to get paid."

"You're lyin'."

Justin wanted out of here. He said, "Search me and see."

They moved in on him. Close. One on each side. Their smell was awful. They searched the saddlebags and leaned in to search his pockets. They kept the few dollars they found in his billfold. As the man on his right straightened up, the kerchief fell off his face, down around his neck.

Justin knew he was looking at Bill "Bandit" Butler. His picture was on wanted posters all over town. He had cut a swath through three states, robbing and killing.

He knew Justin recognized him. "Well, now," he drawled, "that kerchief fallin' is bad luck for you. You know we'll have to kill you." His cold eyes looked at Justin as he lifted his pistol a few inches from Justin's chest.

Before Justin could react, a voice on the bank said, "Drop your guns, both of you!"

The outlaws looked around but held on to their pistols.

The voice that Justin recognized said, "We've got two shotguns and two rifles aimed at you! Show 'em, boys!"

Four masked men moved to the edge of the bank, their gun barrels pointed at the outlaws. "Drop-your-guns-now-or-we'll-shoot!" The outlaws' pistols thudded to the ground.

"Now listen to me good! This man and his family are friends of our'n. You touch 'em again and we'll hunt you down. You can't hide from us. We know exactly which cave you're holin' up in. Now git out!"

The outlaws left in a hurry. One of Abner's men picked up the pistols.

Abner jumped off the bank and held up his hand to help Justin dismount. Justin mopped his face. He was weak with relief. The two men looked at each other. Justin held out his hand. Abner shook it.

"I would have met the undertaker if you hadn't happened by—or did you know…?"

"We heard they was plannin' to jump you. The rest was guesswork. The Good Lord wasn't ready for you yet."

"Thank you, Abner, and all you men." He lifted his face to them. They had dropped their kerchiefs. "You saved my life today. I owe you."

"No," Abner said. "We still owe you one life. Your wife saved my wife *and* son."

Laurel never knew about the outlaws until years later. Justin figured she had enough to worry about.

Justin was again working for the presidential election. Calvin Coolidge had made his mark by being re-elected in 1924. His greatest contribution, Justin felt, was in getting big business established as a force in the country's economy. During Coolidge's term, Herbert Hoover had become greatly admired as Secretary of Commerce. Hoover had become internationally famous for his work as Food Administrator in World War I and for his post-war relief work in Europe. In November, 1928, he was elected as the thirty-first President of the United States.

Meanwhile, Sarah and Adam were enjoying being with other children their age. Their knowledge of the woods made them popular. Soon they had gathered a group that swung on saplings and grapevines, riding out arcs of fun through the air.

One late afternoon in November, however, Sarah and Adam were alone. They took a shortcut through some woods toward home. They broke through a pine thicket upon a small clearing. And there, right in front of them in the fading light was Raw Head and Bloody Bones!

Stark terror seized them. They grabbed each other's hands, screamed, and raced for home. They were sure his bloody hand would seize them from behind at any moment. They fell through the door, still screaming. Their terror transmitted to Caroline and David, who started crying, too.

Laurel finally shook Sarah hard and commanded, "Hush!"

Sarah obeyed, then Adam.

"What's wrong?"

"Oh, Mama, we saw Raw Head and Bloody Bones," Sarah wailed.

Laurel blinked. "Where?"

"In the woods. He was like Daddy said. No skin on his head or body, just bloody all over," Sarah said.

Adam added, "He was just standing there, straight up, like a person. We ran fast. I don't know if he followed us." He glanced at the closed door.

Laurel held them both close 'til they calmed down. Then wiping their hair off their foreheads she said, "There's no such thing as Raw Head and Bloody Bones. That's just a spooky tale. It's not true."

They stared at her. "But, Mama, we seen – saw – him," Adam protested.

"You saw something, I'm sure. Your Daddy will go see if he can find out what it was. Now, go wash your faces I'll get you some milk and cookies."

"I…I'm not hungry," Adam said.

"Me, neither," Sarah added.

Laurel looked at them. "You both got a bad scare. Go rest 'til your daddy gets home."

They climbed into their loft and crawled into their secure straw tick beds. Raw Head and Bloody Bones couldn't get them here.

The next day Justin went looking. His two brave kids were spooked. He walked them to school and told them he would be back for them. He had to settle this thing. He wouldn't have them be afraid to go into their beloved woods. The answer was simple and he was so relieved to find it, he rode Tattoo to the schoolhouse and asked to borrow Sarah and Adam for a little while. As they rode off, together on Tattoo, he explained.

"I found what you thought was Raw Head and Bloody Bones. It would have scared me, too, coming on it at dusk the way you did. But it's not Raw Head and Bloody Bones. There's no such thing. I'm taking you to see this, so you'll know."

"Daddy," Sarah begged. "I don't want to see it again."

"I don't either," Adam said.

"You have to. So you won't be afraid to play in your woods. You can close your eyes 'til I tell you to open them."

They gladly closed their eyes. When Tattoo stopped, Justin said, "Okay, open your eyes."

They looked.

"Tell me what it is," he said. It was still scary, but they were looking at it from Tattoo's broad back, with their Daddy holding on to them.

"It's…it's a skinned animal," said Sarah.

"Yeah," Adam said, "hung up."

"Our neighbor killed a cow for beef. He cleaned and skinned it and is letting it bleed. He'll take it down and cut it up. It'll make some good roasts and steaks."

On the way back to school Justin asked, "Feel better?"

"Yes," Adam said. "You won't need to walk us home."

Sarah hugged him. "Thank you, Daddy."

One evening in spring, they had just gone to bed when someone pounded on the door and yelled, "Help me! Let me in! Hurry!"

Justin jumped up, pulled on his pants and jerked the door open. Lem, the community drunk, almost fell into his arms, babbling and crying.

"Shut the door quick! He's after me! Hurry!" He was shaking like he had palsy. Justin closed the door and turned to help him.

"You're safe in here." Justin helped him to a chair. "Sit down. Who's after you?"

"The devil, that's who!"

Justin stopped short. "The devil?" So this was drunk talk.

He might as well hear the rest of it. "Where'd you see the devil?"

Justin knew Laurel had gotten up and had put on her robe. He was sure Sarah and Adam, in the loft, were awake listening.

"I seen him in the graveyard." The man was clearly terrified. "I need your wife to pray for me. I heard she's a good woman who knows about God. I want her to ask God not to let the devil get me." His voice rose in a drunken wail.

In the small house, Laurel had heard every word. She walked over to him and said, "Lem, I'll pray for you, but you have to be quiet and close your eyes."

She was trying to stop the hysteria.

"I'm afeared to close my eyes, Ma'am. He might jump me from behind."

"No, he won't. Justin will stand behind you with his hands on your shoulders."

Justin obediently did as she said. She took both of Lem's hands in hers, as if he were a child. "Now, let's pray."

Feeling a little safer with somebody behind him and in front of him, Lem closed his eyes.

"Our Father, Lem is scared the devil is going to get him. Help him believe You will keep him safe. Help him to know You love him even when he's drinking. Take away his fear. Help him remember that You are stronger than the devil and that you won't let the devil have him. Amen."

Lem opened his eyes and looked at her, holding tightly onto her hands. He slowly exhaled, his breath pungent with whiskey. In a calm voice, he said, "I plumb forgot that God is stronger than the devil." He was like a child who suddenly remembered something good. He relaxed, but when his fear went, his energy went. He was sinking fast.

"Lem, my wife's fixing you a place to sleep but I need you to answer some questions," Justin said. "Tell me what you saw in the graveyard."

"I done told you. I saw the devil."

"Tell me what happened and what he looked like."

"I was settin' there in the moonlight, leaning agin one of them flat tombstones, having me a pint. I must'a dozed off and sorta' slid down on the ground. Then I felt somethin' touch me and felt hot breath on my face."

He stood up. "I'm…I'm gettin' scared again."

"You know you're safe now. Go on."

"Well, there he was, looking down at me. He," Lem said slowly, swallowing hard, "had red shiny eyes and…and horns…and a beard…I slid out from under him and got up and run." He looked around the room and said to himself, "I'm safe now."

Justin pondered over Lem's tale as he got him to bed. Lem was sound asleep in minutes.

Justin and Laurel looked at each other. "He saw something that scared him pretty bad. I think I'll take the lantern and look around. Do you mind?"

"No," Laurel said. "Lem's out for the night. And I'm curious too, so hurry back."

Laurel sat down at the table to wait for Justin. Sarah and Adam were down the ladder in a blink, beside her whispering. "Mama," Adam said, "what do you think he saw? He sure was scared!"

"I don't know. Maybe your daddy will find out."

"Mama," said Sarah, "I'll remember you praying for that man as long as I live. It…it made him better."

"Yes. He must have believed it because he calmed down."

After awhile Justin came in shaking his head with a big grin on his face. They all looked at him.

"I found him."

"The devil?" Adam breathed, astonished.

"He sure looked like the devil. Had horns and shiny red eyes and a white beard just like Lem said. Guess what it was."

"Daddy…tell us right now!" Sarah ordered.

He started laughing. "It was a billy goat! An old grandpa billy goat! I sure would have been scared, without being drunk, to find that ugly thing hovering over me."

They all looked at each other, laughing, as they imagined it.

The next morning Lem didn't remember anything. He was embarrassed when he woke up with a bad headache in the house of someone he hardly knew. Justin took him to the mess hall for breakfast and some strong coffee before he went on his way. Justin didn't feel now was the time to inform Lem of his encounter with the devil the night before. Someday, maybe; not today.

Laurel was aware of the antagonism of Gertrude and her followers. It was obvious to anybody with eyes and ears. Bess was totally put out with the woman for daring not to like Laurel. She would set off laughter among the camp women, mimicking Gertrude. "I'd like to pull that little tight bun down off the back of her head and…."

"Bess," interrupted Laurel, "you don't want to do any such thing. The poor woman's unhappy and thinks I'm the reason. But I'm not. While she picks on me, she's leaving somebody else alone."

"Don't it even bother you?" Alice asked.

"Yes. It bothers me. I've thought about it a good bit. To please Gertrude I'd have to stop being who I am. So, I just leave it with her and go on with my life."

And her life was full to overflowing. David was almost two and into everything. He was a sensitive little boy who liked being near his mother or Sarah. But he was also happy with Nora or Hannah or Bess or Alice. He liked to play with Alice's daughter, Elizabeth, who was five. Caroline would soon be six and would start to school in August. She played with David and Elizabeth, bossing them around like a drill sergeant. Adam and Tommy were usually busy with boy stuff. Laurel knew that when David was older he would join them.

Cooking for the crew still took a big portion of the women's lives, but cooking for nine men instead of twenty-one greatly lightened their load. During the nine years they had been together they had become a family. They knew and accepted each other's faults, they helped each other, they loved and bossed and looked after each other's children. They had become dependent on each other and refused to think that someday they would separate.

They had all changed considerably. Bess was the most changed and the most vocal about it. Once in awhile she would say, "Remember the days when I was stupid and hated Laurel?" She was now a pretty, lively woman who dressed in good taste. She could read and write. She was an excellent seamstress, a good cook and kept a clean house. She was even learning some practical nursing from Laurel and Hannah. Her life started changing that day long ago when Laurel told her how much God loved her. She had received God's forgiveness, had become "His child" and now enjoyed the love from her Heavenly Father that she had never received from her earthly one. Laurel had introduced her to this new life and, next to Bulldog, she loved Laurel best in the world.

Hannah was still Hannah. Thank goodness! But because of the way Laurel looked up to her, she had developed a self-respect and confidence that communicated her capability in handling life. She was comfortable in her own skin and this brought comfort to those around her.

Alice, in nine years, had not only matured, she had bloomed. Laurel remembered the painfully shy girl with practically no ability and less confidence. Her skinny, pale appearance and fearful manner had made her seem a shadow person. With Hannah's mothering, Bess's teasing and fussing over her appearance, Nora's friendship and Laurel's loving, Alice would never be mistaken for a shadow now. She was more like a wildflower, thriving in a favorable environment. She could cook and sew and keep a clean house. She was a good wife and mother. She had put on some weight and Bess had made her crimp and curl her hair regularly so that it was now a habit.

Nora…Laurel privately thought of Nora as their Gentle, Gracious Giant or their Guardian Angel. Nora had, in Laurel's opinion, been endowed with a special grace peculiar to handicapped people. Nora's unusual appearance was the same, of course, but she had come to terms with herself about it. Laurel's obvious love and praise for her was the sunshine in which Nora lived. She would never forget the first time Laurel had introduced her to some smartly dressed women in Deerbrook. Laurel had said, "I'd like you to meet Nora, one of my best friends." Not, "one of the women who works in our camp" or even "the woman who keeps my children," but "one of my best friends." And they had all had tea together, as if she was normal. It had been a landmark in Nora's life. Something inside her had stood up tall and proud that day and had never totally bowed, cringing again.

Laurel wouldn't allow her to be embarrassed in public. One day some young girls pointed and laughed. Laurel said, "Nora, they don't know any better. When anybody makes fun of you, it's their problem, not yours. Just feel sorry for anybody who is so ignorant! Remember, it's not *you* who has the problem, it's *them*!"

Laurel was so obviously angry and vehement about it, Nora giggled. And almost ever after when someone made fun, she would feel a giggle inside her shoving the shame right out.

One day Laurel said to her, out of the blue, "Nora, you are one of the best people I know. I told my friends at Papa's house that someday I hope to be as good and kind as you and Hannah."

Nora pondered over this statement and treasured it as some men treasure gold. Laurel Worth wanted to be like her. It made her feel very special.

One hot July afternoon all the women were in the mess hall. Hannah and Alice were cooking supper, and Bess, Nora and Laurel were peeling peaches to can. The younger children were playing around their feet. The older children were playing in the woods and the men were on the job.

Suddenly, a ripple passed through the mess hall. It was so slight they each thought they had imagined it. Then another came. Bess asked Laurel, "Did you feel that?"

Laurel stood up. "Yes." As she picked up David, a tremor shook the building so hard, pots and pans clattered to the floor.

"Let's get out of here," Laurel said as the frightened women grabbed up the small children. They ran outside but were terror stricken anew to feel the ground moving in waves under their feet.

"Quick! Everyone into the clearing, away from everything!" screamed Laurel.

"The other children!" Alice said. As if summoned, they all came running pell-mell to reach their mamas.

They heard trees falling before they saw them. "Our men!" Bess said, speaking everyone's thoughts aloud. They looked at Laurel and Hannah for reassurance. Laurel looked at Hannah.

"The men know the woods," Hannah said.

They were helpless as the earth trembled and rumbled and the buildings shook. They stayed in a small group, a makeshift circle, with the smaller children in their arms and the older ones beside them.

Laurel said aloud, "Lord protect us, our children, our men, and the people of our community."

A scream cut through the rumbling. "Laurel Worth, where are you?"

The women saw a strange sight. Gertrude Quattlebaum was running toward them, as if pursued by demons. Her hair had come loose and was hanging about her face. Her clothes were flapping about her as she ran.

"It's the end of time," she screamed. "I'm scared to die!"

She came to a stop before Laurel. "I've treated you bad," she said, panting. "I don't want to face God with the way I've talked about you. I want you to forgive me before I die," she wailed. "I need you to pray for me."

The children started crying. Bess reached and took David out of Laurel's arms.

Laurel felt sorry for the hysterical woman. She reached and took both her hands.

"It's not the end of time, Gertrude. It's an earthquake." She explained as she would to a child in school. "Yes, I forgive you and I'll pray for you."

She held on to the crying woman's hand and prayed, "Our Father, I ask again for your protection for all of us. Gertrude is sorry for the wrong things she's done. Please, forgive her. I ask for Your peace and assurance for her right now. Amen."

As she prayed, the earth became still under their feet and the rumbling ceased.

Gertrude looked around and listened. She backed up a step or two put her hand over her mouth and stared at Laurel.

"You caused the earthquake to stop," she whispered.

"No, I didn't!" Laurel said shortly. "It just stopped! There may be another one any time."

"But you asked Him and it stopped," Gertrude insisted.

Hannah, seeing Laurel's expression, stepped up and handed Gertrude a handkerchief. She then turned to Laurel. "It did stop while you was prayin'."

Laurel was troubled but she knew Hannah was telling her to be quiet about it.

Their thoughts had never left their men, but they checked the mess hall to see if the stove had spilled out any fire and surveyed the damage in all the camp buildings. They found no major problems.

The women had to know if their men were safe. Hannah said, "They'll be just as worried about us as we are about them. They'll come on in as soon as they can."

They all watched the trail near the mess hall, willing the crew to appear. Bess, mollified by Gertrude's apology to Laurel, had pity on Gertrude and offered to fix her hair. She looked a fright.

When Abe and Dirk appeared alone, Hannah rushed to meet them. Abe said, "We're all safe except Justin. He's unconscious. Where's Laurel?"

Abe and Dirk entered with Hannah on their heels. All the women stopped and looked at them to hear the news.

"Laurel," Abe said, "Justin's hurt. A limb fell and hit him on the head. They're bringing him in. He's...he's unconscious."

A spasm of pain crossed Laurel's face. She put her hand over her eyes a moment, then pulled it slowly down over her face as if to erase the pain. Hannah put her arm around her. "Here. Sit down." Laurel sat down on the bench. She felt lightheaded from the fear battering at her senses. She had to get control. She put her head in her hands and took some deep breaths. The total silence in the room brought her around.

"Abe and Hannah, come with me to the cabin," she said. "Dirk, tell them to bring him there. And...and everybody pray."

Jed and Bulldog brought him in on a homemade stretcher made with two long poles and the men's shirts. They transferred him to the bed and waited for Laurel to examine him.

"His pulse is slow," she said. "His eyes are dilated and his breathing is shallow. I think he has a concussion. Jed, take the car and get Dr. Leighton."

Jed went. In a hurry.

Laurel and Hannah continued to work with him. He was clammy to the touch. The limb had hit him on the right side of his head, leaving his hair matted with blood. Laurel cleaned the wound, working carefully around the purple knot that was forming.

They turned him on his side and she made sure his breathing passage was open. She checked his signs every few minutes and called his name repeatedly. He didn't respond.

It was a long wait for the doctor. The people in the community, after finding no major damage from the quake, came to the camp to offer help— and stayed. When Jed finally rode in with the doctor, they found the camp full of people.

Dr. Leighton was very concerned. Justin showed no reflexes. His pulse was slow, his eyes were dilated and he had a watery discharge from his ears and nose.

"Laurel," the doctor said, "You know the signs. He has a severe concussion. I'm sure the brain is swelling some. I'm going to spend the night. We'll need to get him through the first twenty-four hours."

Laurel was relieved. "Thank you. What is your prognosis?"

"Too early to tell," he said, evading her question. "But Justin's a strong man."

For that night and the next day, her world shrank to the confines of the bedroom where Justin lay. She and Dr. Leighton checked him every fifteen minutes. Once when Dr. Leighton went out for fresh air and on to the mess hall for coffee, he came back to find her asleep beside Justin, his hand clasped tightly in both of hers. He let her rest, working quietly as he checked Justin again.

Jed and Hannah stayed through the night in the cabin with them. The rest of the crew was gathered in the mess hall. Nora and Bess took care of Caroline and David. Laurel let Sarah and Adam stay in the cabin. She knew they needed to be near their daddy. They lay quietly on their beds in the loft, crying and trying to comfort each other. One time when Hannah heard the quiet crying, she called them to come down. They crept down the ladder. Hannah and Jed held them tightly for awhile and comforted them.

It was afternoon of the next day before Justin started coming around. Laurel was sitting beside him when she realized he had shifted his head and was staring at her. His look was so strange it frightened her.

"Justin?" she whispered.

"Laurel," he whispered back. "I see two of you." He closed his eyes again and asked, "What happened?"

"You got hit on the head with a falling limb. It knocked you out."

"When?"

"Yesterday during the earthquake."

"I don't remember any earthquake."

Dr. Leighton came in. "I heard voices. I'm sure glad to hear you talking, Justin. Can you look at me?"

"Not long, Doc," Justin said as he opened his eyes. "I see two of you."

His pupils were still dilated, and his reflexes were slow, but at least they were registering.

"You can close your eyes again. Seeing one of me is enough."

"Tell me what's going on," Justin said.

Laurel took his hand as the doctor explained the concussion. "Your brain took a licking and is swollen. If you didn't have such a hard head, you'd have a fractured skull. As it is, you've got a skinned head and a purple goose egg."

Justin lay with his eyes closed.

"How long?" he asked.

The doctor understood the question. "You'll have to lie still a few days and allow your brain to get back to normal. You aren't going to feel like doing much anyway."

"My vision?" Justin asked.

"It will get okay as the swelling goes down."

"Laurel," he said, fretfully, "I don't remember an earthquake."

Dr. Leighton said, "You will after a day or two. That usually happens when you've had a hard knock on the head."

"Was anybody else hurt?" He looked at Laurel.

"No. And no damage to speak of."

"Good!" he said. He closed his eyes and relaxed.

Laurel sent Jed to spread the word that Justin had regained consciousness. Sarah and Adam had not gone far from the house all day. She called them to her and told them. They all hugged each other and cried.

Dr. Leighton gave Laurel instructions and told her some symptoms to expect. Then he went by the mess hall, which seemed to have turned into the community center. He told the crew what was happening with Justin.

"If that limb hadn't hit a glancing blow, it would've killed him. The Good Lord's not ready for him yet."

It was the second time in a few months that someone had spoken those words over Justin.

It took about a week for him to recover. The first time he stood up, vertigo struck and he vomited. His legs were rubbery for several days. One morning he woke up and said, "I remember the earthquake."

Laurel set the clock and roused him from sleep every three hours for a couple of nights. He looked at her at three o'clock one morning through sleepy eyes and said, "Good."

"Good what?" she asked.

"There's just one of you again."

Laurel was made aware again of how much people liked Justin; all kinds of people. Dr. Leighton spent so much time with him, it went way beyond the call of duty. Abner came by one day to check on him. Ethan hovered around so anxiously, she left him with Justin some while she caught up on some other things. After an impatient week of recovery, Justin was up and at 'em again.

The earthquake was actually classified as tremors along a fault line that runs through western North Carolina and Tennessee.

Laurel wondered if Gertrude would retract her confession and revert to her usual obnoxious behavior since she was no longer facing imminent destruction; but she didn't. Her campaign to discredit Laurel was over, to everybody's relief. Her submissive husband even ventured to tell her he was glad she had come to her senses.

In August, 1929, Caroline went off to school with her big sister and brother and Tommy. Laurel always wrote Papa a long letter at the beginning of each school year, keeping him up to date on his grandchildren's academic progress. It was a happy letter, telling him Sarah would start seventh grade, Adam, fifth grade and Caroline, first. Their life was good. She couldn't know that events were evolving nationally that would spin their lives out of control.

Chapter Twenty-five

On a Saturday afternoon in late October, Justin brought home a paper that was full of news about the stock market crash on Thursday. Sam could be counted on to tell Wildwood County the national news.

"It looks like panic has hit Wall Street," he told Laurel, as she was ironing the children's clothes for church.

"What does that mean?"

"It looks like scared investors are selling their stocks at whatever price they can get. Enough people have sold low, or almost given away their stocks to cause a crash."

"What can be done to get it back under control?" Laurel asked as she went to the stove and exchanged a cold flat iron for a hot one.

"It says a group of bankers met at J.P. Morgan and Company and are assuring investors that the market is still essentially sound, despite the unusual losses."

"Do you think this will affect our part of the country?"

Justin folded the paper and stood up. "I doubt it. Usually, it stabilizes before it becomes too widespread. Beck Lumber Company is a long way from Wall Street."

The following week he found out that a group of New York bankers had pooled their resources and bought stock at prices higher than the market value. When, in spite of this effort, the bottom fell out of the market on Tuesday, Justin's optimism felt its first real tremor. He went to talk to Hiram Beck, then on to Henry Sargent, at the bank where they had their savings.

That night he asked Laurel to get out their savings book. "I'm concerned about the crash. It's bound to affect the whole country in some ways. Hiram Beck assured me today that Beck Lumber Company is still operating on a firm footing. Henry Sargent says our money is safe; that nobody has withdrawn money from Deerbrook Bank."

He fished in his pocket and pulled out a scrap of paper. "According to the bank figures, we have a little over five thousand dollars in savings. Is that what our book says?"

"Yes. Five thousand, one hundred and sixty-six dollars."

"We have to make a decision," Justin continued. "I figure we have enough to buy the farm we've been looking at just outside Deerbrook, make the necessary repairs to the house and maybe buy some furniture."

He hesitated. "But I hate to start a run on the bank. It would look bad. Beck Lumber Company money is the backbone of Deerbrook Bank. I guess as long as he feels his money is safe, ours will be, too."

"We've trusted Mr. Beck and Mr. Sargent for ten years, so I'm inclined to trust them now," Laurel said. "Just keep informed."

So life in Locust Hollow continued in its insulated and isolated pattern. As for the effect on their lives, the October crash might have been a figment of their imagination, until one Friday in February. Justin came in from Deerbrook and, without a word, sat down at the table and put his head in his hands.

Laurel rushed to his side.

"Justin, are you sick? What's the matter? Look at me...."

He took his hands away and reached for her. "Sit down, Laurel."

She knew bad news was coming by his pale, set countenance.

"What's wrong? Has something happened to Papa?"

He drew a deep breath. "Beck Lumber Company is shutting down and Deerbrook Bank closed its doors today."

She stared at him as if he were babbling nonsense. "What do you mean?"

"I mean I'm out of a job and...."

She interrupted. "But we can buy the farm and be okay until you find another job."

Then she saw the pain in his eyes. "Laurel, the bank folded! Our money is gone." He stood up and repeated, "*Gone!*"

She stood to face him. "No, Justin, it can't be! We've spent ten years of our lives working to save that money!"

He reached to put his arms around her but she swept him aside. "They have to give us our money! It's *ours*! It's not *theirs*! How can they just keep it? What did they say?"

"Everybody has lost their money. Beck Lumber Company was part of a conglomerate that called in its assets. When that money left the bank, it closed. Nobody can get their money."

"What about the Becks and the Sargents?"

"They're broke, too. Victims of the crash just like we are, and thousands of others like us."

She lifted her chin as he had seen her do hundreds of times when faced with a challenge, but this time it didn't work. Strength seemed to go out of her as she collapsed in a chair and covered her face with her hands.

"Laurel, I have to tell the crew. Beck did scrape up enough money to pay this week's wages."

He took a roll of bills out of his pocket and laid it on the table. "This is the last money any of us will see for awhile."

They looked at each other as their thoughts ranged over the families they had felt responsible for, for ten years. How would they make it? What would they do?

Laurel stood up suddenly and her chin went up again. "Justin, we're acting like somebody died! We're alive and healthy and still have each other. You and the crew can always get jobs. We'll survive this!"

He hadn't realized how much he had counted on this reaction until it happened. Relief spread through him at her in-charge, school teacher voice. He drew a deep breath, drawing in her strength to mix with his.

The families and crew met the news with an unblinking stoicism, developed by years of struggle for survival. Hardship was the norm for them. Knowing there would be no pay, the bunkhouse crew, Abe, Dirk, Zeke and Odell, came back the next week and helped Justin and the others close down the job.

Their last meal together was determinedly cheerful. They talked of inconsequential things. By unspoken agreement, nobody mentioned that their life together was over. Each person carried his sadness privately. Laurel again saw evidence of their innate strength and dignity and courtesy under duress. They all held up for each other.

When they started to leave with their bedrolls, Laurel and Justin had a burlap sack for each of them. It contained meal, flour, sugar, salt, lard, and coffee. When they started to protest, Justin said, "This food belongs to you as much as it does to us. We're dividing it equally among each family. It'll help ease the burden while you look for work."

Justin, Jed, Bulldog, and Tom would keep their families where they were for awhile, until they could find work and places to live. Ethan would stay with them. He was like a member of each family by now, so he had a choice of homes.

Justin and Laurel sat down together to figure their resources and make plans. "When is school out?" he asked.

"About the middle of May."

"Let's stay here 'til school's out. That'll give me time to find a job. I'll start looking this week." He took some change and two wadded up bills out of his pocket. "Put this with the cash you have. How much does that make us?"

She went to a sugar bowl on the shelf and brought back a few bills. "A little over twenty dollars."

"I'll sell the car and call in some debts people owe me for pictures. If they can't pay cash, I'll take food."

Laurel said, "We have enough staples like we gave the crew to last awhile. We also have some beans and corn and peaches that I canned last summer. And, of course, we have milk and butter and eggs."

He stood and pulled her to him. "I promise you our children will not go hungry."

She hugged him back. "I know, Justin. You've always been able to make money one way or another."

Neither mentioned the hovering issue of homelessness. After fifteen years of struggling to reach their dream, it had vanished like a vapor. But they would face *that* another day. Enough was enough for today.

The next few weeks carried a sense of unreality. The men went looking for jobs and places to live. Each weekday afternoon the women pooled their diminishing food supplies and prepared supper together. They drew strength from each other as they sewed and mended, knowing their clothes would have to last awhile.

One evening in March they had just finished supper when they heard a commotion outside. When Justin opened the mess hall door, they saw a yard full of people. The pastor, holding one side of a bushel basket of potatoes, said, "Mr. and Mrs. Worth, the church has brought you folks a pounding—a pound of this and a pound of that! You've meant so much to the community...."

Laurel felt Justin go tense and saw his face tighten as he interrupted. "Thank you, but we can't...."

She squeezed his arm and stepped forward. "Thank you! What a thoughtful thing for you to do! Come in and put the things on the empty table at the back."

They trouped in, talking and laughing. The pastor sensed Justin's discomfort and said easily, "You men have helped roof our houses and repair the bridge and clear off a playground for the school. And you women have been there for everything from a bee sting to childbirth. You've given us so much! We need to do this for ourselves as much as for you."

Justin swallowed his pride and answered simply. "Thank you – all of you. This will help us while we look for work."

With the awkwardness over, the men went outside to visit while the women looked over the food. There were two bushels of potatoes, two twenty-five pounds of flour, cornmeal, sugar, lard, coffee, grits and pinto beans. A big slab of streaked bacon and several cans of salmon confirmed Laurel's thoughts that this had been well planned. "You brought so much of everything."

"We knew there was eighteen people still here," Gertrude said. She handed Laurel two jars and said, "I brought you some peach preserves made with some peelings in them. I heard that's the way you like them."

On Saturday afternoon Abner rode up, hitched his horse to the post and knocked on Justin's door. When Justin opened it, he demanded, "What's this I hear about you'ns movin'?" Laurel was always disconcerted by his lack of formal greeting. He simply jumped right into the middle of things.

Justin reached to shake his hand. "Come in...come in."

"How are Rosalee and the children?" Laurel asked.

"They're fine. Our boy is growin' so fast Ma says you musta' rubbed some fertilizer on his feet when you delivered him."

Laurel just smiled at him and shook her head as she poured them some coffee. She left them to talk while she went to look for Sarah and Adam. They had taken Caroline and David out to play and she knew they would be disappointed if they missed Abner. He was one of their favorite people.

After a time, when Abner started to leave, he gave Adam a large wooden prong with instructions on how to make a slingshot. Sarah received two redbird feathers to go with her eagle feather.

"Rosalee and Ma sent you something," he told Laurel as he went and pulled something from his saddlebag. With a flourish, he handed her a quart jar. "Pure sourwood honey. The boys beat the bears to the honey tree this time."

It was Laurel who wanted to refuse the food this time. She knew how much they prized honey and how sparingly they used it.

"Thank you, Abner. Tell Rosalee and your mother we'll enjoy this for breakfast with our buttered biscuits."

As she prepared supper that night, she thought of Abner's family. She and Alice had some clothes their children had outgrown. They would need to get them to Rosalee before they moved. Tears suddenly blurred her eyes, as they seemed to do regularly these days.

They moved the second week of May, the week after school was out. The four families decided to make an exodus together, because they felt safer and wanted to help each other. The women of the community packed a separate lunch for each family, but nobody planned what happened as the wagons pulled out. The citizens of Locust Hollow spontaneously lined both sides of the road. Sarah, Adam, Tommy, and Caroline climbed down to hug their friends goodbye. Everybody pressed in wanting a last word or a handshake. Laurel's tears flowed freely. It was a bittersweet parting.

And it wasn't over yet. As the wagons entered the stretch of road that ran between two high banks, where Abner had rescued Justin from the outlaws, Abner and his band of men were waiting on horseback, again on each side of the mountain road. Each had a rifle carefully slung away from the group below them.

"Whoa!" Justin called to Tattoo. When the wagons stopped, Justin looked up. "I'm glad to see you boys. What're you up to?"

"Me and the boys want to ride along for a ways, if that's okay," Abner said. "We've been followin' you awhile but we didn't want to spook you."

Justin knew what he was saying. They were providing safe passage out of outlaw and bootleg country. "Yes," he answered. "We'll be honored to have your company."

Adam yelled, "Abner, can I ride with you?"

Abner laughed. "Yeah, I need me a sidekick. But ask your daddy."

"Sure," Justin said. "When that high bank ends and you can get to him." Adam was out of the wagon like a shot, running ahead.

They traveled several miles before Justin called a halt. "I want to talk to Abner," he told Laurel as he helped her down from the wagon. "Let's all take a break."

He and Abner walked together a little way and stopped. "You need to go back," Justin said. "We're out of danger now."

Abner grunted. "A man can't even be friendly without you figurin' somethin's up."

"I know you, my friend. And you know things I have no way of knowing. I wonder how many times you've protected me when I didn't know about it." He held out his hand and said solemnly, "Abner, I want to thank you again for my life. I owe you."

"And I repeat. I owe you and Mrs. Worth for two lives. So, I'll still be in your debt for awhile." Justin impulsively embraced the younger man. And the embrace was returned. There was no need for further words. The bootlegger and the picture-taking man were bound by the strong cords of friendship.

When the wagons reached the place where Justin and Laurel had to go their separate way, few words were spoken. The women hugged Laurel and the children. The men embraced Justin and turned away quickly.

Justin and Laurel would live near Riverside, a small logging town west of Deerbrook. Justin had signed on at the tannery, to provide logs for bark from which tannic acid was made. It would be a two-man operation, with Ethan helping him.

Laurel hated the house from the moment she saw it. It was a lonely shack, perched on a meager slice of rocky ground between the river and the logging railroad. It looked like it had been haphazardly thrown together, misused, then abandoned. She could guess Justin's thoughts as he brought his family into the yard. The place was mute testimony to their reduced circumstances—a far cry from the farm and farmhouse they had planned to buy. Sarah and Adam, for once, had nothing to say. With a benumbed silence, they moved in.

For supper they ate the leftovers from their ample lunch. Adam said, "Daddy, tell us again where the rest of us are."

Justin understood the question. Adam didn't remember ever being separated from the other families. "Jed's family is moving to a farm near Deerbrook about five miles from here. Hannah's and Nora's father is getting old and wants them to move into his big farmhouse with him. Jed's going to be a farmer." He stopped and looked anxiously at Laurel.

"And Uncle Bull…?" Sarah prompted.

"Bulldog and Tom are moving to the other side of Deerbrook, about ten miles from us. They'll still live close to each other, and work together providing logs for a sawmill."

"Is it a long way?" Adam asked.

"Yes, son. By horse and wagon, it's a distance."

Adam stood up and went outside. After a moment, Ethan followed.

Justin had two immediate concerns. Their little bit of cash was almost gone so he must get some logs out to the tannery soon. He also had to put in a crop, and Laurel, Adam and Sarah would need to plant a garden. Everything needed to be done at once.

Since it was almost past time for planting some things, they decided to use most of their precious cash for seeds and plants for the garden first. Justin had made a deal to sharecrop a field near their house. He plowed a corner for the garden, and Laurel and the children planted tomatoes, okra, squash, carrots, cucumbers, snow peas, and onions. Sarah and Adam were good workers. Caroline rode herd on three-year-old David. She may have had the hardest job of all.

The garden gave Laurel her only glimmer of satisfaction. Everything else in their lives was at a standstill, but something was happening in the garden. The orderly rows promised tangible results, and gave her an excuse to get out of that gloomy house.

With Justin's first pay, they bought only the groceries they had to have and spent the rest on seed potatoes and seed corn and beans. They all worked together. Justin plowed, Ethan and Laurel prepared the rows. Adam and Sarah dropped in the seed corn, beans, or potatoes. The bad weather held off until they had the crop in the ground.

Justin and Ethan could now return to the new job, which needed their full attention. They floated the logs down the river to a widened holding pond, where they were plucked out, measured, then put on a railroad car and delivered to the tannery.

Every logger who used the river dreaded a log jam. It was dangerous to walk the floating, rolling logs to loosen the jam. More than one man had died trying it. Justin's answer was to float a few logs at a time; not a river full.

Ethan, at twenty-two, was an excellent logger. He was just as determined to learn to walk the logs as he had been to learn every other logging challenge. Justin was alternately scared or amused by his performance, as he fell in the river time after time. He gradually learned the dance of riding a rolling log and the timing of jumping from one to another. The use of the long pointed pole seemed to come easy to him. One day after Ethan had successfully turned some misbehaving logs, Justin tempered his elation by clapping his hand on Ethan's shoulder and looking him in the eye.

"Son, promise me you'll never take unnecessary risks. If a pond is jammed with no empty spaces, don't go out on the logs. A friend of mine drowned that way. He was a strong swimmer, but he couldn't get out from under the logs."

"I promise," Ethan said.

Justin was driven. He worked from before daylight until after dark every day, logging or farming. On weekends he took pictures. His family felt as if they had lost him.

He believed he had failed them and was less than a man. He should have used better judgment about their money in the bank. They should be in the pleasant, roomy farmhouse instead of this hovel. Guilt and regret were his constant companions, at times threatening to overpower him.

Laurel had distanced herself from him and the children. She was functioning on a level unfamiliar to her family. The vital force that defined her was gone, leaving them all adrift. He was both concerned and irritated.

They needed each other to get through this. He would rather have her temper flashing than this nothingness.

Laurel was aware she was in trouble. She couldn't pray; didn't choose to pray. What good had all the praying and struggling done? And she didn't dare face reality yet and call it what it was. She couldn't take care of anyone else's wounds. She had too many of her own.

It was an alien atmosphere. Their physical dwelling reflected their inner misery. The sun's rays rarely reached the shack through the trees and heavy foliage, and the damp from the river seemed to invade even their bedclothes. As if that wasn't enough, the wretched house leaked like a sieve. The first hard rain had everybody scurrying for pots and pans to put on the beds and furniture. David made the other children laugh. He ran squealing to stand under one leak after another until he was soaked.

Laurel, like Justin, pushed herself to exhaustion. She had never tasted poverty. It was like a bitter poison, sapping her strength and devouring her being. It seemed to shut her down, narrowing her vision of life to survival only. She was pulled up short in every path her mind took by the implacable fact that there was no money. She struggled to prepare decent meals, always aware that hunger was lurking. Her fear drove her and, in turn, she drove Sarah and Adam. Their play and antics seemed an affront, given their circumstances, so she felt justified in keeping them hard at work.

One day as they were hoeing the garden one more time, Adam struck angrily at the ground and said, "I hate it here!"

"Sh-h! Don't let Mama hear you!"

He lowered his voice. "I miss the other families and our friends from school. Don't you?"

"Yes. But I'm mostly worried about Mama and Daddy. They don't talk and laugh anymore."

Ethan watched and understood. He knew deprivation and the barrenness of soul it produced, and he was well acquainted with loneliness. His young life had been full of it until the day he had walked into the Worth Logging Camp six years ago. They had opened a whole new world to him—a world of acceptance, belief in him, laughter and love. He had continued his education and had helped Thad and Jesse with theirs. The loggers had taught him their skills, exacting in their demands but generous in their approval. He would be hard pressed to try to count the things he had learned from Justin, such as honesty, fairness, generosity, pride in hard work and love of life. Justin remained his hero.

Laurel, however, had given him a transcendent gift. She had introduced him to a God who loved him. He would never forget the day he finally understood. His cloak of shame in who he was, which was a second skin he had worn since he could remember, fell away. The bootlegger's son was accepted and loved because God's son had died for him.

Now, perhaps, it was pay-back time. He began by teaching Adam and Sarah how to fish. It seemed more fun than work, but the rainbow trout, rolled in meal and fried a golden brown, were a delicious treat. He and Adam built a rabbit gum; a long box with a carrot in the end that lured in the rabbit. When it started to eat, the trapdoor would close behind it. Fried rabbit with gravy and biscuits was tastier to Laurel than fried chicken.

Ethan was a patient teacher. He helped Adam overcome his aversion to shooting squirrels, convincing him of their need for the food. Adam became a good shot, but he never got pleasure from it. His feelings for the forest animals ran too deep to enjoy killing them for *any* reason.

When, after a few Sundays in their new location, Laurel made no mention of church, Ethan rode out on his own and found one. The next Sunday she and the children went with him, but she sat through it all like a stone.

August brought daily thunderstorms and high water which, in turn, brought problems in floating the logs to the loading pond. High water would deposit logs on a small island in a sharp bend of the river. As the pile built up, other logs would be stopped. When the water receded, Justin and Tattoo would have to get in the river and pull the logs loose to float on down stream. Ethan would clamber onto the log pile and hook the logs to the lines. It was a dreaded job. The swift, icy mountain water, at normal level, came up to Justin's armpits and to Tattoo's haunches. He always snorted and shook his head in protest as Justin led him in.

"I know, Boy," Justin would soothe. "It makes my bones ache, too."

One afternoon Justin allowed Adam to sit on Tattoo's back to see the operation. The skies remained clear above them even though they heard thunder beyond the mountain. Justin was in the water up to his arm pits, guiding Tattoo, when, suddenly, Tattoo threw up his head, shook it and whinnied. Justin responded instantly.

"Jump, Adam! Ethan, get to the bank!"

Justin reached shore trying to pull Tattoo in, just as a wall of water hit. It jerked Tattoo's bridle out of his hand. Tattoo, wild eyed, nostrils flaring, was caught floundering in the tumult of water, logs, and debris. As Tattoo went under, Ethan yelled, "I hooked a big log on just as it hit." Justin knew Tattoo would be drowned or crushed, unless he helped him.

"I'm going in, Ethan! Take care of Adam."

They barely understood before Justin dove into the maelstrom. He stayed deep, under the logs, found the lines and followed them to the coupling. Tattoo's kicking hooves were one of his biggest dangers. His lungs felt like they would burst by the time he unhooked the line with the log on it. He swam toward shore, feeling for the bridle. It was there, suddenly, in his hand! But a heavy blow to his chest knocked the breath out of him. He sucked in water and started strangling, taking in more water. He made a desperate attempt to surface, but the water was filled with logs.

Then he felt a hand pulling him. Ethan had come after him! Holding on tight to the bridle as Ethan dragged him to shore, he lay exhausted, vomiting water. Ethan grabbed the bridle and turned all his attention to getting Tattoo out while Adam, sobbing aloud, worked over his daddy. He pulled Justin's head onto his lap, rubbing his hair and repeating, "Daddy, Daddy...."

As Ethan brought Tattoo out of the water, Adam could sense a change in his daddy. He was still blue and shaking uncontrollably, but his agitation ceased. Tattoo was safe. He closed his eyes and soon started breathing more normally.

The flash flood spent its fury in a hurry and rushed on downstream. Ethan checked Tattoo carefully for cuts, breaks or bruises. He seemed to have escaped serious injury, but was still in a highly nervous state. Justin was the only one to help him with that.

But Justin had his own problems. As soon as he sat up, he knew he had a broken rib. Maybe more than one. The pain cut his breath off when he moved a certain way. He could not control the shaking that was taking all his energy. He knew he had to get to Laurel. She would know what to do. Ethan supported him as they slowly made their way home. They could hear

Adam, behind them, talking quietly to Tattoo as he led him along.

In spite of the fact that he was walking, Laurel knew Justin was in a state of shock. She flew into action. She and Ethan peeled off his wet clothes and put him to bed, wrapped him in a warm blanket, with hot flat irons and a hot water bottle around him to raise his body temperature. As soon as the shaking ceased and he felt warm to her touch, she wrapped his chest tightly with torn strips of a sheet. Now, as she sat beside him, watching his chest rise and fall in a normal sleep, a prayer of thanks rose unbidden. Justin could have died! But he was alive! It was her first step up out of the pit she had lived in for three months.

Justin's work was curtailed for awhile. He wouldn't go to the doctor but he listened to Laurel and gave his ribs time to mend. When Ethan went to Deerbrook to spend some of their precious cash on some quart jars and lids for Laurel's canning, he brought Justin some back copies of *The Wildwood Journal* and a couple of Zane Gray books, compliments of Sam Parker.

"Sam said maybe you'd be fit for human company while you're laid up, if you have something to read," Ethan informed him.

Meanwhile, Laurel canned everything she could get her hands on. It was Sarah's job to wash the jars and help prepare the food for canning. Caroline stayed busy chasing David. One day Sarah, tired from the endless work, said to David, "You better keep moving, little boy! If you stay in here, Mama will put you in a jar."

When they canned everything they could from the garden, they turned to other things. Adam and Ethan brought in blackberries they had picked. One day they came in with two funny-looking bundles made from the shirts off their backs. They had found an old apple tree near their berry patch, loaded with sheep-nose apples. Adam was pleased. He knew they were his mama's favorite.

Adam, at eleven, felt responsible for helping Ethan while his daddy was unable to work. He went to the job with him everyday. His biggest help was working with Tattoo, who surprisingly cooperated. He was usually a one-man horse.

One evening when Ethan and Adam came in from work, Justin was reading the paper to Laurel, while she was finishing supper. A warmth spread through Adam and he looked at Ethan, who grinned at him. Things were returning to normal.

"What's the news?" Ethan asked.

"The depression is widespread. People are in a bad way. I was just reading to Laurel about the hoboes. Whole families are riding the rails, seeking shelter and work. We seem to be better off than thousands of hungry, homeless people."

"Can't somebody help them?" Adam asked.

"This article just tells the problems, not any solutions, son. Everybody seems to be blaming President Hoover for the mess."

Things suddenly didn't seem so bad. They did have a roof, leaky as it was; food on the table three times a day, and clean, warm beds to sleep in. And laughter was returning to their lives.

When the harvest was gathered a few weeks later, they all felt a well-earned sense of satisfaction. They had plenty of corn for meal and fodder for the animals. Several bushels of Irish potatoes and sweet potatoes were stored. Laurel and Sarah had canned enough green beans and corn and tomatoes to see them through the winter. Blackberry jam, grape jelly and canned apples were Sarah's special pride.

When school started, Sarah, Adam and Caroline were ready. They settled in and made new friends. They gathered around the kitchen table at night, under the light of the Aladdin Lamp, to do their homework, while the adults talked or read, or Ethan and Justin played checkers.

Jed, Hannah, and Nora invited the other three logging camp families that had lived together for almost ten years to their farmhouse for Thanksgiving dinner. Everybody brought food, and realized they were blessed. It was a good day for everybody. They soaked up each others' company as eagerly as they ate the food, and made plans to get together more often than they had in the previous months. They had adjusted to daily life without each other, but knew their lives were not complete without regular contact.

As they started to leave, Sarah asked, "Can we come again for Christmas?"

Everybody laughed. Sarah obviously felt at home. It was the right thing to do, so they did it. Their first Christmas of the Depression years was a slim but happy one, made so because they had each other.

In March, Laurel realized she was pregnant. She couldn't believe it, because she was almost forty and her cycle had been so erratic, she thought she was almost through the change. Justin was happy with the news, but she had to talk to Hannah and Nora before she could get her bearings. On Sunday afternoon Justin dropped the family off by Hannah's house on his way to take pictures at a family reunion.

After the usual hugs and news swapping, Laurel sent the children out so the three women could talk. Nora's response was heart-warming. "It's been nearly four years since we've had a baby! I'll come and stay with you awhile and help take care of it!"

Hannah said, "Laurel, this baby will be good for all of us! It'll take our minds off all the bad. The Good Lord knows what He's about!" She stood up, ready for action. "Now, let's see, how can we get word to Bess and Alice. We can't keep this good news to ourselves!"

Laurel felt the tears course down her cheeks. She hadn't considered it good news, but if Hannah declared it so, it must be. She wiped her face, and gave a tremulous smile, as Hannah continued aloud with her plans.

"I'll get word to them tomorrow. We'll all come to your house one day next week and sew baby clothes. It'll be like old times! Which day can we come?"

On the way home, Laurel, for the first time, allowed herself to enjoy the prospect of a new baby. When Justin saw her hand resting flat on her stomach, he reached over and put his hand over hers. They looked at each other in silent agreement. Depression or not, this baby would be welcome.

Laurel and Justin had always had a purpose and goals in life beyond their daily hard work. They believed they made life better for the people who worked with them. They had the prospect of a nice home and farm waiting when they were ready. Now, all that was gone. They were surviving…existing…one day following the other in an endless cycle of sameness…no goals, no plans, no money beyond necessities, and usually not enough for that. *This must be what jail feels like*, thought Laurel, *barriers all around, freedom and opportunity denied.* It was life turned in on itself, a world that consisted of family only, a smaller world than she had ever experienced. And she was bringing a new baby into it. Helplessness to change her circumstances angered and frustrated her. She was caught in the web. She was a victim, along with her family.

Then, from somewhere obscure in her mind came a glimmer of something Papa said about coming to terms with life after her mother died. "I couldn't change my circumstances, but I could change my attitude; I could change the way I reacted to my circumstances." She went still with the impact of it. Had life handed her the biggest challenge yet? How was she expected to meet it? Was she equal to it? Could she choose – for herself and her family – not to be a victim? Did she have the strength to rise to the occasion, for herself and her family?

If Papa could do it with a loss beyond comparison, couldn't she? He had cut a trail through the jungle of despair. Could she do less than follow? It was part of her heritage; part of what had shaped her. Papa had chosen his path and his children had reaped the benefits. She knew now what she had to do.

Her changed attitude, plus her pregnancy, which always energized her physically and emotionally, started restoring their home atmosphere to normal. Justin was coaxed out of his pout, and the children took their cue from their parents. Sarah, an awkward fourteen, and Adam, a strong-minded twelve, remained the buddies they had always been. They still loved their time in the woods. Caroline and David tangled when Caroline became too bossy; otherwise, Caroline's ability to make-believe kept them happily occupied.

The garden was just presenting its orderly green rows and the crop in the larger field was flourishing when they received word that Papa was coming to visit. Laurel had not seen him for three years. They all rode into Deerbrook to meet the train.

From the moment she saw him, Laurel's joy was tempered. Age sat on his face, sculpting his strong bone structure to its essence. An elusive frailty cloaked his large frame. A fierce denial rose from her depths. Papa could not change. He was her source of unconditional love. He understood her. He challenged her. He was her inspiration.

As she watched the next few days, she thought, *Papa always brings*

his own atmosphere, and everybody thrives in it. Especially the children.
Sarah, Adam, and Caroline showed him their school work, and enjoyed his
praise. David Hunter, his namesake, kept him amused by his antics. After
he and Ethan took a long walk one day, Ethan said to Laurel, "Your Papa is
helping me settle something in my mind." He didn't elaborate and left Laurel
wondering.

He and Justin got caught up in their usual political discussions. "The
country seems to be sinking deeper every day in spite of Hoover's efforts,"
Papa said. "His Reconstruction Finance Loans to big businesses, banks,
and railroads should have started helping the economy by now. He has led
Congress to help farmers who were about to lose their farms; and has led
them to pass the Home Loan Bank Act to prevent the foreclosure of home
mortgages."

"I know, Professor. It never seems enough. Hundreds of people, the
paper says, have been evicted from their homes and farms. They're living in
tents, or shacks made from tin, or scrap wood, or tar paper, or cardboard,
whatever they can find. They call these shanty towns 'Hoovervilles.' That's
like a slap in his face."

"Angry, desperate people need someone to blame. Hoover has become
the whipping boy of the press and public opinion."

After they sat reflecting a moment, the professor continued. "It's the
children I worry about the most. Some factories are working children ten
hours a day, paying them less than they would have to pay adults. The
parents allow it, because it's their only income."

His agitation drove him to his feet. "It's stealing their childhood at best,
and stealing their lives at worst. Many children are dying from being
overworked and underfed. They don't have sufficient clothes. It leaves them
prey to disease."

Adam and Sarah had stopped their homework and were listening. Adam
spoke up. "There's this boy at school who's real skinny. He's sick a lot, I
think. When he tries to run at recess, his shoes come apart. I looked at 'em
today, and there's just the top of the shoe left. He has cardboard stuck
inside for the soles and it comes out all the time. He's real embarrassed."

He stopped and swallowed. "I decided today to give him my shoes if it's
okay with you."

Everybody became motionless and stared at him.

He stood, raised his chin, and declared, "I like goin' barefoot!"

Nobody could think of a thing to say for a long time. The three adults looked at each other. Then Justin cleared his throat and asked, "Would your shoes fit him, son?"

"I think so. He's my size, only skinnier."

Justin stood and put his arm around Adam's shoulders. "Laurel, do you have some clean socks Adam can take with the shoes tomorrow?"

She nodded silently, still unable to speak.

Papa went out the door, pulling his handkerchief out of his back pocket.

Over the next few days Papa let Laurel know he understood their circumstances but, as was his style, he put a positive spin on things. "I know how dark things must look to you right now. But I do want to say something to you about your lifestyle. I would not have you change lives with anybody I know. Look at your old friend Isabel. She's had an easy life compared to you, but material things and ease seem to have produced a sterile, boring life, turned in on herself. In contrast, you and Justin, with less, have done more! You have a rich life in all the ways it matters. So far you haven't let the lack of material things bring poverty to your souls and spirits; nor to those of your children. Adam showed us that clearly last night. I've rarely been so touched in my whole life, nor so proud! I didn't know whether to laugh or cry when he stuck his chin up in the air, like royalty defying any commoner to disagree. Just like you, when you're fighting for a cause."

"Do I do that?" she asked, laughing.

"Yes. And you must keep on doing it for all the things you believe in." He grew serious. "It's going to be awhile before the country gets on its feet again. Hard times are here to stay for awhile. I know you and Justin will have the strength of character to come through and bring your family through with all the things that matter intact. I charge you with that responsibility!"

Other than that strong statement, Laurel was painfully aware of a detachment—a distancing—in response to her problems. He was not insensitive nor uncaring. He gently refused to be given responsibility that was hers alone. After a few days of negotiating this strange landscape between them, she understood. He expected her to handle whatever life handed her in a manner that would bring the best for herself and her family. As he had done. He was passing the baton! But her heart cried out silently and secretly and desperately, *I don't want it yet, Papa! You must carry it awhile longer until I am more like you! I'm not ready, Papa!*

One day, over a cup of coffee, he said to her in a casual tone. "Your friend, Chief Lion Heart, and I see each other occasionally. He invariably asks about you. He talks about your strength and your destiny. He believes strongly that everything that happens to you, good and bad, will be used to shape your destiny. I believe the same, only I say it a different way. I believe God will use all things to bring about good if we allow Him to. We have to work with Him."

"What about Justin and his antagonism to God?"

"I believe God will bring Justin to Himself, some way, someday. Justin will cease struggling and know God for Who He really is."

Laurel, tears pooled in her eyes, threw her arms around him. "Oh! Papa! Do you really believe that?"

"I do," he said firmly.

"Then I will believe it, too!"

Hope entered and lit a candle in that dark corner of her mind. She would refuse to cater to the darkness any longer. If her papa said it, it would happen.

When he left, she realized he was going away from her in more ways than one. Her grief was her own. She could not tell anyone, even Justin. But, after awhile, she was also aware of a new sense of coming into her own; a passage of some sort in which she ceased being primarily a daughter, and became instead an adult, a wife, a mother. She was becoming the prime force, herself. Papa had known it was time. She was energized by the challenge, laced as it was with the sadness of seeing Papa grow old.

Soon, the metamorphosis in her was reflected in the family. As he watched her strength emerge again, Justin's guilt and fear were brought into perspective. He could handle the endless hard work as long as she was strong.

Thankfully, the harvest again was plenteous. Justin and Laurel were exhausted with the hard work but thankful for the results. "We should make it fine through the winter, with the cash my logging brings in. And we'll have enough to pay the doctor when the baby comes," Justin said. Laurel knew how important that was to his pride.

The baby chose its arrival time in the midst of October splendor. It seemed to Laurel that the leaf colors had never been more spectacular. She woke about four o'clock in the morning and knew her time had come. Ethan rode first to send Hannah and Nora; then on into Deerbrook after Dr. Leighton.

Justin stayed with Laurel and the children. As they worked together to prepare for the birth, he said, "Laurel, I'm sorry. I wish this baby had a worthy house and better circumstances to be born in."

She straightened from a pain and said, "Justin, this baby is being born in a loving home! This shack is our shelter for now, but we'll do better. And the mountains have put on their most beautiful clothes to greet this baby! So, hush your regrets and help me!"

She still had the ability, at times, to strike him dumb. But her words, in her teacher voice, brought comfort to him. She was in charge until this task was finished. He was quiet as he did as he was told.

It was still dark when Hannah and Nora arrived by wagon. Nora gathered the children, bundled up against the cold morning air, into the wagon to take them home with her. Neither Sarah nor Adam wanted to go.

"You may need us, Mama," Sarah argued.

Justin, pleased by their concern, said, "We'll need you more later than we do now. We have Hannah and the doctor."

Just as they were leaving, Dr. Leighton rode in and swung down, rubbing his hands, "The frost is on the pumpkin this morning. It looks like a young snow in the river bottom fields."

After a morning of hard labor, Laurel gave birth to a girl. Their joy over the normal baby was overshadowed by Laurel's condition. She had lost more blood than she should have. At forty, her womb was worn out with childbearing. He would recommend a hysterectomy after a few months, when she had her strength back.

Justin, sitting by Laurel's bed, deeply concerned at her lifeless color, felt a pressure on his hand. "She is our last," she whispered. "I would like to name her Alexis after my mother. Do you like that name?"

"Yes. But I want Laurel put with it. I want her named after you, too."

"Laurel Alexis," she repeated. "I like it. But I want her called Alexis."

"I'll give the name to the doctor for the birth certificate. Now, you go back to sleep."

True to Hannah's prophecy, the baby was a pleasure to everybody, from Justin down to David. Adam, however, surprised the whole family with his proprietary attitude toward her. For a twelve year old boy, it was the last thing expected.

Nora, as she had promised, came and stayed until Laurel was ready to take up her responsibilities again. Laurel knew her body had to recover and she gladly left Nora in charge of the household. Everybody enjoyed Nora! Even being bossed around by her seemed great to the children. It was as it used to be.

Bess, Hannah and Alice made weekly trips to visit. Bess brought baby clothes until one day she noticed the faded dresses Sarah and Caroline had on. Without explaining, she measured them before she left one day. The next week she brought each of them a new school dress. Both were cheerful plaids, but different colors. The girls were delighted. These were their first new dresses since they had moved from Locust Hollow. They looked so pretty, Laurel's eyes filled with tears.

"Bess," she said, "that's the best gift you could give us. But, I'm afraid you and Bulldog are spending too much on us."

Bess held up her hand. "Do you remember making a plaid dress for a little girl named Joanie a few years ago?"

They looked at each other, remembering. "It will be ten years in July since she died," Bess said.

Laurel crossed the room and hugged Bess. "Thank you for the dresses and for your love."

Hannah and Alice brought food of some sort each time. They all helped with the washing or the ironing or whatever needed to be done, and they took turns holding the baby. It gave them pleasure to shower love on this baby. She was the last one, and love made up for a lot of other things they couldn't give her. "It's okay to spoil you, Little Miss Priss," crooned Bess. "There's plenty of people to take care of you."

Chapter Twenty-six

It was a cold December night when Ethan made his startling announcement to Justin and Laurel. They were sitting around the kitchen table in the glow of the Aladdin Lamp. He and Justin were playing checkers and Laurel was mending. The children were all in bed. He had just won a game, which was rare. He pushed back his chair and said, "I need to talk to you about something."

Laurel laid down her mending and Justin sat back and looked at him. "This may not come as a great surprise to you, Laurel, but it will to Justin. I believe I have been called to preach."

Justin's reaction was from his gut, without thought. "No!" he declared, shaking his head.

Ethan, disturbed by Justin's outburst, looked from one to the other. Laurel smiled at him and said evenly, "Tell us about your call."

"It's been goin' on for awhile. You know I've been goin' to church a lot. I...I guess it's because of the difference it made in my life to know how much God loves me. I want to tell other people about it, so they can have what I have. I think I've got a pretty good case to present to people. I'm a bootlegger's son and helped my daddy bootleg, but God loves me as much as He does you."

Justin was uncomfortable. He straightened and took a deep breath. "Ethan, I respect your beliefs, but you have to give yourself some credit for who you are today. Never mind the bootlegger's son stuff. You're now one of the best. You've worked hard to be who you are."

"I know what you're sayin', Justin, and I appreciate it. But I never could feel quite clean until I understood God's Son died to clean me up. Then He went on to give me strength I didn't have, so I could live right. And I believe

He brought me to you and Laurel so I could learn how His kind of love is lived out in our everyday life."

Justin wasn't winning this one, so he went practical. "So, what do you plan to do?"

"I'd like to continue to live and work with you, and preach on Sundays as I get invitations. Then, after I learn how to preach, maybe some church will want me to be their pastor. I don't know beyond that."

Justin was relieved. "Ethan, you realize you're like a son to us, and I'm sure glad you'll still be with us. I'm sorry for my outburst a few minutes ago. You're a man now, and know your own mind. I wish you success. And you know I'll do anything I can to help you."

The two men stood and embraced. Ethan had tears in his eyes. He said simply, "I know." Justin turned suddenly and left the room.

Laurel stood and hugged Ethan, too. "You'll be a good preacher. I can't wait to hear you."

"I want you to come and listen to me and tell me how I do and where I need to improve."

"I'll be there. So will Hannah and the others when they learn about it."

Ethan shared his news with the other families at their Christmas dinner, at Jed's and Hannah's. The women were not surprised. The men were uncomfortable. At the initial awkward silence, Justin said, "We've come to trust Ethan's judgment through the years, so I vote to trust him now, and give him our best wishes."

Laurel had never loved her husband more than at that moment. The men gathered around Ethan and wished him well. The women hugged him. Irrepressible Bess drawled, "It's about time you got married, too. You'll have to have a wife now to protect you from all the girls in church."

Laurel was pleased the first time she heard Ethan preach. He was nervous but his points were made in a logical, convincing manner. His absolute sincerity and enthusiasm carried him on a wave that caught up other people as it swept along. *And being so handsome doesn't hurt*, thought Laurel, as she looked at the strapping, blond young man. Not long after Ethan had come to their camp at sixteen, Bess had said, "Ethan's face is almost too pretty for a boy." But the maturing years had done their work well. As Laurel looked at him now, she was struck with his face. He was definitely masculine, but there was an open, vulnerable quality, almost an innocence, that drew people to him. She sat, startled, as she realized how this would all work together to make him an outstanding minister. She allowed the joy of it to flow through her.

Afterward, riding home in the wagon, he asked for her opinion. After she had made several positive comments, he thanked her, then said, "Laurel, please tell me my errors and how I can improve. I won't know unless you help me." From then on, she helped with his grammatical errors, and even how to organize his thoughts better. She gave him one word of advice he didn't ask for.

"Ethan, always study and prepare. I hear some preachers brag that they just get up and God fills their mouth with what they should say; that they don't have to study. Well, I don't believe God chooses to work that way, except occasionally. I see Him as an orderly God."

He heeded her advice. Often, at night after the children were in bed, Ethan would sit at the table with his Bible and a lined tablet, studying and making notes, while Justin and Laurel read. Papa, after hearing the news, sent him a set of Bible commentaries and a dictionary. Ethan treated them as treasures, as they illuminated his understanding of difficult passages. One night Ethan said, "Laurel, I talked to the professor about my call when he was here. He helped me some."

Laurel was not surprised. Papa had spent a lifetime doing just that.

Word got around Wildwood County about the young preacher, and Ethan had more invitations than he could handle. It wasn't surprising when, in February, a small church at the other end of the county called him as pastor. He would need to move to the community.

Justin had begun preparing himself for this day when Ethan started preaching. He had been with them seven years, and was twenty-three years old. He had to move on with his life. But he would be sorely missed in more ways than one.

"Son," Justin told him, "I'm happy for you and proud of you. Laurel can't hush bragging about what a good preacher you are."

"My biggest concern is leaving you without help with the logging. You can't do it alone."

Justin said, "I'll work that out. I know I can't replace you, but I can get some help. The important thing is for you to get on with your calling."

It was a tearful time for the children when he rode off. Caroline and David could never remember a time when he hadn't been there. And he was a big brother to Adam and Sarah. Laurel and Justin promised them they would visit him soon. They, and the other families, had plans to take the wagon with some housekeeping items such as quilts, lamps, and canned goods. They were his family, his only family, and they would do right by him.

Justin didn't let Laurel know, but the heart went out of him for logging when Ethan left. It may have been weariness or it may have been that he knew nobody else could work with him as Ethan did. They were so much a team, they rarely had to tell each other what they were thinking. He wouldn't hurry to get some help. He and Tattoo had some work they could do alone. That would give him time to think about the future. He would also go talk with Jed.

By the middle of March, he had a plan that he believed would be good for his family. He would get out of the logging business. Jed was doing well as a farmer, and influenced Justin to try it. He could plant some cash crops that would bring in as much as his logging had done for the past year.

In April they moved to the Rapp Place. Mrs. Rapp, a widow, had put out her two grown sons, both drunks. She had gone to live with a married daughter, putting up her house and farm for rent. When Justin learned that her trouble-making sons had gone to Oregon to seek work in the timber industry, he agreed to sharecrop the fields. He would also pay rent in cash each month for living in the farmhouse.

After living in close quarters so long, the children enjoyed the house. It was old, with broken window panes and a sagging porch, but they had more room. The outbuildings helped. A canning shed stood near the kitchen, still complete with a stove and tables and shelves. Sarah, without enthusiasm, remarked, "Look, Mama. Somebody must know how we spend our summers. They have the place ready for us."

Caroline laid claim to the empty corncrib behind the house. She coaxed Sarah and Adam into helping her and David build a playhouse in it—under her direction, of course. A large, flat rock was their stove, a board on rocks their table, a toe sack filled with straw their bed. Laurel was pleased. She would hear Caroline say, in her persuading voice, "David, let's-play-like …" or in her officious voice, "No, David! Not like that!" Laurel knew these years of closeness were transient. David would not much longer be held under Caroline's sway. The boy in him was breaking out, but for now it was fun.

Justin turned his energies to full-time farming. He planted peanuts for a cash crop. In a small remote section, he planted popcorn, and in a narrow strip by the river, he planted sugar cane for molasses. This was in addition to the wide fields of corn and beans and rows of potatoes. He and Tattoo could be seen day after day, plowing the river bottom fields. Adam was not yet strong enough to push the plow through the earth, but he helped in the ways he could.

Laurel's health was a problem, but she would not face up to it. Her body reserves, depleted from Alexis' birth, could not fully recoup, because each month her abnormal flow depleted them further. Weak and anemic, she went on willpower most of the time. Her normal level-headedness deserted her when it came to her need for a hysterectomy. Justin, Hannah, and even the doctor talked to no avail. She believed she would soon be through the change. They had absolutely no money and she wouldn't put Justin through the embarrassment of not being able to pay the doctor. If they had the money she would rather use it for the family needs. Her reasons seemed endless. Sarah took up most of the slack in the house, and in caring for the younger children. Adam and Caroline helped, but Sarah bore the brunt of her mother's illness.

Their home life, however, was changing for two reasons. The night Adam told them he was giving his shoes away, something clicked for Justin and Laurel. They realized that they had turned in upon themselves. Their lives had shrunk to concerns for their family only. They saw nothing remarkable about the fact that it was their children who helped return them to normal in response to others in greater need. Sarah came in one day from school and announced that she would like to take one of her dresses to a girl who was wearing a dress made from flour sacks, with the writing still on them. Bess and Hannah got involved and made the girl a new dress. They also bleached out the flour sack dress and dyed it with polk berries, producing a rich color between purple and blue.

The other change was inevitable with two teenagers in the house, attracting other young people. Saturday and Sunday afternoons often resounded with horse-shoe and baseball games. Laurel skimped somewhere else in her cooking so she could make lemonade and sugar cookies or gingerbread. After a Halloween Party with treasure hunts, ghosts, apple-bobbing, candy-pulling, and pop-corn balls, the Worth House became the fun place to be. When Justin got up to build the fire the morning after the party, his feet stuck to the floor with every step. That candy pulling must have been a real success! He yelled for Sarah and Adam. They happily scrubbed the floor before they left for school. The party the night before had been worth all the work.

Justin's photography still helped to bring in much needed cash and food supplies. He had always known how much people loved to have their picture taken. He discovered that they would do without other things, if necessary, for that privilege. It worked out well for him and his family. His payment, however, wasn't always orthodox. He was offered everything from a possum to moonshine. He, laughingly, reserved the right to refuse such payment and expected some realism from his customers. Sometimes he never got paid. Sometimes he came home with surprises.

One day the children were playing in the yard when he came down the farm lane, riding Tattoo at a slower-than-usual pace. When they ran to meet him, they saw a white goat following behind Tattoo, being led by a rope in Justin's hand. The goat, dignified as a matron on Sunday morning, seemed to be setting the pace for Tattoo.

"It's a nanny goat," Justin explained. "Go get your mother."

He slipped down and handed the rope to Adam. Then he said to Tattoo, "See, boy, that wasn't so bad! I know it was rough on your dignity, but we made it home."

When Laurel appeared, he explained, "This is payment for a picture debt. I almost didn't accept it, but I remembered the cow is going dry. This goat gives milk."

The children looked at each other and made faces, but Laurel said, "Good! Goat milk is healthy! You'll need to show Adam how to milk her."

They named her Matilda and she adopted David from the first day. Cantankerous with everybody else, she romped and played with him, allowing him to hook her up to a wagon for rides. She even slid off high banks, or waded into the river, at his command. Caroline fussed because David had defected from their constant play together, but Laurel helped her through it. David was being initiated into boyhood by a goat he lovingly called 'Tilda.

Ethan's wedding was the big event of the summer of 1932. Laurel had met Allison a few months before, and considered her a good match for Ethan with her efficient but gentle manner. Both with blond hair and blue eyes, they made a handsome couple. They were married in the church where Ethan was pastor, and would live in the little house the church provided. Justin and Laurel, with the help of the other logging camp families, invited the entire church to their house a few days later for a celebration and household shower. The church group was confused about how Ethan fitted into all these families. Bess added to the mystery when she announced to Allison, "Honey, a bride usually gets one mother-in-law. You're lucky! You get five!"

Ethan explained. "These four families here today took me in when I was sixteen, when my pa was killed. They probably saved me from starvation. But they have given me much more than physical needs. They've given me love and direction in life. They're my family." And no blood family could have shown more pride.

Justin was concerned during the autumn season with the presidential election of 1932, which was upon them. He would serve again as a judge for the Republican Party at the voting place for their precinct. No one was surprised when Franklin Delano Roosevelt was elected the thirty-second president of the United States in a landslide victory.

"Herbert Hoover has been labeled a 'do-nothing' president, when, in fact, he has done a great deal," Justin fretted to Laurel. "It just has not been enough." Deep in its economic collapse, the country would now wait to see what FDR had to offer.

The family was celebrating Alexis's second birthday when trouble arrived on foot, in the form of Bud and Toby Rapp. The rumor was that they had been thrown off their logging job in Oregon because of drinking. Now they wanted to sleep in the canning shed of their old home place. Justin agreed reluctantly. "This is temporary," he told them, "until you can find a place to live."

Bud's and Toby's presence soon brought an uneasy atmosphere, with actual moments of fear. Laurel, at home alone with Alexis now that David had started in first grade, would look up from her work to see one of them watching her as she worked. Sarah, at sixteen, was blossoming into a pretty girl. She didn't understand the revulsion she felt toward them. Even the animals seemed to sense danger.

Justin soon realized they were not just drunks; they were mean drunks. They reminded him of Roscoe Werner who had attacked Laurel. He had made a big mistake in trying to help them. The day he told them to find another place to live, he knew he had made two enemies. They moved on but the malice was thinly disguised. The uneasiness he felt in his gut was soon justified.

Their harassment was always under the cover of darkness and took many forms. One night the family would hear the chickens squawking; another time it would be the barn animals in an uproar. By the time Justin went to investigate, they would be gone. One morning when Laurel went to the bank house to get some canned goods, she found two quart jars broken, with their contents spilled onto the dirt floor. Puzzled, she lit the lantern and surveyed their store of food. To her dismay, she found at least one-third of their hard-earned cans of food missing. The jars had been taken from the back of the shelves and, in the dim light, she hadn't noticed. Their potatoes were also disappearing. The Rapp Boys, it seemed, had found a free grocery store. Justin went that afternoon and got a padlock for the bank house door.

The next day Justin brought home a large dog. Part collie and part shepherd, with long white and tan hair, his appearance was appropriate as he immediately took charge of the farm. Nothing seemed to escape his attention as he made a tour and assessed his responsibilities. Laurel, bemused by his obvious abilities, asked, "How did you get hold of a dog like that?"

"I've wanted that dog for a year, so I did some trading. His abilities were wasted where he was. I offered some corn and roughage for their animals to make it through the winter, but I also offered to make a family group picture. That clinched the deal."

"Good! Maybe, he can take care of our problem."

The children named him Chief and he took care of more than one problem. Bud and Toby understandably stopped their nightly visits. If herding was the dog's instinct, the other animals' instinct was to obey. Even Matilda respected his authority. Under Chief's care, peace returned to the farm. Justin couldn't explain why he felt it was temporary.

Chapter Twenty-seven

Mid-February brought so much snow, people were hardly able to get out of their yards. It had been awhile since they had been snowed in, and Laurel's memory pulled up a page that was rich with the ways Papa and Mama had made such a day special when she was little. She felt unusually close to Papa all day as she remembered basking in his love and security that had seemed almost tangible. She remembered wishing with all her child heart that she could hold the day forever, and it seemed she had – in her memory. She suddenly felt the need to pass the magic on to her children. Before the day was over, the older children had helped the younger ones make a snowman and had supervised sledding down the steep hill behind the house. When they came in, Laurel served them fried apple pies and hot chocolate. When their cheeks were red from the fire, she cooled them down again with snow cream, a delicious mixture of soft snow, cream, sugar and vanilla. They had to eat it in a hurry before it melted.

David climbed up in her lap and summed it all up. "Mama, we had the mostest fun today! Did you see 'Tilda stepping high in the snow?"

About two o'clock the next morning, Laurel awoke abruptly and sat up in bed. She knew, as if she had been told audibly, that Papa was dead. She got out of bed and put on her robe. When Justin stirred, she said, "Justin, wake up! Papa is dead!"

Justin's eyes flew open. "What are you talking about? Did you have a bad dream?"

"No! Get up with me. I just woke up and I know, Justin."

Her white face and strained voice convinced him something was wrong. He got up and built a fire. She sat motionless, staring dry-eyed, as if listening. He came and sat by her, holding her hand silently. She was hardly aware he was there. *This is like a wake*, he thought, *without a body*.

It had been daylight about an hour when Justin saw a rider coming. The horse was making slow progress in the snow. "He's bringing the news," Laurel said. Justin felt a slight shiver pass over him, believing her completely for the first time since they had begun their vigil.

The telegram was brief. *"Papa dead Stop Pneumonia Stop Funeral Saturday Stop Love, Mama."*

It seemed to Laurel that everything, even time, should stop. Papa was gone and the whole earth must, somehow, grieve with her. She watched the family activity around her with a stillness that kept even her children at a distance. As the day wore on, she was aware that Hannah and Nora and Bess were there. Someone helped her get dressed. Justin came and went. She ate and drank when she was told. Otherwise, she might as well have not been there.

In the early afternoon, Justin set a cup of hot, strong coffee in front of her. After she had finished, he took her hand. "Honey, look at me. I've been to Deerbrook checking on things. We can't get to Knoxville for your Papa's funeral. The trains aren't running because of snowdrifts all through the mountains."

He sounded so upset, she squeezed his hand. "It's all right. Papa will understand."

"I sent a telegram to Madeleine, telling her we're cut off and can't be there. I…I can't tell you how sorry I am."

"I know you would do anything possible to get me there, Justin. But, it's not necessary to go. Papa and I have already partly said our goodbyes."

"When?"

"The last time he was here. It was something more understood than spoken. He let me know his expectations that I would pass on what I had been given."

"And you are, Laurel," he said earnestly. "And more! Most of what you give is *you*; not the professor; not anybody but *you*!"

She looked at him in wonder. "But, Justin, it's not pure me! It's Papa and you and life and circumstances and…and God! God causes it all to work together for good. If we let Him." She sat holding his hand, looking at him, figuring something out.

"Even this! Even Papa leaving will be used for good if I let it! Do you see? I will grieve because I don't have him here physically, but he will always be with me. He was here yesterday, urging me to give the children a magic day like I used to have."

She crumpled into Justin's arms and sobbed, "O, Papa! Papa!"

Misery sat on Justin's face as he held her and smoothed her hair. Her tears called forth tears from the children and the women. Crying brought a much needed release to the emotions of the household, and started washing away Laurel's numbness. She became aware of the children's need for comfort, and had Justin gather them around.

She straightened in her chair and spoke almost formally, "Your grandfather was the best man I ever knew besides your daddy. We are blessed that we had him as long as we did. I wish you could have known him better, but we will always have him with us. He'll always be a part of who I am, and I promise to pass that on to you." She smiled and her tone changed. "Yesterday –the fun – the things you did was a gift from Papa."

"How?" Adam asked.

"I remembered how he turned such days into magic, and I wanted the same for you. Yesterday was a Papa-Kind-Of-Day."

April was warmly welcomed after the hard winter. Justin and Tattoo again traversed the fields, opening up the rich earth to receive the seeds for another harvest. Justin was surprised at how much he enjoyed farming. The young children romped with Chief and Matilda. The older three routinely brought in their friends. Justin and Laurel had to watch how they spent every nickel, but so did almost everybody else. They realized they had it better than the majority of families.

Laurel was secretly worried that she wouldn't have the strength to do the garden. Her weakness puzzled her. Watching Chief roam over his domain, she hoped the trouble with Bud and Toby was over.

She knew it wasn't, however, the afternoon when she heard Toby Rapp threaten Justin that he and Bud would put them out of the house. A few days later when they showed up with the sheriff, her fears were realized. When Justin asked her to take the children inside and stay with them, she did so only because she was unable to stand. Her knees had turned to jelly. She was listening, though, and heard Justin come in and go out again.

Adam, in a scared voice, whispered, "Mama, Daddy got his shotgun."

She somehow got to the porch and saw the shotgun leveled on the three men. Justin's finger was on the trigger. *He rarely misses anything he shoots at*, she thought as the world went black and she crumpled to the floor.

She remained in a daze as she realized she was in the hospital and Dr. Leighton was telling her he had to operate….

Justin never forgot his lonely vigil that night at the hospital. He couldn't lie down long. He would become desperately afraid at times and tiptoe in to look and listen for her breathing. He sat most of the night watching her breathe; *willing her to breathe*. More than once, Jed or Ethan brought him a cup of coffee. Several times he was aware of the two men standing nearby. No words were necessary.

Just before dawn Dr. Leighton came in and checked her. "I'm more hopeful than I was last night. She's got a better chance since she's made it this far."

He told the nurse to go get some rest and to leave Justin with Laurel. "If there's the slightest change, let me know."

As daylight silhouetted the surrounding mountains and trees, and crept into the room to caress her face, Laurel sighed and moved her head slightly.

Justin responded instantly. He rubbed her hair back and kissed her on the forehead.

"Laurel, Darling, I'm here. I love you! Can you look at me?"

Her voice was a faint whisper, "Justin…?"

He squeezed her hand.

She didn't move or open her eyes, but whispered, "Children…?"

"The children are fine, Laurel. Nora and Hannah are taking care of them."

She gave another sigh and was asleep again.

Justin called to Jed and Ethan in the hallway. "Get the doctor quick! She just woke up and then went back to sleep." Dr. Leighton hurried in and checked her. When Justin told him about her waking up, he smiled.

"Her signs are better. She's sleeping normally now. In spite of all the odds, I believe she's going to make it. She's not out of the woods, but we can have real hope now."

"Can I send that word to the children?"

"Yes. Tell them their mother is better and has talked with you."

Justin turned to tell Jed and Ethan but could not speak. Tears were coursing down his face and his chin quivered.

Jed's and Ethan's happiness shone in their eyes. Jed said, "We heard the doc, Justin. We're on our way with the good news! We'll be back soon."

The two men ran down the hall. Everybody in the small hospital heard the cheer that went up in the lobby.

Justin went to the window and looked out at the bright morning. The dogwood trees stirred slightly with the breeze. The sky was solid blue and the birds were singing their celebration of spring. Justin's joy was complete. He asked nothing else from life, now that Laurel would live. He felt curiously free from problems. He allowed a formerly forbidden thought to enter his mind. *Could Laurel be right about God? Could He be good, after all?*

Laurel's first awareness in waking up was Justin's presence. Before she could open her eyes she heard his voice and felt his touch. When he kissed her forehead the stubble on his chin and his particular smell comforted her. She was back home from her long journey. She savored the familiar for a long time, then tried to ask about the children. When Justin told her that Hannah and Nora were with them, she was content. Aware that her hand was held securely in Justin's, she slept again.

The April sun was streaming through the window when she awoke. Justin was sitting by her bed asleep. His head had fallen to the side but her hand still rested in his on the bed. She moved slightly and he was instantly awake.

"Laurel…Honey…Are you awake? Can you talk to me?"

Her mouth felt like it was full of cotton. She whispered, "Water…."

Justin gave her small sips of water and washed her face with a warm cloth.

She smiled at him and whispered. "I love you."

"I love you, Laurel, more than I can possibly tell you." He paused, then went on, "I was so scared, Honey."

She said simply, "I know."

Dr. Leighton came bustling in, extremely pleased but not smug. He knew that a power beyond himself was responsible for keeping Laurel alive.

According to all his knowledge about the way the human body works, she should have died. This unknown or unexplainable quantity intrigued him, humbled him, and set his adrenaline flowing.

He checked Laurel and said, "I'm proud of you, my dear. You've made remarkable progress. However, you've lost a lot of blood and your body must have time to recuperate. It's absolutely essential that you rest. Drink the broth and eat everything they bring you, if possible."

"Thank you for all you have done," she said quietly. "I promise I'll do everything I can to get well quickly." His kind eyes looked pleased.

"I know you will. You and Justin put up a mighty fight to keep you alive, and you won!"

He turned to Justin. "After you go tell the children about their mother, you sleep awhile in the room across the hall. It's still yours. Tell the children they can see her briefly tomorrow. No other visitors for a few days."

After he and Justin left, Laurel lay awake awhile thinking of the experience she had just come through. She wanted to share it with Justin but she must be able to think coherently before trying. She didn' know it was possible to be this weak and still be alive. However, it didn't seem important enough to dwell on it.

Her thoughts were totally taken up with what had happened to her on her journey toward death…and back. It had not been a dream, after all. The peace she remembered was still there. Perfect peace! And joy! Something remarkable had happened to her. A significant change had taken place. She tried to comprehend it all, but she fell asleep instead.

When Justin arrived and they had talked awhile about the children, she said, "I need to tell you about my…my journey while it's clear on my mind."

He moved closer and took her hand. "Only if you feel like it."

"Yes. I must tell you."

She looked at him for a passing moment, then started.

"It was somewhat like a dream. I was walking in a meadow. You know the kind I love, with mountains all around. The thick grass was dotted with bluets and violets and dandelions. The birds were singing in the big shade trees scattered here and there. I heard the stream before I saw it. As I went toward it, I knew I was supposed to follow it to its source."

"As I followed, the meadow widened. It was a wondrously beautiful place. A sense of peace and rest surrounded me and filled me. There was a light beckoning me, a welcome waiting for me at the crest of the hill. It…it was right to go on. I couldn't wait to get there."

Laurel paused, looking out the window as if she could still see the meadow and the hill.

"Then I heard you call me, Justin. You called my name several times but I couldn't see you. I realized you must be back in the forest at the edge of the meadow. I knew you needed me by the sound of your voice."

She looked at him and saw tears sliding down his cheeks unheeded. In all their years together she had never seen him cry.

"I did call you back, Laurel, because I do need you. The children need you. And you know we love you."

"Yes, I know. And I love you and the children."

She closed her eyes to rest a moment, then continued.

"I stopped under a beautiful spreading tree by the stream to decide what to do. It seemed like a flash but I relived our life together. Meeting you, our wedding, the children being born, the logging camps. You were with me in it all, Justin. The children were there part of the time. I thought of each of them and the differences that only I know."

"Then," she said very quietly, "suddenly you were no longer there."

She closed her eyes again and was quiet. She could not tell him of the desperate desire she had to keep going toward the crest of the hill; toward the light and the source of peace and rest. But his call and the call of the children were too strong. She chose to go back. As she remembered her sense of loss in not going on, the tears slid down the sides of her face onto the pillow.

Justin had realized by now that he was crying. He was wiping his face with his handkerchief when he saw her tears.

"You're getting too tired. Don't talk anymore right now."

"No. There's something you need to know. I know how you feel about God, but it was God who brought me back to you and the children. I somehow chose to come back but I didn't have the strength by myself. He…He gave me the strength."

She saw a flicker of the old fear in his eyes, and half expected his anger to spill over as it had through the years when they discussed her beliefs.

Instead, he looked at her as if he was trying to figure something out.

"I know, Laurel. Dr. Leighton told me that if you lived, it would be up to a higher power and you."

His old defiance of God was gone for the present but she could sense his groping uncertainty as he continued. "You know I have never understood your beliefs about God. I guess it's because I have always been afraid of Him. That's the legacy my stepmother left me."

He stopped, then went on haltingly. "I'll always be thankful to Him that you're alive. It's confusing to me because I have believed for so long that He meant me harm."

Laurel was quiet but she moved her hand across the bed to take his. She knew the great effort this conversation was costing him. "I'm learning some new things about God, too. I haven't understood Him very well either, even with all my talk and effort."

"I don't understand much of anything, Laurel. But I do know that He gave me and the children our lives back when He gave you back to us." He stood to go.

"You need to rest now. Dr. Leighton will have some choice words for me if I let you get too tired. I'll bring the children to see you this afternoon."

He brushed her hair back and kissed her on the forehead before he left.

Laurel slept again; a good, restful sleep. She woke up as Justin and the children came through the door.

Adam was so overjoyed to see his mother awake and smiling at him, he practically threw himself on the bed ahead of the others. He kissed her and touched her face gently two or three times as he blinked back tears.

Sarah, the practical one, kissed Laurel and rubbed her hair back. She held six year old David up where he could see Laurel.

"Tell her about praying, David," she prompted.

"We prayed for you, Mama, at the woodpile. God told me and Alexis that you would come home soon," he announced.

Laurel smiled through tears as Sarah held the confident little boy down to kiss her.

Caroline was next. She gave her mother a hurried kiss.

"Mama, when are you coming home? I don't like it when you're gone."

Two-year old Alexis kept her head on her daddy's shoulder as she looked wide-eyed but silently at her mother. Justin held her down to kiss Laurel's cheek.

Laurel wanted to take them all in her arms. Instead, she whispered, "I love you very much, all of you, and I'll be home soon."

Justin had been warned by Dr. Leighton to keep their visit very brief. As they left, Laurel said, "Give Hannah and Nora my love and my thanks."

Laurel watched them go with a peaceful detachment. She loved them more than she loved her own life, but she knew now she didn't possess them. It was a good feeling.

She wanted to rethink and try to understand what she had experienced. She had told Justin only part of it. She wasn't sure she could find words to express the part of the experience that had profoundly changed her. It was a private transaction between her and God.

She had chosen to go back, to live, but still held back because she knew she could not live the way she had for the past several years. It was not just the endless, unimaginable, hard work while bearing and caring for her children. It was her approach to life.

She saw with clarity that even though she went to church, had even started a church in a boxcar, taught her children about God, prayed, and felt herself a good Christian – always wanting Justin to share her faith – she had remained in control. She was responsible. She carried the load. She always needed to work things out. She realized with amazement that, for all her talk about faith, she had only wanted God's pat on the head as she plowed through the problems. She had always wanted His guidance, but she had never turned it all over to Him.

She would not – could not – play God any longer in her own life, in Justin's and the children's lives, in anyone's life! This was the load she refused to pick up again. She remembered a deliberate letting go of life as she had always lived it. If that meant dying, then she would die. It was a prayer without words.

At that point of giving herself unconditionally – and everything precious to her – to God, she had suddenly been aware of a Loving Presence in the hospital room. Had Papa come for her? She knew she was awake because she tried to lift her head but was too weak. She did not see or hear anything. Yet, she knew the Presence was standing near the foot of her bed on the left side.

Love surrounded and filled her. She was aware of total love and acceptance at the center of her being. She knew she was of infinite worth to God just as she was. She did not have to earn this love. Indeed, she knew she could not. She also knew she could never lose it.

Somehow, she understood that His transforming love had always been there, but she had been too self-sufficient to receive it. She had constructed her own little world where she was in control, and had kept Him on the fringe, at a comfortable distance to be called on in times of distress.

The Presence remained as she realized that a transaction had taken place. She had laid down the control of her life and the Person who loved her unconditionally had taken over. A profound peace flowed through her, bringing wholeness and joy. She knew she would live to raise her children. And more...much more!

She said softly to herself, "This is reality! This is the way life is supposed to be lived! Why did it take me so long to understand?"

Just before a good natural, healing sleep took her, so weak physically she couldn't lift her head or hand, she thought, *I've never been so alive!*

Chapter Twenty-eight

Jed, Hannah and Ethan were waiting for Justin and the children in the lobby. The children burst through the door, all talking at once. Adam said, "Uncle Jed, Mama talked to us."

"She smiled like herself, too," added Sarah.

Hannah looked at Justin, her eyes full of tears. He nodded and smiled, "Dr. Leighton thinks she will be all right, but she's awful weak."

"Thank God she's alive! She'll gain her strength back soon."

Jed gripped Justin's shoulder. "You know we're mighty thankful, Justin. Now, how about you? Could you let Hannah stay with her awhile and you go home with me and get some rest?"

Ethan spoke up. "I'm not going anywhere until I know both of you are all right. You're exhausted, Justin."

Justin looked at them solemnly. "I just can't leave her yet. I couldn't sleep right now anyway. I've got some heavy thinking to do."

Jed nodded. "Okay for now. Ethan will be here and we'll be back after while. Hannah can stay while you go eat a good meal and rest. I know you're plannin' to stay here all night again."

Justin thought, *He knows when he needs to tell me what to do.* He rubbed his hand over the stubble on his chin and said, "Okay, Jed. I could use a good meal, a bath and a bed for a little while. Hannah, Laurel said thanks to you and Nora for taking care of the children."

Justin hurried back to Laurel's room. He sat close and watched her sleep – and breathe. After awhile he started trying to sort through the problems facing him. It was hard because he still felt euphoric. *Like I've had a swig of good moonshine*, he thought. *Laurel is alive! Everything else seems unimportant, in comparison.*

Yet, he had to be realistic. Laurel would need rest for two or three months. Someone would have to take care of her and the children. They would have to move. He couldn't risk keeping his family there after Toby's threats, but he intended to work and harvest his crop in spite of Toby and Bud and the sheriff. His family and livestock depended on the crop for food during the winter. If those two acres of peanuts made good, he could sell them for enough cash for staples and winter shoes and clothes for the children. He would go talk to Mrs. Rapp.

The spring sun warmed the room and he dozed with his hand on Laurel's. Laurel moved her hand slightly and Justin was instantly awake. She smiled at him. He pushed her hair back and kissed her forehead. "You've had a good rest, Honey. Dr. Leighton will be happy."

"Have you rested any?"

"Yes, I just dozed awhile." He poured a cup of water. "Here, drink a few sips." He held her head up so she could drink.

"Justin, could you wash my face and let me brush my teeth?"

He washed her face and hands with a warm cloth and brushed her teeth for her. They both laughed when he intoned, "Grandma, what big teeth you have!"

"Could you brush my hair? It must be a mess."

"No, Ma'am. You've had enough brushing for now. We'll do it the next go round."

He pushed one rebellious curl back, then gently outlined her face with his finger as they looked at each other for a long quiet interlude.

The nurse came hurrying in with a bowl of broth. She stopped abruptly and said in surprise, "Why, you're the picture taking man!"

Justin nodded. "Yes, I am."

"You've been coming to our house since I was a little girl. I'm Ben Reed's oldest daughter."

Justin smiled. "All grown up and a nurse at that…and a pretty one, too."

She said, "Thank you," as she turned to Laurel and said, "And I've been hearing good things about you. Do you think you can drink some of this beef broth? Dr. Leighton wants you to drink lots of liquids, especially broth and juices."

Justin held Laurel's head up while she drank several swallows. The nurse said, "The hospital has been overrun by people coming by to check on you. No visitors are allowed for a few days, but they leave mighty happy when they hear you're better." Laurel smiled her response.

As the nurse left, she stopped in the doorway and said to Justin, "One of your friends is in the hall waiting to take you home to rest, he says. I told his wife she could stay if she will be quiet. Mrs. Worth must have complete rest."

Justin said, "Will you promise to rest if I leave you and go to Jed's to sleep awhile and take a bath? Hannah will be here with you if you need anything, but you can't talk yet. And, you know Ethan! He seems determined to be here as long as we are. He'll be in the lobby. If you need me send him for me."

"I'll be in good hands, so go rest awhile."

Justin kissed her cheek and said, "I'll be back to spend the night." He reluctantly went to find Jed and Hannah.

Laurel was already asleep again when Hannah tiptoed into the room and sat down by the window. She had brought some quilt squares to work on. She rarely had time to sit down at home.

Jed and Justin bounced along a few miles in Jed's old truck in companionable silence. Jed knew Justin would talk to him about his "heavy thinking" when he was ready. They swung around by Justin's house to let him check on things and get a change of clothes.

As they drove away from the house, Justin said, "Jed, I've got to find another place to live. I need to move before Laurel leaves the hospital."

Jed was surprised. He knew about Justin's crop and his terms with Mrs. Rapp. "Why? What's happened?"

Justin told him about Toby, Bud, and Jim Potts.

Jed didn't get mad quickly nor often, but as he listened to Justin's story, his hands tightened on the steering wheel and his lips drew sideways. It was a danger signal to people who knew him well. He knew immediately what he was going to do, but he wasn't going to tell Justin yet. The man was wrung out, physically and emotionally. He must rest before any plans were discussed.

Jed said, "Toby and Bud both are drunken bums and cowards. And

Toby's got a real mean streak in him when he's drunk, so I agree with you that you can't stay there. Jim Potts is another matter. When this word gets around, and I'll see that it does, he won't be elected sheriff again in this county. You and Laurel have too many friends for that to happen."

Justin said, "I hope not. The people deserve better." He sat up straight and blinked his eyes as if that would help him think better.

"Jed, the way I see it, I've got three immediate problems. I've got to get my family moved. I need someone to help take care of Laurel and the children for awhile. And I have to work and bring in that crop."

He paused a minute and continued, "Would you ask Bulldog and Tom and some of the other men to be looking for me a place to rent, even temporarily. And, Jed, I'm determined to work and harvest my crop. Even if I have to fight to do it. My family and livestock have to have the food this winter."

Jed nodded as he drove up into the yard and brought the truck to a noisy stop by the back door. He turned to Justin. "The first thing you have to do is sleep and eat. Then we'll talk."

The house was quiet as they entered. "Nora said something about her and the kids going on a walk and picnic so you could rest. She dotes on them, you know."

"I know. And they love her, too."

Jed led Justin upstairs to a back bedroom. "Hannah said to put you in here on this feather bed."

Justin took one look at the bed, laid his bundle of clothes on the dresser, sat down and started unlacing his boots. Jed said, "When you wake up we'll have hot water for a bath and a good supper."

"Thanks, Jed. Let's see, it's eleven. If I'm not awake by five, yell for me."

He slid between the sheets and allowed himself to relax totally for the first time in four days. He was asleep in minutes.

Jed left the house quietly to go check on his two acres of corn crop in the bottom land. He needed some time alone to sort things out in his mind. He knew Hannah and Nora would agree with the first part of his plan. In fact, Hannah would probably suggest it the minute she heard about Toby's threats. The other parts could wait until he talked to Bulldog and Tom.

Hannah's father, Mr. Earnest Lee, a widower, had died just a year ago. He had left the house and farm to Hannah and Nora. It was a large house with about fifty acres of good, rich farm land and wooded areas. Jed wasn't sure when he left logging how good a farmer he would be. But he was making a good living at it and enjoying it more than he thought he would. Besides, he figured it was fair for Hannah and Nora and the boys to enjoy living outside a logging camp for awhile.

When Justin woke up just before five o'clock, the awful paralyzing fear he had felt when he thought Laurel was dying gripped him again for a moment. Then he heard the children playing and laughing and remembered that she was alive. He felt the urge again to express gratitude to…whom? To life? To God? But he had never been on speaking terms with God and was confused as to how to start. He smelled supper cooking and felt hungry for the first time since Laurel's collapse.

Jed knocked, stuck his head in and said, "You awake? I put the tub in our bedroom downstairs. We'll fill it with hot water if you're ready, then you can shave at my washstand. I've set out the stuff."

Justin swung out of bed, rubbing his face and smoothing down his hair. "I don't know when I ever slept so hard. I'm ready for that hot water and straight razor right now. And tell Nora that food smells good. I'm as hungry as a bear that's been hibernating."

When he had finished dressing later and stepped into the big farmhouse kitchen, the children swarmed him. They had waited for their daddy long enough. After hugs and kisses they settled around the long plank table for Nora's fried chicken and fixins.

There was an awkward moment. The children were waiting with their heads bowed for the blessing. Jed, who had already picked up the chicken to pass it, said, "Adam, would you ask the blessing?" Adam took a quick look at Justin who nodded his head. His prayer tugged at Justin's heart at the end when he thanked God his mama was better and would soon be home again.

When Jed and Justin arrived back at the hospital, Jed took Hannah to the lobby to tell her about Justin's problems. She listened quietly and said, "Bess, Nora, and I have already been talkin' about taking care of Laurel and the children." Then she told Jed what she thought they should do.

As she finished, she asked, "Why are you grinnin' like that?"

"That's exactly what I figured out, but I knew it would be the hardest on you. I also knew exactly what you would say." He gave her a quick hug.

"Let's talk to Justin now so he won't be wrestlin' with it all night."

She nodded and Jed went to get Justin. When they were seated in the corner of the lobby, Jed, with his customary economy of words, said, "I told Hannah about you needin' to move and we want you to move in with us for a few months."

Justin looked with a puzzled frown from one to the other, "You mean our whole family move into your house with your family?"

"That's right," Jed answered and gave a nod to finalize it. But Hannah knew Justin needed to hear from her, too.

"Justin, you know that Nora and Bess and me are goin' to take care of Laurel and the children anyway, as long as she needs us. We've already been talkin' about it. So, this would be easier than us runnin' back and forth to your house."

"It will be hard, Hannah. We're a big noisy bunch," Justin said. "I don't want to ruin a good friendship."

"Fiddlesticks! It'll be a sight easier than what we done in the loggin' camps. Nora and the boys will be tickled to death. We all get lonesome to be close again," she argued.

"We rattle around in that big old house after livin' all them years in loggin' shacks," Jed added.

Justin stood up. "I don't know how I could ever pay you back."

"You and Laurel already paid us. Ten years worth of watchin' after all of us."

"This offer means more to me than I can tell you." Justin held out his hand to Jed. "Let me think about it tonight"

"We'll help move you," Hannah continued. "Nora, Bess and me will pack up the dishes and clothes. We'll need to put some of your beds and dressers upstairs at our house."

"Bulldog and Tom will help, too," Jed persisted. "We can store some of your furniture in the canning shed by the barn. It's good and dry. There's even a stall for Tattoo in the barn."

Justin looked from one to the other. "It sounds like you've thought it all through."

"One more thing before we go," said Jed. "While you're thinkin' about it, Justin, think about this. If the situation was reversed and we needed your help, what would you and Laurel do? You would've already moved us, that's what! You sure wouldn't be standin' here jawin' about it as long as we have!"

Justin laughed. He knew Jed spoke the truth. They were back on a good solid footing. Jed had just moved the checker where he could countermove without losing face. He put his arm around Jed's shoulder.

"Okay, I don't know if you two are brave or crazy. I'll ask the doc if I can talk to Laurel about it tomorrow. Then we'll work out the details."

Within a week the Worth family had moved in. Hannah, Bess, and Alice packed the kitchen things and clothes under Sarah's supervision. At seventeen, Sarah showed her ability to take care of the family, as she had been doing for the past few months. A senior in high school, she had missed so much school, she wasn't sure she could graduate with her class. She might have to return next year. She planned to talk to her teachers about making up her work now that Hannah and Nora were going to help with the family. And she would try not to miss another day this year.

Jed, Bulldog, and Tom helped move the furniture. Adam handled Tattoo in a manner that made Justin proud. Ever since the time Justin and Tattoo had nearly drowned and Adam had calmed Tattoo down, the horse evidently regarded Adam as worthy of his allegiance. Second to Justin, of course. Adam, now fifteen, felt a keen responsibility to the family, as the oldest son.

The farmhouse accommodated them fine, with a few adjustments. The few years apart had not erased the many years together, almost as a single family. Even though Jesse and Thad were young men now in their early twenties, their pleasure was evident as they slipped back into the role of older brothers to the others.

After a big discussion about Alexis, it was decided that Nora would keep her in her room to sleep and be primarily responsible for her until Laurel was better. Sarah felt responsible for Alexis but was relieved to have help, especially since she seemed to be the mother substitute for all the others. Besides, she would have to work extra hard at home to make up the work she had missed in school. Nora, of course, was delighted to have all "her children" back under one roof. If she could have her way, they would live together 'til they were grown.

It was two weeks before Dr. Leighton released Laurel from the hospital, with a long list of instructions as to what she could and could not do. Dr. Leighton had made it clear that she must build up the quantity of blood that her body needed to function normally. Meanwhile, he didn't want her exposed to even minor germs, because she had nothing to fight with. As Justin read the list of how much she had to rest and about how long it would take to recuperate, he expected her impatience to break out into complaints and concerns about how hard this was going to be for everybody. She had never been still very long in her life. Her calm acceptance with a happiness that seemed almost out-of-place, given their circumstances, was the first clue to Justin that Laurel had come back to him somehow altered.

They settled her into the sunniest upstairs bedroom, out of the flow of traffic. Justin and Hannah gave strict orders as to how often the children could visit. Even so, her presence brought a sense of rightness and happiness and joy to everybody. After a few days, routine was established with the children going to school every day and Justin going back to the Rapp Place to work his crop. And Laurel was at peace about it all.

Justin, however, was not yet to have peace. He soon realized that his problems with the Rapp boys were not over. He came one morning to find the garden trampled and the tomatoes stripped from the vines. He moved hurriedly on to the cornfields to find that several rows of the young corn plants had been pulled up by the roots. At least they had not yet harmed the animals he had left, other than opening the door of the chicken house. He checked the cows, pigs, and Matilda. He and Chief rounded up the chickens. He had somehow believed that moving out would satisfy them and had been taking Chief back and forth with him to Jed's. Now he realized they were going after his crop, if only to destroy it.

Struggling to master his anger and frustration, he went to see Mrs. Rapp about new terms regarding the crop since he was no longer renting the house. His anger was tempered with pity by the time he finished talking with her and her daughter. Mrs. Rapp, in her mid-eighties, fully realized that she had raised two sons who were a menace to society. She was also practical enough to know there wasn't anything she could do to control them. With those two truths established between them, she told Justin she hoped he would somehow succeed in growing and harvesting his crops. She offered to cut down her percentage because of the damage her sons had caused.

As Justin rose to go he said, "I'm legally share-cropping those fields for you, Mrs. Rapp. I just wanted to know if you are still my partner in spite of what has happened with Bud and Toby. I have my answer. You will still receive the share we agreed on before this trouble came up. But I want you to know that I intend to defend that crop and harvest it. I will do what I have to do!"

She held out her hand. "I understand, Mr. Worth."

Justin felt better after talking to her, but nothing had altered the fact that the problem was essentially his. That night after supper he talked to Jed.

"I think I'll go tomorrow and see what kind of legal action I can take. I can't reason with them and I am so angry right now, Jed, I don't trust myself to confront them. I'd likely give both of them a beating they'd never forget, but Laurel would know. Dr. Leighton says she can't have any worry for awhile."

He carefully kept the crop problems from Laurel. Before leaving to spend the night in the canning shed at the Rapp Place, with Chief back on duty, he simply told her that he needed an early start in the fields the next morning.

Jed had been waiting to see if Bud and Toby could leave well enough alone. It seemed they couldn't and Justin had had enough. It was time to call in Bulldog and Tom for the plans he had been considering for awhile. In fact, he would call in Abe, Dirk, Zeke and Odell, to boot. The Rapp Boys had a few things to learn, and what Justin didn't know wouldn't hurt him.

Two nights later, the seven men met at Bulldog's house. Bess cooked their supper and went along to Alice's house, at Bulldog's request. After Jed told them how things stood, they agreed that something had to be done. Jed's strategy appealed to them and when they had finished a long discussion over a good meal and several cups of coffee, they got on their way.

Toby and Bud had tempered their drinking that afternoon, in anticipation of going back that night to destroy some more of Justin's crop. When a group of masked men suddenly burst into their shack, they were sober enough to understand that they were real. They were also sober enough, cowards that they were, to be terrified. Especially since two of the men carried pistols, two carried horse whips, and two carried long hunting knives. The men didn't say a word. They just stood there.

Toby tried to get behind Bud and Bud tried to get behind Toby. Bud finally found his voice. "Who are you and what do you want?"

"Oh, now," Jed said softly, "we can't tell you who we are, but we can tell you what we want."

"What?" squeaked Toby.

"First, let's talk about what you've been up to," Bulldog said. "You've been behavin' pretty bad."

"Whatcha mean?"

"Tell us what you've been doin' to Justin Worth's crop."

"So, Justin sent you!"

"No! Justin don't know we're here and he ain't goin' to know! But Justin has lots of friends in this county. Let's just say that we represent them all. You boys may have to travel West again to be safe."

"How do you know what we've been doin?" babbled Toby.

"People can always tell when a skunk's been around," Abe said. "Always leaves a bad smell. So, tell us!"

"We didn't do much damage," Bud pleaded. "We just want him gone."

"And what about the part of the crop he's plannin' to give to your mother?" Jed asked very softly.

Bud and Toby looked at each other for answers and found none. Their gaze again traveled over the men and their weapons. Bud stood biting his lower lip. Toby's strength must have left him and he sat back heavily on a chair.

The masked men looked at each other.

"Do you think we ought to horsewhip 'em before we shoot 'em?" Jed asked one of the men holding a whip.

"I sure do! Just shootin' 'em outright ain't enough punishment."

"What about usin' the knives on 'em first? I'm in favor of that." Tom fingered the edge of his knife.

Toby groaned.

Bud said, "It's agin the law to do that."

"Oh! The skunk knows the law!" Abe said. "Is it agin the law what you're doin' to Justin Worth?"

Bulldog said, "Well, whatever we do, let's get on with it. Somebody might fall into one of them graves we dug out there in the woods. We've got to finish soon."

Bud and Toby stood as one. Bud pleaded, "Don't kill us! We won't bother Justin Worth no more!"

That sent the masked men into an argument. It was obvious to Bud and Toby that the majority wanted them dead and buried tonight.

Finally, the leader spoke. "There's only one way we'll let you live. You'll give us your oath that you will never set foot on your mother's property again until Justin Worth has harvested his crop this fall and has left. You will give your oath that you will never tell anyone that this meeting took place. And you will be careful never to say one word against Justin Worth. After all, you may be talking to one of us and not know it. That wouldn't do!"

"We swear! We swear!" Toby said. Bud nodded his head vigorously in assent.

"This is more than words. This is a blood oath." The leader turned to the two men with the knives. "Come and draw enough blood for them to understand we mean business. Cut deep enough to leave a scar to help them remember. I don't trust their word."

It took two men to hold each of them, babbling and crying and begging, while the men with the knives forced the palm of their right hands open and delicately drew the edge of his knife across the fleshy part, next to the wrist. Blood welled up in a line. With precision, each man drew another line, causing a red X to appear on each man's hand.

"Let's move a little higher here and cut these veins while we're at it, and save the world a few problems," said one of the men, holding the knife poised.

"No!" screamed Bud. "We'll do what you want!"

Toby was past speaking. He stared at the blood now dripping from his hand and was seized with a fit of shivering.

The men weren't through yet. Jed said to Bud, "Get us two white rags."

Bud scrambled to do his bidding. Jed then ordered them to smear the blood over their hand, onto each finger. He and Bulldog then pressed their bloody hand prints onto the cloths. Abe tacked the cloths up by the door.

"These bloody hand prints will help you remember your oath and remember that this wasn't a drunken dream," Jed said. "Every time you go out that door, you'll be reminded that if you harm Justin Worth in any way, we'll find out about it and we'll be back!!"

Speechless, but eager to please, Bud and Toby nodded their heads.

Bulldog looked at Jed. "So we just fill them two graves back in with dirt for now?"

"Yes. But they won't be as hard to dig the next time. We know where they are when we need 'em." With those words, they turned and left.

Bud and Toby sat exhausted, looking at the red X on their hands where the blood had congealed. Without a word, Bud found the liquor bottle, took a swig and passed it to Toby. They felt they deserved some comfort.

After a few days, Justin began to believe they were going to leave him alone. Nothing was touched, even when he was gone. He decided to wait about the legal action. He had no money for it anyway. One strange thing he couldn't understand was Bud's and Toby's reaction the first time he saw them in Deerbrook. They had always been cocky and blustering. This time when he walked up to the group of men where they were, the two brothers looked at each other and some kind of message was passed. Their fear was evident. It seemed they couldn't get away fast enough.

After two or three more weeks of peace, Justin let down his guard and began to believe that he would be able to raise and harvest his crop after all. That left two major problems left to deal with. Laurel must have time to recuperate and he must find a place to live by the end of summer, in time for the children to start to school in August.

Chapter Twenty-nine

Laurel, meanwhile, was surprising them. She, the prime mover, seemed content to lie still and eat and drink and obey the doctor's orders, so her body's blood supply would build back up. Hannah remarked on it to Justin. "There's a peace and acceptance in her. I thought my biggest job would be keepin' her in bed, but she's been very good. Even with limitin' her time with the children."

Justin was very happy just to have her alive. He sometimes relived his terror when he had thought she was dying. He would never take it all for granted again. He was puzzled, however. He felt it was important that he reassure her that their problems would soon be worked out; that he would soon find a place to live. He found, after a few of these conversations, that she was the one reassuring him.

One night as they lay in bed talking, his anxiety must have transmitted to her in spite of his casual tone. She raised up on her elbow, looked at him and traced her fingers around his face. "Justin, it's okay! You'll find the right house, at the right place, at the right time. I'm sure of it! And, you're exhausted now, so go to sleep!"

He blew out the lamp and she settled in with her head on his shoulder. For awhile after he realized she was asleep, he lay thinking. Her words had somehow loosened the coil of fear that sometimes threatened to squeeze his insides. But there was something else. She had made the pronouncement with certainty that it was going to happen! At least she believed in him. That counted for a lot. But he knew it was more. There was an indefinable difference in her. His arm around her tightened for a moment, then slackened and he slept.

Laurel did believe in him. She also believed in God. She had come back so physically weak she still felt as quivery as jelly, but she knew her real self had never been stronger. She tried to reduce to its essence what she had experienced. She attempted to put words to it and came out with three for starters. But those three were so profound, she was humbled. Love, Joy, and Peace! The three most sought after, yet elusive qualities, in our human experience. She had been immersed in God's love. The results were astonishing in the way she felt about herself and others. If she was of infinite worth to God just as she was, she no longer had to seek His favor continually. But it made her want to live in such a way that would give Him pleasure.

As she looked out at the summer sky, while hearing her children's laughter floating up the stairs, she was suddenly reminded of Papa. That's the way she had felt about Papa! Knowing that she was secure in his love, no matter what, had created in her a deep desire to live in a way that he would be proud of her.

"Papa," she whispered, "I can understand and believe God's love because I had yours to point the way. I can also better understand your great respect for other people. If God thinks I'm of immeasurable worth to Him, He must think the same of others! You knew that all the time, Papa…But we each must learn it for ourselves!"

Joy was harder to analyze. She knew that joy was the force inside of her that made her feel unsinkable. The force that bobbed her back to the surface, like a cork, in spite of what pushed her under. That mighty force assured her that, no matter their circumstances, they would come out on top with all the things that matter intact. Worry couldn't coexist with joy. It skulked away with its tail between its legs.

How could she summon words to describe the utter peace she felt, lying here in someone else's home – because she didn't have one of her own. Receiving charity…when she had always been the one who dispensed charity. The roles were reversed, and there was a rightness, an order to it all. She was so weak still, that she knew recovery would take awhile. Her five children had particular needs to be met. Her husband was without a real job. Terrible circumstances by anyone's standards! But she had passed through some kind of a wicket gate into a new dimension where she knew God had their future planned. They only had to walk it out. And it was an exciting future beyond what they could ask or think! God would do what

373

they couldn't and expect them to do what they could. She was as certain of this as she was of the bed upon which she was lying. Her peace came from that certainty.

Love, Joy, Peace: the divine chemistry that put fragmented lives back together and fused the pieces in place. God's Spirit was in control of her life, and this was the result—the fruit! This wondrous transaction had taken place when she gave up her life to Him. *Why*, she wondered, *had she taken so long?*

Justin, relieved of his constant worry over his crop, was searching diligently for a house. He had promised Laurel a big house when he thought she was dying and he intended to keep his word. He wanted a decent house, large enough for his family to stretch out in, not the ramshackles they had been living in. It was a tall order for a man with no money. But the word went out. Justin Worth was looking for a big house with low rent.

"Justin and Laurel are like magnets," Hannah said to Jed one night when they were alone.

"What do you mean?"

She laughed. "Do you remember how lonesome we was right after we moved here?"

He nodded.

"Well, Mr. Owen, have you been lonesome lately?"

He grinned. "Not exactly."

They both laughed as they thought of the beehive of activity their home had become. "It seems normal having everybody around again," Hannah said.

"It ain't too hard on you?"

"No. I'm enjoying it. And, Jed, I know you ain't religious, but hear me out on this. I believe God has given us this opportunity to repay Justin and Laurel a little for what they done for us for all those years. I feel blessed to be able to do it. Do you understand?"

"Yes, I understand the paying back part. I'm happy about that." His eyes softened. "But, Hannah, you're a good woman. I'm not sure if it's God or you that's in charge of this."

"Oh, I'm sure He's in charge, but He's allowing you and me to help Him."

Jed felt a tinge of discomfort at being called God's helper, but he was an understanding man. He said, "Okay, if you say so. But blow out the lamp now so we can rest and be ready to help Him some more tomorrow."

Hannah lay thinking in the darkness, with Jed asleep beside her, of the happenings of the previous few weeks. Bess and Alice couldn't stay away. They were there two or three days a week to help with the cooking or washing or ironing or cleaning. That meant Alice's children would come home with the Worth children from school. Some evenings Bulldog and Tom came after work and they all ate together. It was like old times.

Ethan, Abe, Dirk, Zeke and Odell lived a distance, but some of them had come each week to check on Laurel, bringing fresh trout or squirrels or rabbits for everyone to eat. Laurel would get tired of the red meat and liver diet the doctor had put her on, so she welcomed the fish and game for a change. Everybody could go up and speak briefly and see for themselves that she was improving, but nobody was allowed to stay for a visit yet.

Ethan was the first exception. When Ethan came it always seemed like a celebration. The young people and children would get to him first; then the women would take turns hugging and asking a hundred questions; then the men. Allison had felt included in this extended, loving family from the very beginning. Their warmth and approval would linger with her for days after a visit.

One Saturday morning when they rode in, they received the usual warm welcome, but Ethan soon asked, "Can I visit with Laurel awhile? Is she able?"

Justin took him by the arm. "She's able. I think you'll do her more good than a bushel of medicine. Come on!"

So, while Allison filled the women in on what their life was like as pastor and wife, Ethan and Laurel immediately dove headfirst into a conversation about how God was working in their lives; what He was teaching them. No preliminary testing of the waters was necessary. They knew where they had left off, so they started from there.

"Are you giving your people a good understanding of the character of God?" she asked.

"I think so. I'm preaching to them about your God, Laurel. The God you helped me to know and love."

"Tell me about it," she said.

As he spoke about his ministry, his face almost glowed with enthusiasm. He told her how he studied as she had insisted; how the commentaries and dictionary from Papa helped him; how Allison worked with him—continuing to help him with his grammar – how people were responding and the church was growing.

Then he pulled himself up short. "Here I am doing all the talking when I really came to see how you are!"

"I'm the best I've ever been, Ethan. I'll be recovering my physical strength for awhile, but the real me is whole in a way I've never been before."

He sat forward, perplexed. "But you've always been the…the most whole person I ever knew. What's different?"

"I yielded myself to God, Ethan, in a way I never had before. It was a deliberate choice. Before, *I* was in charge, asking His blessings on my work, my way. Now I know *He's* in charge and I am to do His work, His way. The difference now is the sense of His presence which brings His love and joy and peace. I've never experienced anything like it before."

"Do you think it's part of escaping death? You weren't supposed to live, you know! You had us all scared beyond reason!"

She answered carefully, for it was a valid question. "I know my euphoria is partly because I have been given my life back. I've thought that through. However, my experience was more than that. Maybe I can share it with you sometime. There was a definite transaction between me and God that catapulted me into a new dimension of understanding His love."

Ethan leaned forward to ask another question as Justin came through the door talking. "I think the women have killed the fatted calf, son, for the prodigal who's been gone too long."

Laurel and Ethan realized their talk time was over, but he would be back. He was intrigued.

"Mama! Mama!" Sarah called as she rushed up the stairs to Laurel's room. For a minute

Laurel was scared. Then she saw Sarah's face. "I'm going to graduate!

I passed all the make up tests!"

Laurel held out her arms and Sarah leaned down to hug her. "I'm so glad, Mama! I was worried I would have to go back next year."

"Sarah, sit down and let's talk a few minutes."

As soon as Sarah was seated on the foot of the bed, Laurel continued, "I want to tell you how proud I am of you, and not just for your school work. I'm very proud of the way you've taken care of the family during the time I've been sick. I thank you for all the hard work. You've had more responsibility than any girl your age should have to deal with, and you've done a good job, and here I am not able to do anything special for your graduation."

"Having you alive is all I ask for!" Tears pooled in Sarah's eyes. "I was so scared you were going to die, Mama. I don't know what we would have done. I want Alexis and David and Caroline to have as much fun growing up as Adam and I did! And they couldn't do that without you!"

"So you think you had a good childhood? Even with these last few years being so hard?"

"I wouldn't change it with anybody I know! Living in the forest…knowing that all those people in camp loved me. Some of my best memories are of Daddy taking us to school on Tattoo."

"Have you told him that?"

"Not recently."

"Why don't you get alone with him and tell him about some of those special memories? It would ease his heart some about his firstborn growing up."

Laurel was in turmoil after Sarah left. She wanted so very much to get out of bed and to plan a celebration for Sarah's graduation. She hadn't even asked her if she needed something special to wear. She sure hadn't been much good as a mother for the past few months and she still had a ways to go before she could function normally again.

She wasn't to fret over it long, however, because Hannah, Bess, Nora and Alice converged on her room that afternoon to tell her their plans. Bess and Alice would make Sarah's white graduation dress. Hannah and Nora would cook a special dinner and invite the former logging crew. They had been there when Sarah was learning her ABC's. Then, they would plan a party for Sarah's friends!

"How does it sound?" Bess asked.

"It sounds like I have the best friends in the world. Thank you for all you're doing for us!" She lifted the corner of the sheet to wipe her eyes. Then she laughed. "I never thought when I met you in that first logging camp, that I would grow to love you so much! Especially you, Bess!"

Bess laughed. "Yeah! I gave you a turn, didn't I?"

"Several turns," Laurel said. "But the best turn was how you turned out."

Everybody except Laurel went to Sarah's graduation. Bulldog grumbled that he hadn't been so spiffed up since he had gotten married. Jed bought himself a new shirt and Tom bought some new shoes. They said they couldn't have their proper, educated young lady embarrassed over them. Justin looked handsome in his old clothes. He had taken Sarah to town to buy a pair of white shoes to go with her dress.

Laurel heard the noisy bunch leave. Then, left alone for the first time, she had a prayer of thanksgiving that their first child had graduated, in spite of the struggles and setbacks. It was a triumph for them all. She thought of Justin's never-ending hard work for his family. She thought of Chief Lion Heart and his prediction of triumph. She thought, of course, of Papa. He would like the person Sarah had turned out to be.

Canning time was upon them again. Laurel fretted because she knew they had to have canned goods to get through the winter. Hannah knew what she was thinking and put her mind at ease.

"Laurel, you would love our cannin' shed. It's out of the way of the kitchen and we can leave everything as it is 'til we get back to it. Now, here's what we're doin'. We're puttin' all our garden food together and cannin' just like we used to do in camp. Then we'll divide it four ways...."

Laurel interrupted, "But...."

"No buts, Laurel," Hannah said firmly. "We're doing this because we want to. Sarah and Adam are doing your share and Caroline has even washed some jars."

She paused. "Bess always puts some of her jars back with yours. She says there's seven of you and two of them and she ain't lettin' Bulldog get fat and sassy from eatin' too much."

She left Laurel laughing. The truth was that they all were putting extra jars into Laurel's and Justin's supply. But Laurel and Justin didn't need to know that.

The day came when she knew she had to get out of bed and start building up to her normal energy level again. Her first meal with the family—with Justin carrying her downstairs—was a happy landmark. From there she went to sitting downstairs an hour at a time and breaking beans or peeling potatoes or whatever was needed that day.

She had been concerned a few times that the children would grow away from her because of her long exile in bed, especially Alexis, who couldn't understand. But her fears were unfounded. Each child, in his own way, showered her with love. Adam, one afternoon, came and sat by her and took her hand. "I'm glad you're better, Mama. Everything is soon goin' to be normal again."

"Going, Adam, going! Don't forget to sound your g's at the end of your words!"

He stood up and threw his arms around her, laughing with delight. "See what I mean?"

"Adam, you did that on purpose!"

"Yes, Ma'am! Just checking to see if you were still the same!" He pranced out of the room. Then he stuck his head back around the door and blew her a kiss.

David caught her up on the news about all the animals, especially his goat, Matilda. "Did you know that Uncle Bull made me a cart to hook up to Matilda? She pulls me around. But I think I'm about to get too big. See?" He stood and stretched.

"You are getting big, David. Are you helping with the work?"

"Yes, Ma'am! I play with Alexis and take care of her while everybody's canning. Nora says I have to 'pertect' her. And Daddy's showing me how to take care of the animals. I like to do that." His earnest little face tugged at her heart. She opened her arms and he went into them. She held him close for a long while.

"I love you, David."

"I love you, Mama. I've been lonesome for you. I'm glad you're going to be well again."

Caroline was eleven and still bossy. *It's difficult being the middle child,* Laurel thought, *so she has to find her own way to be recognized.*

"Mama! I think you're staying up too much!" she fussed.

"No, I'm not. I know when I have to go back to bed." Laurel patted the chair beside her and said, "Come and talk to me awhile."

Caroline perched on the chair like a bird that might fly at any minute.

"Sit back, Caroline, and tell me what's going on with you."

Caroline looked at her almost angrily for a moment, then said, "I'm glad you're better. I hate it when you're sick. Nothing goes right and Sarah thinks she's the boss of everything!"

"Have you helped Sarah as you should?"

"I help some, but I *don't* like to be bossed around all the time."

"So what *do* you like?" Laurel was trying to keep steady in the wake of all these complaints.

"I like to be left alone some, and I like to read. I would like for us to have a home of our own again where there aren't so many people all the time."

"What kind of work do you like to do when you aren't being bossed around?"

"Oh, I don't know. Cleaning house and taking care of Alexis, I guess. I don't like to wash jars, I know that."

"Caroline, look at me!" At Laurel's sharp tone, she looked up quickly.

"This is the first good talk we've had since I...I got sick and all I've heard is complaints. I'm sorry you've had a hard time. But everybody's had a hard time. Do you really think everybody else should be doing all the work, because you resent being bossed around?"

Caroline looked startled, then sullen. She didn't answer.

"Okay, I'll tell you what we'll do. I'll tell Hannah you'll help clean up the house every day, and you'll have certain times when you take care of Alexis. You will report to me. Nobody will boss you around. We'll see how well you do your part. And, Caroline, I want you to know I love you but I don't like your attitude. I hope you can change it."

Caroline got up and, without a word or a glance, left the room. Laurel was troubled. She should have been more loving. She would make it a point to spend more time with Caroline.

It took a little while for Alexis to be coaxed away from all her other mamas. She would look at Laurel, confused, but made no move to go to her. Adam, seeing the hurt in his mother's eyes, took a hand. He carried Alexis in to Laurel one afternoon and stood, with her still in his arms, talking to her quietly.

"Alexis, Mama has been sick and couldn't take care of us for awhile. But she's better now and she wants to hold you in her lap awhile. It won't hurt her. It will make her happy. Okay?"

He set her down in Laurel's lap. "You tell Mama about your playhouse and I'll be back for you in a few minutes."

Alexis sat stiffly, as if embarrassed, in Laurel's lap.

"Where is your playhouse?" Laurel asked.

"In the corn crib."

"Who helped you build it?"

"Caroline and David. Adam and Sarah comes to see me sometimes."

"What do you have in it?" But Laurel, remembering Caroline's playhouse, knew before Alexis told her.

"A stove made out of a rock. A table made out of a board on rocks. And Caroline's going to find me some old jar lids for plates."

"Do you have a bed?"

"Adam is going to put some leaves in a sack for me." She looked at Laurel for the first time. "I need a bed so I can put my baby to sleep," she said seriously, as one mother to another.

"Alexis," Laurel said softly. "Could I hug you and hold you tight for a minute?"

Alexis looked at her solemnly for a moment. Then she leaned over and snuggled. Laurel's arms came up around her and stayed. She didn't even move them to wipe the tears that were running down her cheeks.

Laurel knew Justin was working too hard because he fell into an exhausted sleep every night almost as soon as his head hit the pillow. She longed to somehow lighten his load and told him so one night before he fell asleep. His arm tightened around her.

"You do lighten my load, Laurel, by just being here." He stopped and held her tight a minute before he repeated with emphasis on every word, "By...just...being...here!"

"I'm getting stronger every day. It won't be long 'til we can get back to normal."

"I'm not complaining, Honey. We all want you well. That's the most important thing in the world to us. And hard work never hurt me yet!"

Then one sunny day near the end of July, Ethan sent word to Justin to meet him at Lake Eagle Rest, a small farming community at the western end of Wildwood County. Ethan thought he had found a house for them to rent.

Justin, without a word to Laurel in case it didn't work out, borrowed Jed's truck. He took Sarah and Adam for their opinions. He had come to depend greatly on his first daughter and his first son. After bumping along the curvy mountain road for about twenty miles, they saw a sign that said "Lake Eagle Rest". It was in the shape of an arrow and someone had moved it to point straight up.

They looked at each other and laughed. "Looks like it's pointing to heaven," Sarah said.

"Well, we don't want to go to heaven today," Justin said, "so let's try this road."

They met Ethan at the post office as arranged. He was eager to show them the house.

"One of the men in the church – I had asked them all to be looking – brought me over here yesterday and I think this house will suit your family perfectly."

They came around a curve and there it was: a big brown house with tall windows, and several rock chimneys rising from a shingle roof. It was on a sloping lot with tall oaks, maples, and other hardwoods. Adam let out his breath in a long sigh of appreciation. He and Sarah looked at each other and smiled.

As they got out of the truck, Justin said, "Ethan, I don't think I can afford this place."

"You might be surprised. The owner more or less abandoned this house when the dam broke a few years ago, and the lake washed away. He would rent reasonable to someone responsible who would watch after it for him."

"Where is he?"

"In Atlanta."

"So how do I get in touch?"

"The postmaster has information and instructions."

Sarah and Adam were well ahead, ready to see the inside. When they stopped at the door, Ethan called, "Go on in. It's not locked."

It was the biggest house Adam and Sarah had ever been in. Ethan's excitement matched theirs as he showed them through. "I can already see your family living here. There's plenty of room for all of you *and* all the strays you take in."

Justin put a hand on his arm. "Whoa, son. Let's see how much the rent is first before we move in."

But Ethan liked the gleam in Justin's eyes. He had seen it before. They must have spent an hour looking around inside the house and walking over the grounds, talking and dreaming. As they walked through one last time, Justin was quiet. So was everybody else. Adam and Sarah were bursting to show their enthusiasm, but they didn't want their daddy to know how disappointing it would be not to have this house, so they contained themselves. Ethan, because he had been part of the family for years, understood their feelings.

When the postmaster told him the rent would be eight dollars a month, Justin was astonished. He had expected it to be way beyond his means. He had been paying Mrs. Rapp five dollars a month for that tumble-down farmhouse and he believed he could manage three more dollars a month. He walked away for a few moments because of the emotion that swept through him. This was the big house he had promised Laurel! Only it was so much beyond what he had imagined!

He walked back and said to Sarah and Adam, "Let's rent that house, okay?"

Laughing, they both grabbed him and hugged him, then they hugged Ethan, then each other. The postmaster escaped getting hugged by scurrying back behind his window. After taking care of the business end of renting, Justin thanked Ethan for his help.

"I feel a rightness about this place for you and Laurel. And I have a selfish motive. You'll be closer to me and Allison."

On the way home Justin, Sarah and Adam made their plans. The house had been empty awhile, so the windows had to be washed and the floors scrubbed. That would take some time because it was so big. But they weren't complaining, they hastened to say.

Just before they got home, Justin suggested, "Let's not tell your mother too much about this house. I want her to see it for herself. I know it'll be hard to keep quiet, but do you think we can do it?"

"Yes," said Adam. "But I want to see her face when she walks through it the first time."

"Me, too," added Sarah.

Me, too, thought Justin. *I intend to see her face.*

Chapter Thirty

In August, 1934, Justin moved his family into the big house at the edge of the lake bed, in the community called Lake Eagle Rest. He and the older children, with Bess and Nora, had cleaned the house. Jed and Bulldog had helped him move their furniture. Their belongings looked mighty sparse, but Bess and Nora helped fix things as homey as possible.

When the truck came around the final bend and Laurel saw the house, she could only say, "Justin...!" He stopped at the edge of the drive and they got out and stood with the children around them.

The house sat on a gentle knoll. The yard, full of oaks, maples, birches, and dogwoods, was comfortably covered with moss and natural ground cover that had learned to co-exist with the trees. It was a setting worthy of the sprawling, weathered, brown clapboard house with a roof of curling, mossy shingles where three large rock chimneys rose to a discreet height. And there were many windows – tall windows – trimmed in white.

Laurel didn't disappoint her family. "Oh! It's such a beautiful place! I love the yard...and the house looks as if it just grew there naturally."

"Let's see how you like the inside," Justin said, glancing at Sarah and Adam. He knew they couldn't wait.

They walked through the front door and stopped. A wide hall ran the length of the house. "My goodness," Laurel said, laughing. "It's like a hotel. Look at all the rooms leading off this hallway."

They took time to examine each room, mostly in silence, as if in awe, but Laurel's expression told them everything they needed to know. On the left side of the hall were three large bedrooms, each with a fireplace and tall roll-out windows. On the other side was a corner bedroom, a parlor, stairs to the attic, a kitchen and dining room. But that was not all. At the end of the hall, one large room—a ballroom—spanned the entire width of the house. Laurel and the children turned around and around in wonder. A rock fireplace stood on one side, and David ran to stand in it to show how big it was. Sunlight poured through the row of tall windows on the opposite side.

"What a wonderful room! I can already see the fun we're going to have in here. Look how bright it is now, and…of course, we'll gather around a crackling fire in the winter." She let her eyes circle the room again and turned to Justin. "We could have set one of our logging shacks in here and had space left over."

"Oh, yes. I'm sure we could have."

Adam, anxious to move on, rolled out one of the windows, stepped through and, with a flourish, opened the double glass doors that led onto a porch that ran the width of the house. Ivy woodwork served as porch rails.

They stood on the porch, looking across the valley to the mountain range surrounding them. One mountain ending and another beginning; many sizes and shapes; the ridge line view that Laurel had learned to love.

Sarah and Adam led them down a rocky path that wound through some large, aged oaks and maples to the edge of the sloping grassy yard. The path ended at a low rock wall, beyond which was thick undergrowth such as berry bushes, shaded by many types and sizes of trees, stretching as far as they could see.

"I asked Ethan why this path leads down here and just stops," Adam said. "He told us the lake came to this rock wall. This was considered the front of the house and," he made a wide sweep with his hand, "this whole basin to that mountain range was covered with water."

"It must have been beautiful!" Sarah said.

"It's been about eighteen years or so since the lake washed away. You can tell by the size of the trees," Justin observed.

He turned to Laurel and asked, "Are you too tired to see one more thing before we go in?"

"No. I'm fine."

The younger children were running and enjoying themselves. Sarah said, "Go on. I'll watch them."

Justin led her to the side of the house where another stone path led down to a cove with a copse of trees. Laurel could see a set of stone steps with a wood rail before the path dropped out of sight. Rhododendron and laurel bushes grew in abundance at the edge of the cove.

"You'll like what's down here," he told her.

Right at the head of the cove stood a small rock spring house with a cement walk-around porch and a low rock wall, partly moss-covered, that looked like it was made to sit on. Rock steps led down to the circular rock enclosure around the spring.

"You're right! I do like it!" Her glance took in the beauty of the natural setting in which the rock mason had built his work of art, like a jeweler choosing a setting worthy of a valuable gemstone. "Let's sit and enjoy it for a few minutes."

After a companionable silence, she laid her hand on his and said, "Thank you for providing us with such a wonderful house! It's so far beyond anything I could have imagined or hoped for!"

He looked serious, almost puzzled, as he answered, "Laurel, I can't take credit for finding this house. It's, well, like it was a gift just sitting here waiting for us."

"But you did your part," she insisted. "God made it available and you took His offer."

He studied her expression. "You really believe God had a hand in this, don't you?"

She laughed. "Oh, yes, Justin! I'm as sure of that as I am of your love."

He looked at her in silence. She had rendered him speechless again.

Before they left the cove, they stood together looking through the front opening of the spring at the clear deep water with a sandy bottom. A small orange lizard scampered along the rocks at the water's edge. Justin stooped, cupped his hands and drank. "Good cold water right out of that mountain." Laurel scooped up a drink with her hands and agreed with him.

Looking at a small, spring-fed stream flowing down the crevice of the cove, Laurel said, "We'll need to put our spring box right here in this flat place where the water surfaces and is still cold."

As they walked back up to the house, Justin said, "And, that, Mrs. Worth, is all you get to see until you rest awhile. Hannah packed enough food for an army, I think, so you don't have the worry of feeding us today."

She nodded. This was the longest she had stayed up at one time and her knees were getting wobbly. Soon, she lay still in their new bedroom because her body demanded it, but excitement kept tugging at her to get up and get going. Justin had once said to her, "Your body may be still, but your mind is going about a hundred miles an hour. I can tell by the look on your face." And her mind was traveling now, back through this wonderful house, room by room. She wanted Sarah to have the corner bedroom all to herself; Adam and David could share a room and Caroline could keep Alexis in her room for awhile. And that big room....

Justin, meanwhile, was at the barn. He had brought the animals a few days ago. As he checked on Tattoo, he remembered when Ethan showed him this place. After seeing the house, he had asked, "Does this fine place have a barn?"

"Now you know I wouldn't show you a place without a barn. I'd hate to see you put Tattoo in one of those bedrooms," Ethan answered.

Justin grinned. "Then where is it?"

Ethan had led him back past a big garden plot that was grown up and choked with weeds. Almost hidden by trees stood a barn that looked better than most houses. It was the same style as the house and had double doors that evidently had accommodated large carriages and several horses. Justin stared while Ethan tried to keep back a smirk. He knew how Justin would feel about this barn.

"I couldn't put Tattoo in there," Justin said seriously. "He'd put on airs and stick his head up so high I couldn't get a bridle on him."

"I thought about that," Ethan replied in the same level tone. "But I realized that Tattoo would only think it his due. By now he probably thinks he's human, anyway."

Now Justin, stroking Tattoo's face, realized how happy he was to have a place like this for his beloved horse. "Ethan was right, boy. You're standing here as calmly as if you've been used to this all your life."

The cows seemed content in their stalls. He would move the pigs out as soon as he could build a pen. The chickens would stay around the barn. He didn't have time to build a separate hen house now.

Later, at supper, Justin said, "You'll have to see the barn tomorrow, Laurel. And there's a big garden area."

The younger children couldn't talk fast enough to tell of one more thing they had discovered inside or out. After awhile, Justin said, "Whoa! You can't all talk at once! We plan to live here awhile, so you'll have time to tell us everything."

Everybody seemed pleased with the bedroom arrangements. Especially Sarah. In seventeen years she had never had a room of her own.

"I want to see the back side of the house, off the kitchen, before dark" Laurel said. The back porch was only a foot or two off the ground, in contrast to the other two high porches. She could already imagine sitting and breaking beans or peeling potatoes while she had her magnificent view of the mountain range. A long shelf would have to be built between two of the posts to hold the water pails and wash pans.

Across the back yard from the kitchen porch stood a smaller house, the same color and style as the big one. Laurel said, "Let's look at that house. Tell me about it again."

"Ethan said it was the servants' quarters. I told him I didn't know what we would do with it, and he said, 'Knowing you and Laurel, it'll be full of people before long.'"

It was a square-shaped house with a sitting room, kitchen, and two bedrooms. "Our rent includes the use of this house, too. I asked to make sure," Justin said. "For so many years, we hardly had room to turn around. Now, we've got a different problem! More room than we know what to do with!"

"I'm sure we'll find out what we need to do with it," Laurel said.

As they headed back to the big house, Justin said, "There's something else I want to show you."

Two doors led from the back porch into the house. One opened into the kitchen; the other into a hallway at a right angle to the large hallway that ran the length of the house. He led Laurel up the wide stairs to the right. At the top was a large room with two tall windows facing the stairs, and two smaller windows behind the stairwell. Justin walked around to the left of the stairs and opened the door to a small room that was not much bigger than a closet.

"I had trouble believing this when I found it, Laurel. Look! It's a perfect darkroom to develop my pictures!"

She peeked in at the dark interior and turned and threw her arms around him. "You've never had a darkroom! This house was surely built with us in mind!"

That night after everybody was settled in, and Laurel was asleep, Justin lay thinking. He had found a house worthy of his family and had moved them in. He had fulfilled a solemn promise. It had been one of the most satisfying days of his life.

The next few days were spent getting settled and making new discoveries about the house. Two large bathrooms, one on each side of the hall, had been stripped of their plumbing and fixtures. As she and Laurel looked them over, Sarah said, "We could fit a small bed and chest into either one of these to make a child's bedroom. But, since we don't need any more bedrooms," she finished with a flourish, "what is your pleasure, Ma'am?"

"Let's turn them into closets for linens and quilts and extra clothing that doesn't fit into the bedroom closets."

And so it went for several days. Everyone had to tell something else he or she loved about the house. At lunch one day Adam said, "I love to go barefoot in this house. These floors are so smooth! No splinters!"

"These are hardwood floors," Laurel told him. "With finished lumber."

"Your mother grew up in a beautiful house almost as big as this one," Justin said.

"She did?" David's eyes were big.

"Yes," Sarah answered. "Adam and Caroline and I were there before her papa died."

That evening when they were cooking supper, Sarah commented on the size of the pantry. "Look, Mama, this is more than a closet. Why would they have shelves this wide along the wall?"

"It's a butler's pantry," Laurel told her. "The butler and maid would prepare the serving dishes in here."

"Well, bless my soul," said Sarah, "all we need now is a butler and maid."

The fact that they didn't have enough furniture to fill this house didn't seem to bother anybody. They had beds to sleep on with plenty of cover and a table to eat from with plenty of food. With the Depression still gripping the country, that was more than most people had.

One cool night, after a thunderstorm, the family gathered in front of a fire that Adam had built in the big fireplace in the big room. Quilts on the floor made a cozy seat for the younger children. As the flames cast flickering shadows across their faces, Justin said, "I found out about the schools today. Adam, you'll need to ride the bus to Riverside High School. It's about a ten mile trip. Caroline, you and David will walk about a mile to Lake Eagle Rest Elementary School."

"My school?" asked Alexis.

"You aren't old enough for school, Punkin," Justin said. "Besides, your mother needs you here with her."

She looked solemnly at Laurel. "I'll take care of you, Mama."

Sarah was quiet. She knew she was needed here awhile before she could plan her future.

Justin continued, "I also asked about the nearest church…." He broke off as they looked at him with obvious surprise. He had never before shown any interest in a church. Nobody said a word, however, so he finished. "I knew you'd want to know. It's across the lakebed. If you walk around the road, it's two or three miles, but they say there's a trail that cuts the distance in half."

Adam said, "Sarah, we'll have to scout out the trail next Sunday."

David looked earnestly at Justin. "Daddy, can we live here forever?"

"I hope we can live here until all of you are grown." He looked at Laurel. "I made a promise to your mother that I plan to keep. No more moving around every year or two."

Everybody was quiet, digesting the novel idea of permanence. Then David said, "Good! I'll tell Matilda tomorrow."

Interrupting the laughter that followed, Justin said, "David, why don't you go around and tell all the animals. Chief and Tattoo need to know, too."

He got up. "That reminds me. I need to check Tattoo."

As he went out, Sarah said, "He just likes to tuck Tattoo in at night."

Alexis yawned noisily and Sarah responded, "I think it's time Miss Priss gets tucked in, too. Caroline, can you take her?"

"Yes. Can you come and help me light the lamp in our room. I'm reading *Alice in Wonderland.*"

"Oh, good," Laurel said. "Let's talk about it tomorrow."

"I think I'm going to bed, too," Sarah said. "I want to read some in *Little Women* tonight."

Adam, not to be outdone, added, "I'm reading one of Daddy's Zane Grey books."

After they all kissed her goodnight and trouped off to bed with their lamps and their books, Laurel sat in the cozy glow of the firelight and the Aladdin lamp. Her eyes traveled over the furnishings grouped around the fireplace. When they had moved into the Rapp Place, Justin retrieved the furniture they had stored when they moved into that first logging camp. The Victorian sofa and Chippendale tables, along with their reading chairs, were well-worn by now. Her roll-top desk had weathered the logging shacks. A few years ago, Justin had bought a used oak library table for the children to have a place to do their homework.

Surrounded by the familiar, Laurel walked back through her memories. Primitive, isolated logging camps...unending hard work...losing their life savings...homelessness...her illness... Outwardly, it sounded like a journey of protracted defeat. Inwardly, she knew better. It had actually been a march of triumph. They had overcome.

The fear she had faced years ago that she would lose her identity – her real self – in the demands of the logging camps had slunk away in the face of her faith and determination. She not only had survived; she had thrived. Chief Lion Heart's prophecy had come to pass. With an overwhelming sense of gratitude, she realized the long, hard years had forged a woman of strength. Iron had somehow, somewhere entered her soul. She knew she had been fashioned into a whole person, by God's love, through circumstances that might have destroyed her. She also knew that what she had learned would not be wasted. She had a destiny. The glow inside her soon matched the glow surrounding her. Justin came in quietly to find her wiping her eyes.

"Are you okay?" He sat down beside her and took her hand.

"I'm more than okay, Justin. I can hardly contain my happiness."

"Do you want to tell me your thoughts?"

"Yes. Before Papa left the last time, we had a serious talk. We were in that terrible shack between the river and the railroad, having our hardest time ever. I remember Papa's words clearly. He said, 'I know you and Justin have the strength of character to bring your family through these hard times with all the things that matter intact. I charge you with that responsibility.'"

She looked at him for a moment. "We've done that, Justin, by God's grace and power. We have all the things that matter intact. I'm so proud of our children. Papa would like them."

"And you are alive...that's what matters the most." He brought her hand up to kiss it.

"I somehow know this house is important to our future. When God gave me the strength to come back, I *knew* I would live to raise our children. I also *know*, with the same certainty, that He has a purpose for our lives beyond our children. I believe this house will help fulfill that purpose."

"*Our* lives? What possible use could *I* be to God?"

"That's for you and Him to work out."

He didn't protest or pursue it. His ambivalence toward God, since Laurel's crisis, was new territory to him. His wall of self-protection, built by fear and scorn, had been breached. God had given Laurel back to him and the children. Justin, somehow, didn't fear Him any longer.

When he put his arm around Laurel and pulled her close, she smiled at him with the confidence of a woman who already knows the end of the story.

*   *   *

To learn how Laurel's and Justin's new destiny together is fulfilled, and to complete the thirty-five year saga of the Worth family, please read the sequel, *Mountain Song,* which should be published in a few months.

NOTES

"The Serenity Prayer" is attributed to Reinhold Neibuhr, who in turn attributes it to Friedrich Oetinger, 18th century theologian.

The hymn, "O, Come to the Church in the Wildwood" was written by William S. Pitts in 1864.

The poem, "Why Should the Spirit of Mortal Be Proud" was written by William Knox, a Scotchman (1789-1825).

All Scripture references are from the King James Version of the Bible. They are, in sequence in the book, as follows:
Psalm 121:1-2
Psalm 68:20
Philippians 2:13
Song of Solomon 2:11-12

Printed in the United States
54891LVS00004B/178-237

9 781413 721256